THE ESQUIMAUX

Tom Tivnan

SILVERTAIL BOOKS • *London*

This edition published by Silvertail Books in 2017

www.silvertailbooks.com

Copyright © Tom Tivnan 2017

1

978-1-909269-67-5

Tom Tivnan was born in Massachusetts and educated at the University of Massachusetts and University of Strathclyde. He worked as a bookseller and journalist in Rome, Budapest, Hamburg, Edinburgh and Glasgow before settling in London in 2007.

To my mom and dad – who would have been proud

I.

Discovery

North Atlantic, 1816

'Jesus Fuck Almighty,' John moaned, 'why have You forsaken me?'

Or that is what he wanted to moan, but couldn't, beaten by exhaustion and a tongue wallowing in deprivation. With each waterless day it had swelled, filling his mouth, the tip protruding out of cracked lips. John loved to talk, yet now his tongue, engorged and lazy, refused to work. The prayers, monologues and exhortations to Above all came out as mumbled mash.

He grabbed his tongue and tried to manually form the words, but couldn't.

He slumped back on the kayak, flinging his arms out, the tips of his salt-encrusted mittens dipping on either side into the sea. He looked at the water just inches from his face and fought the urge to drink again. The last time, the last few times, had made him cough and retch and had only made him thirstier.

He remembered a line from that poem Father Kelly had taught him, one he never really appreciated until now: 'Water, water everywhere/Nor a drop to drink.' Despite himself he laughed. He thought of Mary and what she would say if she could see him now. *Idiot*. That was one of her favourite English words, one she would scold him with, but stressed with a smile, elongating each syllable comically, often accompanied by her throaty chuckle — eee-dee-ott. He had heard that word over and over. Idiot John, you let the fishing line go, again. Idiot, John, you could have killed that seal. And he could almost hear her now: you idiot, John, you *eee-de-ott*, you strap enough meat onto the kayak for a week, but only bring one pouch of water.

John had realised his mistake after a day of constant paddling, when he had drunk the last of the pouch and searched for another.

He had thought of turning around, but only briefly. There was no one there for him now. His only way was forward. Forward to Paradise. Father Kelly had often pointed it out when they were out walking in the early morning, John following Mary's lead, the priest slipping and sliding on the snow, clumsily bringing up the rear.

'There, children,' he would say, with the convulsing and twitching that always got worse when he was excited, 'to the right of the sun. There is Paradise.'

John and Mary would look impassively towards the horizon as Father Kelly shook and blinked away tears. 'Ach, Jesus fuck Almighty, sure it's not the Lord goddamn God in heaven paradise, but as close as you can get in this life: Sligo Town.'

Sliiii-gooo Town, John repeated in Father's rolling, lilting way as he sat upright and paddled towards Paradise.

A slap of cold water jerked him awake. The sky was gloomy-grey, the sea rough, the kayak careening into troughs that curled and stretched high above. He made to paddle again but found his hands were empty. He half-heartedly reached for the back straps for a replacement, but knew he had none.

You idiot, John, you *eee-dee-ott.*

He clutched the sides of the kayak and used his body weight to steer into the waves. He managed to slip under one wave, then another, plunging through and emerging on the other side, trying not to open his mouth and drink when under.

He pitched along until, popping out of one wave, he was propelled back and downwards by something solid. He gagged, corkscrewing in a reverse barrel roll until the kayak righted itself and propelled him to the surface. Dazed, John wiped and blinked away the water and salt then looked into an eye.

The eye was brown and large, as big as John's two fists. It glared with what seemed like both confusion and irritation. Then it shut, and the creature's barnacled head plunged into the sea followed by the arch of a fin back and then the fluke, a black crucifix that rose and rose, quivering for a moment before slipping down.

As it vanished John noticed the harpoon stuck just above the fin and the length of cable trailing behind. He felt the animal surge underneath the kayak, sensed the sway of its body, heard a low singsong moan. John shot through another wave and saw more eyes, men's eyes trained intently on the rope, in a boat not a great way off. His heart beat a triple-time flutter and a great swell of joy escaped from his lungs in a whoosh. Deep down he had already shucked off any notion of rescue, of seeing another living soul. Of living. Yet here they were a-fore him; a miracle.

They were white men mostly, but not all. They all had the wind, sun and saltwater-cured faces of every sailor he had ever met. A man was poised at the front of the boat holding a long spear, its tip jutting forward. Others crowded behind the harpooner, their heads craned over their shoulders, useless oars upended in salute.

All were fixed on the whale. The last man, red of hair and scarlet of face, was a blur of motion as he wrestled with the tiller, fussed with the pulley that held the cable and screamed — at the men, at himself — his neck corded, froths of spittle flecking his mouth.

With a bolt of panic, John realised none of the sailors had even so much as glanced in his direction and the boat angled away from John's kayak. He tried to cry out but all that came out was a tamped-down groan. He splashed with his hands in the sea, bashed on the kayak's hull, attempted to scream with a ravaged throat.

The redhead paused and looked about with a furrowed brow, as if hearing something a great way off. He scanned either side to the horizon, then turned away from the whale and locked eyes with John. He stared across at John blankly, then blinked slowly several times. His flow interrupted, the oarsmen looked back to the tiller, then followed the redhead's gaze. The whole crew half-stared at John, half-looked over their shoulders at the whale.

'Well,' the redhead said at last. 'We meet a fellow traveller on the road.'

The cable slackened and the whaleboat slowed. With a burst of strength John pushed his kayak until it came to a rest close to the whalers, the two craft see-sawing up and down on the waves. John forced his lips into an approximation of a smile, croaked an unintelligible greeting.

'"Alone, alone, all all alone/Alone on a wide wide sea",' the redhead muttered.

John's eyes shimmered with delight and he responded: '"And never a saint took pity/On my soul in agony".' He collapsed back, his vision swirling and blackening.

The men regarded him uncertainly, scratching their beards. 'The fuck he say?' the harpooner asked.

The redhead shook his head and made quick calculating looks fore and aft. 'I am mystified. Some heathen Esquimaux gibberish, I should think. Pull him in.'

'But the fish—' one of the oarsmen started.

'Is sounding and I reckon we have a moment or two. Pull him in now, I said. And make his vessel fast.'

Dimly, John perceived several hands reaching towards him and he was lifted up, his body folded over and crammed into the bottom of the boat amidst the sailors' feet.

The redhead regarded him for a long moment. 'Whatever are you doing way out here, sir?' he said almost to himself.

John tried to respond, but before he could the cable pulled taut and twanged forward, burrowing through white foam. The boat buckled, then jumped ahead and all was movement and yelling before John slipped into the dark.

North Atlantic

John shot awake. Two men bent over him, one inches away, another a step back. They were covered in blood, it matted their hair, it saturated their clothes. Only their blue eyes bright as night stars shone clean.

The nearest one, the redhead from the whaleboat, thrust a cup in John's face. The bloody hands that offered it reeked, the smell forcing its way up John's nostrils. John screwed his face up and gagged, and though he could tell the cup held water, fresh water, sweet, sweet water that his body screamed for, he shrank back.

'Take it away, Millar,' the man furthest away said. 'He's scared.'

'Sure, sure, Mr Coffin, sure,' Millar mumbled, scratching his nose, his chin and his underarm in rapid succession.

Mr Coffin squared his broad shoulders and rubbed his gut. 'See, they get scared easy, these fellows. I saw a lot of Esquimaux folk back on my last trip up Greenland. That was during the trouble with the French, you see, and we holed up to hide from a privateer. Primitive folk, un-Christian folk, your Esquimaux. The women though are, heh-heh, very accommodating. There was one I took up with, aye, she was oh, she was—'

'Yes, yes, Mr Coffin,' Millar interrupted, now scratching the back of his neck. 'Should he not be drinking something? It is extremely perplexing that this man, so obviously in an advanced state of dehydration, will not drink.'

'They don't have what we would call Christian morals, see. Anybody can hump anybody. Another man's wife, another man's sister, it don't matter.' His voice grew soft, distant, he looked away. 'Another man's brother.'

The cabin door burst open, daylight streaming in. Millar and Mr Coffin straightened. A man nodded curtly to them and strode towards John's bunk.

'This is the visitor,' the man said. A statement not a question.

Mr Coffin nodded. 'Aye, Cap'n Chase. One of them Esquimaux folk you might get in these waters. See, I was just telling Millar here about my time with them, during the trouble with the French.'

The Captain stared intensely at John for an uncomfortable minute, his glittery eyes reminding John of his mother's in her final, feverish days. He took the cup from Millar and offered it to John. John looked at the cup and then at the man's coat. It was red, of a vibrant sort he had only seen in certain sunsets. The shirt underneath was white as hilltop snow. John seized the cup and drank it down in one. The Captain promptly handed the cup back to Millar who refilled it.

'He seems to have taken to you, Owen.' Millar smiled at the Captain, who shot him a withering look. 'Taken to you, sir. Captain Chase.'

The Captain looked back at John. 'He trusts me. He knows me. He must be him, he must be him.' Then louder to John: 'Hello, sir, my name is Captain Owen Chase of the whaleship *Wessex*. You are very much welcome aboard.'

John stopped drinking momentarily and attempted to say, as best as he could with his swollen tongue, 'Greetings to you, my dear sir. My name is John.'

The Captain stepped back and shook Millar by the collar. 'Did my ears deceive me, cousin? Did you hear what he said?'

Millar stared hard at the Captain for a long moment. 'It was quite garbled, I really could not comprehend him. Captain.'

'I think he said "thank you" in savage-speak,' Mr Coffin said. 'I picked up quite a bit of their lingua. See—'

'Be still, Mr Coffin,' the Captain said. 'Can you not see he is trying to speak again?'

'My name is John, very pleased to make your acquaintance,' John repeated, even less clearly.

'Good gracious God! Did you both hear that? It is what I, we have been searching for. Did you hear it, cousin?' The Captain clutched the front of Millar's shirt. 'He said, "I am a son of Ham!"'

North Atlantic

A gentle shake, progressing to a hard nudge, ending with a punch to the shoulder – and John awoke with a groan.

'Ah, you've arisen.' Millar stood before him, a cup in his hand.

As John accepted it, Millar continued to speak, slowly as if to himself.

'So, my son of Ham, you enjoy a good kip, don't you my ham-some devil? You are meant only to drink a little, Captain's orders. He says you shouldn't give a man dying of thirst too much initially or the intestines swell and — bang! — they burst. I find nothing of that in any of the literature at my disposal, but it has to be said there is a paltry collection on this vessel. So I will have to take my cousin's, and the rest of my shipmates', word for it. But, mind you, from a natural philosophy perspective seeing a man's viscera explode would be quite an interesting phenomenon to witness. An interesting phenomenon, indeed.'

He bent closer, whispering, 'But just between you and me, Hambones, they are an ignorant and superstitious lot, my fellow Argonauts. Still, in times like these I will bow to their experience and let nature run its course.

'So, you should eat something. Something sweet and easily digestible that will help the blood and the humours. Here's a bit of plum duff from the Captain's personal stock. I would be remiss if I did not try a bit first before you, to ensure its suitability.'

Millar took two healthy mouthfuls. 'Oh, merciful Christ, that is rapture. I hope you stay to your sickbed. I have not eaten as well this voyage.' John smacked his lips and raised his head. While he was semi-conscious he had had a sense of constant buzzing, an incessant drone not unlike the first few weeks in summer when the flies come out near the banks of the rushing river, so thick they clog your nostrils and you have to cover your mouth to breathe. That sound was this voice.

John felt better. His tongue was more or less normal size, his lips not so cracked. He patted his belly and croaked: 'That smells wonderful.'

Millar stopped mid-sentence, the spoon perched midway between bowl and mouth. A dollop of plum duff slid off the tip of the spoon and plopped back into the bowl.

'Plum duff, did you call it? I would like some, if you please,' John said, reaching out.

Millar handed John the bowl. Ignoring the offer of a spoon, John tipped it back and drank. It was warm, sweet and gluey.

John handed back the empty bowl and belched loudly. 'Thank you very much.'

'As a one-time student of languages, I am fluent in several tongues. That, I believe, is English.'

John nodded, his head thumped. He wanted more water.

Millar pointed to himself. 'Barzillai Millar. Yes, Barzillai Millar. Late of the Island of Nantucket, later still of Newburyport, Massachusetts.'

'I am called John.'

'John? Wishing to cause no offence, but that is a strange name for a man with your provenance and skin colour. Shouldn't you be called some incomprehensible Esquimaux name like Owlakook, or Nookochook or something like that?'

'John is my confirmation name.'

'Into what?'

'The Holy fecking Roman Catholic and Apostolic Church.'

Millar's eyes lit up, the skin around them creasing as he smiled. 'Ho, ho! Well, the Papist missionaries taught you English exceedingly well. Singular, but well. What is your real name then?'

John thought a moment. It was not the easiest of questions, for he had used John almost since the day Father Kelly arrived among the People, but it always felt slightly off, like an over-large parka he would have to grow into. But the name his parents gave him also felt false. Especially now. 'Saccheuse is what my mother and father named me.'

'Sash-ah-hoosah?'

'Saccheuse.'

'Sack-house?'

'Nearly.'

'What shall I call you?'

8

'Why don't you call me John?'

'People call me a variety of things. Barzillai is a handful, a mouthful, even. Ha! Bizarre Millar, some say. The Captain calls me Ginger Nut, Bizarre the Red, Flame Hair. Friends I allow to call me the diminutive, Barz. I particularly like it when they elongate the "Z". Barzzzz. Has a touch of the Orient, the Glorious East, I think. Would you agree that it is irrelevant what people call you as long as they know who you are?'

'I . . . I believe that sounds somewhat reasonable.'

'Excellent, for the Captain, you see, thinks you told him you were a son of Ham.'

John furrowed his brow. 'Ham? Noah's son?'

'A scholar of our Good Book, as well. My dusky friend, you are full of surprises. Yes, Noah's son.'

'That would be the cursed son of Noah? The one who sees Noah naked and is cast out? Why, pray tell?'

'I do not have an answer to that which will perhaps satisfy or make any sense. It has to do with miracles and madness — often the two are intertwined. Still, the answer lies with our dear Captain, and I think for the moment we should not disabuse him of his assumption about you. He is slightly unbalanced in his faculties just now and his dear wife made me promise that I should do what I can to watch over him, and disabusing him, I think you might agree, will upset the balance.' John shut his eyes. He had told himself on the day he sewed himself into his kayak and paddled away with not one backward glance at the only home he had ever known, that his destination was Father Kelly's Sligo Town. A pilgrimage of sorts; something penitential. Yet deep down he knew he would never reach it (for in truth he did not really know how to get there). The endless sea would be where he went to die.

John opened his eyes and wondered if, in fact, he had already died. Father Kelly's explanations of what exactly constituted the afterlife were always rather vague. Perhaps purgatory would be a millennia-long voyage on this craft, being forced to listen to the rantings of a ginger lunatic. Well, it was deserved.

John said: 'Where is the ship going?'

'The Captain has not yet informed us. I hope we go back to where

9

we are supposed to be. We are meant to be in the Pacific, as far away from here as you could possibly be.'

'You hunt whales?'

'That is the main purpose of this vessel, but we have sighted three and killed just one, the one we were chasing when stumbling upon you. The hunting of whales has been only a secondary goal for the Captain. No, it seems he has actually brought us on a quest.'

'For what?'

'Ha! That will bring you no end of amusement, my dear John. We have been looking for a long-lost son of Ham. We've been searching for you!'

Barz told John he had been five days aboard the whaleship *Wessex*. When John thought about it that seemed right — there was a sensation of time passing, of slightly perceptible changes between night and day, of visitors, of meals and drink.

Barz stressed over and over the need for John to prolong his stay in the cabin.

'Right now, you see,' Barz said, gnawing on a wheel of cheese, 'we are both living well. We set sail without anyone in the medical line, and being the only one with any advanced book learning, I was given the job of caring for you. Thus, here we are luxuriating in the Captain's commodious quarters, a comfortable bunk for each, and, unheard of for the likes of me in the four oceans and seven seas, our own seat of ease. Oh, to be able to loosen one's bowels and not have someone, inches away, yelling for you to hurry up. As for you: you are not dead. You're resting, relaxing, gaining strength day by day. Me: I am here to watch over you, finally eating some decent food, exempt from the duties out there,' now pointing with a hunk of salt pork he had picked up, 'that I am disinclined to do. Let us not upset the applecart.'

John agreed that it would be a bad thing to upset any cart. He was still unwell and he liked being waited on. John enjoyed hearing Barz speak, straight through for most of the day. He talked of home, stressing names that had a familiar chime: Mass-a-choo-settss, Co-choo-it, Nan-tukk-itt. But John really liked the ones that sounded so foreign: Bah-stun, Cam-brij, New-bed-fuhd.

Barz yammered away, barely stopping for breath. He was like Father Kelly when the priest first arrived, screed after screed, talking non-stop, using words that even John couldn't really catch. There was a resemblance to the good father which made John smile inwardly: both were redheads, wiry, thin and taut, quick with a smile, but there was something underneath those smiles — a quiver, a twitch of the eye — that could change at a snap. John settled back, content to listen to the monologues, letting Barz's words stream by.

They were only occasionally interrupted by a visit from the Captain. Barz, hearing the tramping boots and the soft knock, would make John lie back and affect feverishness, splashing a bit of water on John's face.

'How is he?' the Captain would whisper.

Barz's voice deepened with authority. 'Improving. But fractionally. Hippocrates recommends fresh meat. You may have to slaughter one of your hens. Feed a fever, Captain, is our best course here. And some wine might help as well. The claret.'

'Who is this Hippocrates you keep mentioning?' John asked after the Captain had left.

'Ah, well,' Barz laughed. 'A genius of a Greek, two thousand years dead whom I have scarcely read. Those with little formal education are always impressed by the ancients.'

Barz threw himself on the cot and licked his lips. 'Oh, we shall have roast chicken tonight. How long has it been?'

North Atlantic

Day after day John stayed in the Captain's cabin, chatting to Barz and feigning insensibility when the Captain crept in.

He was eating again. In his last days with the People, he had had little, ghosting around from hut to hut, wraith-like and delirious, trying to cadge a bite here and there, not getting anything, not caring. The food, which Barz kept telling him was the best in the ship, wasn't as good as he was used to — he could see why many seamen looked so unhealthy — but it put a sparkle and brightness back in his eyes.

He felt sorry for the Captain. His face was earnest and trusting, patiently waiting for John to regain the strength to speak. 'It is wrong to deceive that man,' John said after the Captain tiptoed out after another visit. 'Surely, it is wrong.'

Barz put his bottle down, wiping a dribble of Burgundy from his chin. 'There is no deception if there is no hurt. Wrong? John, my friend, we come from different countries, different worlds, different cultures. Is it wrong for an ordinary man such as I, such as you, to finally sup at the table for which we are worth? To finally get our true rewards? We are wretched folk: a penniless whalerman and a savage, no offence, a savage, plucked from a certain frigid sea death. Yet even so, are we not God's children? Do we not deserve the best? If God gives us the tools, the ability for subterfuge, does He not mean for us to do so? I, my friend, am tired of waiting for my reward in the next life.'

As it had often been with Father Kelly, John knew the words but somehow felt he was missing their essence. He lapsed into silence.

There were frequent interruptions. A shout for all hands, a clanging bell from on deck and Barz would slam his bottle down and grumble, 'You would think the sun would not rise and the world would not spin if we did not adjust those fucking sails.'

A bang of the door and Barz would be gone, often for hours, returning lathered in sweat, roughened hands covered by a sticky black substance. John hated the time alone. Barz's voice prevented him from thinking about being boxed in, the airlessness and unceasing movement. To distract himself he would try to read, picking up the

only book in the Captain's cabin, the Bible. He found himself reread-
ing the passages about ships — Jonah, the apostles in their fishing
boats and, of course, Noah. But then the *Wessex* might dip, making
his stomach flip and gurgle, swooshing along with every pitch and
shudder.

There was little to distract in the cabin. A plain wooden table and
chair, a small row of glass windows that opened to the sea but were
most often boarded up. A skylight overhead battened down and
closed. A few shelves whose contents were locked and bolted away.

Yet there was a painting of a woman on one of the walls. John was
not unfamiliar with portraits; Father Kelly carried two small minia-
tures. They were, the priest would say, 'of me Ma and Da'. John didn't
get to see them often because whenever Father Kelly would extract
them from his breast pocket, he would devolve from small sniffles to
a low gulping, 'Oh, Father, forgive me, oh forgive me.'

The cabin's portrait was a woman dressed in white, a cascade of
black locks falling down, framing pale skin, though her hair was cut
short, perhaps cropped, at the back. She was sideways on, lips slightly
parted, looking upwards with big, startling, almost amber eyes with
flecks of red, a combination of colours that John thought could not
exist in real life. Her expression seemed troubled and thoughtful.
John would get out of the cot and shuffle over, placing his fingertips
over the woman's cheek. John wanted to bring her into his arms and
make it all better.

John was dozing after Barz had left for his 'infernal fucking other
duties' when he was pulled out of sleep by the stamping of feet. This
was not like the usual footfall, the rushed boom-boom-boom accompanied by hollering and hallowing. No, this stamping was rhythmic
and regular. A definite beat. Then he heard above the stamping the
strains of the fiddle. The fiddle that he knew so well, the happy sing-
sawing which he associated with every ship that visited the cold deep
harbour.

He sprang out of his cot and, for the first time, opened the cabin
door and stepped out. It was night-time, the ship illuminated by softly
glowing orange lanterns scattered on her arms. The entire company
was gathered in the waist. The fiddler sat on a barrel near the side,

scratching out a jaunty tune. About fifteen or so men were gathered in the middle, stomping away in a hurly-burly swarm. A few were on the sides passing around a jug. Only the Captain stood apart near the helm, looking out to sea, his hands clasped behind him.

John knew the tune, he had danced to it several times on different ships. With a whoop of glee he ran towards the crowd, giving the Captain a jovial clap on the back as he went past. John jumped into the midst of the men, and cavorted around smiling and laughing. A few of the men stopped, the fiddler skipped a beat. But John's smile and exuberance were contagious and soon all were smiling and dancing.

As the song ended, John wiped the sweat from his glowing face, patting the backs and shoulders of the other dancers. The Captain rushed to him.

'Glory be,' he said, pumping John's hand. 'Millar, you have convinced me of the ameliorative effects of music and dance, but surely this is a miracle. Mere hours ago our Esquimaux was bedridden and delirious.'

Barz looked at John sullenly, then back to the Captain. 'Yes, Captain. But mayhaps this show of spirits is a bit of over-exuberance brought on by his fever. I would suggest he should go back to the cabin.' The Captain shook his head. 'Nonsense, Millar. You may be our *in loco medicus*, but I can clearly see a miracle. Tell me, sir, how do you feel?'

'Please, Captain, the music is glorious. More dancing, please.'

The Captain's eyes shifted downwards. 'Yes, but perhaps it is far too cold a night, for even you, to go about as God made you. Mr Coffin, get the man some clothes.'

Mr Coffin was standing near his Captain's shoulder, his eyes also cast downwards. 'Yes, sir,' he said rather wistfully.

'Well, you pretty well spoiled things, eh, mate?' Barz said sourly.

John looked at his feet and frowned. He opened his mouth to explain that his response to the music the previous night was as involuntary as drawing breath, but stopped short when he looked up. Barz's face — that lively, friendly, smiling face — had changed utterly, distorted into rage.

Barz bared his teeth, biting down on his bottom lip so fiercely it looked as if he might draw blood. 'Well,' he said at length. 'Get dressed. We'll take a turn. The Captain wants to meet and talk now that you are . . . cured.'

They left the Captain's cabin and walked the length of the ship. In the clear light of day, with all the men crowded on board, John felt that ship seemed delicate — a fragile dried leaf in a wide expanse of sea. Last night it had seemed the deck was part of the horizon, like it went on forever. He returned the smiles of the crew, who looked up from their duties to steal a quick glance before being ordered back to work. Barz's face darkened as they walked on. A couple of times he turned to say something to John, but broke off, whirling away abruptly, his fists clenched by his sides. He and Barz circled the ship and returned to the cabin they had left.

Finally Barz hissed, 'Cap'n will see you now.' John had never seen Barz in the clear light of day and he was fascinated by his face. There were patches of red rashes, an archipelago of little islands spreading from chin to forehead, that became brighter the more agitated he got.

'What age are you?' John asked.

'Five and twenty. Why?'

'You seem older.'

Barz leaned forward and squeezed John's arm. 'Remember something. His state of mind.' Barz tapped his head for emphasis. 'His faculties have been rearranged and disturbed. Do not prey on them.'

Before John could answer he was shoved through the door.

The cabin had been completely transformed, so quickly that John was disoriented — was this really the same place he had just come from? The bunk was stowed away, a desk had been put out in the middle of the room on which a map was spread over, chairs were set out, and chests had appeared. And Captain Chase was behind the desk, smiling broadly. He sprang up and ran around the desk, taking John's hand in his.

'Hello, my dear sir. Hello again, I should say. I would like to take this opportunity to welcome you aboard the whaleship *Wessex* formally. How are you feeling? Have you recovered?'

John smiled. 'I am well.'

'Good, good.'

The Captain held John's gaze for a long searching moment, which John met before having to turn away. John cleared his throat and pointed at the portrait on the wall. 'Is that a good likeness?' he asked.

'Ah, yes, my good wife,' Captain Chase said somewhat vaguely. 'My dear, blessed wife, Isobel.'

'Her hair is . . . interesting.'

'Yes, my wife has some, shall we say, inclinations.'

'Inclinations?'

'Beliefs about the role of the fairer sex in our society. That shortened hair at the back . . . it borders on manliness, does it not?'

'Well, I am not altogether certain—'

'You see, she believes she should be able to wear it as a man, and not have to hide it in a bonnet when going about her business out of the house — that is one manifestation of it. I indulge her amusing little whims.

'But come, sir. Where you hail from, I surmise, political and philosophical discussions of the rights of men and women such as my dear wife loves to bring up ad nauseam are few and far between. Please, let us sit down.'

The Captain whirled nimbly around the desk, fussily whipping the tails of his green coat back before he sat down. The way he moved was somewhat theatrical, and John had the distinct impression that every part of those movements were considered, perhaps even practised. He remained standing until the Captain motioned to the chair. John sat down heavily and almost immediately felt his stomach lurch; he had not gained sea legs when he had been abed. He found it worse now as he sat in the chair, overly conscious of, and fighting against, the ship's roll. He became momentarily mesmerised by the pendulum movements of the lanterns hanging behind the Captain's head. John snapped out of it when he realised the Captain was gazing intently at his face.

John fidgeted in his seat, until he could bear the silence no more. 'I am very grateful, sir, for you having rescued me.'

Captain Chase shook his head. 'I dare say that I am the one who is grateful. For you have been delivered to me. I was told to find you and here you are.'

John frowned, reaching behind the chair to grip one of the legs. He felt he had to anchor himself to something solid. 'That was . . . fortunate for me. Who told you?'

The Captain smiled. 'I was told by someone known to us both.' He then glanced upwards and John followed his gaze, staring perplexedly at the thick broad ceiling beams.

'Yes,' the Captain continued. 'And now I must ask you to tell me where to go.' He placed his fingertips lightly on the map. He looked downward, encouragingly, at the map then up at John again. John studied the map dubiously for a few moments.

The Captain searched John's face. 'Forgive me, perhaps it is the wrong one. This is the South Pacific, of course, where most fertile whaling grounds are, but maybe it is wrong, all wrong.' He threw the map off the table violently and replaced it with another stowed nearby. 'The North Pacific. No? What a fool I am!' And again ripping the map off. 'The North Atlantic. Just point to where we should go.'

The Captain looked beseechingly at John. John hesitated and placed his finger somewhere in the middle of the map. The Captain stared hard at where John was pointing, then placed his hand next to John's, their fingertips just touching.

'In this very place?' the Captain asked.

There was such vulnerability in the man's face, John thought. He did not want to disappoint him, but he had gone too far. 'Yes,' John said, at length.

'Well, now,' the Captain whispered, then yelled, 'Mr Arthur, Mr Arthur. There you are, took your time. Tell Mr Coffin to set a course for 45 degrees North North-east.'

Cotton Arthur was forty-three and looked a weather-beaten sixty. He had whaled since the age of eleven, survived three shipwrecks, a harpoon wound that left a semi-circular smile on his neck, fourteen hurricanes, seven typhoons and six cases of the clap. Much had passed before his grey, watery eyes. Yet he blinked several times, opened his mouth as if to say something, turned to leave, then back again.

He cleared his throat. '*North North-east?*' he said, each syllable more uncertain than the one preceding it. 'Sir?'

'Were my instructions somehow unclear, Mr Arthur?' the Captain said. Then turning to John, after Arthur had left, a soft: 'North North-east, yes?'

By the time John emerged with the Captain onto the deck, the ship was already turning. The crew were running down from the yards, most with bewildered expressions on their faces.

And as they stayed North North-east, the bewildered expressions gradually turned anxious, then sour.

On the third day, Barz brought John below decks, speaking to him low and urgently. 'Do you know where we are going?'

John motioned in the general direction the ship was sailing.

Barz rolled his eyes, bit his lower lip. 'Yes, but where are we going?'

'I pointed to the map. He asked me to.'

'Do you know what we do? We hunt whales. But not just any whales. The spermaceti, the leviathan of leviathans. He, and she, can now mostly be found in the Pacific Ocean, Magellan's pond, which, I am afraid to say my good sir, is in the opposite direction of where the ship is sailing.'

John waited, and Barz went on, the rash on his face brightening, 'You must tell him you made a mistake, you must convince him that your first instinct was all wrong.'

'I just don't understand,' John said. 'Why would he listen to me? Why am I pointing the way?'

Nantucket

Owen Chase believed in Christ the Saviour and the Good Lord above. Fervently, just as long as Jesus, the Father and the Holy Spirit delivered his ship into port stuffed with whale oil. And thus far, the Holy Trinity did, bless them, for ever and ever. Amen. But the Holy Trinity had help. Owen at various times prayed to Yahweh for a stiff wind, Allah for deliverance from Barbary pirates, beseeched Shiva the Destroyer to spare the *Wessex* from a cyclone. His beliefs were catholic — Catholic, even, as he once sailed through a typhoon shouting out the rosary with one of the Papists on board.

Owen stood on the crosstrees of the *Wessex*'s mainmast, one hand nonchalantly caressing the mast, balancing on the nine-inch round yardarm, the only thing between him and seventy-five feet of air to the deck. He watched the men bustle about beneath him, rolling casks from the Nantucket quay to the ship.

His heart was singing. Here he was happiest — those sunshiny joyous moments of delicious anticipation before a voyage.

The previous night, as they lay under the covers, he said to Isobel that preparing the ship for sea was like their courtship.

She had been lying pressed against him, languidly post-coital, whilst she idly traced figures of eight on his chest. Her finger froze. 'Victualling and stowing ballast aboard the *Wessex* is like our courtship. Is that what you are saying, husband?'

She paused before the last word, lingering over it in a way that made his stomach drop.

Owen never was good with words, at least not with Isobel. Of course he did not mean it was like their courtship, just the feeling was, that sort of heart-pounding excitement. He blinked several times. 'No, no. I am misrepresenting my thoughts yet again. I—'

She placed a finger on his lips, shut her eyes and half smiled. 'No. Do not. Do not speak.'

She then kissed his neck and climbed on top of him again.

Owen let go of the mast and inched out on the yardarm. The pole bent with his weight and he bobbed up and down, balancing hands outstretched on either side. He turned towards the town, and could just about see Isobel looking out at the ship from the widow's walk on the top of their house. He was teasing. Isobel was fearless in most things except for heights. Seeing him on the rigging always sent her into a panic. He stopped bobbing and rode the final vibrations of the yardarm until it stilled. He looked down at the men, across the wide arc of the harbour and up at the overcast sky. Then there was a blue-bright flash and he somehow knew, even as he was blasted out into the air and perceived a distant roll of thunder, that he had just been smote by the Hand of God.

Isobel wished Owen would drive the men to fit out the ship quicker. There was the possibility, if they did not finish by tomorrow evening, they would not leave until they had the right tide in a week's time. She always loved the sight of her husband's ship warping off the pier and sinking the island behind it. It meant peace, many months of it. Of course there was part of her that loved the sight of him coming back as well. An old Nantucket saying: 'Abstinence makes the heart grow fonder.'

On the first day of his return they would not even make it to the bedroom, meeting at the front door, all lips and tongues and fingers and ripped stays and torn breeches. They would make their way through the house, fucking on the reception hall floor, on the sitting room day bed, standing on the first-floor landing, until finally reaching the four-poster bed.

She loved the smell of him then, redolent of the ship, of sea and salt and tar and wood. Odours she never thought were particularly agreeable on their own, but when they mixed with his scent, they were irresistible.

She ran over things. Owen Chase was the handsomest man, still, she had ever laid eyes on. Eyes so startling bright and blue that it was almost uncomfortable to look directly into them. A pouty mouth that she had to physically restrain herself from kissing the moment she set eyes on him — she had had to pinch herself in the leg to get back to her senses when he took her other hand in her father's drawing room on that fateful day six years previously. And yet. Owen Chase at nine and twenty was the youngest and one of the most successful whale captains on Nantucket. And yet. Owen Chase was generally kind to her, was a good provider, treated her with solicitude and warmth. And yet. And yet. And yet.

They had married on Empyrean Rock, the largest of the Felicity Islands, just before the start of the last war. Her Church of Scotland missionary father and former Doctor of Divinity at Edinburgh University was an imperious, domineering man — in the lecture hall and with his students. Yet he was befuddled and cowed by his two daughters, almost helpless to resist whenever they wanted anything. And Isobel, desperately, desperately wanted to get off the claustrophobic Felicity archipelago, and it only took a little persuading for him to agree.

When Owen Chase first strode into their house on the Felicity Islands, he had seemed so charming, erudite and handsome. Dashing, more like. When she looked at his face, with the tiny scar on his right cheek that only served to accentuate his features, she thought of sword fights, boarding ships on the Spanish Main, yardarm to yardarm battles, courageously ploughing through storm-ravaged seas.

She longed to run her fingertips, her tongue, along that scar. Owen too, was enraptured. They conspired to find time, every moment they could, to be alone together. He delayed the *Wessex*'s departure for one tide, then another, until he could delay no more. He dropped down on a knee in front of her in the garden. 'Isobel,' he stammered, 'I know we have not known each other for long —'

'Oh yes, Owen,' she blurted out before he finished. 'Oh, yes.'

She had realised her mistake somewhere in the middle of the Pacific. Owen could seemingly not talk about anything but whaling. What had seemed so fascinating back in Empyrean — the art of the hunt, the terror of a hurricane, the variables of oil pricing — was now tedious. Whaling itself was dangerous, certainly. Weather and the hunt had their perils, pirates were a worry, and depending on the state of affairs with Great Britain, impressment by a passing Royal Navy frigate was a concern. By the time they reached Cape Horn, Owen began retelling his anecdotes. A claustrophobic life in Empyrean was traded for one on Nantucket. In the Felicity Isles, her father and the other missionaries talked of little but converting the heathen. Nantucket was a town that talked only of blood and money and killing. Yes, God was mentioned frequently — the island was mostly Quakers — but it was about God delivering the whale, to be ripped apart and drained of its juices to be converted to oil and cold hard cash.

And now, Isobel could see Owen was trying to make her nervous with his cavorting on that thin strip of a yardarm. 'I hope you fall,' she said quietly to herself, then pinched herself in the thigh and shook her head, horrified she had said it.

She was about to put the spyglass down when the bolt of lightning blasted Owen off the top of the *Wessex*.

'Your husband,' Dr Jeremiah Franklin intoned portentously, 'has been knocked insensible.'

Isobel was sitting at Owen's bedside. She looked at his bluish face, his eyes blackened and swollen shut. His fists were balled up tightly and, no matter how hard they tried, they could not straighten his fingers out. His breathing was shallow, far too shallow.

She turned and faced Dr Franklin. He was Benjamin Franklin's great-grandson, a fact Jeremiah often managed to introduce moments after meeting new acquaintances. Though he often did not have to broach the subject himself because he emphasised the likeness by wearing his hair long with a pair of rounded bifocals perched superfluously on the tip of his nose. After a moment or two, people would say: 'Why, sirrah, you are the spit of our dear Mr Franklin.' The affectation was not without practicality; his practice prospered — his was the busiest on the island — because Nantucketers wanted to come close to a little Founding Father stardust.

Dr Franklin put a consoling hand on Isobel's shoulder. She stared at it until he took it away. She pinched the bridge of her nose, blinked her red-rimmed eyes. 'He has been knocked insensible? Is that your considered opinion, Dr Franklin?' she said drily. 'I am amazed at your powers of diagnostication.'

'Well, well, I . . . ' Dr Franklin flushed scarlet, his eyes ranging around the room as if hoping a rejoinder could be read off one of the paintings on the walls. Wit, alas, had not passed down through the

Franklin generations. He took a handkerchief out and wiped his bifocals, putting them back on quickly. 'Your husband was struck by
lightning and fell some 100 feet to the harbour. He is in a deep coma.
He lives because he did not hit the deck, but I am amazed he lives yet.
Give him quiet, a dark room and he may rouse himself. Or he may
not. I do not know, in truth.' Isobel shuddered slightly as the doctor
slammed the door behind him. She watched Owen for the rest of the
night, hardly moving in her chair, her heart skipping a beat whenever
his breathing became too shallow.

A soft deferential knock on the door made Isobel start, confused by
sunlight drifting in through the window. She must have nodded off.

'Ma'am,' Nancy said, poking her head into the room. 'Mr Mather is
here. He has come to see how Mr Chase is faring.'

Isobel blinked at the maid. 'Mr Mather is here himself?'

Nancy nodded. 'And he doesn't look too chipper, if I do say so,
ma'am.'

'I shall be down soon.'

Isobel had not seen Ezekiel Mather in perhaps half a year. In fact,
she had heard the old man, victim of some incurable, unnameable
wasting disease, had not even set foot out of the house since Christ-
mastime. He was the owner of the *Wessex*, and eight other
whaleships, one of the many old souls on the island who somehow
managed to square rampant, lusting commercialism with Quakerism.

He had always doted on Owen, and was extremely solicitous to
Isobel, but only, she suspected somewhat uncharitably, because Owen
brought home his ships laden down with oil. Still, she appreciated his
plain-talking manner and lack of artifice. 'At my core, ma'am,' he said
to her once, 'I am a mean skinflint. A tough old son of a bitch, you'll
pardon my language. I reckon I'll need to account for that when I meet
my maker.'

Few had seen him these last six months, not even Owen. Ezekiel
did his business through Mrs Hummock, his fearsome, devoted and
brutally efficient housekeeper (and, it was assumed widely, his lover)
who would call around with documents for Owen to sign, manifests
to go over. For a time, Isobel had thought the housekeeper had actually done Ezekiel in and was running the business herself.

23

'My dear child,' Ezekiel said, as Isobel entered the downstairs drawing room. 'My dear child.'

He rose, slowly and with effort. She was shocked at how much he had aged. He was a giant of a man, about six and a half feet tall. His shoulders, still broad and strong when she last saw him despite his seventy-five years, were stooped. He was thinner, his black coat hung as loosely as the turkey wattles under his chin. She took his hands and he winced slightly. His meaty paws engulfed her hands, but had lost their former strength, were arthritic, all knuckles and gnarled veins.

'How does he fare?' he asked, with such naked concern her heart melted.

'Let us go see him,' she said.

Ezekiel sat in the chair next to the bed, leaning slightly forward, hands resting crisscross on his cane. Isobel perched on the window sill, watching the old man. He stared fixedly at Owen, his mouth slightly agape, seemingly bewildered and entranced.

Ezekiel looked over at her suddenly and she blushed and turned away, feeling as if she had intruded upon an intimacy.

'I often wonder how one gets here,' Ezekiel said.

'Sir?'

'It seemed like yesterday I was battling leviathan in the South Pacific, brawling in a Montevideo cantina, enjoying the ever so accommodating native ladies of the Sandwich Islands, begging your pardon, ma'am.' He shot a quick glance at Isobel. 'We do these things when we are young and at sea. Not your husband, I am sure. The accommodating native ladies bit, I mean. But now.' He looked at his hands. 'Useless and weak.'

'I have seen many young men die, in my time,' he continued. Isobel sucked in her breath and Ezekiel raised an apologetic hand. 'I am sorry, my dear. I do not mean to alarm you. The Good Lord shall not abandon your husband, of that I do hope.'

A dry hacking cough, then a long pause as he gathered strength. 'Nevertheless, young men do die in our business. I have sent so many to their deaths. Not of a purpose, you understand, but as a matter of course. Taken by weather or whales. Natives or disease. And will I have to answer for *that* in the final reckoning? 'And yet, sometimes

I wonder if God does not punish more those whom He spares. In my looking glass of a morning I see someone I do not recognise. It is astonishing, astonishing how decrepitude marks us. And look—'

Here Ezekiel held out hands again which quivered and trembled. 'Try as I might I cannot hold them still. My body is no longer under my control. It seems . . . it seems like I was young just a moment ago.'

Isobel stepped closer to him. 'Mr Mather, I do not know what to say.'

A ghost of a smile. 'I am not looking for answers, my dear. Not earthly ones, any rate. When one is dying, one looks to God for answers, but He seems not inclined to talk.'

'Oh, Mr Mather, you are not . . .'

'Please, child. Indeed I am, we both know that to be true. I have spent the most of the last six months in bed, trying to call to account my life. Praying. Looking for answers, getting none. Looking for a miracle. For a sign. And this is God's answer. A young husband, fighting for his life.'

Ezekiel pursed his lips, leaned forward and with a trembling hand touched Owen's forehead.

Owen's eyes snapped open and he inhaled in a great gulp like a pearl diver emerging from the water. He jack-knifed up to a sitting position, breathing heavily. Isobel and Ezekiel stood, open-mouthed as Owen looked at them as if not knowing them. Then he grabbed Ezekiel's hand, sat up, and brought himself eyeball to eyeball with the old man. 'Oh Ezekiel my brother,' he croaked. 'You will know the things I have seen, the things I have seen.' Then he slumped back.

'Owen!' Isobel cried, suddenly brought out of her shock, and rushed to the bedside but was blocked by the old man's bulk.

'What did you see? What did you see?' Ezekiel whispered urgently.

Isobel squeezed past Ezekiel. 'Owen.'

Owen looked at his wife vaguely, then piercingly at Ezekiel. 'A vision, I have seen a vision, brought to me through ice and fire. I am to deliver unto you a son of Noah. He will show me the way, and then show you the way. For he is out there' — here pointing northward — 'for he is out there and it is through him deliverance rests.'

Owen had collapsed back on his bed and slept peacefully for several hours, a half-smile on his face. He woke with Isobel, Ezekiel and Dr Franklin gathered around the bed.

'Friends. My wife.'

Dr Franklin bent down, a candle in his hand. He stretched one of Owen's eyelids open, brought the candle close, peering in. 'How do you fare, Captain?' he said.

'Prime, thank you, Doctor, prime,' Owen answered in an all-hands-on-deck-voice.

'How is your head?'

'As clear as it has ever been. And I beg your forgiveness but I must take your leave. I must go to my ship.'

As Owen rose from the bed, the three tried to restrain him – but he was too strong. He threw off his night shirt, the two men looking away, and went to his wardrobe. 'What date is this?'

No one answered and he asked again, turning around and looking at Ezekiel. Ezekiel told him.

'I have been away for three days, then. We must be at sea in another three. How has Mr Coffin fared in fitting out the ship?'

'There has been a cessation of activities,' Ezekiel said. 'As we were undetermined about your health.'

'Well then, I must be away as quick as possible.'

Owen shook both men's hands, gave his wife a peck on the top of her head and bounded out of the door.

A few hours later, Isobel stood on the quayside, watching in wonder as Owen ran about across the deck of the *Wessex*, pointing, shouting and directing the men. 'Hup to it, lads,' he yelled, 'hup to it! There are whales to kill and a mission to complete, and we won't get to see lollygagging like this!'

The crew, though pulled from most of Nantucket's taverns and whorehouses after the unexpected day or two of freedom, worked with fervour, spirits raised by Owen's reappearance.

Ezekiel was a few paces away from Isobel, half supporting himself by his cane, half by resting against one of Mrs Hummock's generous hips. Isobel tugged at her bonnet and pulled it off, ignoring Mrs Hummock's tutted disapproval.

'Are you to allow this, sir?' Isobel said.

Ezekiel had been smiling as he watched the commotion on deck, which faded slightly when he turned to her. 'I know it beggars belief,' he said. 'Your husband has regained, or even doubled, his former strength. We cannot ignore miracles, we cannot ignore divine will.'

'He does appear transformed. But, sir, surely it is too soon, surely he needs to be examined before exerting himself even more.'

Ezekiel shuffled so he was facing Isobel directly. 'Ma'am, your husband has received a message from God, struck down by lightning on a cloudless day—'

'Nonsense, you forget that I was watching. Storm clouds were gathering.'

'Mr Coffin there' — here a nod of the head towards the mate — 'said to me it was a clear, sunny day. I was indisposed at home and cannot verify. Apologies, but you are no mariner, my dear, and I trust what Mr Coffin had to say. Besides, did you not hear your husband? "It is through him deliverance rests".'

'I believe he also said that that deliverance rests on him procuring the son of Noah who by my reckoning has been dead some six thousand years.'

'*A* son of Noah,' Ezekiel said. 'Not *the.*'

Mrs Hummock put a hand on Ezekiel's shoulder. 'Sir, your choler is rising. You know what the doctor said. Please, shall we take our leave?'

Ezekiel nodded and the two limped away, Mrs Hummock shooting Isobel a dark look over her shoulder. Isobel spun on her heel, turning back to the *Wessex* in exasperation. The men, indeed, seemed driven and propelled by some kind of enthusiasm. Even Owen's brainy, disreputable, work-shy cousin seemed energised, and was lustily winching a netful of boxes from the dock, applying himself with far more vigour than she had ever seen him do any task. Barz eventually paused to rest for a moment, wiping his forehead. He glanced in Isobel's direction, caught her eye and gave her an ever so slight guilty shrug before returning to work.

North Atlantic

Barz leaned close to John. 'We were all caught up in it, all of us, you see. When we pulled him from the water he was dead. Blue, no heart-beat. But then he coughed and he started breathing again. But still he would not wake. And there he was three days later burning with something inside that made us all believe. We were swept up, took leave of our reason.'

John opened his hands as if presenting himself. 'And now he has found me.'

'You are a son of Noah, then?' Barz asked.

John suddenly felt a pang, saw the faces of his mother, father and Mary swim before him. Barz looked at the prow of the *Wessex*. Little frostings of ice and snow had begun to gather on it as the ship dipped into the sea. 'We need to be away from here, in warmer climes. Please speak to him.'

A few moments later John was admitted to the Captain's cabin, reciting carefully the phrases Barz had scripted: 'Captain, I have made a mistake. I believe we need to round the Horn and head for the Galapagos or the Sandwich Islands.'

Owen laid a kindly hand on John's shoulder. 'No, no. I know this crew, I know the men, I know what they have been saying to you. Their faith comes and goes, they are not resolute like you and me. They think they will try to get you to change what the Almighty has charged us to do. No, we go with God, go with what God has told you. North North-east we stay.'

And so they remained North by North-east. The *Wessex* was buffeted by howling winds, tearing down from the Arctic. Day upon day, the company was in constant activity, fighting to gain every sea mile.

The more the crew fought the elements, the more John could feel them turn. The smiles he encountered when he first careened onto the deck to sing and dance, descended gradually into grim frowns.

John's heart sank. He could abide almost anything bar being disliked. He tried to win them over. 'Hello, my good sir,' he chirruped to Isaiah Sheppard. 'What are the uses of this contraption?'

Sheppard, lean, withered with a face fissured with wrinkles, slowly reeled in the logline which measured the speed of the ship. He turned, held the log reel in his hands, squinted at John so a thousand tiny tributaries to his main wrinkles erupted on his face. 'If it weren't for the Captain, this contraption would be used to be shoved up your arse.'

Later John sauntered up to the second mate Matthew Joy, singing out 'Give you joy, Master Joy,' his ironic 'we're all shipmates and in this together' sally about the 'moderate breeze' (a 50-mile per north-easterly that made the *Wessex* tip on a 45-degree angle) dying on his lips when Joy glanced at him with murderous hate.

After two weeks even Barz had stopped speaking to him. John would end up spending most days near the masthead, watching the *Wessex* crew struggling with the elements and the deep blue-grey water churning into white foam by the prow.

Solace was evening meals with the Captain in his cabin, warmed and lit by whale oil light. 'Well, Mr Sackhouse,' Owen had said a few days after the ship had turned northwards, 'the men have turned against you.'

John smiled uncertainly. 'They are not as welcoming as they have been, sir.'

'Men, humanity in general, are a fickle lot. Very few people are constant and true. This I found out very quickly in my life, and whalermen in particular are more variable than most. They twist and turn and go whichever way the wind blows them. It is the rare man who stays the course or remains loyal. This I value more than anything. This I see in you.'

At table, John had noticed, Owen had the habit of not looking you in the eyes, until he wanted to drive a point home. Whilst he talked, his attention danced somewhere a foot or so above your head, only to hawk in with those piercing eyes at the crucial moment. John could not figure out whether this was artifice — a theatrical trick — or a strange combination of diffidence and confidence. Yet, it seemed to work.

'Yes, Captain,' John squeaked, doing his best to hide the tears forming. 'I am with you entirely.'

Owen looked away when he noticed his glistening eyes.

'Forgive me, Captain,' John said.

'Owen, please. Captain on the deck, but you are not one of the men here, Mr Sackhouse. I would like to think of you as a friend.'

Here real tears began to form and Owen quickly said: 'Erm, um, listen. May I ask you a question? Why is a dog like a tree?'

John blinked. 'I don't know, Owen.'

'Because they both lose their bark once they are dead.'

Owen nodded, smiling. 'Bark, dead, you see. No? No? Well, then I will tell you a story. When I first met Isobel, my wife, we went to a ball held at her father's missionary house. It was a ceilidh, an energetic series of dances that whip you round and round. Towards the end I said to her: "My dear, do you not get dizzy doing these ceilidh dances?" And she said: "No sir, I do not, for it is just the way of the whirled." You see it, Mr Sackhouse? The way of the *whirled*.'

John looked at Owen impassively. 'How about this one,' Owen went on, not only undeterred but enlivened. 'Two gentlemen were standing on the quay in Boston town when a woman passed them. One of the gentlemen said to the t'other: "That is one of the most beautiful women I ever saw." The lady, overhearing him, turned round and replied: "Sir, I wish I could return the compliment." "So you might, Madam," the gentleman replied. "And you would tell a confounded lie as I did."'

John nodded glumly. 'Now I'll tell you a story, Owen. And it relates to naval matters, so you may find it diverting. Some time ago, an Irishman and an Englishman were condemned for piracy in London, and as is general in these cases they were to be executed over the Thames. Upon the time of the execution, the tide was remarkably high. As the executioner was trying to tie the Irishman's noose, the rope slipped and the condemned plunged into the river and, being a strong swimmer, made it to the other side and freedom. Then, said the Englishman to the hangman: 'Sir, you had better make my rope fast, for I cannot swim and, if I fall in, I shall surely lose my life.''

The two men looked at each other for a long moment before bursting into laughter.

'Wonderful, Mr Sackhouse, wonderful. I shall have to remember that one.'

'Thank you, Owen. And please, call me John. Those are very good jokes; I salute you. It took me a while to understand the whirled/world twist. Tell me, where have you heard them?'

'Heard them? Tosh, they come from my own noggin, don't they? I just make them up in the long hours whilst I'm stamping across the quarterdeck. Yet what of you, Mr Sackhouse? Where did you hear that little beauty?'

John smiled thinly. 'From a friend and teacher. He told me a lot of the Englishman and Irishman variety. He said the roles are reversed if you travelled across the Irish Sea.'

'What of your people, John? Do you have jokes?'

'Do we? Indeed, every year at a huge gathering we have a competition for the best joke-teller, which I humbly can tell you I once won. But I am afraid, they do not do well in the translation.'

'Tosh. I am sure it is all in the telling. Pray, relate one.' Owen's eyes glowed in anticipation.

John looked upward, trying to work out how best to say it. 'One day in late autumn a man and a woman became husband and wife. After the ceremony, night drew in and they laid down for the first time. When the wife woke up at first light, she found she was six months pregnant.'

Owen's smile remained rigid as he waited for the punch line.

After a pause, John said: 'That is the joke. You see, the sun goes down for almost half the year where I am from.'

'Ah, yes. Very good, ha, ha! No, very good, I just did not twig the reference there. Very droll, very droll indeed.'

'Yes, droll,' John said, somewhat deflated. At the gathering where he told that story, there were roiling cascades of laughter, even Torok barking like a seal until tears streamed down his cheeks. 'May I say, Owen, that I would not have taken you as a joking man.'

'No?'

'No. You are rather . . . formidable on the deck. Forbidding.'

'I'm pleased you say that, actually, because that is what I like to call the theatre of the quarterdeck. I have to appear as if I am God Himself. Remote, untouchable, *unquestionable*. How would it look if I revealed my true self to the men; would they hop to it, would they sail *North North-east*? No.'

'Can you always stop playing God? When you leave the quarterdeck, when you leave the ship?'

Owen drank deeply on his claret. 'This, John, is something I have asked myself many times.'

Sunday meals were uncomfortable, however, for it was tradition for Mr Coffin to eat with the Captain, and the first mate would spend most of the time glaring at John — his round, yellowish, rheumy eyes shimmering with rage in their sockets. Mr Coffin would stay as long as he dared, before his rage seemed at a tipping point and begged to be excused.

'Your Mr Coffin does not care overmuch for me,' John said a moment after the first mate slammed the door behind him after one of the trio's first Sunday meals.

Owen slurped the last of his bumper of claret. 'A good first mate,' he said, 'craves order, discipline and is at his very heart, resistant to any change. I have asked him to adapt. He is not taking it well, but will get over it in time. And your snug little cabin is, rather was, his. This has riled him.'

The bawling voice of Mr Coffin raging at a sailor who apparently had not sanded the deck properly, broke in on them. John waited a few beats after the diatribe and said: 'I was unaware I had taken his lodgings. How long should I expect him to be upset?'

'He will become his old self again in perhaps nine months or so.' Owen paused a moment before hooting with laughter. 'Oh, John, your stricken face was most precious.'

John folded his arms, turned away and frowned at the door as Mr Coffin unloaded another barrage of abuse at some poor unfortunate. Owen reached out and touched John's arm. 'My dear sir, I do believe you are discomfited.'

John squared his shoulders. 'I must move my lodgings.'

Owen half smiled. 'Berth.'

'I cannot move my birth, I was born amongst my people.'

Owen stared at John for a moment, a half smile on his lips. 'Are you playing me, sir? At any rate, aboard ship we sleep in a berth.'

'Yes, you sailormen awake every day out of your berth as if reborn.

But I shall not be distracted, Owen — I will need new lodgings and Mr Coffin returned.'

Owen's smile broadened. 'Aboard ship, you *request* something like that from the Captain, you do not demand.'

'Oh, apologies, Owen, I—'

'John. Do not fret. You have given me a good turn. Mr Coffin's querulousness has become tiresome. And Mr Coffin's vexations mean he is not driving the men as he should. Of course, he has commandeered Mr Joy's cabin. Mr Joy is now berthing with the harpooners, and is also resentful. Shit, as my old Captain used to say, flows downhill. But where can you sling your hook?'

'Perhaps with Barzillai? We did form something of a bond during my . . . recovery.'

'You would do that for the *Wessex*, John? You would do that for me? You are a marvel.'

'It is but a trifle, I assure you,' John said, squeezing backward in his chair as Owen had lent forward to shake his hand with somewhat alarming force. John's gaze roved around the cabin, hoping to alight on a new subject of discussion. 'I confess that I have been reading your book, Owen.'

'My book?'

John sprang over to Owen's desk where a thick folio lay. 'Yes, this book here,' he said, rifling through a few pages. 'Though, I have to say you are something of a poor narrator: "4th April 1816. Tremendous choppy sea. Hove to upon spying one spermaceti. Killed it. Reuben Hussey, able seaman, lost three fingers. Shower of shooting stars during the dog-watch. Not more than three hundred seen." A hunt, an injury, inclement weather and a celestial phenomenon, all dispatched in less than fifty words.'

'I employ facts in the log, nothing more.' Owen had followed John to the desk and stood considering him for a moment. 'I confess I did not know you recognised your letters. Can you write as well?'

A flush spread across John's cheeks and there was a flash in his eyes. 'Don't be absurd, of course I can write. Why, I was told I could do so better than most university men, I—'

'I meant no offence,' Owen said, raising a hand in surrender. 'It is a rare thing on this crew.' He rummaged through a sea chest, and handed John another log book, this one blank. 'Perhaps the *Wessex* needs a second, unofficial log. You can put your thoughts on this journey into here. It will be most educational.'

John caressed the book, then clutched it to his chest tightly. 'Oh, Owen. You are the kindest of men.'

'You may not think I am so kind after you've bunked with Mr Millar and his mates.'

'Surely his accomodations are not much different than yours or Mr Coffin's.'

Another hoot of laughter from Owen, one of deep, genuine amusement.

Mr Coffin, smiling widely, escorted John out of Owen's cabin, bringing him past all three masts. And then after the last mast they opened the hatchway. The groan of the hatch stifled a hearty round of belly laughs from within.

'Well off you go, Son of Noah,' Mr Coffin laughed, his hand on John's back, nearly toppling him down the ladder.

John clambered down, his arms full of a hammock and his clothes. The hatch banged shut and, as his eyes adjusted to the gloom, he could make out five men, one of whom was Barz.

'Well, well,' Barz said. 'Cast out of Eden.'

John stood with his arms full, smiling a bit uncertainly.

Finally, Barz went on: 'Yes, here you are now, put into the most vile, smelliest and worst berth in the ship, forced to live with all the other first-timers, green hands, long layers, outcasts, or worse, coofs.'

'Coofs?' John asked.

'Yes, the worst crime of all. We are those who had the misfortune to have been born somewhere else than the glorious island of Nantucket. That's Jim O'Malley, thrice damned for being a New Yorker, Irishman and Papist. Isaac Al-Ali, half Mohammedan, half Jew, enslaved, then escaped. Howard Howarkaliki, from the Sandwich Islands and Joe Cole of Boston whom we call No Nose, for apparent reasons.'

Smiles, nods and in No Nose's case, a strange half-snort greeted John.

'But,' John asked, 'aren't you the Captain's cousin? Do you not get special dispenses?'

Barz smiled. 'Owen's familial obligations fall far short of the obligation to the crew. A ship, my dear Esquimaux, is full of hierarchies and subtle politicking that would not go unremarked in the court of the Borgia. If I were to get, say, a decent berth on one of my first voyages and me not a native Nantucketer, well, it would bring a near mutiny amongst the men. Still, I get the company of these good fellows.

'You interrupted incidentally, Mr Sackhouse, just as we were about to set down for a libation. Would you care to join us for a drink?'

Greenland

John's early memories — long before Father Kelly, when he still thought of himself by the name his parents gave him — were of blood: running rivulets, juddering spurts, pulsing arterial cascades. Dragging paths of crimson cut through snowdrifts, red bubbles floating upwards from churning water. His mother holding him with arms slicked in caribou guts, her tacky fingers painting his face. The anoraks and mittens of the adults covered, first bright then slowly changing into a cruddy brown. In the huts, the slimy undersides of hanging skins, the windows blocked by seal intestines still clotted and caked.

John hated blood. The smell sickened him and the feel of it — particularly when it carried body heat — repulsed him. When he was very small he would run away screeching whenever even a drop touched him. For a while, this amused his parents, it was the family joke: *Look at our brave little hunter!* But as time wore on, they stopped laughing.

One morning, in his eighth year, John's father Qataag announced he was going to bring John out.

His mother Slipal, half dozing under the cover of pelts and furs, yawned.

To hunt? she asked.

I know he is young, too young, but . . .

Qataag finished his sentence with a half shrug and a wrinkle of his nose.

Mary, then still called Umuk (for this was before, long before, Father Kelly arrived) sprang out from under the pelts.

Take me, too, Father, she yelled. Take me, I'm older.

Qataag looked at her, a curious half-smile on his face, chucked her playfully under the chin. No, no, he said, not unkindly. Just Saccheuse. Your brother is one who will hunt.

Later, as they packed up on the sled, John perched uncertainly on top of the gear, Qataag turned to Slipal. She touched his arm, rubbed it gently and looked down on him — for she was a head taller than her husband — with concern.

Are you all right? she asked.

Qataag shrugged. I know he is young, he said, but he must learn. He is far too much like my father.

They set off, John riding in the sled, his father running along beside, whipping the dogs forward, frequently untangling the leads. They travelled to a frozen-over inlet a good distance from the camp. A few of the People were spread over the expanse of white all hunched still as stone, harpoons suspended and ready.

Qataag led the team to three breathing holes, examining each, touching the edges, sniffing over the surface, until deciding on a fourth a long way from the others. He left the sled far from the hole, slapping and kicking the dogs into silence.

Qataag nodded towards the man furthest away.

You can see Torok there, he said. He's a hunter with bad luck. Luck, good or bad, rubs off. Stay away from him.

He spat fiercely then began the lesson, showing John how to silently make the opening larger. He then drilled a smaller hole and inserted his harpoon.

He moved his face close to John, speaking even softer than usual.

Now, he whispered, you have the most important part. Lay down on your belly in front. Still and quiet. And when a seal comes up for air, yell as if your lungs were on fire.

He patted John on the head and smiled, then pressed into his harpoon, somehow at once loose yet taut. John lay down spread-eagled, his chin resting close to the water. He was still and quiet. Then he fell asleep.

He was woken by a thrashing sound and a brush of whiskers on his face. John shrieked and his father responded, thrusting the harpoon home. The struggle lasted what seemed like ages, Qataag fighting with the harpoon line, alternately playing it out then reeling it in. Finally, the line slackened completely and the seal was hauled out onto the ice.

The seal was still alive, moaning and panting heavily, John so close he was warmed by its fishy breath. Qataag used the heavy cudgel, the blow splattering seal brain and blood onto John, who yelped and frantically clawed the matter off his face. The others were now gathering around. Torok, the last to arrive, was scowling until he saw John's reaction. He guffawed.

Ho-ho-ho, he boomed, pointing his harpoon at John. I see Bright Eyes takes after his namesake. Qataag, you'll be lucky if you don't live long, this one won't bring you any meat when you're old.

Qataag turned around slowly, clutching his cudgel tightly, but Torok was already moving away. Later, in their hut, Qataag grabbed John by the shoulders, speaking urgently.

You mustn't be afraid to kill, he rasped.

The tone alarmed John. Everything about his father, except his granite hands and weather beaten face, was gentle. Especially his voice, which was like stroking the softest fur.

But now it was rough and coarse: We have to eat. You can't be afraid. I know you like the meat.

This was true. John especially loved the chewy blubbery bit of seal fat that was just underneath the skin. It was just that meat was always brought to him, fed to him by his mother. He knew that he was eating a thing called 'seal', and he had seen these seals alive and frolicking about, but he never really connected the smell of blood with the getting of that meat. Killing in and of itself didn't bother him. He astonished the others with his long and accurate rock throwing; he was able to bring down birds that were out of reach of even the adults and plunk a hare at 200 paces. He would never shirk from playing Crack and Pop, that game where they rounded up a few skuas from the crags, the young ones that couldn't fly away. John could break this and snap that easily enough. But when the blood started to flow he shrank away, threw his bird down, trying to hide his revulsion. Not that the others would ever notice. Torok's two sons Kelak and Sapok enjoyed it, their faces glowing and frenzied. But once Mary, slowly killing her bird, observing its pain indifferently, looked up suddenly, catching John as he was stifling a retch.

Discarding the carcass, she yelled: Come, we'll go to play with the dogs.

She started off, caught John's eye and smiled. Kelak and Sapok followed — they were always following Mary — running down the crags after her.

Qataag brought John out again and again after the first hunting trip. To the rest of the People it seemed to work. Every time John was strapped down to the sled, he and his father would return so laden down with kills that the dogs were overcome with a blood frenzy. The People would yell and pick John up, parading him around in triumph.

Brave little man, did you kill all these yourself?

Now we see who the *real* hunter in the family is!

Qataag played along through forced smiles. The boy was charmed, sure, and his luck only increased as he got older. John would kill prey without meaning to: losing his balance near a breathing hole and accidentally harpooning a seal that he didn't know was there; tripping down a gorge and dislodging rocks that crushed a great buck caribou; forgetting to fasten the net on the creel, which released a school of freshly caught mackerel, which in turn induced two fat narwhal into beaching themselves.

John was careless, sloppy and inattentive. And it didn't matter. Each incident infuriated Qataag. As John took more and more prey, his father's irritation increased, punctuating lessons with jabs towards John with his hunting knife.

You must learn to hunt correctly.

Yes, Father.

Your luck will run out someday.

Yes, Father.

You cannot hunt on luck alone.

Yes, Father.

A belly won't stay round on luck.

Yes, Father.

Each rebuke cut into John. He wanted to please his father so much. And his father was right. Hunting took courage, skill, but most of all, patience. John could not bear stalking caribou for days or waiting by a breathing hole for hours on end. A few minutes on his own, his mind would wander — he liked to stare up at the sky a lot, dreaming of flying away with the birds — and the next thing he would know, an animal would appear and inexplicably impale itself on his spear.

John and his father's last hunt together was in that fallow time between the great walrus herds of summer and the teeming narwhal pods of winter. The two were in an umiak, paddling for half a day after a young grey whale. Finally they were able to get close enough to risk a harpoon strike. Qataag said that he would do all the work, throw the harpoon, play the creature out to tire it, then finish it off with his lance. All John would have to do was to keep hold of the rope, especially when the moment came for the killing hit when his father would let go of the rope to get all his strength behind the lance. John nodded eagerly. He was always excited during the first part of the hunt.

You must do this right, Qataag said, looking intently into his eyes. You must be prepared. I will be ready, Father.

Qataag grunted, then turned and threw the harpoon with quick beautiful grace. Then they were off, the confused and angry whale towing the umiak. Even bouncing along in the fragile craft with only its rickety skeleton of whale bone and thin layer of walrus skins separating him from the frigid ocean, John soon lost interest and began thinking of Seetiak.

She was from the south end of the island and John had seen her at a gathering last summer, noticed her immediately from across the campfire. She wore a great shock of hair over her eyes like a mask, which she would brush away when she laughed, revealing eyes that danced and sparkled. John spent the greater part of the evening moving places closer to her as people got up and moved about the camp. Finally, sometime during Allaq's long song *The Char Fisherman* — the one he rarely got to finish as Torok would start to bellow, Shut up, you are putting me to sleep — Seetiak's little sister moved and John nonchalantly got up, pretending he was going away, decided against it, and sat next to her.

She brushed away her hair, stared at him levelly, those eyes shining with mirth. I have heard you are a great hunter, though you seem to be the most indecisive, she said. Then she laughed.

John conjured up that moment — the trilling laugh, the spark of mirth in her eyes — over and over in the months since, often consuming him, making him drift off into a reverie. He thought of it now on the chase with the whale, then he imagined showing her all the blubber they were going to bring home, when her people visited the encampment after the Gathering, how impressed she would be.

As the whale was tiring, John spotted two great skuas wheeling overhead. Seetiak loved skua. John quickly stood up, reached into a pocket for a couple of stones and threw two perfect strikes, both birds splashing down next to the boat. As he reached for them, the boat lurched and he heard a cry of anguish. His father had at that moment let go of the harpoon line to pick up the lance. The whale, perhaps sensing a shift, dove, taking the harpoon and the entire rope with it. The animal surfaced a way off, injured but able to escape.

For several heartbeats all was suspended. John was stretched halfway out of the boat, trying to reach the birds with an oar. Qataag stood with the lance in his hand for some time. The tip of it pointed at John, wavering in Qataag's hand ever so slightly.

Neither spoke. John gestured apologetically at the birds. His father put the lance down and slowly turned away towards the front of the boat.

John picked up the birds and they rowed silently back to their camp. They ate the birds wordlessly — John had begun to say he had caught them for Seetiak, but thought better of it — and went to sleep.

The next morning they broke down camp and hitched up the dogs. There may be caribou on the outer hills, Qataag said, finally speaking. I am going alone. This is what I have been talking about for so long. I think your luck has run out.

His father's face was impassive, but John could sense somehow a brightening of his mood.

Yes, Qataag repeated, your luck has run out.

John would always think of that moment, the slightest of smiles on his father's face as he turned. John watched him for many moments, hoping for a last glance back. But no. His father trudged purposefully ahead with a lightness of step, disappearing over the ridge, and was gone.

A thrill would go through the camp whenever the ships came. All of the people would be excited — barring Torok, who would bray about his hatred for them. But then, Torok grumbled at most things. Singing again, he would sigh whenever Keetiak brought his drum out. I shall stuff my ears with blubber. How many times will we hear this stupid tale? he would bark in irritation when Kaasassuuk the One Armed began the story of how he fought three bears all at once.

And then when a ship would appear in the bay: Here they are to bring the pox and fuck the women.

Still, he was often the first on board, ready to trade anything — meat, fur, a few minutes with his daughter — for a mirror, beads or something shiny.

Once when John was young, he had run away from Mary, run for so long and so far he had forgotten why. Soon he was lost, tumbling through the scrub near the cold, deep harbour, until he burst out near the shore to see his father, Torok and the brothers Amaruq and Taqukaq stopping in the midst of hauling some nets out of the water to watch a ship drop anchor. Qataag looked back at the boy, smiled broadly, then frowned. The ships were more likely than not to be safe, but still. There were stories, mostly from long ago: fights coming out of nothing, misunderstandings turning bloody, some of the People going on board and never coming back. So the People were careful with a strange ship, the women and children staying clear until ensuring the sailors could be trusted. But the cold-deep harbour was far from the encampment and it was safer to keep John nearby than to let him loose to get lost or who knows what else.

Plus, John was besotted by the ships — he had been taken aboard four or five. Qataag weighed what was more tolerable: Torok's scorn at John getting underfoot when they climbed aboard the ship, or Torok's outright abuse for John's inevitable wailing tantrum if the boy was left on shore.

Qataag extended his arm to John and said, Let's go meet the seamen, son.

John jabbered excitedly as they paddled the kayaks out, but was stifled with awe as they touched the side and he looked up at the cliff face of wood and smiling faces staring down. He clung to his father's neck as they scaled the side of the ship and clutched his hand tightly as they first moved about the deck.

John was soon distracted, breaking off to stare slack-jawed at the vast

42

wings of sail and the puzzle of rope that kept them in place. He was about to untie a rope to see what would happen when there was a sudden roaring. Torok and his father were trying to remove something from the deck, but the sailors didn't want them to have it. There was pointing and shouting and, while each side understood the raw emotion, the substance of the words was lost. John, rooted to his spot, his hand frozen and clawed against the rope, realised he understood it all.

He tugged at his father's sleeve. He said, They can't let you have that because it helps them steer the ship.

Then to the gap-toothed sailor closest, 'If we can't have . . . object . . . there. Knives, kindly.'

The sailors, his father, Torok, and the two brothers all stopped, eyes boring in on John. The long pause was broken by a tall, wiry man in a long green overcoat who had been deferred to by the seamen. 'Well, fuck me down,' he said, scratching at his fulsome black beard. 'You're a clever little shaver, you are. We should seal the deal with a wee guzzle.' He brought the bottle he had in his left hand to his mouth, the cork making a *wuuhpop* when he extracted it with his teeth. He held it out for Qataag to take.

He says I am a smart . . . child, John said excitedly. He offers you a drink—

I understand that much. Qataag cut John off, taking a long pull from the bottle and passing it on.

Some time later, the People left the ship to a hail of merry good-byes. Qataag and John scrambled down first, Qataag quickly securing his son in the kayak before speeding off towards the shore. The others followed at a more languid pace. A laughing Torok got caught in the rope ladder and had to get help from Amaruq to extricate his foot, while it took Taqukaq several tries before he found the cockpit on his kayak and gingerly placed himself on the seat.

John watched as Torok, Amaruq and Taqukaq followed in his father's wake. The trio were bunched together, so close their paddles would sometimes click-clack when they touched. They were speaking lowly, eyes sometimes sliding towards John.

John, seated in front of his father, looked up and behind at Qataag, whose face was inscrutable.

The others cannot paddle straight, John ventured.

Qataag nodded, but did not look down at John. He said, The sailors' drink is strong, some it affects keenly.

Qataag ploughed deeper into the waves and the kayak surged forward. John's stomach sank. He had felt joyous, if strange and out of sorts as they left. He had done an astounding thing. More so, he had been helpful. Of use. He thought his father would have praised him, chucked his chin, ruffled his hair.

I do not know what happened, Father, John said. It came to me all in a rush. I don't know if I'm clever as that man said, it just came naturally. I wonder—

Stop talking, Qataag said, his eyes hard on the shore. Do stop talking.

It was not long after the entire party made it back to the huts that John's gift was the talk of the People. It was not completely unexpected: John's grandfather, his namesake, could talk to the men in ships as well.

Around the fire that night Torok rumbled, The eyes like his namesake, a sorcerer like his namesake. Bad will come to us and him, you shall see.

The next day, John and Mary were throwing rocks at a single wispy tree a few hundred paces outside the encampment. John had hit it ten times in a row, five apiece with each hand, when Utuk approached. He was a head taller than the rest of the People, and was painfully shy, almost guilty about his height, could barely look others in the eyes. He had lighter skin, too, the son of a Danish missionary on the south end of the island, who fell in love with Utuk's mother in the midst of teaching her the *Ave Maria*, abandoned the mission, and died on his first hunt when disembowelled by a walrus.

Utuk sidled up. He cleared his throat, shuffled his feet, affixed his gaze at some point about a foot or so above John and Mary's heads. What are you two doing?

John picked up a flattish stone and threw it behind his back. It hummed towards the tree, taking off a chunk of bark when it hit.

Well done, Bright Eyes, Utuk said.

I can do it with my eyes closed. Watch!

John scrunched his eyes up dramatically, pitched another rock towards the tree, again taking off a bit of bark.

You peeked, Mary said.

I didn't!

Utuk chuckled. Peeking or not, still very good.

He looked at John and Mary, then quickly back to that point above their heads, cleared his throat again and spat. I was on my way to hunt, he said.

Mary pointed far across the encampment in the opposite direction. Isn't that your sled there?

Utuk nodded. I've taken the long way. I was just wondering, just wondering if you could hold these for a moment.

He thrust his toggle-headed harpoon and lance into John's hands, who held them for a moment. Utuk took them back, mumbled thanks and scampered back towards his sled.

The next day Iluq and Chu, the squat, garrulous twins — barking seals with legs, Qataag called them — convinced John to touch their bows before they left to go auk hunting. As they were eating that night, he told his father about Iluq and Chu.

Qataag stopped chewing, eyes sliding to Slipal.

Why are they doing this? John asked.

His father swallowed, sucked his teeth. For luck. For a blessing. Whatever you do, don't tell the shaman. Don't let the shaman see you.

Why not?

His father shuffled over to John, speaking lowly. Because he has cause to fear you.

Why?

Qataag pursed his lips, reached into the folds of his shirt and pulled out a pocket mirror. It was a thing his father treasured perhaps more than any possession, though he would hardly admit it. John would often catch his father at odd moments, somewhat dreamily looking at himself with it, but when he realised he had been discovered, he would quickly put it back in the secret pocket in his shirt, making sure it was tightly tethered to its leather string.

Look, Qataag said.

45

John made to grab the mirror, but Qataag pulled it back. I said look, do not touch.

He held the glass up so that what filled the mirror was John's eyes, first one, then the other.

These, Qataag said slowly, are different than anyone else's.

John did not have to be told that for he had been made aware of it ever since he could remember. The People, strangers, anyone he first encountered, talked about the glow, the twinkle, the brightness of his eyes. John had no looking glass of his own — and it was impossible to cadge looks off of his father's — but he had looked deep into them many times in any reflective surface he could find, had Mary stare deep into them to tell what she saw. They were not dark brown like Mary's and his parents, but certainly they were not *bright*. It was just that, within the brown of his eyes, there were marbled whorls of other colours, a mid-summer sky blue, a shallow lagoon green.

People say that they are quite like Grandfather's, John said.

The mirror disappeared into his father's shirt. Exactly like, I should think, Qataag said. And he had the gift that you have, as you know. Your grandfather and the shaman's father . . . did not get along.

But that was Grandfather, and I am me.

Qataag gripped John's arm. The shaman will not see it that way, son. Do not let him see the others coming to you for blessings. It will not be good for you. For us.

John thought his father was overreacting. If the shaman, and the People for that matter, thought there was something magical in what he did they were sorely mistaken. In retrospect, he realised that in the four or five times he had been aboard ship, he had been hearing and gradually understanding their language. The sensation was like someone shouting from far away and not quite catching what they were saying. But finally it was as if that person was now speaking close to him, and it fell into place.

He yearned for more. Most days at first light he would race up the crags to scan across the wide expanse, hoping to spy a sail dotting the horizon. If he did, he would rush to the probable anchorage point, heart fluttering. And, oh the bounty when aboard! He soon discovered that, more often than not, on each ship there would be multiple languages and dialects, with their own rhythms: the fluting, up and down DA-da-DA-da of the Northmen; the nasally bark of the Yan-kee; *les Français* who seemed to be trying to eat their words. And on and on. He tried to understand, devour them all.

But it was hard work. For the first few times, John left the ships feeling headachy and nauseous, unable to speak his own language properly for days. He felt he drained something out of the men, not just a new language but a certain melancholy. The sailors had the same weather-beaten faces and raw hands of the People, but they all seemed much sadder. Trapped aboard their wooden islands, most were missing teeth, had noxious breath, and stank of filth, their skin the colour of disease.

But as time wore on, his sickness abated and John began to recognise that there were happy ships amongst the sad, several that all the People looked forward to seeing. The most popular was the *Thomas and Ann,* which came twice a year with Captain Veitch and his cheerful crew. That was the last ship John had interpreted for, just weeks before leaving. On the final night of their mooring there was a huge feast, two big fires, a man from the ship with a fiddle, all the people singing and dancing and eating. John had his first grog that night, cup after cup until he had to lie on the deck, the stars pinwheeling across the sky. The last thing he remembered was seeing Mary dancing between Torok and a scabby-looking sailor.

Father Kelly always avoided the ships in general, but those with the flag of three crosses made him particularly nervous. Once, seeing one of those ships from the top of the crags, he came running down to the encampment twitching and screaming about the Royal FECKIN' Navy before heading down river inland. The priest was back in the hut when John returned, but still jumpy, half-hiding under his blankets. John unveiled a hatchet for Mary, a pewter mug for himself and, lastly, a battered, water damaged but perfectly readable copy of *Paradise Lost* for Father Kelly. The priest shot out from under his covers, gleefully snatching the book.

'Sweet dear child,' he laughed, 'how did you come upon this marvel?'

John shrugged. 'I sang for it.' He waited for Father Kelly to ask him what he meant, but the priest was greedily flipping through the book.

It was strange, because John only had to sing a few songs to the surgeon of the ship, a scrawny, ill-looking grey-skinned man with wide frog-like eyes. The surgeon excitedly scratched little markings on paper, his head bobbing along as John sang.

John often got books for Father Kelly — the priest had arrived with only a Bible and, apart from 'dear sweet feckin' drink', it was what he craved most. He mostly had to settle for things of a scientific nature: Jacobsen's *Considered Remarks Upon the Observation of the Transit of Venus*, Lawrie's *A Pamphlet for the Discussion of the Use and Misuse of the Chronometer*. Father Kelly would accept these gifts with a sigh. Occasionally there was a reader aboard who would be willing to part with something like Coleridge or Swift, which the priest would smile and twitch gratefully over. *Paradise Lost*, however, sent him into a swoon of ecstasy.

Father Kelly read aloud to John and Mary, spasming and guh-ha-hahing, at one point exclaiming after a long laugh, 'Oh, dear Milton, why do you give Satan the best lines?'

John interrupted, asking something that had been gnawing at him for some time: why do these men in killing ships — you could some-times smell the whales' blood through the floorboards — need to trade for meat?

Father Kelly shook his head, annoyed and impatient. 'Feck, son, we simply are not like you.'

John sighed. 'That is what you say when you don't like my questions.'

Father Kelly turned back to the book, but John had another question.

'Why are things written down?'

Father Kelly's spider-web-cracked spectacles twitched on his nose as he answered, 'To remember.'

'We remember perfectly well and we don't write things down.'

'But a book can be passed on from generation to generation.'

'Can everyone read?'

'Hardly.'

'Then you have to have someone read it, to tell it to others.'

'It is also for enjoyment, for pleasure. You like to read.'

This was true, but it made John uncomfortable. It had taken a long time for Father Kelly to teach him. Despite his gift, Mary began reading much sooner, as methodical and patient with learning as she was with hunting. John would look at the pages for a moment, half-listening to Father Kelly and, when it didn't come, he would start dreaming of something else. He struggled until one day the whole thing snapped into place and he saw how these little black and white markings meant the things that he could say. After that he read a lot, whenever he could. But he felt guilty about it all. Many of the People thought John somehow foreign, otherworldly, not like one of them. Reading was, in a way, doing the worst thing of all: not sharing.

John tried to explain, but felt he couldn't, felt the priest wouldn't understand. Eventually he just frowned.

Father Kelly, impatient, turned back to his book. 'As I feckin' said, we're just not like you.'

THE LOG BOOK OF JOHN SACKHOUSE, ESQUIMAUX

9th May 1816

Entry, my first. My first entry. First entry, my.

All seem correct to me. If I speak, the words come out as intended, more or less as they should, properly speaking. Writing them down, howsoever, is different. I have not written my letters since Father Kelly left. The stylus feels clumsy and foreign — an enemy in my hand, an enemy in my hand. I know what this entire entry will be — but this blasted pencil lags behind my mind — almost working against what I am trying to convey. I want it, all of it, out now on the page.

Mayhap it is because my wits are somewhat 'mazed at being thrown into this ship with men I do not know, and ways of living I have trouble deducing. It is a song whose rhythms I know but the words I cannot quite catch. I am not doltish. I know that there is some sort of hierarchy here with Owen and Mr Coffin at the top. But other than that, I am at a loss. They do seem to be governed by the ship's bell as if it is some monstrous god whose language I cannot decipher. *Bong.* Wake up and scrub the deck. *Bong Bong.* Break your fast. *Bong Bong Bong.* Retire to your beds.

But why do they need to be told anything at all? Among the People, my old People, it was straightforward: hunt, build, mend, sew and you live through another winter. These men are not unused to their lives being at threat – they live on a ship and are amongst constant danger. But they mostly tend towards sloth. They shirk, they laze, they look for any subterfuge to get out of their duties. Perhaps they enjoy being abused by Mr Coffin?

And the food! It is hardly the best, but it is prepared for them by Cookie and young Master Weeks without anyone else lifting a finger. And the quantity! I could hardly believe when I went down to the bottom of the ship: barrel upon barrel of what is called salt pork (something that approximates meat), ship's biscuit (hardened discs which taste like wood and are eaten heartily though often are crawling with insects), peas (mushy paste of pale green) and on and on.

There is months and months' worth of food down there. And is that the reason? Does lack of want lead to sluggishness? A lack of desire?

On the latter, actually no. The men desire much drink, much sexual release. Much of their days are spent in schemes of how to steal more than their usual ration of spirits. And nights, after the lamps are dimmed, are devoted to much self-pleasure. But they are so furtive about it, each of my mates pumping underneath their blankets when the others are meant to be asleep, although they all are awake and most know the others are engaged in the same nocturnal activity.

But one must not speak of it! This I learned today as I said to Joe Cole, the nose-less incomprehensible Bostonian: 'You certainly had a long gallop to the finish line last night, Joe.'

'Eh?' Joe said. 'What's that, Mistah Sackhouse?'

I smiled, trying to be ingratiating. 'Your self-abuse last night, I mean. There you were, still bashing away long after your fellows finished their emissions. I fear for the state of your member!'

Rather than some jolly banter, Joe scowled, said 'I nevah!' in a harsh whisper then shouldered by me, his face aflame.

11ᵗʰ May 1816

Though I cannot fathom these men, they seem to accept me. I do not know why as I have no particular role here — other than being the Captain's good luck charm – and as I am with Barz's 'coofs', I gather I am to be part of their boat when we go a-hunting whales.

Yet the men are disinclined to teach me much of the workings of the ship. Partially this is because I am wilfully not a fast learner. It is not that *I* am lazy or a shirker. But I am not equipped for the manual arts, especially if they seem to me to be extraneous busy work. So I have machinations. Ergo: the morning task is to scrub the deck with water using great stones. It is tiring work — on one's hands and knees and the action makes the back and arms ache ever so much. All I had to do was scrub against the grain of the wood a few times in Mr Coffin's presence, then affect not to understand his instructions and dumb show mime.

'I tell you what, Mr Sackhouse,' he said, speaking loudly and slowly as if to a child. 'I'll give you a very special duty.'

'Indeed, sir? I would be most happy to help in any way.' I hoped there was no trepidation in my voice. Mr Coffin had been much kinder since I was no longer in his cabin, but he still strikes me as a man for whom malice can linger.

'We need another lookout, another pair of eyes, as it were.'

'Oh,' I said, my mouth suddenly dry. I glanced at Obed Lacey in the crow's nest. He was a hawk-eyed gangly youth whose voice was just breaking and never ceased to amuse the crew with his low-to-high, screeching and fluting calls from above: "Sa-HAIL fuh-IVE points off the STARboard bow!' or 'A-HAUL IS we-ELL!' I am not afraid of being on high if rooted to the firmament — on a mountain edge, say. But the crow's nest is on a spindly mast which sways from side to side on just the slightest of breezes. The notion of being up there made all swim before me for a moment.

Mr Coffin noted my look upwards. 'Oh, no. You shall be a special lookout, down here on the deck. As you know where the whales be, I believe the best vantage point for you will be here at the level of the sea.'

I was beginning to warm to Mr Coffin. 'May I bring my books and writing implements as I scan the horizons?'

'Of course. For a special assignment as this you mustn't continually *look out*, you would strain your eyes.'

I bowed to Mr Coffin and as I left the rest of the coofs Barz watched me with a smirk on his face.

13th May 1816

This is my third day of 'look out' duties and I have not spotted anything, but have read and scribbled much. And I have set up a nice nest of my own. I dragged one of Owen's more comfortable chairs amidships near the galley and the warmth of Cookie's oven. I wrap myself up in a blanket, my feet stretched out on a low barrel, a hefty tome or my log book in my lap.

About mid-way through my 'watch' a shadow blotted out the sun. 'My, my, this is a cosy spot, Son of Ham.'

Barz stood a-fore me. He held a bottle loosely in his right hand. His face had that spreading pink rash and glossy sheen which I knew meant he had had a few swigs. I sat up and he plopped down on my low barrel and offered me the bottle. I considered. Barz still seemed cross with me after breaking our subterfuge with the Captain and he was quick to anger, to boil to a rage in an instant, from a trifle. I had found that acquiescing seemed to be the best balm for his dark moods. And he tended to get particularly testy when one refused to drink with him. I find myself wondering if he has always been like this. Is it the spirits? Is it some defect in his character? What drives his anger? I grabbed the bottle, tilted it back, felt the fire course down my throat.

'You are a man after my own heart, John Sackhouse,' he said.

'Merely doing as instructed, Barzillai,' I said.

'Ha!' He looked benignly over the rail and out to sea. 'It is an odd life being at the whims of others.'

I made no comment other than an ambiguous 'hmm' which I hoped he would take as agreement. I was not certain what he meant — his life, my life, all life? 'How did you pass your days 'fore coming to us?' he went on.

I did not answer. His question brought me back to hut and home. Of the warmth of the fire, Mary's trilling laugh, Father Kelly's lopsided smile. Of that night.

'You must have been free as nature first made man,' he said, leaning close to grab the bottle back from me. He tapped my forehead with the index finger of his free hand. 'You do not know the gift that your mind is untutored. I am weighed down by the difficulties of learning and university. Your faculties are still pure, letting you lead a virtuous and unblemished life. You are so fortunate.'

I burst out laughing. 'Book learning seems to result in ignorance not wisdom.'

He shot me an angry look and I cursed myself for he would soon be a-boiling, but we were interrupted by a curdling shriek.

'What in the devil?' I said.

The keening continued, the squeal growing louder and higher in pitch. 'The pigs,' he said. 'I reckon that idiot is making a right mess of it.'

He stood and I followed him to the front of the *Wessex* where the sad coterie of animals – a few pigs, the chickens and a goat – were penned. Cookie and Master Weeks had suspended a sow upside down from a winch, a rope lashed fast around its hind legs. Cookie seemed to have had a couple of bashes at killing the poor creature – there were two gashes across its throat but still it bucked and shrieked and only a small amount of blood oozed out. Meanwhile, the beast's wails were spooking the other pigs and the goat still in the pen, who were crowded in a corner oinking and bleating piteously. As we neared, the blood-smell hit me, causing my legs to buckle, and I had to grab the rail to stay upright.

'What's the ruckus, Cookie?' Barz yelled as the man went in for another go on the pig's throat.

Cookie turned to us, mouth agape. He was a compact muscular man, hirsute of body with fur-like patches of jet-black hair escaping from collars and cuffs. Yet he was balding, which accented his main feature: a white scar which traversed the entirety of his forehead. The wound was wide – about the width of my thumbnail, made more grotesque by several inexpert and irregular stitch marks. This, I've been told, was the result of the *Wessex*'s last tour when a huge splinter from a shattered cross-tree embedded itself in the man's head. Cookie had previously been a competent whalerman, a dab hand with a flensing knife, and pleasant enough company. Surviving was a miracle but it left his wits a-scrambled and he existed on only two planes: a dull-eyed listlessness or a seething rage. The crew called the two moods Cookie Be-calmed and Hurricane Cookie.

'Uh, Mr Millar,' Cookie droned in his monotone. We were in a Be-calmed phase. 'Meat for the feast.'

'I think we need instruction, sir,' Master Weeks piped up.

A flash in Cookie's eyes. 'I'll show ya instruction, you wee shite.'

He moved to strike Weeks with the back of his hand, but Barz stepped between them. Weeks was the only first voyager on the *Wessex* (besides myself) and, having just turned ten, was the youngest aboard. He was also Cookie's nephew. Whether it was the familial connection or a young lad's lack of wherewithal, Weeks was often a bit forward with Cookie and thus the recipient of most of the older man's ire. But the boy, an exuberant, runty little blond-haired thing, never seemed to be much bothered by his uncle, skylarking about the ship soon after even the worst screams and blows.

'Calm yourself, Cookie,' Barz said. He pursed his lips and pulled out a sharp and heavy instrument from his pockets. He knelt next to the thrashing pig. 'You need to respect the animal, put it out of its misery.' He touched a point on the animal's neck. 'The carotid artery, here. It takes but a matter of seconds.'

He plunged his blade in and blood gushed out. In one or two shudders it was over.

'Thank you, sir,' Weeks squeaked and Cookie grumbled a gratitude.

Barz nodded, turned away looking troubled and downcast, rearranging his features when he came up to me. 'I say, Sackhouse, you look positively green about the gills. A little blood doesn't scare you, does it?'

'Ha, of course not,' I scoffed, moving away from the blood smell down the other end of the *Wessex*. 'A little shift of the ship made my stomach gurgle a bit, nothing more. Uh, a feast, eh?'

'Yes, a whole roast *cochon à la Isle de Sandwich*, oh!' Barz stopped. 'That was meant to be a surprise. Evince astonishment when the Captain tells you.'

14th May 1816

I was summoned to Owen's cabin today.

In the days I have been bunked with the coofs I have not had much intercourse with Owen. While on deck, he has impressed the need for me to respect the sanctity of 'the god-like authority of the Captain'. While he is at his duties there are to be no jests between us. No banter. No intimacy. I do miss it so.

'Ah, yes, Mr Sackhouse,' he said sternly when Arthur showed me to the door. 'That will be all, Arthur. Now, Seaman Sackhouse, I have something to ask you, something extraordinarily serious.'

His face was stern and forbidding. My heart sank – had I done him an injury? He said: 'Why can a married man be like a fire? No, you have no answer for me, sir? Shame on you. It is because he angers his wife by going out at night.'

I nodded. 'I will answer by my own question. If a young lady fell into a well why couldn't her brother help her out? Because how could he be a brother and assist her too?'

Owen's eyes twinkled. 'Did you know that back in Nantucket town one evening, Mr Coffin was once caught short and went to make water upon a house. He did not see two young ladies looking out of a window close by him until he heard them giggling. He asked, "Ladies, what makes you so merry?" "O! Lord, *Sir*," said one of them, "take no mind. We will laugh at any little thing."'

'I will tell you something my old friend Father Kelly once said to me. The good father was a great punster and his friends would challenge him with divers subjects to make them up on the spot. One once said, "My subject is George III." "I cannot oblige you," came the reply, "because a King is not a subject."'

We burst out laughing. Owen jumped up and clasped my hands in his and held on tightly. 'Oh, John my friend, it is good to be able to talk to you freely. How fare you with Barzillai's coofs?'

How exactly was I to answer that? I sleep close-packed with six men whose nocturnal trumpets, eructations, snoring and masturbating are not conducive to sleep. And the pungency! Most of the men on this ship stink, not just because of the lack of washing but the diet, the drink and something else rotten inside. Being closely quartered with them can be noisome. And my bunkmates are coarse and rough. Some scare the bejaysus out of me. And yet, I am not shunned, I am accepted. 'On the whole, tolerably,' I said.

'I see Mr Coffin has you employed to good use.' I rolled my eyes, and Owen broke in, 'Do not be offended, he merely wanted—'

'I take no offence. I am better employed reading and writing and safely out of the way than tripping over those who know better.'

'But, John my friend, you have the most arduous task of all. It is through you that we are being led for the promised land, or sea, if you will. We are still sailing for it, yes?'

My hands began to shake from nervousness and I had to make fists to still them. 'Owen,' I said at last, 'I know not where any whales are.'

Owen began nodding vigorously. 'Mm-hm, mm-hm, yes, yes. Of course, you do not know *intellectually*. It is instinctual. As surely as one does not know how to breathe, it just happens. But you have set us on your path, I am sure it is right.'

'That is a remarkable amount of faith in me.' I could not stop my voice from breaking, tears welling in my eyes.

My emotion discomfited him. 'Ah, ahem. Not just faith in you, but our Lord and Master. But I warn: others, and I mean the crew, may not be as faithful as me if we are not immediately successful. We must stay the course.

'Now I have a surprise for you. We will be having a feast in your honour!'

'A feast, Owen?' I opened my eyes wide, let my jaw fall. I had been practising an 'amazed' face. Barz said it was most genuine.

'I see you are surprised. We shall have a pig roast. The pigs are my private stock and would never be slaughtered so early in a voyage, nor, I confess, would I share them with the entire crew. But Barzillai said that a pig roast was a particular delicacy of your people.'

I had never seen a pig a-fore setting foot on the *Wessex*, a fact Barz and I had discussed a couple of days ago. 'It will be like going home again,' I said.

15th May 1816

The smell nudged me awake and I found myself smiling with pleasure from a smoky-sweet-sour odour filling the cabin. I did not know where it emanated from, but it made my mouth water, my stomach rumble. My cabinmates were, unusually, absent. They normally did not arise until Mr Coffin came barrelling through with inventive curses that at once insulted the men's mothers, laziness and masculinity.

In a trice I was on deck. In the waist, the carpenter and smith had erected a fire pit and roasting spit. Our unfortunate pig from the other day was staked through, being slowly turned over blazing coals by young Weeks. It was the source of the wonderful smell and I was pulled towards it.

A knot of men was gathered 'round and an intense debate was under way. 'Cookie, Cookie, Cookie,' Barz was shouting above the din, 'you have it all wrong. Our man here' — he clapped Howard Howarkaliki on the shoulder — 'is a Sandwich Islander, home of the pig roast. He says it needs a slow roast. A lower fire, a higher spit.'

'You fuckin' telling me how to run my galley, Millar?' Oh, dear. It was Hurricane Cookie, running a furious gale.

Barz held his hands up. 'I merely wanted to avoid bouts of the screaming flux for all aboard. I bow to your superior culinary acumen.'

'Aye,' Cookie said, spitting a great wad of phlegm into the fire with a *sssss*. 'As long as this foolish boy keeps it turning, she'll cook all right.' Here he took his carving knife and swung it flat side on at Weeks. The boy normally would have ducked, but he was caught up with the spit's handle. He moved but not quickly enough and the blow clipped him on his head, sending him sprawling to the floor.

'Hey, watch that, Cookie,' a couple of men said, stepping to help the boy.

'Now, now, now, lads,' Mr Coffin barked, moving into the waist from the quarterdeck. 'Too many cooks here. We don't need fifteen of you to roast a pig, do we? Let's set the lot of you to a-decorating.'

The men dispersed with murmurs. Weeks returned to the spit, watching furtively as Cookie paced back and forth in front of him, muttering darkly.

I was going to say a word to Cookie when suddenly Mr Coffin was in front of me. 'Mr Sackhouse, we can't have you preparing the meal for yer own special feast, now can we?'

I manoeuvred to the first mate's side, and said lowly, 'Mr Coffin, that boy is hurt. He is being abused.'

Mr Coffin led me aft. 'Discipline is part of this life, Mr Sackhouse. When I was a wee lad, I was boxed about the ears pretty well in my first run or two.'

'Weeks does not look like he is being edified by being hit in the head by the flat of a knife. Can you not do—'

'No I *cain't*. You see, the galley is Cookie's domain. If I come down on him, on how he runs things, especially in front of the other men, well they're apt to say "what about Mr Coffin, we don't like the way he's running things". And then it'll go up to the Captain and the whole line of command becomes nothing. You see?'

I did not see. I only saw a boy scared by a tyrant.

'Now why don't you rest up a bit? Or, better yet, how about another watch on your special look-out duties?'

Mr Coffin's tone had taken a patronising air and I fought an urge to kick him in the nethers to wipe the smugness off his face. Over his shoulder I could see most of the rest of the crew setting up the tables and chairs and erecting the tent (we were dining al fresco). 'May I help my fellows, Mr Coffin?'

'Today, I don't see why not. It's your feast, after all.'

'Mr Sackhouse, to me!' Owen yelled.

The Captain, Mr Coffin, the second mate Mr Joy, Barz, one of the McKeever boys (they are near identical brothers — who remind me of big slabs of meat on legs — one of whom commands one of the whale boats, but I cannot tell them apart) were at the small head table underneath the tent. The rest of the crew shared a longish bench.

All was convivial, perhaps made more because by the meal not yet appearing in our midst. Howard Howarkaliki's advice on slow roasting was finally heeded by Cookie, for after a couple of hours or so the pig was burnt on the outside, raw in the middle. The change of method meant delay, which the Captain smoothed over by digging deep into the spirit closet.

At our head table, bumper after bumper of wine was downed, while the men were given full strength grog. After only a few moments, I was light-headed, one turn of the clock and my eyes were vibrating in their sockets, barely keeping focus. Our carousing and merry-making failed to completely drown out Cookie's carping at poor Weeks.

Finally, a nod to Owen from the cook and the time was upon us and I was called to the Captain's side.

'Men,' Owen intoned, holding his glass aloft. 'We are on a voyage of untold riches.' Here a roar in answer. 'And who is going to lead us but our Son of Ham.' He pointed to me and there was much hooting and hollering and my face burned with pleasure. 'So, I thought we should celebrate with a side of Ham for the Son of Ham!'

Owen had obviously hoped for a big laugh, but there was one mild chuckle and a lot of strained grins. 'For the pig is a ham, you see, and . . .' he faltered. 'Anyway, I give you our roast.'

Now there were genuine laughs and claps. Cookie emerged from the waist, carrying the pig upright on the spit by himself as if marching with a flag. He was struggling, listing from side to side, barely supporting the weight, his movements made trickier by copious amounts of fat oozing off the animal.

'Cookie, where is Weeks?' Owen demanded. 'Why are you carrying the pig by yourself?'

'Don't need 'em, Cap'n,' Cookie grunted. 'Useless boy.'

'Laycock, Banks, lend him a hand,' Owen yelled.

The two men, who were sat closest to Cookie, sprang up. But at that moment the *Wessex* lurched, a quick tilt to the side, which coincided with Cookie stepping into a slick of pig grease. Cookie stumbled and with a quick three-step shuffle to port hit the rail and, clutching the pig fervently as a lover, tumbled into the drink.

An hour or so later, I had joined Owen in his cabin for a drink. I thought him unduly morose and told him so. 'An unfortunate end to our meal,' I said. 'Or, rather beginning! But no matter, sir. Cookie will only lose a few toes and fingers, Barzillai said. And perhaps an ear and the tip of his nose. The expediency of the rescue in these icy waters should be commended. We may have lost a pig roast, but we saved the man.'

Owen smiled tightly, filled his glass from the decanter. 'I deeply regret that ham/Ham sally.'

'Come, Captain Chase! In a few months, nay weeks, this will be a humorous anecdote.'

'You don't understand, my dear, dear John.' He spoke so quietly I had to lean forward to catch what he said. 'This is an omen; this is a sign to the men. They are full of superstition. If we don't find any whales soon, things will get dangerous for you.'

II.

The University: Or, the rise and fall of Barzillai Millar

Newburyport, 1806

'Look — the proper gentleman!' Lord Cranston Millar cried. 'Don't he look marvellous, Hetty?'

Barz had just alighted on the landing of the grand staircase, shifting uncomfortably in his new purple suit of velvet breeches, a matching coat with inlaid gold fleur-de-lis, and an overly complicated ruffled mauve shirt that took him ten minutes to button. The vigorously buffed black of his shoes glittered, the gold of his buckles twinkled. He felt discomfited, not least by literally standing in someone else's shoes. They pinched horribly and were — like the suit he was wearing and almost every article of clothing that was packed in the dunnage on the coach that stood outside the front entrance — once the property of the Chevalier de Bourbotte, a French courtier who had his head removed during the Terror two decades previously. His father undoubtedly had acquired the good Chevalier's wardrobe by less than above-board means from his many semi-legitimate shipping concerns. Cranston had presented them yesterday to Barz as his belongings were being packed.

'Stay, son, stay, ladies,' Cranston had thundered, as Barz and the maids fussed with his perfectly respectable, perfectly sober, perfectly New England collection of brown, olive and black suits. 'You will not need those commonplace things.'

Cranston puffed himself up as his two 'agents of business', Gresham and Alberts, came into Barz's room with the Chevalier's ensembles. The two men were slabs of muscle — bulls incongruously stuffed into clerk's black coats — who normally bowled about the quays of Newburyport seeing to the less delicate of Cranston's arrangements with clubs, knives and daggers worn ostentatiously on their belts. Yet Gresham and Alberts minced into Barz's room, their terrible scarred and battered faces beaming, carrying the clothes aloft and displaying each suit with a fastidiousness that would have outdone the Chevalier's Parisian tailor. Barz had never seen the like; the clothes were colours which he had rarely seen and struggled to name — vermillion, teal, magenta.

'I am speechless, Father,' Barz gulped, with the horrible sinking feeling that his father might not be playing a prank and he would actually be expected to wear these monstrosities.

'No, no, do not thank me,' Cranston said, his hand thrust out theatrically. 'Going down to the University you need to make an impression, Barzillai. And what better way to do so than in clothes made for the court of Versailles.'

Barz knew, with the intuition of the teenager who was soon to be the new boy coming into a course mid-year, exactly what sort of impression these suits would make. 'Father, I do not think—' he began, but stopped, seeing Cranston beginning to well up.

Stern, remote and formidable in his public roles as the owner of both the biggest shipping concern and distillery in Newburyport (Cranston's Old Reliable Rum was a popular tipple throughout the *North-east*) and the town's representative in the Massachusetts assembly, behind closed doors Cranston was prone to wild outbursts of emotion. Anything could start the cascades: a mewling kitten, a lachrymose ballad, a particularly beautiful setting sun — but he was most susceptible to extreme emotion with anything concerning his dear and doted-on only son.

'I do not think,' Barz began again, 'I could have ever hoped for such a gift.'

Now, as he stood on the landing, Barz was regretting his tact. Along with being uncomfortable, the snug fit of the Chevalier's suit emphasised more what he was: a weedy 15-year-old, too soon playing the part of a grown up.

Hetty, the former Henrietta Calhoun, stared up from the front door where she and her husband stood. 'Sir, does he not look adorable in his tiny jacket?' She gave out a little shriek, moved towards Barz as he reached the ground floor, giving him a rather forceful pinch on the cheek. 'I could just eat little Barzillai up, I could. Yet, I should not say such things to you, Barzy-warzy. You are going away to become a man.'

Barz scowled. Hetty was Cranston's fifth wife, just three years older than Barz himself — it seemed only yesterday she was the slightly gawky girl a few years ahead of Barz at Mrs Lethem's school. Since Cranston had brought her home she had played the lady of the manor with a grand, officious and what Barz found especially galling, matronly style. She scolded Barz, she condescended to him, treated him as a child. Yet this was a girl — and girl he could not help but think of her as — he himself had once kissed after school when he was ten and she thirteen. Hetty was dared to do it by Lucy Edes, and thinking about the dry, closed-mouth clumsiness of it, followed by Hetty and Lucy's trilling laughs as they ran away, still brought a blush to Barz's cheeks.

Barz did not want to go down to the University, he did not want to leave his friends or his father, but at least he would not have to suffer Hetty anymore. Or that memory. With her safely out of sight, he could stow that kiss and the trilling laugh into the small cupboard of his mind in which he shut every one of his bad memories, locked up tight.

Still, Barz judged half-grimly and half with a triumphalist lift in his heart, if past experience was anything to go by, Hetty would not be around for too long – for there seemed to be something of a curse on his father's loins. His own mother, Dorothea Benskins, then Martha Slipsmiths, then Emilie Taylor, then Mercy Bass were all carried off in childbirth with Barz the sole offspring to live more than a few weeks. Barz's entire life, it seemed, was punctuated with episodes of sitting in the drawing room, listening to screams from upstairs while worried midwives and servants bustled around.

Cranston embraced Barz tightly, treading on one of the Chevalier's glossy shoes. 'Oh, dear, oh dear, my boy,' he said, starting to blub.

'Well, Father,' Barz said quickly. 'I am terribly excited to get away.'

'The coach can wait a moment, Barzillai,' Cranston said, composing himself and ushering his son into his study. 'I have a going away present.'

Cranston called it his 'study' but the space was of a grandeur that one might associate with the receiving rooms of the Palace of Whitehall or Frederick the Great's Sanssouci. Fifteen-foot-high ceilings, stuffed bookshelves on the two long walls, a gleaming table with spaces for twenty chairs suitable for the negotiation of peace treaties and at the far, far end, underneath the huge arched window, Cranston's heavy, fortress-like desk (Barz always pictured it in his mind with sunlight streaming onto his father at work, choral evensong coming from somewhere in the distance).

The study was forbidden territory for much of Barz's early life, the door perpetually locked when the room was unoccupied, bolted shut when Cranston was within. It was when he was ten – just a day after Hetty's kiss, actually — that he was first summoned to the inner sanctum. It was a late autumn evening, the solemnity of the occasion underscored by the low candlelight and Cranston's formal dress.

Cranston scrutinised his son for a full minute after Barz sat down. 'You are young, Barzillai,' he said at last. 'But, ready, I do believe.'

He dangled a long, heavy solid key in front of Barz. 'Here is the key to this room, one of only three in existence. Guard it well. And here is the ledger for my practice.' He opened a large green binder which contained itemisations of clients defended, wills written out, lawsuits instigated and payments received for all. 'This is what the tax and revenue collectors of the Commonwealth of Massachusetts get to see every year. Now, I will show you the ledger for our other business interests.'

His father patted him on his head and ducked underneath his desk, removed a bit of carpet and knocked a floorboard loose, extracting a compact, thicker ledger wrapped in oilskin. 'This we keep away from the tax and revenue inspectors of the Commonwealth. In fact, if there is that day when the tax inspectors or excisemen come knocking and I am not around, this you burn but only at the last possible moment. Now, repeat that to me.'

Barz, ten years old but now feeling twice his age, swelled with pride. 'If the tax inspectors and excisemen come and you're not around, I burn this ledger, but only at the last moment.'

'Good lad, good lad. Now let me show you the ledger's secret code.'

In the ensuing few years, Barz wondered why his father bothered with the secret ledger. There was not a person in Newburyport that did not seem to know that their representative in the state legislature ran an import/export business that was outside the law; indeed there were few in the area that were not employed either directly or indirectly by his father's shady businesses — including the state's Custom and Excise man in town, Mr Wycombe.

'If I can give you any advice,' Cranston once said to his son, 'be prepared for all eventualities; never tell anyone more than they need to know; expect betrayal, and always be prepared to scarper at a moment's notice.

'If I could keep all of my accounts and outgoings and incomings from smuggling—' here his father paused; he rarely used that word and when he did he put his hand on his belly like it caused indigestion '— in my head I would, but I cannot. The ledger it must be. But it must remain our secret. Our disposable secret.'

'Here,' Cranston said almost shyly, pushing a box across his desk to Barz.

Barz ungracefully fought with the too-long arms of Chevalier de Bourbotte's coat and the frilly sleeves poking out of the cuffs, before finally securing the box. He opened it slowly. 'Your marked deck of cards,' he whispered.

Cranston nodded. 'And my loaded dice. They served me well enough when I was your age.' He smiled and patted Barz's head. 'You will be mixing with Cabots and Lowells and Quincys and Adamses. Most of them inbred fools, of course. The irony of our supposed revolution is that we merely shrugged off one ruling class and replaced it with another, one lacking in style and grace. Why would you want the House of Hanover, the Dukes of Norfolk, the Earls of Essex when they can be replaced by our band of pinched preachers, tight-arsed lawyers, slave-fucking heathens and dishonourable nincompoops who now run the Republic?'

Barz sighed inwardly. The Rant was starting. Even in his callowness, Barz realised Cranston's ill feeling for the New Men of the nascent country had far less to do with politics and far more to do with the former Colonial government's administrators' eagerness to be compensated for overlooking the many activities of the Millar empire.

'Wycombe,' Cranston spat the Customs man's name. 'Who does he think he is, with his airs and graces? A man can hardly make a decent profit these days.'

Cranston brought himself up short, looking at the billy club gripped in his hand — the one he kept inside his desk and had once brought down on the head of a burglar who tried to break into his safe in the dead of night. He turned to his son who had the waxy look about the eyes of the congregation around twenty minutes into Reverend Sharpe's Sunday sermon.

'Well, yes,' Cranston harrumphed. 'At any rate. These fools are the ones who run the country and this Commonwealth. And their sons, your class-mates, will be the ones who run it in years to come; it is best to try to use them to your advantage. Now, sir. Repeat what I have told you about life at the University.'

Barz closed his eyes and said flatly as if he was reciting the multiplication tables: 'Book learning has limited use in later life. Study, assuredly, but only enough to get by. Cultivate advantageous friends and acquaintances. If you cheat a man at games, especially a friend, ensure he does not become aware.'

Cranston's eyes filled with tears and he choked down a sob. 'Good, my son. Now let us be off.'

Cambridge, 1806

Barz had imagined the University as a magnificent series of edifices
— gleaming spires, a library to rival Alexandria's, marbled colonnades
amongst which scholars would engage in intense debate — not this
somewhat squat collection of lopsided brick buildings. The college
green was expansive, he granted; roomy enough for the hundred or
so cattle currently ruminating and shitting upon its grass.

The herd seemed the only members of the university community
on the premises. Though the term started in three days, he was
assured by his father that most of his class-mates would be on campus
'making merry, getting up to japes'. Barz was glad it was deserted,
however, for he still was clothed in the Chevalier's ensemble and was
looking forward to the moment he shook himself free of Alberts to get
back into his own togs.

They had shipped down in the *Wampanoag*, his father's fastest
cutter. The 40 miles or so from Newburyport to Cambridge would
have taken a day by coach, but his father had refused as there were
four turnpike tolls to pay en route. That would have put Cranston out
of pocket by some one or two dollars — 'an unconscionable expense,
my boy,' he had raged at Barz, 'for the principle of the matter is the
roads should be free. Did we not fight a war for freedom? Did I not
spill blood for my country in order to remove the shackles of this kind
of tyranny?' Barz knew better than to point out that the only blood
Cranston would have spilled during the Great Rebellion was if his
barber nicked him whilst shaving, and that the simple cost of the crew
the *Wampanoag* meant the journey south was probably costing
Cranston $20 more than if he just paid the tolls.

Immediately after the *Wampanoag* sunk Newburyport and
Cranston and Hetty were no longer visible waving from the quay, Barz
clambered down to the hold to his dunnage. He was about to spring
the lock on a trunk when he heard a throat clearing behind him.

'No, no, young sir, if you please,' Alberts said. 'Your father emphasised that he wanted you to arrive at the University dressed like a true
gentleman. It was his particular wish that I deliver you so.'

'Well, Alberts,' Barz now said, turning away from the cows on the green as nimbly as he could in the Chevalier's pinched shoes, 'I am delivered. Shall we go to my lodgings?'

Ten minutes later, Barz and Alberts arrived at a second-floor corner room in Massachusetts Hall. They fumbled with the door knob and heard a yelled, 'Just a moment, just a moment,' from within.

A hulking man — a trifle larger than Alberts — stood with his back to the door, hurriedly covering something on the desk near the window with a cloth. He whirled around and Barz realised he was somewhere around his own age — sixteen, seventeen at a push — with a roundish baby face made even more youthful by its anxiousness.

'Oh, thank goodness,' the boy squeaked in a high-pitched voice incongruous in that massive body. 'I thought you were Dr Wigglesworth, come to catch me out. Please, would you close the door?'

Barz and Alberts hesitated, not at the request but at the fact that the man/boy made it by gesturing with his hands, in the left of which he held a cat's head, in the right a bloody cleaver. Alberts, his face pale, dropped Barz's trunk and muttered, 'I will get the rest of your dunnage sir, and leave you gentlemen to get acquainted,' before slamming the door behind him and clomping rapidly down the hall.

'You must be Millar,' the boy said, transferring the cleaver to his other hand, juggling cat and cleaver easily in his big paw. He shook Barz's hand vigorously. 'Thomas Sparhawk.'

Barz's hand came away tacky with blood. He held it aloft uncertainly as he did not want to wipe it on the Chevalier's coat. 'Yes, I am Millar. Barzillai Millar. I am sorry, I cannot help but notice that you hold a cat's head, one rather recently separated from its body.'

'Ah, well spotted. Stray, you understand, I won't have you thinking that I go around Cambridge town knocking people's beloved pets on the head. At least, I think it was a stray . . . '

'What are you doing to it?'

Sparhawk motioned Barz over to the desk and whipped off the covering. The rest of the cat lay in a dish, with scalpels and forceps lined up next to its body. 'I am in the Anatomist Club. We, ah, anatomise. We are a somewhat outlaw society. Yes, we may tinker with our cadavers whilst in the operating theatre under the strict eyes of Dr

Warren. But it seems absurd that we are prevented from doing so in our spare time. So we Anatomists have taken it on ourselves to procure specimens to work on after hours, as it were. Dogs, cats, the odd pig. Once, a bear.'

Barz looked over to the other side of the room, with its cluttered desk, full bookshelves and made bed. Then to this side, clearly his part of the room. 'Would this be my desk, then? The one with the rest of the cat on it?'

'Ah, apologies. But all for the furtherment of science, you know. Hand me that scalpel, will you, and we will see what made this old boy tick.'

Wanting to forestall that moment, Barz said, 'Tell me, where is everyone else? Your, I should say our, class-mates?'

'Oh, there are but twenty or so which have arrived. I suspect the rest will trickle in over the next month or two.'

'But the term starts in three days.'

'Hm, yes. Attendance at lectures is often neither mandatory nor expected, you'll find. Most of those who are in situ are currently in the university brew house — Yawkey stole the key off of one of the porters — drinking the president's supply dry. I can take you there, but first would you mind assisting me with cutting up Mr Geoffrey here?'

'Mr Geoffrey?' Barz cried. 'You know its name?

'Fear not, he led a good and long life. Now, shall we get on?'

Barz never made it to the brew house. How could he? From the moment he lifted the lancet to help Sparhawk with the dissection of Mr Geoffrey he was utterly changed. Sparhawk's deft cut along the animal's torso, along with a disconcerting faint ripping noise, was like the parting of a curtain to reveal another world. For here, suddenly before him, was the cat, its inner workings, the very creation of life. All of the Almighty's genius opened up to him. Simply wondrous. Or rather, he had those grand thoughts after he recovered from his initial swoon at which he had to grip the sides of the desk to avoid pitching onto the floor.

'Are you quite well, Millar?' Sparhawk had asked. 'I admit Mr Geoffrey is a trifle gamy. Fear not, you will get used to the smell.'

'Just a slight turn,' Barz said, mopping his brow. 'I have of course seen the odd pig or lamb being butchered, so I have the rudimentaries of anatomy, but this . . . '

He trailed off, his hand fluttering in the air in ineffectual explanation.

Sparhawk looked at Barz for a beat or two, his expression sober. 'This is not butchery.'

'No, I didn't mean—'

'I did not think you did. But I wanted to underscore this point: we are explorers, Millar, intrepid discoverers of the untold mysteries of natural philosophy. Think, thousands of years of human understanding and we — through application, inquisitiveness and the great god reason — are in the vanguard.'

And they were off. Two, three hours passed in an eye-blink as Sparhawk and Barz's journeyed through Mr Geoffrey's musculature, nervous system, internal organs and secretions and excretions.

Eventually they sat back, tired but sated.

'Rum, then!' Sparhawk sprang up and rummaged around amongst his things emerging, clinking and clanking, with two banged-up pewter mugs and a full bottle of Old Reliable.

Seeing Barz's arch half-smile, Sparhawk paused. 'Oh I know it is not the best,' he stammered. 'Rotgut, to be sure. But it does the job.'

Barz nodded. 'It does many jobs, I can assure you.' He turned and looked at Mr Geoffrey, who was not recognisable as himself anymore, with his various innards and outers, scattered on the desk in neat piles. Barz shook his head. 'It is miraculous.'

'No!' Sparhawk cried as he slopped the rum into the cups. 'It is nothing of the sort.'

'I merely meant—'

'Yes, yes, it is certainly captivating, seeing the inner workings of all God's creatures, most particularly when first encountered. But we must resist the urge to attribute the wordage of mysticism around it. This is scientific inquiry, my dear Millar. There is nothing "miraculous" about taking nature and taming it.'

Barz looked down, partially to avoid the intensity of Sparhawk's gaze. He took a healthy swig, felt the familiar burn. Overly sweet, this

72

batch, which meant it probably came from the Ipswich distillery, managed by Ridgeway who, despite Cranston's admonitions, continued to be heavy-handed with the molasses.

'Are you not fond of cats, then?'

'Why, I have quite an admiration for *felis catus*. As a species they have often been unjustly persecuted through superstition and ignorance. And Mr Geoffrey here was quite frisky in his time.'

'Hang on, you knew this beast?'

'He was, I should confess, my beloved childhood pet. And died, to stop that look on your face, from entirely natural causes after a long and full life.'

Barz looked uneasily at Mr Geoffrey's now stripped down skull, the empty eye sockets staring accusingly back. He turned the skull so that it looked away. 'Then, how can you dismember it – him – so?'

Sparhawk reached over and plucked up Mr Geoffrey's skull, tossed it up in the air and, on catching it again, held it aloft in his palm, Hamlet regarding Yorick. 'I shall confess something else to you, Millar, but I beg you do not tell a soul. I was a bookish lad—'

'You astonish me, Sparhawk.'

Sparhawk smiled quickly. 'Yes. Bookish and bullied – well, bullied until I grew about a foot and a half and gained several stone in my twelfth year – and I lacked friends. I can perhaps safely say without fear of contradiction that Mr Geoffrey was my sole friend and boon companion.'

Barz squirmed in his seat. 'Ah, well, that is most unfortunate.'

Sparhawk shook his head as if to say 'no matter', and refilled Barz's mug. 'I say this to illustrate a point. Mr Geoffrey — the creature who would nuzzle me, perhaps sensing when I had had a particularly trying day with my fellows — ceased to be the moment the poor thing shuffled off its mortal coil, leaving just this sack of bones, this organic mechanism. This' — here he pointed to the tissue and flesh and bone and blood on the tray — 'has nothing to do whatsoever with my Mr Geoffrey.'

'Oh come, in death the physical apparatus that carried Mr Geoffrey throughout his years surely has some relationship to who he was in that life.'

'Apparatus is the key word, Millar. Yes, apparatus, equipment, a machine merely. And one that is no longer linked to him.'

'Yes, but this is a beast. A "nuzzly, cuddly beast" in life, but a beast nonetheless. You would not say that about a person and his or her body.'

'Ah, but I would! Doubly, trebly so. Our whole ritualisation of the corpse reeks of the rankest pagan superstition. Here we are, Millar, cutting up Mr Geoffrey and not some worthy gentleman or gentle-woman who has donated their remains to the University. And why? Because people daren't do it. They are hamstrung by outmoded beliefs.

'In fact, Millar, let us make an agreement. When we expire, when we are hopefully old and grey, whichever of us is called to our Maker first, the other should perform a dissection on him.'

Barz took a gulp of his drink, felt the burn through his throat, spreading downwards through his body. 'I fear the Old Reliable may have gotten to your head.'

'Why?'

Barz stole a glance at the bottle's label. 'I can think of a number of obstacles, not least that I imagine our family and heirs may object to the one of us carting the other off to slice and dice.'

'Hang them, we shall put it in our wills. A rock solid, stone-clad bequest.'

'I am here to study rhetoric and language in the main, with a view to be admitted to the Bar and to take over my father's, ah, various businesses. I will not be a medical man.'

'Nonsense, Millar. First you are presupposing that you will outlive me.'

'I am younger . . . '

'And I am stronger, fitter, a bull. Your reedy frame and frailer con-stitution will undoubtedly mean you will be carried away by consumption, pleurisy or yellowjack. I am also worried about that in-cipient rosacea that has flared up across your face at just a few cups of rum. I daresay you will be lucky to eclipse forty years of age.' He stepped closer to Barz, looking him up and down. 'By the way, do you have any pain in your neck, glands or back?'

'Why, a little in my back, but I thought that was due to travel. Why?' Barz felt his back, his head.

'No reason, no reason. But mostly, I say nonsense because you have *it*.'

'What "it"?' Barz clutched his throat.

'It. A thirst for knowledge. Boundless curiosity. The law, rhetoric or God help us, the arts or humanities, are fine for those who are clever enough but who lack true understanding. You will not waste yourself on it. No, Millar, you will join me in the vanguard to rid this country of superstition with reason.

'And I will outlive you, and take great pleasure in dissecting you. I am already imagining that first incision into your pale, cold flesh.'

Cambridge, 1806

9th February 1806

The Most Honourable Cranston Millar

My dear sir,

Apologies for not answering your letters with due speed. I realise I promised to write frequently, Father, but my first weeks here at the University have hurtled by with hardly a time to pause for breath, let alone to pick up pen and paper. My room-mate, one Thomas Sparhawk, is an agreeable fellow though a scholarship boy (as I gather, his father owns a not very productive smallholding in that miasmatic shitehole Worcester), and much devoted to study, so I see him little.

My first night here I was truly inaugurated into College life, joining my fellows for a carouse in the university brew house. Thomas Yawkey — his family hails from the wilds of Georgia and I initially presumed this would mean he has no better manners than an orang-utan, but he is a consummate Southern 'gennelmun' and owns several plantations and scores of slaves — had liberated the keys and I got acquainted with my classmates whilst enjoying some of the finest porter I have ever had. They are a good lot, Father. Stephen Sewall, the Congress-man's son, is a considerable wit. Abel Osgood — of the Osgood shipbuilders — is a dab hand on the pianoforte and possesses an excellent singing voice. Phineas Gore (who, by the by, told me *sotto voce* that his father Christopher is to run for governor in ought eight) is by all accounts a genius at Greek, but more impressively is able to drink three whole bottles of port in a sitting and not feel the least affected.

And in these three weeks, I have become particular friends with Amos Cushing — you know his father the Senator, of course. He is the president of the Packachoag Society, which I have been honoured to be allowed to join. For some unfathomable reason we are named after a band of savages wiped out by the pox around the time of King Philip's War and are ostensibly a speaking society — or that is what we tell the tutors. We do, it is true, begin each meeting with a cursory stab at a philosophical, theological or literary debate: can good morals exist without religious motives? Are the writings of the late Scotsman Dr Hume calculated to destroy the goodness of all mankind? Are the opinions of Mrs. Wollstonecraft Godwin true — that women are equal in intellect to men?

And other such equally weighty yet ultimately nugatory topics. Soon, however, perhaps after the fourth or fifth bumper, we weary of intellectual pursuits and commence to follow our motto: *Vivimus ergo nos edere et bibere et futuere*. We are usually at Moore's or Bradish's where we sup on roast pig or duck, drink the tolerable local ale and, particularly at Moore's, consort with the local wenches.

I am writing this of an afternoon having just risen with a band of gypsies playing in my head and a sere tongue. Last night, we Packa-choagians met at Bradish's to discuss: Is there any reason to suppose the pope is not the Anti-Christ and a man made of sin? As you can imagine, we were all swiftly in accord on that score (no, there is no reason at all) and thus began the evening's revels.

We were soon joined by one Greene, an Englishman and distant relation to Osgood. He was a genial fellow — to start. But then he procured several bottles of gin which he began quaffing rather vigorously and then he proceeded to get somewhat caustic in manners, particularly on the subject of Our Grand Republic. We are savages, apparently, a provincial nation lacking any sort of culture. He rattled on in this line until the gin fully took hold and he slumped in the corner near insensible, repeating over and over to no one in particular whilst clutching his bottle: 'Do you know we call gin "Strip Me Naked" in old England?'

We were turfed out around three of the clock — even dear old Mrs Bradish has limits to her patience — carrying Greene along with us (he was to stay at Osgood's lodgings), the Englishman still mumbling about 'Strip Me Naked'. Which gave us inspiration.

We proceeded to roll him about in one of the University pig sties, conducted him to President Kirkland's house (the light-fingered genius Yawkey had stolen the keys a few nights before) and laid him spread-eagle in the president's bedroom. President and Mrs Kirkland, it transpires, are heavy sleepers. Greene was discovered shortly after six; Cushing told me Mrs Kirkland's scream could be heard across campus, but I was too deeply wrapped in the arms of Morpheus to confirm this.

Your affectionate son,
Barzillai

Post Script

Though I am getting along tolerably well at cards and games (much thanks to your going-away gifts), would it be possible to have an increase in funds? My new fellows live terribly high and I feel I need to keep up, as it were, to remain in their affections.

Barz shook sand over the letter and watched the ink dry. How was he able to be duplicitous and dissemble so easily? And why was he writing as if he were the Duke of Buckingham? 'My new fellows live teeerrrribly high,' he said aloud in a genteel English accent.

'Wha's that, Millar?' Sparhawk said, rising woozily from his bed. Over the past couple of days, his room-mate had been trying to discover a better mixture of drugs for operations and was experimenting on himself. Tonight, he had ingested a blend of cannibas indica, laudanum and ground mother of pearl.

'Nothing. Go back to sleep.'

Cranston's letters had arrived every other day, with a few notes from home — Hetty inevitably with child, Gresham recovering from a knife wound to the thigh, Alberts caught in flagrante with old Mrs Ackroyd in her kitchen — but mostly they were pleas for news from the University. How was Barz getting on? Was he making friends? Was he ingratiating himself with the Cabots and the Lowells and the Adamses? With each unanswered letter, Cranston's tone became more worried, more strident, demanding news.

He had not answered because he was unsure how to without disappointing. He knew those fellows, or at least of them, and this Packachoag Society — the strutting cockerels of the quad — but never associated with and hardly spoke to them for they seemed such an irrelevance.

He stayed up until three or four that first night, talking to Sparhawk about books and ideas and the great worthies of thought like Franklin, the Lavoisiers or Sir Joseph Banks and how they, Sparhawk and Millar, would someday be the equal to them all.

He awoke the next day, sprang from bed, planted his two feet on the ground to thrust himself into the hurly-burly of thought, enquiry and reason. However, his progress was thwarted by the official proscription of courses for, as an institution, the University seemed to have very little interest in Barzillai Millar's education in particular and indeed, education in general.

For the first couple of days, Barz gamely attended lectures and was astounded at the lack of interest from the students, and a corresponding greater lack from the lecturers. The first he attended was with President Dr Kirkland himself, that Classicist whose fissured, granite face itself hinted at antiquity. The good doctor rattled on for two hours without pause on Plato's *Symposium*. Yet it was a strange display: his eyes fixed on the windows at the back of the lecture hall, his cadence rushed as if he were trying to race to the end and his voice pitched a great rumble in order to drown out the chattering group in one corner, the whoops and angry moans of the winners and losers of the high-spirited game of whist in another, and the roaring snore of one fellow who reclined over three chairs, not five feet from President Kirkland's podium.

And that was the University student body giving a lecturer respect. Over his first couple of days, he witnessed a knot of upperclassmen openly smoking and passing a jug of rum during young and wispy Reverend Doctor Osgood's rambling screed on Lot's wife; an underclassman named Holt, with the help of two collies, guiding a herd of sheep into Professor Burlington's Peloponnesian War symposium, the poor beasts' distressed bleats joined by cacophonous 'baaahhing' from the students; and old Doctor Sumner having to scuttle, then break into an undignified run across the quad, to avoid a barrage of rocks thrown at him by the well-lubricated members of the Debating Society.

Sparhawk and Barz had been skirting the opposite edge of the quad on their way to the library when the volley was unleashed.

'My God, they are pelting Dr Sumner,' Barz yelled. 'With rocks!'

'Hm, yes,' Sparhawk said. 'Something of a tradition for all of the doctor's half century of teaching at the University. I believe he has only been conked four or five times. A much easier target, though, now he is approaching his eightieth year.'

'But, but, where is the discipline? How do they get away with this?'

Sparhawk stopped walking, half-turned to Barz, blinked several times and peered closely at him. This was Sparhawk's tic when examining some new, curious discovery. 'You are a babe in the woods, Millar, truly.' He nodded towards the Debating Society, now slapping backs and red-faced with laughter. 'That well-fed jowly fellow's uncle paid for those two buildings. That pale, carrot-topped spotty one is the son of the current Secretary of State. The stipend from the weaselly, runty one's grandfather's will pays the salary of good Doctor Sumner and the entire faculty. Discipline? Millar, you are precious. To the library!'

Ah, the library. It was the epicentre of their world. Barz's true education, his intellectual stimulation was not in the lecture hall but outside it. He had come here on the second day, proceeding up the steps from the quad's bright sunshine and din of braying seniors and juniors mixed with the mooing of ruminating cattle to the low-lit and curtained calm of the library's main reading room.

The door closed behind him and a new world opened up. Seeing all the books lined up over three storeys, he felt weak in the knees. Cranston did have his sizeable library but Barz did not have access to it as the bulk of the volumes — purchased by the yard and on the cheap during the War from a Loyalist bookseller who had to leave the country in a hurry — had hollowed out pages and were stuffed with secret documents, jewels, hard cash in numerous currencies and other contraband. Yet here was the greatest accumulation of knowledge in the New World, all ordered and processed and filed and annotated between the pages of these books. When he would open a heretofore unknown book, it felt like tapping into someone else's mind, their very soul.

Much of his and Sparhawk's education had a furtive, *sub rosa* element. Whilst the rest of the student body were roistering in taverns, Sparhawk was taking Barz to a midnight trip to Doctor Devries' coal cellar for the dissection of a corpse fresh from Paupers' Yard; or sneaking into the bell tower of the Old North Church to conduct electricity experiments with ex-Professor Paxton in a howling thunderstorm; or attending a talk by well-known atheist Thomas Ingram in the bowels of Filene's Coffeehouse under the guise of the North Cambridge Temperance Society Annual Meeting; or skulking to the North End hovel of Signor Qualigia who taught the forbidden modern languages of Italian, Catalan and German (if the Ancient Greeks or Romans did not speak it, the University was not interested in it); or in the library well after-hours, guided by the deputy chief librarian Mr MacQuarrie, scouring through the University's *libri illiciti*, tomes deemed to be so detrimental to morals even most dons were forbidden them.

All of these tutors were geniuses, but men of former parts, with a clinging whiff of disrespectability. Devries expelled from Utrecht for deism; a wayward Paxton experiment had fatally electrocuted a University pupil; Ingram debauched a fellow Cambridge don's wife; Qualigia, it was rumoured, murdered three men in a Neapolitan blood feud; MacQuarrie the embittered grandson of a leader of the last Jacobite rebellion, whose descendants were forbidden from ever going back to Scotland. 'Whatever you do,' Sparhawk had whispered to Barz when first meeting the latter, 'never in his presence mention Culloden, the Act of Union, King George, or England. Never.'

The small group who were in Sparhawk's circle, the others in 'natural philosophy's vanguard', kept their extra-curricular activities to themselves. When the gang encountered each other on University grounds, they gave the barest of nods. They were the most secret of societies.

Early one morning, after about four months at the University, Barz and Sparhawk were ambling back to Massachusetts Hall after a particularly difficult dissection with Doctor Devries. It had been a sailor's body — Scandinavian, judging by the clothes — thrown up on the shore off Nauset Point and found in a snow drift. The body was still half-frozen, the legs a particular trouble requiring two men on either side, sawing away as if felling a sequoia. The two friends walked bleary-eyed, huddled against the chill, their boots crunching snow, their coats hiding blood-spattered shirts.

'Oh, Jesu,' Sparhawk muttered.

'What?' Barz followed the other's gaze up the path. Yawkey and Gore were trailing in the wake of a student Barz had never seen before. He was smaller than the other two, but Yawkey and Gore were bent low on either side, to better speak into the new boy's ears.

'My previous room-mate, Cushing. Amos Cushing. Of *the* Cushings. He had been rusticated to Stockbridge with the Revered Doctor Anthony Ward.'

'Rusticated?'

Again, the slow half-turn, blinking and peering in close examination, the tic Sparhawk seemed to employ several times a day with Barz. 'A babe in the woods, indeed ... When one of the student body has transgressed against the laws of the University, his punishment is to be lodged in some rural parish with an alumnus reverend. The country airs and the close instruction of one of our more godly alums is meant to put one back on the straight and narrow.'

Barz shook his head. 'If you can pelt the chair of Hellenic and Ancient Roman Studies with rocks seemingly without censure, what do you have to do to get rusticated? Kill a man?'

'Depending on the man, you could probably get away with that. Rustication generally concerns those who have committed a sin of the flesh. Or, more accurately, committing it and leaving something of an evidential nature.'

Sparhawk mimed a pregnant belly with his hands. 'The wife of the landlord at the Dog and Duck. These things can be squirreled away most often, of course, but the husband was somewhat put out and made a ruckus to President Kirkland.

'Asinine, do you not think? Yes, the animal urge is in us all; in fact, "animal" gives it a pejorative tinge, let us call it the all-too-human urge. Yet, why does no one have the barest understanding of the reproductive system? Good God! Coitus interruptus! An English greatcoat! Oral stimulation! There are many ways to avoid the begetting of bastards, do you not think, Millar?'

Barz had not really contemplated the matter before, but wished Sparhawk would quiet a tad; a gaggle of tutors trudging to the Dining Commons on the opposite path turned to see what Sparhawk was getting excited about. The other three students were almost upon them, and as Barz could now truly see Cushing, his immediate thought was 'goodness, he is beautiful'. Yes, he thought, beautiful not handsome. Like a statue of Apollo come to life — flowing blond locks, startling blue eyes, a pouty mouth.

'Thomas,' Cushing said, smiling broadly as he and his two courtiers were within a couple of feet.

'Cushing,' Sparhawk said neutrally as the two shook hands.

'I am returned,' Cushing said, spreading his arms wide.

'I trust your stay in the great West of the Commonwealth was edifying.'

'It was certainly edifying for Reverend Ward's daughter, Sparhawk,' Yawkey boomed in his deep baritone, punctuated with an over-elaborate mime of thrusting hips, at which Gore dissolved into hysterics, a high-pitched *tee-hee-hee, tee-hee-hee.*

'Gentlemen, you do me a grave disservice,' Cushing said sternly. 'Reverend Ward has *two* daughters. And an extremely comely wife.'

Now gales of laughter, the highs and lows of Yawkey and Gore's timbres sounding almost pleasantly harmonious. Cushing turned back to Sparhawk with a lift of the eyebrows as if to say, 'And why do I bother with these fools?'

'And who is this, Thomas?' Cushing asked, without looking in Barz's direction.

'Barzillai Millar, my new room-mate, Amos Cushing,' Sparhawk said after a pause. 'Cushing. Millar.'

Cushing pivoted nimbly, reached out and shook Barz's hand, placed his free hand on Barz's shoulder and almost imperceptibly pulled him close. For a moment, Barz was lost in the bright blue of Cushing's eyes and the gentle tug of his hands. For that moment, Barz felt the most important person on earth, and that nothing existed except he and Cushing.

'Welcome to the University, Barzillai,' Cushing said. 'I trust Thomas is treating you well.'

'Ever, ever so well,' Barz stammered. 'He has shown me some most interesting things.'

'Ah, the mysteries of the universe and all that, wot?' Cushing trilled a laugh, which conjured up images to Barz of a warm fire on a winter's day, crushed velvet against the skin. 'Thomas, and I say this with more certainty than anything I have ever said in my life, is a genius. A Franklin, a Jefferson.'

Cushing released Barz's hand and Barz suddenly become aware of Sparhawk hovering nearby, Gore and Yawkey still elbowing each other in mirth, the quad, the world.

'Thomas, why do you not join us in the Packachoag Club tonight?'

'Thank you, Cushing, no.'

'Barzillai, do convince our Thomas to come along, or maybe just yourself. It is grand fun, we talk, we debate, we drink,' and here Cushing tapped Barz's chest playfully, 'and it is ever so philosophical.'

'Perhaps I will,' Barz said eagerly, before catching Sparhawk's dark look. 'Although, we shall see.'

Cushing spun away, Yawkey and Gore scurrying behind him. 'Ten of the clock,' he called over his shoulder. 'Bradish's.'

'Well, he seemed a rather nice chap,' Barz said as the three moved out of earshot.

Sparhawk eyed Barz for a moment and then strode off. Barz had to run a step or two to catch up.

'What is this Packachoag Club?'

'A complete waste of time,' Sparhawk answered.

'Shall we go? It sound like it would be a laugh.'

'You hardly even know what it 'tis.'

'Well, Cushing seemed quite charming.'

'Aye, and so is the devil.'

Cambridge, 1806

'No, that will be all, Mr MacQuarrie,' Barz said to the hovering shadow to his left, thinking it the librarian. 'Thank you.'

'What is the meaning of this?' came a low growl.

Barz snapped his head up. Cranston stood at his side.

'Father, I . . . ' Barz stood up, dropping his book, upsetting the candle.

Cranston snatched at the candlestick, catching it before it over-turned. 'I went to your lodgings,' he said. 'Your man told me I could find you here, in the library. On a Friday evening. At study.'

'I am truly sorry, Father, but—'

'At study,' Cranston repeated, spitting out the word, making the candle gutter. 'On the way over here, I passed by Wilkin's Tavern which was awash, awash, I say, with your fellows engaging in riotous discourse. I passed Bradish's and perceived young Cushing, Gore and Yawkey lolling about outside, obviously in their cups. These are the friendships you should be cultivating, Barzillai Millar. Yet, here I find you—'

He righted the candle, putting it back on the table with a *thunk*.

'I am truly sorry, Father, but—'

Cranston motioned up and down the empty aisles of the library as if it were a house of ill repute. 'At. Study. Now, sir. You are to be away from this desk, this instant. This instant!'

When Barz hesitated, Cranston collared him and propelled him out the door, down the steps of the building.

'Father!' Barz cried, struggling to free himself from Cranston's iron grip. 'Please, let me explain.'

Cranston considered his son for a moment, then loosened his hand-hold. 'Very well.'

'I, I am sorry to have lied to you, but I was swept away.'

Cranston pursed his lips primly. 'In the wrong direction.'

'I have learned so much in my time here. About so many things: the movement of the celestial bodies, the arguments against the en-slavement of the black race, the conduct of electricity in a vacuum, the anatomy and physiognomy of man. The, the—'

Barz became tongue-tied. It was so very hard to convey the gush, the mass of things, the very universe, that was exploding in front of him.

'Anatomy,' Cranston said flatly, after seeing Barz would not continue. 'You have been studying medicine.'

He pronounced it *med-suhn*, in the old-fashioned English manner, with a tone of disgust that made Barz's blood chill. 'Not formally, you see, Father, but rather informally.'

'To what end? Perhaps you think you will become a lowly country surgeon, lancing boils off the arses of farmers, or bringing their braying brats into the world? No, this will not do, sir. You will cease this . . . meandering . . . this moment. You will attend to your future.'

Barz kicked a rock back and forth, before looking up into his father's face. 'No.'

'What?'

Cranston whispered that so softly, Barz could barely hear it. Yet it was worse, more terrifying, than Cranston screaming at the top of his lungs. But Barz pressed on. 'Sir, I must follow my own heart, my head. I am, dare I say, gifted, at academe. I do believe I could make a difference in whatever path of natural philosophy I choose. I could help mankind, I could make a difference. Do you not see, Father?'

Cranston was nodding during this speech, not looking at Barz but down at his cane. Barz's heart lifted. Perhaps he was winning Cranston over. Then there came a flash of silver in the lamp and moonlight.

Barz blinked. He was on his back, Cranston looming above, the silver tip of his cane pointed at Barz's face.

Barz half sat up. The jaw ached where the cane had caught him. One of his back molars was loose. 'You struck me,' he said, rubbing his jaw. Cranston had never raised a hand against him, in fact was not a violent man in general (that is what Alberts and Gresham were for) and Barz had been coddled and spoiled most of his life.

'I have never been more disappointed,' Cranston said stiffly. He kept the cane extended, the silver tip hovering a few inches from Barz's face. 'You will get off of your feet, get into some respectable clothes and march yourself over to Bradish's within the next half hour.'

'No.'

'What?' Again, low and dangerous.

'No, I will not. This is like a religious calling for me. Don't you see?'

Barz struggled to his feet to plead further, but as he did, Cranston delivered a crunching blow to his midsection which expelled all of Barz's breath, quickly followed by an uppercut that lifted him off the floor and again deposited him on his back.

'Do you think this is some sort of children's game?' Cranston whispered. And then he screamed, 'Alberts!'

Alberts appeared out of the shadows. 'Clean Master Millar up, put him in a respectable suit of clothes and hustle him to my carriage.'

Alberts lifted Barz up gingerly, almost apologetically. 'Come now, young sir,' he whispered.

'Do not ever cross me again, Barzillai,' Cranston said, still looking down at the spot Barz had fallen. As Barz was led away, he poked the loose molar with his tongue, tasted the iron tang of blood.

Fifteen minutes later Cranston was pushing Barz out of his couch onto the street in front of Bradish's. It had been a tense wordless ride, Cranston continually shifting and fidgeting, not looking at Barz.

'Now, sir,' Cranston said, his bulk filling the window of the carriage, his face florid. 'You will go into that house of somewhat ill repute and will meet your fellows. You will converse, you will drink, you will make merry. And you will be left at the University over summer term—'

'But, sir—'

'You will not come home this summer term lest I am satisfied you have made an impression on your peers. I will have people watching, as I have discovered I simply cannot trust you.'

Barz rolled over and the smell of sour claret and putrid beef stew was like a punch to the stomach. Lurching out of bed, he threw open the window. His belly flipped, heaved and gurgled but he was unable to expel anything.

He reeled back into the room and collapsed onto the bed. Sparhawk primly picked up Barz's vomit-stained jacket and folded it on a chair, wiping his hands as he turned away. 'You are systematically laying waste to your wardrobe, Millar. Soon you will have to return to those Versailles fripperies.'

Barz covered his eyes with his arm. 'Cushing wagered I could not drink a dozen double bumpers in under one half minute. I did. Then he wagered I could not do it again. I did. Or at least I believe I did.'

'Two days ago he wagered that you would not run naked through Doctor Peabody's lecture.'

'I did disguise myself with a Guy Fawkes mask.'

'But you did not disguise your pubis mons. As one of only three underclassmen with your distinctive red hair, you might be prepared for an inevitable discovery. The previous week Cushing dared you to swim in the Brew House vat.'

'And?'

'The vat is ten foot high — you could have drowned.'

'I would have died with a smile on my face.'

'And I do not know what sort of wager he gave for you to come back with all those rug burns on your face and torso last month. "Best not to speak of it," you said.'

'What of it?'

'Tell me, do you ever wager Cushing for him to do something abominably stupid? Or are you the little jester for his sole amusement?'

Barz sprang up and angrily marched across the room to his wardrobe, searching for a clean shirt.

'Barzillai,' Sparhawk said softly. 'It is three months since you have come anatomising.'

'I am through with anatomising and all other frivolities.'

Sparhawk shook his head. 'Hm. Doctor Jacobus, *the* Jacobus from Leiden, will be speaking to a small group of us on the transit of Venus at the library after hours. You are welcome to join.'

'I cannot. The Packachoags will be meeting at Mother Crab's.'

'Really?' Sparhawk could not hide his disappointment. Mother Crab's was not the least insalubrious brothel in the North End, but near enough. Yet, it was a favourite amongst University men as the proprietress, Madame du Poesy, had a soft spot for young academicians, and would quickly sniff out and expel any University administrators skulking about trying to catch their charges. Madame was hardly matronly, but nicknamed (not to her face) 'Mother' due to that worthy John Hancock's frequent visits to her, when the great man's cries of 'Spank me, Mother, spank me harder!' could be heard through the premises. And Crabs? Well, Madame du Poesy, she of zee over-pronounced Frainch ack-zent, was in fact born plain old Sarah Crabtree in Hampton, New Hampshire.

'Yes, really, Sparhawk. Wine, song, lasses. Merriment with like-minded fellows. That is what I am after. Not enduring the droning of a superannuated drooling Dutchman. I want to live life, have revels, fuck women. Not beetle around with some monkish celibate who perhaps can only get his member tumescent when he sees a dead corpse.'

'A dead corpse? Opposed to what, pray? A live corpse?'

'Always the pedant. I admit my wits are dulled this morning. Yet, I am bored of all that. I am bored of you.'

'That redness. That unhealthy weal of rosacea and psoriasis on your face, most pronounced on your cheeks and forehead. It will reduce if you cut down on your drinking.'

'Leave me.'

Sparhawk bowed slightly and went to the door. He paused as he was leaving. 'Bavarian, by the by. Jacobus hails from Munich originally, although he is, or was, of the Hebrew faith. He merely lectures at Leiden. And he is not yet forty. I do not know if he drools; I shall report back.'

Barz braced himself for a slam, but Sparhawk closed the door gently with the barest of clicks. His hands shook in anger; he wanted nothing more than to punch Sparhawk's kindly-looking sanctimonious face. He knelt by the bed and pulled out a case of Old Reliable.

'Hello, Father,' he said, grabbing a bottle and unstopping the cork with his teeth. He took a deep pull.

The door to Mother Crab's burst open loudly, causing the fiddler to skip a beat. Barz did not turn, however, as he had his hands full with a plump lass named Game Shirl. He sat on a couch, Shirl on his lap, and was pouring a trickle of claret down her chest which he would lick up as it approached her ample cleavage. Yawkey and Gore sat on either side of Barz, fumbling with employees of the house called Caris and Chastity. Cushing stood behind the couch, drinking a mug of grog, smoking a pipe and watching.

'Oooo, young sir,' Caris trilled to Gore. 'They must teach you ever so much at the University. I am being fair swept away on tides of ecstasy.'

'In the end, Miss, I believe you will be disappointed,' came a voice from above. 'Gore here has never engaged in congress, and I will wager the act will be clumsy, inexpert – although, for you, mercifully short.'

The University men looked up. 'Sparhawk!' whooped Cushing, a bright gleam in his eye. 'You have come!'

'Yes,' Sparhawk said. 'Astute as always, Cushing. I was setting out for a lecture tonight, when I said to myself, "Hang it, what I really fancy is a right-old gambol with the Packachoag Club brain trust."'

'And so you are here,' Barz said.

'And, so here I am,' Sparhawk answered gravely. He turned to a young, pretty Crab-ite who was sauntering past with two mugs of punch. 'I beg your pardon, Miss. I see you are bringing refreshment to that longshoreman, who may be your . . . companion . . . soon. Now, I have not seen his member, of course, but I am also certain that the pink tinge of his eyes, the mouth ulcer and the discoloured fingernails means he has been exposed to the Neisseria gonorrhoea bacteria. Please, be on your guard.'

'Oh, sir, I—'

Gore stood up, laughing mirthlessly. 'Don't worry if you die of the pox, love. Sparhawk here will be there to cut you open and examine your insides, won't you?'

'I, I—' the girl faltered and scuttled quickly away.

'Now, my dear sweet Caris, it is time for the seeing-to of your life,' Gore said, glaring at Sparhawk.

Sparhawk sat down in the seat next to Barz and Game Shirl, his eyes following Gore and Caris. 'I wonder if Gore has perceived the overly pronounced Adam's apple of his paramour.'

'You are companion-less,' Cushing purred in Sparhawk's ear and immediately sauntered off through the room calling for Madame du Poesy.

'What are you doing here?' Barz hissed.

'Why, making merry and later enjoying vigorous coitus with one of these fine ladies,' Sparhawk said.

'This is not for you, Sparhawk.'

Sparhawk looked directly into Barz's eyes. 'Nor you. However, I was thinking about this little charade tonight in the spirit of enquiry. Rather than listening to the good Doctor Jacobus discuss his astronomical observations, I could be in the field, as it were, with anatomical research. Do English greatcoats actually prohibit the spread of venereal diseases and unwanted pregnancy? You could help me, Barzillai. I brought one for you as well. No offence is meant, miss.'

'None taken, ducky,' chirped Game Shirl. She then sniffed. 'Egads, what is that?'

'Sheep intestines, miss. Wholesome sheep intestines.'

'And Barzy here is going to put that on his General Washington before it goes into me?'

'If, uh, Barzy, so wishes.'

'Please, Thomas,' Barz whispered, 'go home. Go back to the lecture. Go away.'

'Nonsense, this is natural philosophy writ large. We will forge some new field research together.'

Barz frowned as Game Shirl hopped off his lap and led him up the stairs. Sparhawk held a glass aloft. 'The happy couple,' he toasted.

Cambridge, 1806

He was awake, face down in the road, his nose wedged between two cobbles. Barz rolled over with a groan. Two matrons, bustling along the sidewalk with liveried African servants in tow gave him a sideways glance – noting, with a look of inevitable resignation, his University gown.

He seemed to be on the lower end of Beacon Street, as John Caulker's Bookshop lay directly in front of him. The eldest John Caulker himself (for there were three generations of John Caulkers in the business now) was unlocking the door.

'Ah, Mr Millar,' Caulker said in a conversational tone, his eyes betraying nothing, perhaps used to seeing a young gentleman poleaxed across the road. 'We have the Herodotus for you.'

'Thank you kindly, Mr Caulker, I am indebted to you,' Barz managed to croak from the cobbles. 'I shall call later to retrieve it, if you please.'

'Very good, sir. Good day.'

'Good day.'

Barz crawled to the kerb and arranged himself gingerly into a sitting position. His best breeches were ripped at the knees, the left sleeve of his jacket torn, the collar hung on by a couple of stitches. The knuckles on both hands were red and scraped raw. There appeared to be dried blood on his hose. Checking himself over, once then twice, he began to suspect it was not his.

As he walked slowly back towards his lodgings, Barz felt the fear. Last night? What in God's name had occurred? He remembered it had begun well enough with some fizz as the members of the Packachoag Club gathered around the fireplace in the upper room at The Muddy Charles. The conversation flowed, witty, urbane and quick, too quick – Barz a half syllable behind it all. He laughed as best he could, arranged his face into being agreeable, and drank until the nervousness went away, his rapidly emptied glass always quickly filled by someone at his elbow.

Then to the dinner with the endless speeches — dear Sparhawk on Milton; Cleland on beauty; Brecon on the dung beetle — the toasts, bumper after bumper.

And then? Mostly blank but a few images as in a half-forgotten dream. Urinating in the side corner of a coach. The boots of the coach driver — surprisingly well-made, highly polished and pristine, he remembered that distinctly — kicking out at him. A flurry of angry red faces in front of him, a blizzard of fists.

The bell across The Yard tolled nine and Barz picked up his pace. He was late for Rhetoric. He arrived at the Bedley Hall and pulled the door open, which responded with a long complaining creak. Barz winced, though he knew the sound would not interrupt Dr Grebe; the old man mumbled through his lecture, his eyes just inches above his notes, never varying from his text.

Yet Yawkey, Gore and Cushing all snapped their heads at the noise, staring hard at Barz. Sparhawk was just behind those three, and his look of despair and pity made Barz slink into his seat at the back. The lecture was interminable, unintelligible, Barz sweating alcohol, his stomach gurgling, his head pounding; he reeked of the street.

A rustle of bodies and he snapped to; he must have dozed. Barz let all the other students file out, until it was just him and the thick-lipped, pop-eyed vaguely frog-like Dr Grebe, snaffling around the podium gathering bits of paper. As the old man trudged out, he nodded vaguely at Barz, as if he was a scarcely remembered acquaintance, not someone whom he had perhaps seen most days for the last several months.

A slow walk outside and all of the Packachoag Club were near the stairs in a knot. Barz breathed in deeply. 'Well, Packachoagians,' he sang out. 'I was certainly not at my best when I awoke this morning.'

Cushing had had his back to Barz, but now turned around slowly. A nasty welt ran across his right cheek, and was at the stage where it turns from pink to yellow before bruising to blue. He eyes were hard as stone. 'Nor was I, as you can see. Millar.'

'Amos . . .' Barz said uncertainly, trying to remember what had happened, trying to slow down those brief images that flashed in his head.

'Millar,' Cushing cut him short. 'You . . . laid hands upon me.'

'I must have mistaken you for your mother.' Not a ghost of a smile, not a chuckle from the Packachoags, certainly not from Sparhawk, who was looking at Barz with a worried frown, then glancing at his boots as he poked at a stone. 'Please, fellows, I am jesting of course. I know things might have become a bit raucous, but surely you realise I was in my cups.'

'But you laid hands on me,' Cushing repeated, in an affronted schoolmasterly tone.

If there was one thing that Barz could not abide about Cushing it was this — his affectation of having the manners and the mores of an English baronet with all those codes and airs and graces. The notion that a gentleman must not engage in physical violence other than at sport or when he was called out was rather ridiculous at the University as the students were all — out of necessity of the frequent contretemps with the townies — practised brawlers.

'You are a hypocritical,' Barz began slowly, 'God forsaken, son of a whore.'

Cushing turned to the knot of men. 'You see, fellow Packachoagians. This guttersnipe — *peasanticus rusticus* — resorts to the language from whence he and his family come: the gutter.'

Blood pounded a drumbeat in Barz's ears. He concentrated on his fists, clenching them hard, the knuckles becoming whiter and whiter. And then a blackness came over him.

The next thing he knew he was being restrained by three others — Sewall, Osgood and Lowell — strong lads all, with iron grips. Cushing was gathering himself up from the ground, wiping blood from his lips, shocked and enraged.

'He has done it again,' Cushing squeaked. 'Hold him fast.' The hold around Barz tightened and Cushing nodded to Gore, who delivered two quick punches to Barz's midsection, followed by a donkey kick to the chest.

Barz doubled over and he could feel the grip of the three who held him slacken. 'No,' Cushing said, 'keep holding him fast. You—' this to Yawkey, who was watching with a sneering sideways leer '—give him what for.'

Yawkey hesitated for a moment, but saw the intent in Cushing's eyes, and stepped forward, delivering a cuff to Barz's head that made his ears ring.

'Now all you others,' Cushing roared. 'Have a go.'

And they did, one after the other, some with more enthusiasm than the others, but all not holding back. Finally, Barz was let go and he collapsed on the ground.

'You, too, Sparhawk.'

Barz looked up blearily. Thomas stood slightly outside of the pack, looking as if wanting to run away. Barz nodded to him slightly, as if to say, 'It's all right.' Thomas assented with an alacrity Barz had not foreseen, stepped towards him and all went black.

Barz blinked awake, a drummer playing a tattoo on his skull. Sparhawk swirled in and out of focus nearby.

'I thought it best,' Sparhawk said, in a whisper that hurt as much as a shout. 'Knocking you insensible. Rather than let the beating continue.'

'Kindness disguised as cruelty.'

'Something of that nature.'

'What exactly happened the other night?'

Sparhawk shook his head. 'You were . . . uncontrollable. I tried to stop you, but did not succeed. You have not been yourself these last, well, several months.'

Barz looked at the wall. 'And you have been constant, Thomas?'

'In trying to keep you out of trouble, I have been constant but largely unsuccessful. Having to be in society with these Packachoags in order to try to cushion your fall has been most difficult.'

'I am so sorry, Thomas.'

'Think nothing of it. But . . . Barzillai, you need to get away.'

'To where? I cannot return home.'

'Perhaps you would like to accompany me to Worcester this summer.'

Barz laughed, then clutched at his ribs. Had some been broken? 'To work the farm?'

'No.' Sparhawk sat down and shook Barz's shoulder excitedly, eliciting a groan. 'Oh, forgive me. No, not to work the farm. Over the past year, my father has allowed me to build a most prodigious laboratory in one of the outbuildings. I have few responsibilities on the farm — he has gotten on quite well without me since I matriculated. We will be free to experiment and anatomise to our hearts' content.'

'My father . . .'

'Does not need to be aware. Write him just before you leave and say you had a last-minute invitation from Yawkey to join him on his plantation. "Dear Father, I hope you will excuse this irregularity, but it was perhaps a once in a lifetime opportunity to engage with the cream of Southern society". He will fall for that tripe. We can have Yawkey intercept the letters from your father. And by the time he writes back and the letters cross, it will be term time again!'

A smile crept across Barz's face. 'It could work. But I would be out of funds.'

'The Sparhawks have you covered on that. So it is agreed!'

'Yes, yes I think . . .'

'Excellent. I would advise a low profile until we leave in two days' time. Avoid Bradish's and avoid Cushing.'

When at Bradish's the Packachoags always commandeered the Continental room on the second floor. It was not the tavern's grandest space, but it had advantages of situation: from the peephole in its main door, there was the perfect aspect over the mezzanine to the tavern at large; best to spy any University faculty in their rare forays to corral wayward students. There was a large window within, which led directly out to a flat roof, from which there were three escape routes — down to the alley below, a vault over to the back yard of the stables, or an easy jump to the roof of the General Ward.

Barz had hauled himself up to the flat roof from the alleyway and sat watching the Packachoag meetings from its edge, in the darkness just outside the glow of the lamps inside. The window was open, but owing to the general tavern noise below him, Barz could only hear the Packachoags' voices when they became particularly boisterous. He sat watching the dumb-show, sipping from Cranston's Green Devil — a new rum and absinthe concoction — occasionally dodging the lit ends of cigars pitched out the window.

He stayed and watched the pantomime even as a summer rain started. Do I, did I, look as stupid as they all do? he wondered. My face glistening with sweat, red as rare lamb, piggish mouth oinking with forced laughter? Although Cushing never seemed to feel the heat, and was always just outside the centre of things, egging people on, then standing back.

Suddenly Yawkey and Gore began shadow-boxing and the group all crowded round, miming the events of yesterday's beating, step-by-step. Barz gulped a long burning draught and made to go, but Gore — obviously playing 'Barz' — squealed loud and high-pitched. A mist descended and, in two strides, Barz was at the window, flinging the sash upwards and jumping into the room. The Packachoags froze.

'Fellows!' Barz roared. 'Did you think to start the evening's revels without me? A toast to our good Society!'

He drained the Green Devil and turned the bottle over so he was holding it in his left hand by the neck.

'Back for more, peasant?' Cushing sighed and then nodded languidly at Osgood and Sewall, who were at peephole duty at the door and were positioned behind Barz. The two rushed him.

Barz reached in his jacket and extended his arm quickly towards Osgood, who had reached him first. 'No, no, no,' he said. 'The object I am holding next to your carotid artery is called a lancet. A push, the slightest of pushes, and you are liable to bleed to death in five to ten seconds.'

He applied slightly more pressure to Osgood's neck, manoeuvring the two towards the end of the room with the rest of the others.

The Packachoags, not least Osgood, eyed Barz and the lancet nervously – all save Cushing, who had turned his back and was lighting a cigar from one of the candles on the mantle.

As he sucked and puffed vigorously on the cigar, he said: 'And this . . . display . . . helps you how, Millar?'

Barz blinked and swayed, then pushed Osgood backwards, still holding the lancet out. Then he brought his weapon down and started scratching his initials on the table.

'You have not worked that out, have you?' Cushing said. 'If you are looking to get reinstated and back in our good graces, this is hardly the way to go about it. You were blackballed tonight, incidentally. Unanimously. And this hardly helps your post-University career, does it? Osgood's father — you know Osgood, do you not, you were just threatening to slice his neck? Well, his dear old father controls the Bar. You shall never be admitted to it.'

It began slowly after a beat, a barely perceptible, 'heh, heh,' rising to a full chuckle, and then Barz threw back his head and laughed, a crescendo rising to the cackling whoops of a madman.

Even Cushing seemed unnerved. 'Come, come, man, depart, it, it is for your best interests,' he stammered. When Barz stood still, Cushing shook his head. 'Hang it, there is only one of him with a flimsy weapon. On him!'

The Packachoags hung back.

'Yes, have at me, my fellows,' Barz growled. 'And it is two weapons, by the by.'

He twirled the bottle of Green Devil over, grabbed it again by the neck and smashed it on the post to his left. As he did so, Barz was dimly aware of the door opening behind him.

'Millar, stop—'

All slowed. Some of the Packachoags in front of him were cowering, some wide-eyed looked beyond him. Cushing smirked directly into Barz's eyes. Barz turned. Sparhawk was stumbling back into the hall, clutching his neck, blood geysering over the walls. Barz rushed to him and ineffectually tried to staunch the flow from the green shard of glass protruding from his neck.

Sparhawk looked not at Barz, but somehow beyond him. 'Carotid, Millar,' he sputtered. 'Mark it. Two seconds, three seconds. Mark the time, I say! Four seconds, five . . . '

Newburyport, 1808

'Are you listening to me, sir?'

Barz kept reliving it, trying to staunch the flow of blood as others scrambled for help. 'Eleven, twelve, thirteen . . .' then the eyes dilating, fixing into a permanent disbelieving, disappointed look.

'Are you listening, God damn you!?' Cranston bellowed, kicking out at Barz's chair.

'Yes.'

Cranston took two turns around the length of his office. 'There will be no inquest, no serious inquest, at any rate. The story has been agreed that it was a tragic accident. Someone, no one knows who, dropped a bottle, the shards flying unaccountably into the neck of Mr Sparrow.'

'Sparhawk,' Barz said.

Cranston carried on, not hearing. 'I do this not for you.'

'You astonish me, sir.'

'I do this for this house, my business, our future. I cannot have us tainted by your folly, though Lord knows most of the University knows what you have done, and thus their families, the—'

'Cream of society,' Barz finished.

Cranston shook his head at his son, walked to the end of the office and stared out the windows. From the gardens, Barz could hear the faint cooing and baby-talk of Hetty and the wet nurse. Hetty had not only survived childbirth, but thrived, delivering unto Cranston obscenely healthy twin boys.

'Sons and heirs,' Barz said lowly, now two steps behind Cranston.

Cranston whirled around, startled. He had not heard Barz approach. A red weal was spreading across Barz's face; there was something in his eyes which made Cranston retreat a half-step. Barz's hands hung loosely at his sides, a matter of inches from the billy club on Cranston's desk.

Affecting not to hurry, Cranston reached across the desk and rang the small bell. 'Ah, Gresham, there you are, took your time. Prepare the carriage for Hetty, the twins and I. We shall leave sooner than expected. And leave that door open, would you, it is terribly close.'

He rounded the desk, keeping it between himself and Barz. 'We go to the Boston house. The legislature is in session, as you know. Normally, I wouldn't trouble myself with the duties of office, but I have to be there to help repair what you have done to this family's reputation. In three days' time you will ship on the *Squanto*.'

The *Squanto*. Barz's heart sank. It was, he knew, loaded with cotton, hemp, timber, maple syrup and salt cod. From there it would go to West Africa to deliver to British and French outposts, and to stock up on blacks to sell in the West Indies. And from there, back home with cane sugar and molasses for the Old Reliable business.

Four of Cranston's fleet were involved with the triangular trade; it was five until the *Blackstone* was captured by pirates off Cape Hatteras just days previously. Cranston hardly advertised that a significant portion of his empire derived from the selling and killing of his fellow human beings and even seemed slightly discomfited by it. But the money, the money that rolled in from it! Yet it was the unmentionable part of the business; the captains and crew of the slave-ships were in the whole a tainted lot, looked down upon by the smugglers and borderline pirates Cranston generally employed. As a young man, Alberts had made the West Africa to Hispaniola run. Barz had once asked him about it, and something rumbled deep beneath that hard, granite face. He twitched his eyes and all he would say was, 'Never again, young sir, never again.'

Barz looked squarely at Cranston. 'I shall not do it.'

'You will, sir, you will,' Cranston answered. He softened slightly. 'I am disappointed in you, Barzillai. But this is how you can repay me. You need to take responsibility for yourself.'

'But the University—'

'Is impossible for you now,' Cranston cut in. 'Do you not realise that, you imbecile? Even if I would pull every string and call in every favour and grease every palm, you have, let us be blunt here, slain a fellow student. You are finished there. Perhaps you may return to your experiments as a hobby. There will be time aboard the *Squanto*, and there will be many maritime things to distract you, I am sure. But your time at the University is ceased.'

Barz nodded and strode out of the room. Cranston called after him, but he paid no heed, sprinting up the stairs and into his room. He shut the door softly behind him, shoved the key in and locked it, the click reverberating in his ears.

During the course of his talk with Cranston, someone had packed most of his clothes into two sea chests that stood in the corner. His wardrobe, he noticed, contained all of the Chevalier de Bourbotte's clothes; they were not in the chests. Not quite the thing for the seagoing slaver, then. He brought out the purple number with the gold fleur de lis which he wore on his first day to University and laid it on the bed.

He reached under the bed and brought out his leather medical bag, took out a scalpel and scissors. He slowly and methodically sliced the suit into one-inch strips with the scalpel, from which he made one-square-inch swathes with the scissors. He piled it all on the bed, then grabbed it in his arms and threw it upwards, leaving his arms outstretched as he spun round in flurries of purple and gold.

Barz listened to the tramping back and forth downstairs, the yelling, the cursing, the hullaballoo of packing and loading two carts and a coach and four. Then more last-minute barking of orders, Hetty bidding good-bye to the servants, the slamming shut of the main double doors. The neighing, clip-clopping, rapidly receding farewells, and a long pause of silence. Then a loud 'thank fuck' from one of the footmen. The Lord and Lady were gone.

Barz thought he would feel some sort of relief, but did not. There was merely a growing sense of unease. He re-read the same paragraph in his book for about the tenth time, largely thinking that he was completely alone in the world.

A clip-clopping and a crunch of wheels on the gravel drive. Was Cranston returning? No, it was a heavy wagon and it turned into the stables; provisions for the house, no doubt.

Barz was re-reading the passage for the twentieth time when there was a knock on his door. 'Beg pardon, Mr Millar,' Jefferson, the 'thank fuck' footman said, sticking his head in. Not yet twenty, Jefferson had recently made the decision to grow a mustachio, in order to give more gravitas to his duties. But it came out in uneven ginger clumps and the result made him look young and silly.

'What is it, Jefferson?'

'There is a package for you, sir.' Still the footman hovered, not entering Barz's room.

'Well, bring it in.'

'It sits in the stable, with its deliverer. He said he would only open it for you. I, I . . . '

'Spit it out, Jefferson. And why are you so pallid?'

'I asked him what the contents were, then. And this just ain't right, sir. It just ain't proper.'

Barz crunched hurriedly across the gravel drive. With each step Jefferson hung back a bit more. Barz threw open the stable door and a tall, broad-shouldered man stood in front of a dray cart, his arms folded behind as he looked at the sole cargo: a large cask.

The man turned round and Barz started — he was the very spit of Thomas. 'Mr, Mr, Sparhawk?' Barz asked.

'George Sparhawk,' he confirmed, squeezing Barz's hand firmly. 'You are Barzillai. Just as he described you. Your psoriasis has not cleared up, I see.'

Barz could not meet Mr Sparhawk's searching gaze, staring down at the older man's well-made if unfashionable mud-splattered boots. Barz said: 'There is a hole in my heart that will never be filled, sir. I do not know how you are coping. I am so sorry.'

Mr Sparhawk bowed deeply in thanks. 'A waste of a promising life. Were you there with him, at the last?'

Barz met his eyes as best he could. 'I was in the . . . vicinity.'

'Tell me what exactly . . . ' Mr Sparhawk broke off. 'No, no. I shan't torture myself. I know the coroner's report to be a sham.'

'I, I have not read the report, so I cannot be sure.'

'No matter,' Mr Sparhawk said after a pause and a searching glare. 'The truth would make no matter to my conscience. Nor return my son.'

Barz opened his mouth once, twice, thrice to speak but stopped. He turned to the cart. 'What are you bringing me, sir?'

'Your bequest. Well, not an official bequest as he was not yet of age, of course. But Thomas told me of this on several occasions, and had his will drafted to be signed the moment he reached his eighteenth.

And I mean to follow his wishes. Oh, the subterfuge! Weighting the coffin in with rocks, dissuading his mother from having one final look at his body before the funeral.'

'Thomas is in there?'

Mr Sparhawk half-turned to Barz, blinked several times and peered closely at him. The Sparhawk tic was nurture not nature. 'Thomas led me to believe you were far sharper than you are demonstrating, Barzillai.'

'But it has been two weeks.'

'He is pickled like Lord Nelson. Preserved, more or less.' Mr Sparhawk stepped to the cask, placing his hands upon the sides. 'I was not always the shit-kicking, clod-hopping farmer you see afore you.'

'Oh, please, sir, I do not in the least—'

'My father was a bright man, indentured servant when young, but an autodidact. He did everything he could to try to secure me a place at the University. But the flux carried him and my mother away when I was sixteen and I had my four younger siblings to look after and my fate was sealed.' A smile. 'Thomas caught the book learning bug early and I moved heaven and earth to get him to the University and ensure that something to do with the book would be his life's work. I did right by my son in life. I will do right by him in death. And you will, too.'

Mr Sparhawk gave the slightest of bows, turned and walked out of the stables.

'Mr Sparhawk, your cart, your horse,' Barz called after him.

'Have it delivered to me,' he called over his shoulder.

'But your journey back?'

'I will walk.'

'All the way to Worcester?'

But Mr Sparhawk was out the gate, rounding the corner and then gone.

'Jefferson!' Barz yelled. He turned back to the main house and could see Jefferson, Mrs Ackroyd the cook and a few other servants crowded behind a side door. 'JEFFERSON!'

Jefferson tentatively stepped outside, the others fleeing back into the house. 'Yes, sir?'

'I will need a stout, long table — it must be above six foot — brought into the stables, several hands to help me with the, ah, package, some extra lamps, the brown bag in my room which contains my instruments and one of my note-books.'

An hour later, Sparhawk's body was stretchered out on the table in the middle of the stables, whale oil lamps burning brightly above him, cutting through the gloom. It was like an ancient offering to the gods.

It had taken a while to wrestle Thomas onto the table for in the end Barz had to do it alone. When the cask top was opened, Jefferson fainted dead away and Musgrove and Elliot, the two foot-boys, pelted straight out of the stable and onto the road, perhaps terminating their employment forever.

Barz bolted the door and walked back towards the ring of light. He unfolded the instruments case and found the items in remarkably good nick. Had Thomas been cleaning and sharpening them? He took his time selecting the best, longest scalpel and then, for the first time, dared look at Thomas's face.

'I am sorry, dear, dear Sparhawk,' he said, before inserting the scalpel just below the neck — three inches from the death wound — and slicing down Sparhawk's torso.

'Sir?' Alberts asked, hovering at the door. 'The *Squanto* sails upon the tide.'

Barz sat on his bed, fully clothed, greatcoat on, tricorn in hand. 'Is all ready?'

'Packed and stowed.'

'My father?'

'Detained in Boston, I'm afraid, sir.'

'Then what have we to wait for?'

Alberts bowed and led Barz down the steps to the carriage waiting in front. 'That is not my luggage,' Barz said, stepping inside.

'New sea chests, sir. I thought they would be more appropriate. They are monogrammed, you see. Very seamanlike.'

'Thank you, Alberts. Very kind, as always.'

When younger, Barz thought that the boats in Cranston's fleet might have leapt out of storybooks, akin to gold-laden Spanish galleons, predatory pirate ships or the trimmest, smartest ships of the lines. Now, as they approached the harbour, he saw them more as ledgers on a manifest, squat tubs whose sole purpose was to move money and misery from A to B to C. They were not the racehorses or stallions of the seas, but the donkeys, the burros.

The *Squanto* was the fleet's biggest, its flagship if ever it could be called that, 300 tons and already deeply loaded and nearly ready to disembark. 'Time and tide waits for no man, sir,' Alberts said as if by rote, his square head filling the window. Barz realised he had shrunk back into the carriage, twisting his gloves in his hands. He nodded and followed him up the gangplank and on board. Alberts shouldered a path through the busy, riotous deck, presenting Barz to the quarterdeck.

'Captain King,' he growled. 'Here is Mr Millar.'

The Captain, reedy, tall, with mahogany skin the exact hue of his rusty hair, turned to Alberts, then to Barz, looking at him with unfeigned disappointment. 'Ah, Mr Millar. We are nearly underway and I thought that you, perhaps, might not be coming.' Barz knew of King, or Captain Queen as he was known, due to the high-pierced shriek he employed when vexed. 'If you could get him stowed, Mr Alberts, I would be grateful.'

Alberts bowed, then motioned to the boys with Barz's dunnage to go down the hatch to the third mate's cabin. Barz and Alberts were right behind.

'Well,' said Barz as he stood in the cabin, stretching his arms out to test the width. 'I reckon that is not above five foot six. Hardly commodious.'

From above came a shrill whistle, the cry of 'All hands! All hands!' and the tramping of feet.

'I suppose I must go?' Barz said, but Alberts held him back, a hand on his chest, until the last of the sailors rushed by to go on deck. 'This way,' he said quietly, leading Barz aft and into the Captain's cabin.

'Close that door behind you,' Alberts said, then hurried Barz to the windows, unlatching the largest. Alberts whistled and a moment later, Gresham rowed out from under the quay in a longboat.

'Gresham?' Barz cried. 'And with my dunnage?'

'We must do this quickly, sir,' Alberts said.

'What's this about, Alberts?'

Alberts looked down, then out of the window as if trying to urge Gresham forward. 'You were never to make it far, Mr Millar. Captain King was to arrange an, uh, accident. A lamentable loss at sea, but given the dangers of the trade, not completely shocking.'

A momentary plunging chill went through Barz, he felt as if the blood all suddenly dropped to his lower extremities. A heartbeat or two later and it all came roiling and boiling back up, his face turning crimson and he gnashed his teeth. 'This will not stand, Alberts! When Gresham helps me make my escape, we shall immediately tell my father.'

Alberts looked squarely at Barz.

'My father . . .'

'Hetty is with child again, young sir. The twins are hale and hearty as your old man.'

Barz slumped back heavily on the Captain's desk. 'My father would not . . .'

'No time for sorrow, young sir. I have written to your cousin in Nantucket under the guise of your father, asking him to take you aboard, "for seasoning in the noble whale trade". I have briefly sketched out your . . . predicament . . . so have urged the utmost secrecy. He has agreed. You will be safe. Or safe as any man can be on a whaleship.'

'Safe. Without family. Without friends.'

'You can build your own family, young sir. You can survive and thrive. But you are not without friends.'

Barz smiled, blinked back tears. 'Thank you, Alberts. Thank you. But what if this Captain writes to my father? What if Captain King tells of my disappearance?'

'Have you ever known your father to open his own correspondence? It is either myself or Gresham who do so. And King, much as he is a cruel, bloody-minded cunt, did not want any part of this. He will tell your father you went overboard in the middle of the Atlantic and were lost. Just as planned. Now out you go, young sir. And good luck.'

Nantucket, 1810

The brass knocker echoed through the house.

Isobel looked up, cocked her head. Undoubtedly it was old Mrs Nickerson next door, coming for what would become a long natter, or perhaps Sally Hankredge enquiring after the order for the Iroquois Tomahawk (a design of Nancy's, it had a handle at the other side of the business end which vaguely resembled a hatchet blade). Mrs Hankredge had popped by several times since she placed the order two weeks ago to check on the progress — she wished to make sure the handle was a good hilt for 'an optimum of purchase' — but was becoming a drudge. Nancy and Kathryn were out. Isobel decided with a twinge of guilt not to answer the door.

The caller was undeterred, continuing with a series of sharp raps, with barely a pause between. Isobel sighed, set her tools down and strode into the house. She reached the door with a half-formed apology to either Mrs Nickerson or Hankredge on her lips. It was not either of those two ladies but a man. Though he had been knocking insistently, he now stood with his back to the door, down at the bottom of the stoop.

He wore a dusty black coat, one sleeve of which had been sewed back on, poorly, with red thread. His breeches were only slightly more respectable while his hose sagged and did not quite tuck into the knee. A sea chest which once might have been blue but was now a washed-out grey, was next to him, upended drunkenly on its side.

Isobel waited a moment for the man to turn around and acknowledge her, but he did not, continuing to stare out to sea.

She coughed. 'Yes?'

'Captain Chase,' the man stated flatly, half-turning when he spoke, but not looking at her. 'I am here to see Captain Owen Chase.'

Isobel blinked in disbelief. If some shipmate of Owen's did not know how to speak to her, then this minky bampot could go hang. She slammed the door and stomped back through the house to the shed.

After a moment the knocking resumed but Isobel ignored it, concentrating on her work. She was soon lost, enraptured in the art of creation.

'You there!' a voice blared into her reverie.

The sailor must have scuttled around the alley between her and Captain Gardner's house – for there he was, behind the fence. Isobel quickly put her work into the shed and strode toward the man.

'Sir, your manners have hardly improved. Begone or I shall call the constabulary.'

'The constabulary?' The man laughed, mimicking her accent. 'Och, aye, you doo tha', lassie.'

He placed two hands on the fence, and after much grunting managed to clumsily vault into the yard. Isobel took a half step backwards to pick up her awl, then stepped boldly towards him.

'Ah, ah, ah,' he said, putting up his hands, half-defensive, half-conciliatory. 'I fear we have gotten off to a bad start. I do apologise for my rudeness, but my journey has been long and I am rather fatigued. But, I am expected. Allow me to introduce myself. I am Barzillai Millar, and I am here to see my cousin, Owen.'

He grandly swept off his hat, did a courtly bow and replaced it. 'And you must then be cousin Annabel.'

'Barzillai Millar?' Isobel repeated. 'You are very late.'

'Am I? That is unfortunate. Would you tell me where I might find cousin Owen?'

'Somewhere near the Azores just now, I imagine. Come, we shall get you refreshment as you are so fatigued.'

He was very late, indeed. Eighteen months late, so much so that Isobel had entirely forgotten they had been expecting Owen's cousin for his latest voyage. She ushered him into the sitting room and cocked an ear, anxious for Nancy and Kathryn's return. He would not sit still, he scratched at various rashes on his face and underneath his shirt. His whisky-breath filled the room.

'My girls are out, to return shortly. Very shortly, I should think,' Isobel said. 'Would you like a cup of tea whilst we wait?'

'I shall take sweet wine if you have it, gin if not, and some Madeira cakes and lemon biscuits.'

He said this with his back to her, examining the bookshelves. Isobel found herself contemplating picking up the bust of Sir Walter Scott and bashing Barz over the head.

He turned around. 'Well?'

She controlled herself. 'I do not believe we have either Madeira cakes or lemon biscuits.'

'Improvise, then.'

Her eyes widened, her nostrils flared – but somehow Isobel calmed herself and walked to the kitchen. Her improvisation was jam cakes — Kathryn had made them in the morning — and a bit of cherry wine, which she had made by her own hands. Before pouring a glass of wine out, she considered spitting in the decanter but she paused and marshalled her anger. 'You are above the fray,' she said to herself. 'Above the fray.'

The half an hour or so that elapsed before Nancy and Kathryn returned was trying. 'I had understood you were coming from Newburyport, Mr Millar,' Isobel said. 'We were expecting you a year and a half ago. You were detained, then?'

'Obviously.'

Isobel sipped her dish of tea to save herself from flinging it at him. Barz refilled his cherry wine, sloshing it over the top of his glass. 'If I may ask, where have you been?'

A healthy slurp of the cherry wine. A yawn of boredom. 'Tither and yon, cousin, yon and tither.'

The back door banged and, hearing Nancy's impatient tread, Isobel muttered, 'Thank Christ.' Then, louder as she sprang out of the room: 'Help has arrived at last, Mr Millar.'

'Ah, ma'am!' Nancy exclaimed as Isobel entered the kitchen. 'I fancied you would be in the shed.'

'Owen's cousin is here and I must have him shifted out of this house as soon as possible. Hello, Kathryn.'

'Hall-ooo, Missus,' Kathryn sing-sang as she glided into the room, hands full of boxes.

'See to the gentleman in the parlour, please, Kathryn. Remove the glasses and the plates, I do not care if he is in mid-sip or his gob is crammed full of jam cake. Nancy, we need to find him lodgings. Could we have Jemmy shift his dunnage to the Tri-Pots, Mrs Kenny's or perhaps — yes, Kathryn?'

Kathryn stood uncertainly in the doorway. 'It's just, Missus, just that the gentleman is in a deep snore. And seems to have, uh, relieved himself in his trousers and onto the damask chair, is all.'

Isobel woke at half five the next morning, keen to get to the shed. She crept through the quiet of the house, but stopped short as she reached the bottom of the staircase and sniffed. Coffee. Was Owen home? Impossible. But he was the only one who drank it in the house. She followed the smell to his study. She opened the door with a smile, saying, 'How have you returned without waking me?'

Barz sat at Owen's desk, a sea-going physiology book open before him. 'Oh,' he said, closing the book.

'You have found the coffee, Mr Millar. I am unsure how good it is, I do not think anyone has drunk any since my husband went to sea.'

Barz's hair was combed, his beard kempt, he had put on a clean shirt, breeches and coat. He looked away, abashed. 'It is tolerably good, thank you. I gather my behaviour last night might not have been exemplary, Mrs Chase. For that I humbly apologise.'

Isobel studied him for a bit. He looked a scared little boy, now turning doe-eyes towards her. 'Yes, you may not have been yourself.' She caught the title of the book on the spine: Maddox's *The Common, Un-common and Extremely Rare Complaints and Diseases of the Sea-Farer*. 'Interesting reading.'

Barz scratched the rash on his forehead but then, seeming to admonish himself, took his hand away. 'I have some training in the medical line, which may be of use when next your husband sails.'

'Well, he may be back before you know it. The last message I had said he was homeward bound. Now, if you will excuse me, I have some matters to attend to.'

'A captain's wife must have to keep herself extremely busy when her husband is a-sea, I imagine.'

Isobel smiled and left him.

'Ma'am, he has been in the wine cellar yet again.'

Each morning, Mr Millar was up early, contrite, polite and keen to make amends for his 'rudeness in lubrication' the previous day. Yet, by about midday he would have developed a glossy sheen on his face and become particularly keen on Kathryn, pestering the poor girl as she scurried about the house trying to do her duties. By five bells he would have become cantankerous, the cloud of anger that surrounded him darkening, the more refreshment he took, until it would break as he dropped into a sleep so deep he would have to be carried to his room.

At luncheon on the third day of his stay, Isobel said: 'Well, Mr Millar, it has been a great pleasure having you, but I trust you have arranged your lodgings.'

He reached across the table and filled his glass to the brim. 'Oh, yes, Annabel. I have been told it will be available tomorrow.' After about his fourth or fifth drink, he would call her Annabel.

Isobel did not rise to it. 'I am glad for it. It would please me to keep you here, but of course it would hardly be proper for you to remain with my husband away.'

'Very true. Even with the short time I have spent here, perhaps your reputation may not survive at all. I am indebted.'

For the umpteenth time inthe last three days, Isobel was seized with a vivid, violent fantasy, this time of taking her knife and plunging it straight into one of Mr Millar's eyes. 'Your lodgings,' she said at length. 'Tell me about them.'

'Mrs Patterson tells me she has rooms available.'

'Patterson? I know no Patterson who lets rooms. Mrs Patrick? Mrs Palmerston?'

'Yes, it is Mrs Palmerston. On Centre Street.'

'Mrs Palmerston's lodging house is on Coffin Street.'

'The very one.'

Seven days this went on with a room, somehow, someway, not materialising, whilst Barz slowly made a sizeable dent in the house's drinks supply. This did not excessively annoy Isobel, nor his rudeness at table. She was from Edinburgh; a meal would hardly be complete without some drunk and surly man souring things. It was his practice of always being *there* which grated. She would turn into the darkened study and a soft 'hello' would startle her, and there he would be tucked into a corner. Or she would come down the landing of a morning, sigh contentedly that she had the house to herself for at least some moments, turn the corner and he would appear silently in front of her, as if conjured out of nothing.

'Ma'am, I say again, he has been at the wine cellar!'

'Nancy,' Isobel said wearily. 'I thought you had padlocked it.'

'He must have picked the lock. There cannot be above five cases left.'

Isobel did a double take. 'I don't believe you, it would be impossible for him to drink that much.'

'Can I not count? Have I not been in charge of the pantry and cellar these many a year?'

'Yes, yes, Nancy. Where is he?'

'I have no idea, ma'am.'

'Go try to find him, please. Have Kathryn pack his things this instant and put them on the front stoop. Let me go check the wine cellar.'

The 'wine cellar' was a rather grand name for what was, in fact, just a modified root cellar. Yet, Owen had expanded it during his last stay at home and at capacity it could hold a good 1,000 bottles. The padlock opened with a heavy chunk, Isobel propping up the door before she went down. At the bottom, she picked up the long corkscrew, striking empty after empty rack, the tapping sound overly loud in the confined space. 'Dearie me,' she said. 'He has been at it.'

'Boo,' a voice said lowly just behind her. Isobel spun and held the business end of the corkscrew out, its point almost grazing the lower end of Barz's throat.

'No,' he said. 'Not there. That's the trachea. You push and you may just end giving me another orifice in which to breathe. Here is what you want.'

He guided her hand upwards, placing it on the side of his neck. 'This is what you want,' he whispered. '*Carotis communis*. About sixteen seconds it takes to kill a man when it is severed.'

Blood thrummed in Isobel's ears. Her hand did not waver. 'Your things are being put out front. You must leave.'

Barz closed his eyes and pressed into the corkscrew so that it made an indentation in his flesh. Then he broke away suddenly and scrambled up the stairs.

Isobel slumped back heavily, breathing hard. 'What the devil?' she whispered.

A noise. He was here again, clomping back down. She straightened, stepped back, held the corkscrew out again. Barz reached the bottom of the stairs, looked at her for a moment, crouched down and scooped up four bottles in his arms before rushing out of the house.

'These are beautiful rooms.'

Barz rolled over. Mid-morning sun streamed in through the windows, between which sat a man on the leather chair. He blinked and had to remember where he was. Cambridge? No, that rooming house in Nantucket. Mrs, who is it again?

'I daresay that Mrs Sherman has some more expensive lodgings on the island.' The man smiled. He looked like a slimmer, more handsome version of Sparhawk. 'Actually, I know so.'

'Who are you?'

'Your benefactor, Barzillai Millar,' the man said, taking a couple of sheets of paper out and examining them closely. 'And it is my good name you have been living on this past month since my wife removed you from our household. Look at these bills that I have received! Lodgings, food, drink, the gaming table. '

'You are Owen? Owen Chase?'

'Yes, Owen Chase. Captain Chase to you it is, at your service. My credit has certainly been at your service.'

'I, I fully intend to pay you back as soon as I am able.'

'Oh, you will indeed. In fact, you already are! Starting this very moment you are in my employ. I have, I should say, been back these five days. And in two and a half days the *Wessex* sails again. Until then, you will be my dogsbody, my servant, you will run messages, you will help with the requisitioning and the victualising of the ship.'

'Well, I am not sure I am quite qualified.'

'A man of your parts will learn very quickly. My wife tells me you are also knowledgeable of medicine, which will prove to be handy on board.'

'Again, I am not entirely qualified to—'

'It will reduce costs.Incidentally, I tallied up the decimation of my wine cellar and that will come off your wages. If you dance, you must pay the piper, as they say. Let us begin. I should say part of your duties willrequire you to be at my beck and call – and God help you if you are not sober and sensible when I need you.'

Owen had stood to his full height, and seemed to burn with righteousness, filling up the room. 'And I mean now, Barzillai Millar, right this instant,' he said in his all hands voice. 'Get your sorry shit-stained carcass out of this bed. This instant!'

III.
A-Whaling

North Atlantic

It was getting dangerous.

As the *Wessex* had surged mile after mile north into colder water, flying in the face of increasingly worse weather and the received wisdom of 200 years of sperm whale hunting, John steadily became the least popular person on board. It had got to the point where he could not go the length of the ship without being roughly jostled, have one of the crew accidentally drop something — usually heavy and metal — near his feet from one of the yardarms, or to nearly be punctured by a harpooner's practise throw gone very wide of its target.

Even Owen's unshakeable faith was wavering. John was no longer invited to the Captain's table, no longer even brought into the cabin for informal chats. Captain Chase seemed to barely be able to stand the sight of John, subtly yet deliberately looking the other way whenever he saw the Esquimaux come on deck. Yet the course was not altered; Owen kept the ship surging relentlessly onward, past mountains of ice and into a curled fist of Arctic winds.

John was acutely sensitive to his shipmates' feelings. He doggedly went about the duties that were required of him — more doggedly than ever, more doggedly than he ever did any work — then retreated to the safety of his hammock as soon as he was able. His fellow outcast coofs were sympathetic after a fashion, but soon they began to detest the sight of the man who was taking them away from money — for every sea mile North North-east they travelled was like dollars dropping over the side — and possibly to their deaths.

The weather turned colder, windier, stormier. The crew would be called out in shrieking winds, wrestling with frozen sails, and even the normal tasks of sailing became increasingly fraught.

The shoves, bumps and thumps became nastier. Often these were unavoidable: it was a small ship, there were many men. But as days progressed, each push and prod had a little more oomph behind it. John felt most vulnerable going to the head. Whenever he would go, sitting on the rough plank, a few inches of oak between him and the sea, the water often washing up and covering him, a shipmate came up and would try to dislodge him. John took to pissing over the side, in the odd bucket when he could get the chance. But when he had to sit down, that was the worst. Once, Deavers, whilst he had been squatting, took his seal suit (which John had taken completely off as was the normal manner) and threw it over the side.

'Beg pard'n, Esquimaux,' Deavers growled. 'Seems I dropped your little fur night dress over the side.'

After that John usually only went to the head in the dead of night. He crept forward one foggy midnight, and just as his buttocks hit the rough wood plank they sprang.

'At him, lads,' someone whispered harshly.

The two McKeever brothers and Caleb James, the three biggest and brawniest of the crew, encircled him. John looked around frantically, but the men blocked his way to anything that could be used as a weapon. He aimed a mighty kick at one of the McKeevers then tried to run around him whilst yelling for help. But from behind, James clapped a hand over his mouth, the McKeevers snatched his legs and, in a blink, he was pitched over the side.

But they did not throw him far enough. As he fell, John twisted and grabbed the under-rigging with one hand. He dangled for a long moment, a short drop to a certain icy death, one he perhaps would have embraced a little while ago. But not now. He pulled himself further into the rigging, looked up at the McKeevers and James. They were cursing lowly at each other whilst scrambling around the deck. Then Jim McKeever popped up and heaved a belaying pin, which whistled by John's ear. James then bellied over the ship's rail, an iron bar clutched in two hands. He began to swing it overhead like a wood chopper. John shook his head, yelled 'No!' and swung his body up, his feet meeting James' elbow with a sickening crack before the man could bring the bar down.

James yelped in pain and the bar pinged off the *Wessex*'s side, plopping harmlessly into the water.

'You'll have to stick him,' said a familiar-sounding voice from behind the three men. 'Get it over with, you idiots. And fast.'

'You got the harpoon?' Jim McKeever said.

John McKeever nodded, hefting it to strike when they all stopped. 'Did you hear that?' James said as he rubbed his elbow. *Thoosh*.

The elder McKeever muttered, 'Aye, I did.'

And then again. *Thoosh*. And again. *Thoosh*. *Thoosh*. John twisted his body in the rigging so he could turn toward the sound a few points off to starboard. The mist cleared away slightly and there, not a far way off, was the whale. Or whales. A great giant pod of them, innumerable.

'Jesus God Almighty,' John McKeever said, almost to himself. 'Did you ever see such a sight?'

The sounds of the breaching and belching for air — *thoosh, thoosh, thoosh* — became almost deafening, so loud they woke Obadiah Templar in the crow's nest who set to screaming: 'She blows, she blows, she blows!'

John looked up at the McKeevers and James. 'Perhaps you fellows would like to give me a hand.'

Barz came from behind them, looked down at John dispassionately, as if weighing the odds of a whist opponent's hand. At last he said to the others, 'Well c'mon, you idiots. Hoist him up.'

John sat in the coofs' boat glaring at Barz. Barz tidied the rope and pulley at his feet, fussed with the harpoons, looked up at the side of the boat, anything to avoid John's fiery stare.

At last, Barz said: 'I thought it would be for the best. For all of us. You, too. I haven't got time to explain. What you do now is just row.'

'You tried to murder me,' John said. 'Actually, you did not have the courage to murder me. You had others try to kill me.'

Barz nodded and looked away. 'You need to row.'

Gripping his oar tighter, John stood up and smashed it into Barz's head, brains bursting out the side. John dropped his oar, hefted a harpoon, stuck it into Barz's belly until it came out the back and embedded itself into the boat's gunwales. John reached into his boot and pulled out the bone knife, slicing through tendons and arteries in Barz's neck until he reached the spinal cord.

John blinked. All three imagined scenarios actually made him smile. But then he looked around at the other men. The ship so far from anywhere. Live to fight another day, he thought to himself, relaxing the grip on his oars, loosening his shoulders. Live, live, he thought, live for another day.

The coofs' boat, the smallest and least seaworthy, had been the last of the four to splash into the water. There was a febrile excitement that spread from man to man, boat to boat, blood and money in the air. John shrank deeper in his seat and shivered. Though the sun had peeked through, burning the fog away, it was still cold, yet he seemed to be the only one that could still feel it.

The whales: how many there were, John could not tell. As many as a school of minnows. The sea was alive as these great hulking beasts breached and burst through the water. He had only ever hunted grey whales in a small umiak, with at most four people. These animals, some as big as the *Wessex*, were all armoured with barnacles, looked dangerous, deadly.

The crew had to be quiet. As they moved about the boats, the men used careful, exaggerated movements like they were trying not to wake a sleeping baby. Though silent, they were somehow more communicative than ever. Nostrils flared, eyes locked, gestures were extravagant.

They chopped slowly through the sea, rowing for about half a mile. The boats kept a good distance from each other, spreading out to attack separate parts of the pod.

The Captain's boat reached the whales first. John stopped a moment to watch him at the prow of the boat in clothes as white as an angel and in a clean, jerky motion heave at a huge basking bull. The harpoon arced toward the beast, the rope fluttering behind, and went home with a sort of sucking sound. The whale went from luxuriously basking to thrashing upwards and down, tugging the boat away from the pod.

Barz's face, full and purple with rage, filled John's vision. 'C'mon,

John,' Barz yelled, his face purple. 'Row, damn your fucking eyes, row, you cunt. Put your back into it.'

John put his back into it. Whilst they rowed, the others looked warily about. Whales sometimes charged and ran, were capable of stoving a boat in two with the merest flick of a tail. Mr Coffin's boat now was striking a whale and then a few minutes later the McKeevers' boat struck, and still the great pod did not run.

It was the coofs' turn now and Barz steered towards a great bull, lying slightly apart from the rest of the pod. As they closed on their prey, the men's breaths grew more rapid, shorter. Howard, the Sandwich Islander to John's left, started grunting. John stared at Barz, whose face was pink as he worked the tiller, his eyes boring over John's shoulder at the beast that lay dead ahead.

'Right, all right, all right, No Nose,' Barz said, lowly, almost to himself as No Nose let go of his oar to grab the harpoon, and shuffled to the front of the boat. 'Be swift, be true, now my son, let it loose now, my son. Now!'

No Nose jerked the harpoon away and it flew home, embedding itself close to the blowhole. The whale let loose with an underwater scream which travelled across the sea and up through the planks underneath to John's boots and ran right through his entire body and seemed to burst out his eardrums.

'Stow your oars!' Barz yelled.

The whale dove and John watched the entire length of harpoon rope play out, uncoiling so fast that it started smoking in the pulley under Barz's feet until he began dousing it with water. The rope pulled taut and the boat leapt forward, cleaving through the sea. John's oar, still dipped into the water, almost shot out of his hands. Barz and Howard helped him wrestle it onto the boat. With the oar safely aboard, Barz puffed up in size and authority, bellowed into John's face, 'Did I not tell you to stow your fucking oars?'

John shrunk back, clutching the bench as the whale towed them along. It seemed like an interminable ride, the most precarious sled journey he had ever been on, all bumps and hops and skipping along at breakneck speed. Twice after cresting a wave, the boat was airborne, John seeing a chink of light in the boards as they separated momentarily. Eventually, the speed slackened and No Nose was able to stick the beast two and then three more times. Still, the whale towed them, yet its wake changed from white foam to a blood-red trickle. It finally stopped swimming and floundered, a laboured breathing escaping through its blowhole.

Barz whispered, 'Now, lads, let's finish him off.'

The others picked up their oars and pulled towards the beast. 'Careful, lads,' Barz said, 'he might be near his time, but he might not be done yet.' They touched the side of the whale, but it hardly reacted. No Nose and Howard stood, took hold of the lances and began spearing the whale, prodding it for that killing spot.

The whale was turning in the water, moaning, groaning as No Nose and Howard hacked. John covered his ears, but the creature's agony surged through his body. He could take it no longer. He turned, barged his way to the front of the boat, took a lance from No Nose and jumped towards the whale.

He bounced off the side of the creature, sliding down a bit, but managed to get hold of a ridge of barnacle. He shimmied up the beast's slick and oily back. It was listing; John could feel the reverberations from its laboured breathing travelling upwards through his whole body. John took off his one of his mittens and placed his hand near a jagged gash in its hide where blood was rushing out. He kept the hand there, let the blood wash over it, stifling the shudders coursing through his body.

He gave the whale a last pat, then sketched the sign of the cross with the lance tip mumbling: *Nomine Patris, Filii, et Spiritus Sancti*. He rocked back and forth and plunged the lance down with all his might, just to the left of the dorsal fin. A delayed second, then the creature bucked one final time, blood and gore and viscera exploding out its blowhole, showering John as it died.

As they towed the whale back, dragging its unbelievable weight, John looked down at his hands. The blood was drying, but not quickly; it was thick, gelatinous. John paused for a moment, brought his hand to his face. The blood was more deeply pungent than any other blood he had smelled, animal or human. John sniffed again at his hands, and surprised himself that he did not retch.

'Put your back into it,' Barz said to him, but mildly as if a joke. Barz had the sated look of someone who had eaten a mouthful over his fill. He smiled benignly at John. 'Towing the fish back, you'll find, is the worst of our tasks. You think you are done with it when you kill the beast. But, like reaching the top of a mountain — you still have to walk back down.'

The coofs' whale had towed them closer to the *Wessex* than any of the other boats and they were first to bring their catch alongside. John watched as the others expertly split the head of the whale open, the jelly inside going from clear to milk white when exposed to the air. The Captain's boat came alongside them, the crew laboriously tugging an even bigger animal.

Owen stood at the prow, his harpoon dripping blood, yet his own clothes were clean as if they had just been freshly laundered. He stretched out his hands towards John. 'Son of Ham, my son. Son of Ham, our saviour. John, my friend. You have delivered us to the promised land as I knew you would.'

The Captain's boat touched gently against the side of the coof's whale. The Captain reached over into the whale's head cavity, pulling out a dripping handful of gunk. 'White gold,' the Captain muttered as he unfastened his trousers, revealing his engorged, tumescent penis. Owen slathered it, began stroking and within a few moments he grunted and sent a series of spurts into the whale's head. John slid his eyes towards Barz, who smiled uncertainly. 'Owen is under the impression that that is good luck. Apparently, this is an old custom of the sea.'

John looked out at the hundreds of whales. 'For every one?'

Barz nodded solemnly. 'The customs of the sea are inviolable.'

For ten days and nights they hunted the whales. Hunted might not be the precise term. Picked. Selected. The slow pod of spermaceti rarely moved, seemingly unconcerned that these men were killing them off one by one.

'It's just like goin' to the shops, eh lads?' No Nose chuckled to the others sometime during the fourth day. And they all laughed, John too, cackling like a madman. It was constant activity; the men hardly slept, ate or paused, propelled by the adrenaline. There were so many kills that they stopped trying the whales out — boiling down the blubber to get every last bit of oil. Instead they just scooped bucketful after bucketful of spermaceti from the whales' heads, then cut the massive bodies adrift, the ship surrounded by an ever widening goo of blood and oil.

John looked in horror as the body of the first whale was cut adrift. 'You are not going to use the rest of it?'

Barz shook his head. 'No need.'

'All that meat. All that meat.'

IV.
The Amazing Mr Sackhouse

Nantucket

'Ma'am, ma'am!'

Nancy burst through the door, the newest He's at Home Lady's Friend model — Pacific Island Chief — in her hand. Isobel was packing the next day's shipments for New Bedford and Fall River, forty-two orders ranging from the Malay Caliph to the West African Prince, all different in length, girth and design.

Isobel turned round. 'Nancy, what is the matter? Ah, you have finished, then!'

She took the Pacific Island Chief from Nancy. It was six inches long, on the thinnish side, carved out of whalebone. Isobel arched an eyebrow. 'Circumcised?'

Nancy's voice turned professional. 'Why yes, ma'am, my model was. It was a surprise for me, no doubt. Still, I think it improves the line and some of our customers were wanting something in the middle sizes. But, ma'am, I came to tell you: the *Wessex* has come in.'

A half-smile from Isobel. 'Nonsense, Nancy, she has only been gone three months.'

'Did I not see it with my own eyes rounding the Point?'

Isobel blinked a couple of times, looked out the window. 'Are you sure it was the *Wessex*?'

Nancy squared her shoulders, her eyes widened, her brow furrowed. 'Am I not a native Nantucketer? Have I not been on this island my entire life? Can I not tell one vessel from another as I can tell my family apart? Why—'

Isobel held her hand up. Nantucketers and their knowledge of ships. Let them start talking about it and that's you for half an hour.

'And 'sides,' Nancy barrelled on, 'Jemmy Martin was with me and he had his spyglass and said the same.'

'Jemmy Martin?'

Nancy's face flushed, and not with shame Isobel thought, but pleasure. 'The point is, ma'am, that she'll be docked in three hours.'

Isobel took a despairing look around what had been Owen's study and had become, as it did each time he put to sea, the headquarters and distribution centre of the He's at Home Company – Inventors and Proud Purveyors of the Original Lady's Friend. The room was full of order forms, boxes, about 150 Lady's Friends in various stages of production, and all manner of raw material: wood, ivory, whalebone.

Isobel puffed her cheeks. 'The ones boxed and ready for dispatch let us bustle down to Mrs Kitteridge's boat just now. The other ones we can put in the shed. Let's hurry, now.'

They covered the half a mile to the Long Wharf quickly, Nancy barrelling onward in her side-to-side swaying gait that was not unlike a seaman on his first few days on land, Isobel walking, half running to keep up.

'You were not mistaken,' Isobel said softly when they were able to see the bay and the quays spread before them. Isobel rarely could tell one ship from another, but she knew the *Wessex*, with its funny, lumpy middle berth and its harlot red mermaid prow. And there she was, being brought in by a pilot boat about a few cable lines out. She could make out Owen in his gaudy scarlet coat — bought last year from M. LaCroix of Rue du Faubourg Saint-Honoré and of which he was inordinately proud — standing atop a side rail, leaning casually over the sea, a shortish dark-skinned man next to him, the two looking to be in some animated conversation.

The quay was packed. Most returning ships got some rowdy reception; friends and family were normally front and centre, and even at the busiest season there were many unemployed and idle whalermen who would stumble out of the taverns to give a ragged cheer and say hello to old mates. The owners of course would be there anxiously awaiting the final tally. Yet when word spread that the *Wessex* was entering the harbour, it seemed that the whole town had filtered down, even the whalermen who should be fitting out or unloading their own ships.

Three months a-sea and already returning. As Isobel moved through the crowd she caught snippets of anxious talk. 'What do you think, ran aground somewhere?' 'You reckon she came upon a blow and couldn't go on?' 'No, she looks fit enough from here. Maybe the yellowjack.' 'Or even the plague?' At the last suggestion, a section of the crowd involuntarily stepped back from the edge, allowing Isobel and Nancy a way through the crowd.

Ezekiel Mather was at the edge of the quay, half-slumped against Mrs Hummock, looking grey and insubstantial, a wavering spyglass clamped to his eye. He acknowledged Isobel with a resigned nod, then turned back towards the *Wessex*.

'Perhaps,' he said in a small voice, 'I should have not let your husband set to sea. But I was so sure, I was so sure.'

'Whatever has happened, sir, God has delivered them back home.' Piety, Isobel had long ago discovered, was the language the Quakers of Nantucket responded to the best.

Mrs Hummock pursed her lips, adjusted her grip around Ezekiel. 'It has come to no good, I can feel it in my bones.'

Ezekiel shook his head. 'Still, she is so low in the water, as if laden with oil. But that cannot be, it is too soon. And yet, I can see the men just now, they seem in rather high spirits. And who is that blackamoor on the quarterdeck in conversation with Captain Chase?'

Felicity Islands, South Pacific, 1809

'These natives,' Isobel's father rumbled, blowing on his Cullen skink, 'they freely fornicate within our midst.'

'Indeed, sir, it is one of our greatest of trials,' agreed the Reverend Mark Tait. 'But I do believe that if anyone can deliver these savages to Christ, it is you.'

The Reverend Dr Campbell grunted. His square face was, as usual, downcast, but Isobel recognised the slight twinkle in the eyes: he was pleased. She could not fathom her father sometimes. He had a towering intellect, had taught rhetoric and natural philosophy at Edinburgh University, and normally suffered no fools — unless they were simpering sycophants. The Reverend Tait hardly let an hour in the day elapse in which he did not tell Dr Campbell he was Christ's warrior — 'as if the archangel Gabriel come to life' or 'John the Baptist born again'.

The Reverend Tait had been one of Dr Campbell's acolytes at university, his constant sweet nothings worming their way into not only Dr Campbell's heart, but Alison's, his eldest. Alison and Reverend Tait married just two months before the good doctor brought his two daughters halfway across the world to this sweltering archipelago in the Pacific.

Talk at every meal eventually veered towards fornication. The weather first (stifling, but it was God's will to bear it), the food next (the native cooks could hardly manage to cook proper porridge, but a small thing to be endured), then fornication, always somehow edged towards the subject by Reverend Tait complaining of the wantonness of the natives.

Isobel looked at Alison, who rolled her eyes towards her husband and their fathers, as if to say *what a pair of dafties, eh?*

Twelve years older than Isobel, Alison had inherited their father's blocky face — it made her handsome, not pretty — and his intellect, his turn of phrase, his caustic wit over the dinner table, three characteristics which had tended to scare off suitors. They could overlook a lack of comeliness, but not intellectual superiority.

Isobel loved her sister, mostly because Alison intuited that what

Isobel craved most from companionship was quiet. When alone they spent much of their time together in a comfortable silence, often drinking whisky on the veranda of an early evening (the bulk of Alison's dunnage consisted of books and ten crates of Tallisker), reading and writing.

'Ah, there he is, my lovely husband,' Alison said on one of those days, a loose smile on her flushed and pink face. The Reverend Tait was about a half a mile off, easy to spot in his black cloak, gesturing with his hands as if practising a sermon. 'Perhaps he is rehearsing platitudes to feed Father over tea.'

Isobel sniffed her whisky before sipping. It smelled peaty. Of home. 'Why on earth did you marry him, Ali?'

It was a question Isobel asked often in the bantering playful tone she took with Alison, who would bat it back with a dry irony: 'for his vast fortune of £100 a year'; 'for his wit that would have shone brightly even in Madame de Pompadour's salon'; 'for his poetry-inflected wooing'. But whether Alison had drunk the right amount of whisky, or something was in the humid air, she answered, 'He asked. I refused. He asked again, I refused again. And on and on. By the tenth time, I was just tired. I did not have many other choices, as you know. And would never do with this phizzog, and tongue.'

'Oh, Ali . . .'

'Tut, tut, my dear, we should not insult our intelligence by saying what is not true. I am not blessed like you.'

'Ali, please, I—'

'Yet why *marry* is the question, of course. I shall admit it was only because I was curious about sex. The Reverend Doctor Tait's motives for my hand were so obvious: to get near Father. That I wanted not his hand but tadger, I wager, is something he would never had thought.

'In the end, it is a spurious reason, marrying for sex. At least in other places in the world you don't have to be so constrained.'

Here Alison glanced back towards the house, then sat forward. 'And he is an oddly cold man, my Reverend Tait, despite his obvious preoccupation with the mating habits of the Felicity Islanders. Physically, I mean. To the touch. Even his penis. It is rather off-putting, I assure you.'

Isobel had noticed that, whenever forced to take the Reverend Tait's arm or hand, it was cool and clammy, even in the monstrous heat. And he rarely perspired, except when he raised the topic of fornication at table. One dollop, then two, would form on the ridge of his nose, then trickle down to his lips.

Reverend Dr Campbell swallowed a hunk of fish and considered the fornication of the natives. Yes, he was a Church of Scotland minister and missionary, but first and foremost he was a natural philosopher — reason and enquiry were his true gods. Throughout Isobel's life, he had talked of the sex practices of humans with the same scientific, and non-doctrinal detachment that he did of the pine marten or flying fox.

Isobel slid her feet under her chair. When the fornication talk commenced, she knew what was next. Reverend Tait's foot would scuttle underneath the table, desperately in search of her own.

Many of Isobel's days were spent in elaborate plans to avoid Reverend Tait, or at least avoid his cool touch. Yet he seemed adept at bumping into her in the drawing room, brushing her hand whilst he dealt at whist, being the first to offer an arm while promenading to church. A few days previously in the grotto behind the manse, Isobel was picking flowers and she stood up.

'Hello, sister,' someone breathed on her neck.

Isobel jumped. 'My goodness. Reverend Tait. How did you come to be standing next to me, without appearing in a puff of sulphur?'

She smiled briskly and made to leave, but the Reverend was staring at her intently, blocking her way. 'I knew you would be here, Isobel,' he said earnestly. 'I have followed you to this private grotto, which could be an earthly Eden or Hades, I know not which.'

'Reverend Tait, please unhand me.'

The Reverend looked at his arm which had snaked across Isobel's waist as if it were unconnected to his own person. He fell to his knees, prostrating himself before her feet.

'I have married the wrong sister,' he wailed.

'Get hold of yourself, sir,' Isobel hissed, having to leap over his back and scuttle through a tangle of fronds to escape.

Reverend Tait was attempting to coerce Isobel's father to prolong

the conversation. 'I have heard it said, dear sir, yet I can scarce countenance it, that the natives indulge in' — here pausing to try to look
Isobel in the eyes — 'the sinful practice of mutual onanism.'

At the words 'mutual onanism' Alison's eyes lifted from her Cullen
skink. They had taken on the soft dewiness they always did on these
discussions, drifting over to the hulking, tattooed form of Manu
Tatupu, who, as the manse's head of household, stood in attendance
at every meal. And who, Isobel knew, Alison visited every afternoon
in his room while the Reverends were out visiting the tribes.

Isobel could see her father about to weigh in at length on mutual
onanism. She interrupted: 'Is it not unbearably hot in here? Unbearably close?'

Reverend Dr Campbell paused. 'It is indeed, child. But it is what
we must endure as God sees fit.' He tugged at the sleeves of his formal
heavy black coat, made for draughty Edinburgh drawing rooms. 'We
must endure.'

Manu Tatupu was then at the Reverend Doctor's elbow: 'Oh, Mr
Reverend Doctor. There is a sea captain at the door who wishes to pay
his respects. A Captain Chase from the Americas.'

Nantucket

John was itchy. Ever since Deavers threw his seal suit overboard, he had been stuffed into whatever hand-me-downs he was given by the crew. Overlarge nankeens, trousers that only reached mid-calf, billowy shirts made of worn sailcloth. Only after the success with the whales did his shipmates reveal what dab hands they were with the needle and thread; he had been dressed in relative finery ever since. Still, all the clothes were made with strange coarse materials seemingly designed for discomfort; the wind blew through the fabric too easily, and he felt colder and wetter and more miserable.

Today he sported some of the Captain's finest clothes, lovingly altered and fitted out to John's shorter, stouter frame by Deavers himself. 'We need to present you to the island proper-like, Mr Sackhouse,' he said, touching a knuckle to his head, not daring to meet John's eye.

Proper-like or no, the polished boots pinched his toes, the breeches bunched obscenely at the crotch, the fire-red jacket was stiff and the top hat made his head sweat. And his under linen had been washed in sea water — thus the all-over itchiness. Yet, no matter how uncomfortable he felt, he could not help but admire himself in the looking glass. Dashing, was how Barz put it, as he brushed John's coat down earlier that morning. John could not disagree.

As the *Wessex* edged towards the harbour John grew quiet. He could hardly believe the immensity of the town — the homes were ten times the size of his old hut, made of solid stone and wood, looking permanent and immovable as mountains. A forest of ships' masts stretched across the harbour, eddying in the water. And across the town and packed together on the quay was the greatest mass of humanity he had ever seen.

John swallowed. 'So many. So big.' Owen looked at John curiously. 'Sure, our island community is prosperous — in fact I believe the most prosperous small stretch of land on God's green earth, per head, if you see — and may be busier than some. But we are on but a little speck, truly. You should see New York or Philadelphia. Or Old Europe where London and Paris both have near enough to a million people.

And I have stopped at ports in China and the Far East that rival that. Barbarous places full of malodorous primitives—'

Owen bit off the rest of his sentence, his eyes sliding quickly over towards John. But John was gawping at the town, trying to count the number of folk on the quay, trying to envision what a million people would look like. He shook his head when he realised he could not, and smiled. 'I would, Captain, like to see those places.'

A hail from shore, reedy and a bit tremulous, yet clear all the same. 'Ahoy, the *Wessex*.'

Owen had seen Ezekiel as the ship was piloted in. He knew the old man must be fretting, but also knew something about the theatre of coming to port, particularly with a hold full of oil.

Owen climbed further up onto the top of the taffrail, unclubbed his ponytail to let his long locks free, made sure his coattails were fluttering in the breeze. He let the moment drift along, could feel the expectant eyes trained upon him.

Finally, he said, almost offhandedly, 'A speaking trumpet, if you please, Mr Arthur.' The helmsman, hovering nearby, handed it to him before he could finish. 'Oh, thank you.'

Owen brought the trumpet to his lips, but then put it down. 'No, I shan't need it.' Then in his roaring basso profundo: 'Ahoy, Mr Mather. I hope I see you well.'

The tremulous voice again from the quay, this time a bit exasperated. 'Are you clewed up? Returning for repairs?'

'I am afraid I have to disappoint you on the voyage, sir.' Here a mumbling from the shore, and several curious glances back to the quarterdeck from the *Wessex*'s crew. 'I know, sir, that you are a scrupulous owner, mindful of costs. It grieves me to tell you that we have completely run through our store of staves and hoops because we had to make so many barrels – to fill them up with whale oil!'

The joke was limp but true — the *Wessex* had used every bit of wood and iron in its hold to fill barrel after barrel. So much so, that after the hold was full, the Captain stowed some in odd places within the lower deck and in the officers' cabins. However lame a sally, it was received rapturously on the deck, with bellowing laughter, hats thrown in the air, the ships' boys dancing.

A long wait to finally dock and when the Captain strode out first, John trailed behind. Owen strutted down the gangway, arms spread wide, embracing the applause, and John hurried to catch up as the crowd surged forward. He then stopped short when he saw just over Owen's shoulder a woman. Not a woman, actually, but THE woman — Owen's wife from the picture in his cabin, who looked at that moment beautiful, almost celestial.

Isobel, for of course he knew her name, was smiling though not jubilantly. Wryly, John thought, as she watched Owen strut, as if she knew the Captain was playing a part, being the showman. What was it Father Kelly used to say? 'Some want to be the groom at every wedding, the corpse at every funeral.'

Isobel stepped toward Owen, but her husband turned first to pump the hand of an extremely tall elderly man who was standing next to a roly-poly little woman who shrieked: 'Oh, I knew it was a resounding success, did I not say so, Mr Mather? Did I not say so?'

Isobel sighed and looked away, her gaze wandering back to the *Wessex*, the harbour, then to John. She looked away from his stare, a sweetly-shy quick downward movement of the head, before lifting her chin back up. John gave her a quick smile, glided around Owen and approached her, reaching out his hand. He moved slowly, tentatively and she initially drew back. Finally, she let him touch her, looking at him curiously.

Her face was warm, soft. John said, 'Forgive me. You are the woman from the portrait. Your eyes do have that exquisite colour. It was not an artist's fancy. I can scarcely believe it.'

Isobel made to say something than stopped, as if unsure of herself. She kindly removed his hand. 'I don't believe you set out with my husband, sir,' Isobel said at last.

John touched Isobel's elbow, edging her away from the melee. Owen was being hauled up on the shoulders of two brawny whalermen as the crowd closed amidst a chorus of 'huzzahs'. The rest of the *Wessex*'s crew were now trudging off the ship to a maelstrom of noise.

'Your husband saved me from the sea,' John said, staring at Isobel. He had completely forgotten about the crowd. 'I am bearing a gift for you. We extracted from within one of the whales this rock.'

He fumbled in his waistcoat and procured a large goldish sweet-smelling almost spongey lump. 'This is ambergris,' she said, taking it from him. 'It is most valuable. At this size, near to a small fortune.'

'I was struck that something this beautiful could come from inside such a creature. The Captain gave me one, and I stood holding it in the light of the weak sun and it kept shifting colours, yellow and gold and amber. That is what your eyes look like.'

Isobel looked at John levelly — they were the same height — and smiled archly. She removed her bonnet, tousled her hair. 'Are you in the habit, Mister . . . ?'

John did not offer his name, just continued to look at her. 'May I ask your name, sir?' she went on.

'John Saccheuse.'

'Well, Mr, erm, Sackhouse, are you in the habit of making inappropriate comments to the wives of your shipmates?'

John was about to answer when the sun was blotted out. A thin giant of a man, looking down at him piercingly.

'Mr Mather, hello,' Isobel said. 'Allow me to introduce Mr Sackhouse, whom my husband appears to have encountered on his voyage.'

'Mr Sackhouse, is it?' he said, smiling broadly. 'Is that the name you're using?'

He clasped his large hands over John's, the fevered grip of one close to death. He pulled John close, gave him an overlong bear hug. John had a brief thought of his mother, the same desperation in the hands. 'You are here at last,' the man said, his voice tinged with a deep emotion, the source of which John could not quite place.

The old man broke off and looked about the quay. The entire town was pouring down to get near the *Wessex*. Two well-dressed men in black held back from the crowd, eyeing John speculatively.

Ezekiel's eyes narrowed. 'I see my competitors Mr Ellis and Mr Kane have taken an interest in you. Come, sir, let us go to my house. We have much to discuss.'

He spun John around, shouldered through the crowd with surprising strength, breezing past Mrs Hummock who, flustered and flapping, turned round and followed in their wake with studied dignity.

133

Nantucket

After just a few minutes, John got up from his seat and sat cross-legged on the floor. The Mather drawing room was spare but John was oppressed by the shininess. Everything gleamed: the polished hardwood floor, the looking glass on the corner, the ebony side table, the grandfather clock.

Ezekiel had been speaking excitedly and rather at random, telling of the exotic ports of call from which he had picked up each of the objects in the room. He trailed off when John sat on the floor.

Mrs Hummock leaned towards John, speaking slowly and loudly as if to a doddering dowager aunt. 'It is custom to sit in the chairs in this country, Mr Sackhouse.'

'The. Chairs,' she added even more loudly, grasping the back of an empty chair.

John shook his head. 'The chair is of poor design. The back is curved so that you have to sit unnaturally straight. The lack of padding means it is hard on the buttocks. Although I am not as commodiously built in that area as you are, Mrs Hummock.'

Isobel laughed, covering it up as a cough. Mrs Hummock started to sputter. 'My butt—' then changed tack, whispering in wonder: 'But it's a Thomas Chippendale. From England.'

Ezekiel stood. 'Come, let us join our guest and sit as he does. He does have a point about the lack of comfort of these chairs. And your backside, Mrs Hummock, to be fair.'

The old man slowly descended, John wincing at the popping of bones and joints. Mrs Hummock squirmed in her chair, finally getting out to sit as demurely as she could.

'Mrs Chase?'

'Thank you, Mr Mather, I believe I will remain as I am.'

'As you wish.' Ezekiel turned to John. 'Now, Mr Sackhouse. Tell me about your voyage.'

John told him of being adrift and insensible, being saved by the coofs' boat, the Captain, the change of course, the journey north.

'North-North-east,' Ezekiel whispered, amazed.

John continued, told about nearly being thrown overboard, to gasps from the two women. Ezekiel was nonplussed. 'I have seen worse. Men get superstitions about other men. Think them unlucky. Go on.' John told them about the immense pod of whales, the non-stop killing. Owen expunging into the whales' heads.

'What?!' Isobel said.

Mrs Hummock covered her mouth. 'My word.'

'Does this happen all the time?' Isobel asked.

'Perhaps, Mr Sackhouse,' said Ezekiel, colouring slightly, 'we shall omit the, the, less than crucial aspects of your tale. Tell me where this immense shoal was.'

Ezekiel went on before John could answer. 'Of course, it is immaterial. Worldly. But I trust you will not tell anyone, particularly Messrs Ellis and Kane where it was.'

'I assure you I haven't the foggiest idea.'

Ezekiel tipped him an appreciative wink. 'The perfect answer, Mr Sackhouse. The perfect answer. Tell me, though. How did you come to be adrift in the sea?'

John thought a moment, shifted uncomfortably. He stared at his hands, started wringing them. When he looked up again, he realised he must have drifted off, lost in those awful memories. The others were looking at him warily, an awkward silence hung over the room. John cleared his throat. 'I had no home, no one to go to.'

'Cursed and cast out of your father's house,' Ezekiel said, looking at John significantly.

'Something along that line occurred, yes,' John said slowly.

A knock at the front door. No one moved for a minute. And then another knock. Ezekiel turned to Mrs Hummock. 'Where are the servants, Mrs?'

'All off celebrating the *Wessex*'s return, as per your order,' Mrs Hummock said with some asperity.

'Shall I answer that?' Isobel asked, rising.

'No, no, not at all, Mrs Chase, please do not trouble yourself,' Mrs Hummock said. 'It's just that, just that . . . you couldn't give us a little start, could you, Mr Mather?'

Mrs Hummock rocked from side to side and Ezekiel gave her an extra push. She tumbled over onto her side, rolled over twice before managing to regain her feet. She patted herself down primly and went out of the room.

A moment later she showed Owen into the parlour. 'Mr Mather,' he began, and then stopped at the sight of his employer and John sitting Indian style on the floor. He regained his composure. 'Mr Mather, I give you joy on the most prosperous of voyages. I see you have met the man most responsible.'

'Mr Sackhouse,' Ezekiel said, emphasising the name archly, 'has been telling me the tale.'

Isobel watched the men stare at John. She recognised that look, wanton and lusty, the way some men look at women. Owen had not acknowledged her, had barely looked her way. 'Owen,' she said softly.

'Ah, Isobel. I had expected you to meet us on the quayside.' He spoke flatly.

'I was there,' she answered, stung. 'You may have not noticed me as you were embraced by the mob. And, as you can see, I accepted Mr Mather's kind offer to sit with Mr Sackhouse.'

'A hand, if you please, Mr Sackhouse,' Ezekiel said, stretching out his arm. John helped him to his feet. When he touched the older man, John felt him shudder. 'A most righteous grip,' Ezekiel said, almost to himself. 'The hand of God. Mrs Chase, I shall be a trifle rude and ask your forbearance. Your husband, Mr Sackhouse and I must discuss business and I fear it will be some hours. Mrs Hummock, would you be so kind as to show Mrs Chase out?'

The meeting was indeed to be some hours. Owen had brought manifests, the ship's logs, a lump of documents which the two and Mrs Hummock waded through.

John's attention soon wandered. He got up and ambled over to the great bay window with its view of the other great houses of Nantucket ringing around the square. In the centre sat a great squat church with a spire sticking up as tall as the *Wessex*'s mainmast. How were these great edifices built? he wondered. It must have taken lifetimes. Why do they not fall down?

'Are those horses?' he asked.

The other three looked up from the documents. 'Those beasts there,' John went on. 'Pulling those carts.'

Ezekiel craned his neck. 'If they can be called such. That is Stephen Dobbie and his ancient bays, not long for the knacker's yard. They don't have horses in your country, Mr Sackhouse?'

John shook his head. 'They have been described to me. I have read about them in books. I never thought I would see them. Nor churches, taverns, cobbles on the streets, street lamps being lit. What a wondrous vista you have from outside this very window.'

Ezekiel nodded. 'You are truly godly, Mr Sackhouse. Seeing the divine in the commonplace.'

'Oh for goodness sake, Mr Mather,' Mrs Hummock said, thumping the table. 'Is it not Newton Street? A road you have walked on for most days these last sixty years. May we get on with the business to hand?'

The three hunkered down. John stayed at the window as the day darkened and the lamps were lit behind him. Newton Street seemed incredibly busy. Most of the town seemed to be walking by. Some nonchalantly strolled by the Mather house, glancing inside, as if business happened to take them by. Others gathered outside and openly stared at John, who waved cheerily to them all.

Mrs Hummock scratched excitedly at a piece of paper, dabbing her pencil into her mouth as she worked out the sums. 'Now if these records are accurate—'

'My records are always accurate,' Owen cut in.

'Indeed they have been up to now, but begging your pardon Captain Chase, even the most scrupulous of commanders can sometimes make a mistake and the final reckoning isn't done in my book until the last drop of oil is measured out. But given that prices have risen substantially in even the past few months since you left, owing partly to the war, this haul should come in at . . . $125,223.'

She put her pencil down with satisfaction. Owen smiled, but Ezekiel was looking over at John. 'Did you not hear, Zekey – Mr Mather? That is by about twenty-five percent higher than our greatest haul and only in but a tenth of the usual time.'

Ezekiel nodded. 'I heard loud and clear. I am contemplating what that means.'

Mrs Hummock looked as if someone had brained her with a belaying pin. 'That means, I believe, that you have had your greatest success ever. By twenty-five percent.'

'Yes,' Ezekiel said mildly. 'But does God care? What does He want me to do? That man alone can tell me.'

John was still watching the street. 'Your Mr Kane and Ellis remind me of crows.'

Ezekiel started. 'What?'

'Yes. Their beaky noses, the black clothes, the way they strut about, hands behind their backs. They have been outside for some time.'

Ezekiel jumped up from his chair. 'Bastard sons of whores. How dare they? Trying as ever to claim what is not rightfully theirs. Close the shutter and step away from the window, Mr Sackhouse, lest their very gaze bedevil you.'

The old man was sweating, panting heavily. 'I fear I have had a turn. Mr Chase, I trust you will put Mr Sackhouse up in your house, just for this night.'

Owen had been looking over Mrs Hummock's maths, was tracing a finger over the $125,333. 'Oh, but sir, I thought you would put Mr Sackhouse here. My cousin is staying with us and I had thought, since you had ample room . . . '

'You are forgetting I used to live in that house, Captain Chase,' Mrs Hummock said. 'That still leaves you with another spare bedroom. And I thought I heard Mr Millar say he would be staying at the Three Crowns.'

'Oh, did he? Then I would be happy to oblige, Mr Sackhouse.'

Ezekiel looked down at John. 'Mr Sackhouse, I would be obliged if you could wait on me in two days' time. On the Sabbath. There are several people I would like you to meet.'

He turned to Owen, speaking lowly. 'Keep him close. Do not let anyone visit with him. And go out the back way.'

Nantucket

'Thank God it's you,' Isobel said as Owen and John came into the house. 'There has been a steady stream of visitors wanting to meet Mr Sackhouse.'

'I'm afraid we will have to disappoint them,' Owen said.

The three stood awkwardly in the reception hall, until Isobel led them into the sitting room. John went straight to the settee, laid down, hands behind his head.

Isobel smiled. 'Do make yourself at home, Mr Sackhouse.'

'Comfort is a rare commodity aboard ship, I find, Mrs Chase. This is bliss.'

Owen and Isobel lingered by the door, close but not touching. 'Will you be all right on your own here, Mr Sackhouse? I need to discuss a few things with my husband. Nancy and Kathryn, who work for us, are attending to some duties elsewhere. They will return soon.'

'I assure you I shall be fine. I imagine you'll be having what we used to call . . . ' John paused looking upwards to concentrate, '. . . the welcome home fuck.'

Owen straightened and looked out the window. Isobel coloured.

'Is that not the right phrase? The return rogering? The coming back coitus? Homecoming humping?'

'I entreat you, Mr Sackhouse—'

'The seeing you again seeing to?'

Isobel continued. 'Please, Mr Sackhouse. We shall see you soon.'

John waited until he heard their footsteps retreating up the stairs. Then he went straight for the polished walnut sideboard and opened it up, and was entranced by the glittering plates inside, gold rimmed and blue etched with a scene of a whaleship trying out a fresh kill. He picked up one of the sets of tiny cups and long silver wooden-handled knives and put them into his pocket.

To the kitchen next. John sniffed. His nose was assaulted by a number of competing smells: sweet, sour, salty, and several things he could not recognise. He followed them to the end of the kitchen and opened the door to the cool larder and stepped inside.

'Jesus fuck Almighty,' he breathed softly to himself.

John had often tried to conjure up what Father Kelly meant by heaven, and one of John's thoughts was of an endless supply of food, a land of plenty, free from want. What he was standing in now did not match his fantasies in terms of abundance, but far exceeded it in variety. There were salted meats hanging from hooks, legs of mutton, sides of ham, hunks of beef, links of cured sausages; in a large box in the corner were all manner of salted fish, some a strange flat shape he had never seen before. One side of the larder had shelves of vegetables in such colours: fiery orange, mustard yellow, hot red and rich purples. He picked up a red ball of a fruit and squeezed, pips and juice running down his hands and forearm.

Then to the baskets of leaves on the far end, their odours so varied and heady they drove him to his knees. When he touched them he felt he wasn't grabbing handfuls of leaves but smells: peppery spikiness, cloying honeyed sweetness, summer freshness. He crushed the green leaves together in his hands to make a paste, spreading the coolness over his face.

He stumbled to another wall with jars labelled strawberry, raspberry, apple, elderberry, blueberry. He sniffed at a strawberry jar, put a finger in and tasted it. The sweety-tartness ran through his body from his tongue to the tips of his fingers and his toes. He felt his heart skip a beat and gripped the side counter to keep from falling.

Another thing Father Kelly had once said: conceiving of heaven was impossible because it was too much joy, too much pleasure for human minds in their earthly bodies to handle. John understood the feeling of too much joy now. He had to leave the larder; he could endure no more.

He took the strawberries and a hunk of ham and sauntered down the hall.

He opened another door and stood stock still in wonder. Rolls of maps were spread on a desk, a globe stood in a corner, but around the walls: the books, sweet merciful fucking Christ, the books. More than he had ever seen, more than he could hardly even imagine existed. Thousands.

He ran his hands along one wall of them, fingertips tracing the spines. Many were of the type he would grab for Father Kelly off visiting ships: *My Life Among the Natives of the Sandwich Islands* by 'A Yankee Whalerman'; Steele's *Elements of Sail-making, Mast-making and Rigging*; Dalrymple's *Essays on Nautical Surveying in the Barents Sea*.

John found a thick, well used copy of *Paradise Lost* and laid it on the desk, crushing some rolled-up maps in the process. He dipped the ham into the strawberry jam and ate, tearily transported back to winter evenings of what Father Kelly used to call 'just the four of us': the priest, Mary, John and the blind poet.

A knock on the front door. John sprang up, rushed down the entrance way and whipped the door open. Mr Ellis and Mr Kane were standing on the stoop. John thought they looked like the number ten: about the same height, Ellis rail-thin, Kane corpulent, almost spherical. The two looked startled.

'Er, um,' Ellis said, doing a little double step. 'I was expecting Mrs Chase or Miss Nancy or Miss Kathryn to answer. You must be, er, um, Mr Sackhouse of whom we have been hearing so much. Allow me to introduce ourselves—'

'You are Mr Ellis and Mr Kane,' John interrupted. He bowed and the two smiled, an obvious natural act for Ellis, Kane doing so with much difficulty. 'I have heard much of you. From Mr Mather. You are the two bastard sons of whores. Or is it whoreson sons of bitches?'

The smiles wavered. 'Er, um,' Ellis peered at John, sniffing at him. 'I am sorry, sir, but I do believe your face is slathered with mint.'

John touched his face. 'Ah, *mint*, is it? Yes, it is slathered with mint.'

A pause of a second or two, and Ellis went on, 'Well, no need to stand on ceremony. At any rate, we were hoping to call upon Captain and Mrs Chase to welcome him home and toast his success.'

'I am afraid the two of them are fucking at the moment.'

Ellis looked at his feet, muttering 'Er, um.' Kane guffawed, burst into his first genuine smile and clubbed his partner on the sleeve. 'Let's cut the horseshite, Lambert. Mr Sackhouse, it is you we are here to see, as I think you may know. Would you like to join us at the Tri-Pots Tavern for some ale, chowder and a bit of a talk about your voyage?'

John's eyes lighted up. 'A tavern? I would very much like to join you.' He ducked back inside, grabbed his top hat, the copy of *Paradise Lost*, and ran out the door.

'The Old Thatch in Killeagh.' Father Kelly had been leaning back on the pelt, hands behind his head, eyes closed. When homesick, the priest reminisced about taverns, pubs and inns. 'They serve this particular ale, sort of red coloured in certain light, an agreeable burnt oaty aftertaste. More often than not, there is a pig on the spit, and you can just peel off crackling when you want.

'The Cobblestone in Dublin. Near Smithfield. A rough area, of course, full of poxy doxies. But there is always someone with a mandolin or a fiddle or a song in the corner. They serve this stout by the name of D'Arcy's. Chocolatey almost, but light as a feather.

'But, GUH, GUH, The Harp and Bucket in Sligo Town. The prince of pubs, the tsar of taverns. The ceiling is made of tin tiles — I kid you not, have you ever heard of such extravagance? And the Sligo whisky, it's sugary, earthy, a joy.'

'What is the countryside like?' John asked.

'In Sligo? Oh, green, beautiful, rolling hills, dramatic sea cliffs, I suppose. You know, the kind of thing that often sends poets into swooning ecstasies. But let me tell you about the roast dinners at the Harp . . . '

Father Kelly would have approved of the Tri-Pots, with its comfortable booths, a cast iron pot of chowder over the fireplace filling the room with home and hearth and comfort. It was one of the brightest rooms John had ever been in, the whale oil lamps burning clean and bright.

Kane led them to a booth in the corner. The three sat by the window, a warm summer breeze carrying the salty sea air in. The merest of nods from Kane, and the landlord brought over three pints.

'Sláinte,' John said and took a healthy gulp.

The two men raised their mugs and sipped. Ellis used his thumb and forefinger to gently rotate his glass a few times before speaking. 'Er, um. We understand that you have had the most extraordinary of voyages. And that you, Mr Sackhouse, are responsible for that success.'

'I seem to have been.' John drained his mug and Kane ordered him another.

A sudden loud hallooing arose from the door and a group of the *Wessex*'s men, including the McKeevers and Barz, rolled in. They were sweaty, red-faced, and had obviously been spending their first few hours ashore making themselves very merry indeed. On seeing him, the *Wessexes* started chanting 'Sackhouse! Sackhouse! Sackhouse!' and a fresh round of drinks appeared on the table. John toasted the men, even the McKeevers, but found Barz was gone.

Kane said: 'Mr Millar has gone out the back way and I suspect we have little time. I shall lay our cards on the table, Mr Sackhouse. You seem to know the location of newfound grounds of spermaceti, the most rich and . . . tractable, of which I have never heard. We want you to bring us to those shoals. For that we will pay you a significant sum of money.'

John sank his fourth mug of ale. Another appeared in front of him, courtesy of one of the *Wessexes*, followed by a barrage of tremendous if friendly-meaning blows on his shoulders. He looked across at Ellis and Kane, his eyes buzzed back and forth in their sockets, and the two men vibrated in front of him for a second until he blinked exaggeratedly and they stilled.

'Money,' John said very slowly and carefully, 'is a rather good thing to have in this world, I take it. And I shall take it, but there is something else I require. But,' and he looked up at the front door, 'that will have to wait, for here is Captain Chase.'

Nantucket

'Come on.'

Owen brought John out of the back door of the house, and the two skirted down the garden, vaulting over the fence that separated the Chase property from the Husseys'. They kept low, skirted through one garden, then another, avoiding a snarling mastiff, until emerging through a hedgerow on a road out of town.

The church bells in town tolled a mournful sound, John thought. It was the Sabbath, the first time he had been out of the Chase house since he had met Ellis and Kane at the Tri-Pots.

'Those men want something from you,' Owen had said as he ushered him away from the tavern that night.

'You astonish me, Owen,' John answered. 'They seemed like the most agreeable, trustworthy of fellows.'

Owen shot him a look, staring hard, a half-smile creeping on his face. 'Let me ask you a question. If all the seas in the world dried up, what would old Neptune say?'

'Who is Neptune?'

Owen sighed expansively. 'For a man of so many parts, you have huge holes in your learning, dear John. He was a god whom the Romans thought ruled all the seas. So I ask you again, what would old Neptune say? "I really haven't got a notion."'

John, despite himself, giggled. 'Let me tell you a little story, Owen. An Englishman goes out in society with one of his hose inside out. His friend asks him why it is thus, and he answers: 'Why, sir, because I have a hole on the other side.'"

John's house arrest had not been unpleasant. He had read, been fed – his almost every need catered to. With Owen busy down on the docks supervising the unloading of the *Wessex*, he talked mostly to the women. Nancy was cheery with a spiky streak, Kathryn pleasant but dozy. Isobel was less easy with a smile, more serious, but when she laughed the room lit up. Which she did not do much, John realised, when Owen was around. After those first few hours at home after their voyage, she seemed irritated by Owen's presence.

Isobel had seemed almost relieved as John and Owen left that morning, heading for their appointment with Mr Mather. John expected to go to the shipowner's house, but Owen led him out of town. A mile, then two.

'That's Benjamin Forester's farm,' Owen said, pointing to a series of neat stone and wood buildings off in the distance. A herd of cows ambled away from the biggest building, the dong-dong of their bells chiming lowly. 'The centre of the island. Sixty years old and he has never once left.' Owen shook his head. 'He is mad. There he is.'

A burly man walked out of the barn, waved cheerfully to John and Owen.

'Working on a Sunday,' Owen said.

'And?'

'It's illegal.'

'On the ship we worked every day.'

'Needs must. It is illegal here. On the books, anyway. About twenty years ago, Minister Coleman — who was always a stick his nose in it whoreson son of a bitch—'

'He was both a whoreson *and* a son of a bitch?'

Owen frowned, and went on with a slight grate of irritation in his voice. 'Minister Coleman came right up to the door and started haranguing Ben. Ben went inside, got his smooth bore and shot a round off about a foot above the Deacon's head. The Deacon came back with the constable. Ben said that he worshipped God in his own way and sometimes that meant milking his cows on a Sunday. The constable agreed. Ben's argument was probably helped that he had brought out two shotguns along with his rifle.

'Still, worshipping in your own way is a sentiment that most folk on the island would agree with.'

They walked by the Forester farm. They came to a crest and descended into a vale – and there lay the biggest stretch of wood on the whole island. The vegetation on most of the island had reminded John of home. Gnarled little trees that were beaten down by wind and salt water. Stunted bushes with spiky leaves and branches that seemed tough and almost aggressive. However, the tiny valley they were now walking through must be protected against most of the elements: there were proper full-sized trees, the trunks of which had the girth of the *Wessex*'s mainmast. The wood was alive, humming with bees. Birds flitted between wildflowers which, John realised, with a jolt he felt in his stomach, smelled just like Isobel.

They walked into the wood, following the bend around a corner, and came to a rough stone hut, around which a couple of horses were tethered. John recognised Ezekiel's horse and buggy.

'What is this place?'

'A few of us call it the Cathedral of Nantucket,' Owen said.

As they got closer, John heard what sounded like the buzzing of an enormous hive.

'They've started,' Owen said and pushed the door open.

About thirty people were in the hut, seated on planks of wood nailed to each of the four walls. They didn't acknowledge the door opening, were all humming, rocking back and forth, eyes closed. It was hot and close from the press of bodies. John and Owen found space on one of the benches and sat. John was next to a man who was rocking back and forth, an animal noise coming from somewhere deep inside. The hairs on the back of John's neck rose; he reached out and touched the cool damp stone behind him, dug his fingers into the crevices, trying to anchor himself to something tangible.

Someone struck a match and lit a whale oil lamp that hung in the corner. Ezekiel stood in the middle, eyes closed, arms outstretched. He was shaking and rocking more violently than the others, seemed taller than ever, the swaying light making his skeletal face angular and beakish like a terrifying bird of prey.

Ezekiel started shouting, in a voice that was far too loud for the tiny room: 'Here he has come to us, a Son of Ham!'

The others rocked and hummed more violently, even Owen at John's side. John dug his fingers even deeper into the stone, wanted to vault out of the door but found he could not.

Ezekiel stepped aside and revealed a small table with two massive death-pale ivory chalices. 'Come to me, Son of Ham! Come to me!'

John hesitated and Owen pushed him towards the middle. He stumbled into Ezekiel, who rather than frail and delicate, seemed now as solid as a mainmast. Ezekiel's eyes were still closed, but he gripped

John's shoulders with steely talons. 'Now bless us, Son of Ham, in blood and oil. We too have been cast out from our fathers, doomed to roam the world, but we can be redeemed if bathed in blood and oil. Bless us.'

Ezekiel steered John to the table. He could see, and smell, that the chalices were full — of whale oil and blood, the blood from what source he could not tell. John started to retch, but Ezekiel held him tighter, shouting 'Bless us!' his eyes popping open for the first time, boring into John, mad and frenzied.

He forced John's hands towards the chalices, dunking the right hand into the blood, the left the oil. 'Bless us,' he rasped again, jerking John's hands upwards until they painted Ezekiel's face red and glistening. 'Blood and oil,' he sighed, then quivered as he let go of John's hands, and slunk back.

The rest of them were now upon him, crowding him. 'Bless us! Bless us!'

In a panic, John dipped his hands in the chalices and began anointing the people's faces around him, pushing them away as he did. But still they came. He cried out, not knowing why, in a number of languages: 'Blood and oil. Blut und öl. Sangre y aceite. Blod og olie. Sanguine et de oleo.'

The room spun and John could hear Ezekiel shouting above it all: 'He speaks in tongues. God speaks through him in tongues.'

John woke on the floor of the Cathedral of Nantucket. It was empty, the table and chalice taken away. Light streamed in from the open front door, where Owen stood, back to John, hands clasped behind his back, looking out to the wood.

Owen turned. 'You . . . swooned. I thought it would be best to leave you until you recovered.'

He helped John to his feet and they walked out of the wood and did not speak until they got to near Ben Forester's farm. Forester was outside, shovelling hay onto a cart and turned to wave to the two of them again.

'There's Ben Forester, working on a Sunday,' John said. 'He must be mad, eh?'

Nantucket

Isobel watched John and Owen leave with relief. Early on in their marriage, Owen had tried to get Isobel to come to one of these Quaker/Shaker meetings. 'As a daughter of a minister of the Free Kirk of Scotland I cannot oblige you,' was her firm reply. 'You do understand, my love?'

Owen had been at the door of their house, his hat cradled in his hands. They had returned just days earlier from the Pacific, the culmination for Owen of fourteen months at sea where his every order and whim was carried out quickly and unquestioningly.

'Ah, yes,' he said, swivelling back and forth. 'Will you be going to the Friends, then?' The Society of Friends, the 'official' Quakers and not Ezekiel's offshoot, were the dominant religious order on the island.

Isobel shook her head. 'Like your Quakers, I choose to worship God without the need of an intermediary.'

'Ah, yes. Of course.' Owen placed his hat on his head to go out, took if off and came a step inside, then doffed his hat vaguely at Isobel and strode into the street.

There was some loyalty to her father and the kirk, to be sure. But there was more loyalty to her father, who had imbued her with a scientist's natural scepticism. The Reverend Doctor Campbell never seemed in tune with belief or any creed, per se. The kirk was a means to an end, a route to his professorship at the university which enabled him to become a natural philosopher. The chance to go to the Felicity Islands was really an opportunity to study the island's flora and fauna and human inhabitants; he left whatever preaching there was to Reverend Tait. Isobel's abiding memories of her father and the island were helping him put specimens of insects, birds, plants and small mammals into spirit jars.

But her decision not to accompany Owen was more because she had fashioned her own particular belief system, her sole adherence to the Great Mary, Mrs Wollstonecraft herself; *A Vindication of the Rights of Women* was her Bible. Women had forever been denied their rightful place and only the Great Mary seemed to be putting herself above the parapet and railing against it. She realised at times this became almost fetishistic; she carried a miniature of Mrs Wollstonecraft at all times, brought it out in times of trouble, communed with it like a Catholic with a rosary. She would often look down at the image of Mary in miniature and model her own features into that heroic but somehow doomed Wollstonecraft look.

She had been introduced to Mrs Wollstonecraft by chancing upon *A Vindication* in her father's library. Her father was hardly an adherent to the rights of women or the equality of the sexes, yet he had a first edition of the book. In fact, his library was mostly full of authors and tracts which he disagreed with, oftentimes virulently. He was never more at home than when he was engaged in battle with a book, both of the mind and physically. Thus, whilst Isobel read Mrs Wollstonecraft, she had to try to ignore her father's furiously deep-marked marginalia of which 'Thou liest, harridan!' and 'Get thee to the devil, harpy!' were some of the milder interjections.

Most of what the Great Mary wrote about men and women chimed with what Isobel thought. Men the 'stronger' sex? Empirical evidence seemed to suggest otherwise. Yes, perhaps stronger in the broadest physical sense: running faster, throwing farther, lifting more. But weak mentally, unable to function for themselves, morally swayable, easily manipulated.

As Nancy once said after a rather brutal break with Jeffrey Chandler, the second mate of the *Wigwam*: 'What are they good for besides that which dangles between their legs? And this He's at Home' — here she flourished a half-finished double-ended Don Juan — 'won't erupt after twenty seconds and be useless for the rest of the night.'

Owen did not have that trouble — he could keep going no matter how many times he, er, erupted — but Isobel agreed with Nancy's general principle.

But, oh, if the Great Mary could have travelled and seen Nantucket before she died! This island at first was a trial to Isobel: initially friendless and horrifically lonesome, she missed Ali and her father so much. But it was rendered at least tolerable because it was as close to a gynotopia as you could get on this earth. Yes, the men's names were on the top of some of the shipping company letterheads, but not all.

And those that did have men in charge generally had a Mrs Hummock-type truly running things. Because the men were away so often, and for so long (and often died in the line of duty), it was women who ran the town council, who were largely responsible for the spiritual well-being of the island, who owned the shops and the houses. Let the men have their little fantasies about being bosses when afloat; they were ruled by their wives when they came back to the island. Was there any more of a Nantucket moment, than seeing a burly ship's Captain, home after many months' a-sea facing down storms, hulking ocean-going beasts and menacing natives, meekly following his wife as she bustled around the shops, ordering him to pick up this and that?

As to religion itself, Isobel had a way of worshipping completely of her own construction, little to do with the Church of Scotland. She believed in a force that moved the world, a perfection, something ineffably good that all should strive to be. She never allowed herself to dwell too deeply on it, for she knew it was woolly and ever so intellectually unsound. But she could not reconcile any religion — from Christendom to Mohammedanism — with good, or what she could describe as good: equality for all. So there had to be something else, some other religion that no one had discovered yet, because the logical conclusion was that there was no god. Wasn't it?

The Kirk, then, was a useful excuse. It spared Isobel having to attend services with Owen, or have a forthright discussion, as he was, to use a phrase her father would trot out to those he thought were not the brightest candle in the chapel, 'not entirely equipped for philosophical discourse'.

Besides, she learned that Owen was not a Quaker, but belonged to Mr Mather's, as Nancy called it, 'Shaky, Flaky, Quaky set'. A cell that Ezekiel and Mrs Hummock started up when he and his former friend Deacon Brodie got into a fistfight over, the story goes, the Deacon's rather traditional view of Mr Mather and Mrs Hummock's rather untraditional living and sleeping arrangements.

Not uncoincidentally, the people around the Shaky, Flaky, Quakers were those connected to Mather in some way commercially: his sea captains, his warehousemen, ship builders and suppliers.

Isobel waited about ten minutes after Owen and John had left, then rushed out to the shed and opened it up. She took out the Torino, a special order for Mrs Delahunt of Mystic, Connecticut, wife of the purser on The *Headwind*. It was made of narwhal tusk ivory and Mrs Delahunt, in her letter, had specified 'that above all it is girth, not length, which I require'. Well, thought Isobel, she was going to give her some girth, indeed.

Isobel took out her hammer, chisel, fine sander and chamois cloth and began working away on the tusk, humming to herself. This work made her happy, she liked taking some material and seeing within it the shape it was to become and slowly, with her tools, stripping all the extraneous bits away until there it was: this creature new-born. She liked what the tools did to her hands — roughened them, callused them; she wore each scratch, scar and yellow pad of skin with pride like warrior marks.

She was, of course, making objects for ladies to pleasure themselves with. Hardly, she often thought when she held her newest He's at Home Company creation in her hands, works that would rival Bernini or Canova, or any of the sculptors' work she had seen on her trip to Italy with Ali and her father prior to setting sail for the Felicity Islands.

'But,' she concluded after expounding lengthily on the subject to Nancy as the two were sipping flip, watching the sun set after a lengthy, productive day in the shed, 'I would argue that our objects are as lovingly and skilfully made as anything Signori Bernini, Canova or any sculptor has done.'

Nancy, whose eyes had glazed over the instant Isobel had said 'have I ever mentioned our expedition to Italy, Nancy?' (for indeed Isobel had, oh God yes, indeed she had), leapt up. 'Another glass of flip? I shall not put so much rum in this one, I think.'

Whatever satisfaction Isobel felt at her, ah, commercial work, what made her heart sing the most was sculpting tiny, intricate objects. She whittled, carved in wood, ivory, whale bone and was always thrilled to see new shapes emerge from this raw material. Just before Owen had returned, she made a replica of the *Wessex* out of an eight-inch block of teak. Working with a magnifying glass, she went down to minute detail, her rigging, the spars, even put a tiny Owen at the helm. She couldn't find it in his study yesterday; she would have to ask him if he had moved it.

Her heart skipped a beat when the garden gate banged open, but she relaxed when Nancy called out, 'Sorry I'm late, Mrs Chase.' Nancy was slightly out of breath and flushed. 'Old Deacon Brodie was in a frightful lather this morning.'

Isobel smiled, glad to see the girl. 'Nae bother, Nancy, we have about three hours free, I should suppose.'

Nancy sat on a stool next to Isobel, unrolled her tools from a leather satchel and set to work on an Ebony Stranger. 'Everyone was abuzz this morning about our little Esquimaux. Deacon Brodie, of course, preached about the pernicious Savage not having true wisdom, or some such nonsense. But before and after it's all anyone could talk about. Mr Ellis and Kane were sniffing about, seeing if I would tell them anything, the whoreson bastards.'

'Nancy, do not speak ill of two of this island's finest citizens,' Isobel mock admonished.

'Ah, one of the cheeriest sights of my life was when I saw you kick Mr Kane in his bollocks when he tried it on with you when Mr Chase was away.'

'That was a fine day.'

The two women worked in companionable silence. 'So,' Nancy smiled. 'How was Mr Chase's homecoming?'

Isobel rubbed an abrasion on her thumb. 'Disappointing.'

'Three's company in the house?'

'No, I don't think Mr Sackhouse's presence is the matter. You know I have said that Mr Chase is rather dutiful, not altogether there sometimes, in terms of spirit?'

'Mm-hm.'

'Something has happened even more since the lightning. I think it has changed him.'

Nancy put down her tools, mouth agape. 'You don't mean he's been de-masted? And so young?'

'No, it isn't that. That something is happening up here,' she tapped her own head with the chisel handle. 'He told me the blast purified him. That he is happy to fulfil his husbandly duties, but all the while he was thinking of "higher things".'

'Merciful Christ. Well . . . it was a shock. It probably has confused him for a while. It'll get better.'

Isobel nodded. She wanted to tell Nancy more, but what could she say? It was never right with Owen. He always seemed to regard her enjoyment of it all as something to be tolerated. She could not help that she wanted it, needed it in her life. And he seemed put off by her womanliness, asked her to shave down there before they did anything, asked her to clean and scrub until 'everything smelled fresh and clean'. Homecomings and good-byes were about the only times he truly seemed to want her.

'Have you ever thought about the biggest mistake in your life, Nancy,' Isobel said, 'and wondered just how you are going to get out of it?'

Nancy looked across the garden, up at the sky, then back to Isobel. 'I often think it's the wise woman that doesn't get married. Still, Mr Chase will be away for many months at a time. And there is always He's at Home.'

Isobel laughed. 'Indeed.'

'Oh, I didn't mean it that way, ma'am. I meant the business.'

'I know exactly what you meant, Nancy.'

Nantucket

'You are not going out of doors like that?'

John stopped short, looked wildly about his person. 'I beg your pardon?'

Owen ticked off each transgression with his cane, the silver tip glinting in the sunlight. 'Sir, your breeches, your waistcoat, that unconscionable hat, the dreadful lack of symmetry, the blend of colours which rather than complement seem to be at war with each other. It may have done aboard ship, but not in town, even a town as this.' He collected himself. 'Forgive me, my friend, this is entirely my doing. The first thing we should have done when you set foot on this isle was to get you properly attired.'

He hurried John out of the house. As he was hustled past the parlour, John caught a flash of Isobel seated on her day bed, her face pressed resolutely, determinedly into a book.

Stepping from the shaded cool of the house, John felt the heat of the day hit him like a kick to the stomach. Just a few steps down the street and he was dripping with sweat, the sun hovering above, relentless and insistent as if it bore him a personal grudge. His legs wobbled, his head swam. He tore off his cravat, ripped open his shirt, bursting the three top buttons.

Owen cried, 'What are you doing?'

John looked up and was surprised at Owen's mixture of alarm and seeming affronted. 'Is it not exceedingly hot?' John asked.

Owen glanced to and fro rapidly, doing up John's shirt, expertly whipping the cravat back into shape. 'Look around.'

They had advanced about a hundred yards from the house and had approached the edge of the Common. Great hulking houses — including Mr Mather's directly opposite — sat smugly around the open space. A small flock of sheep grazed in a far corner, and several couples promenaded around the outskirts, men in black and top hats linked arm in arm with parasol-toting women.

'Tell me what you see.'

'Well,' John said, scanning about. 'I see Mr Ellis watching us with a telescope.'

Owen looked over towards the Ellis pile at the far end of the Common, and Ellis was indeed in his large picture window, a glass trained in their direction. 'Your eyes are sharp, John. Let us move away.'

They turned away from the Common, heading into the centre of town. 'No, the point I was trying to make is that most of the people around that Common, in fact every man jack of them, is dressed as I am. Not as well as I, not in a way that so adequately suits their figure, carriage and status. But they are all dressed as if nature and the elements do not exist.'

John looked back. The men in particular looked uncomfortable, films of sweat covering their broiled pink faces. He nodded. 'Is that stubbornness or stupidity?'

'Here is what I will say is the difference between savagery and civilisation. I trust you know I do not mean to offend.'

'How could I be offended by your utter denigration of my previous life without having intimate knowledge of it?' John said dryly.

'Good, good man!' Owen said, gripping John's shoulder warmly. 'The difference between savagery and civilisation is that we in the civilised world marshal nature, we make no allowances for it. We here are clothed as we are because civilisation demands it, and we do not adjust, no matter if it is a few degrees too warm and too cold. We suffer, we endure and in the end we conquer.'

John thought about one of the walrus hunts he went on when his father was still alive. In late winter the herds gathered on the rocks near the Far Shore to breed, and the People would knock a few off, usually waiting to do so when the beasts were at their most vulnerable — enthusiastically fucking — to strike. John's father's brother Giquo had harpooned a great bull whilst the poor beast was giving a cow a seeing-to. It was a tremendous strike, so true the beast had been struck dead instantly.

The rest of the herd dropped from the rocks into the water, bellowing in alarm as Giquo approached the slain walrus. But it was not yet dead. Just as Giquo arrived, it gave a final savage triple shake of its massive head, ripping at Giquo with its tusks and knocking him into the icy water.

The men scrambled after him and finally managed to hook Giquo and pulled him up on the rocks. Remarkably he was not cut, but it did not matter. His parka was so shredded he was almost bare chested and he was soaked through to the skin. To creep up on the herd they had had to leave the kayaks one hour's hike away. There were no spare clothes, no possibility of a fire. Giquo breathed shortly and sharply; he looked a trifle bewildered but mostly rather irritated. John's father knelt down and held his hand. The men gathered round and watched him die. John counted. It took 123 heartbeats.

John wondered how much civilising it would take to conquer that kind of nature.

'There are further reasons for going about thusly clothed,' Owen went on, warming to his speech. He threw back his buff blue coat to reveal the magnificence of his ensemble: the detailing in the ivory buttons, the paisley waistcoat, the workmanship of his silver-buckled shoes inlaid with ambergris. 'Am I a preening peacock? Mayhaps, I am. But that is the point. A peacock preens and displays to establish himself as better than others, to lay a marker down about his worth, and, of course, to attract mates. That is what this is.'

Owen laughingly spread his arms out to fully display himself and did a comic shuffle dance. 'Feathers. Or more accurately armour, as glittering and inveighed with as much pomp and circumstance as knights at a joust.'

Two voices in unison to the left. 'Afternoon, Cap'n. Hello, Mr Sackhouse.' As John had watched Owen carry on, he had spied Jamie Wren and Stephen Ritherdon, two oarsmen on Mr Cotton's crew, amble out of an inn. They had at first made to make their acknowledgements, but seeing Owen prancing about in a un-captainly way, had done an awkward do-si-do, colliding into each other as they tried to back away.

Owen's warm smile instantly turned to glacial reserve. 'Ah, Wren, Ritherdon. I trust I see you well?'

'Yes, sir,' Wren said, kneading his cap in his hands. Ritherdon had no cap but copied his shipmate's kneading motion. Ritherdon said: 'And we would be honoured to serve with you again. And, of course, would be all the more delighted if Mr Sackhouse here was joining us.'

John was fairly sure that Ritherdon was the one who, in those dark days before the *Wessex* found the pod of whales, dropped a 20-pound killick from the crosstrees which buried itself into the deck where he had been standing but a second before. Dreaming of the sudden *whump* and the image of the killick's prongs embedded ten inches into the wood had startled John awake several times since. He was not particularly desirous to see Ritherdon on a long journey again, but merely nodded his head.

'Well, men, we are anxious to get away as soon as possible,' Owen intoned rather severely. 'But owing to Mr Sackhouse here, we are inundated, positively inundated, with tip-top whalermen clamouring to join us. You two served very well last voyage but there were several times you were wanting—'

'Oh no, sir!'

'You in particular, Ritherdon.'

'I was only poorly a couple of times, sir.'

'Poorly as the result of drunkenness which caused you to be slack in your duty. Nevertheless. Never the less. I will consider your conduct on the whole voyage and will make a decision very soon as to whether you will ship with the *Wessex*.'

The two bowed and mumbled their thanks, once, twice, thrice and scurried away. John watched them go. 'Did you mean that?'

'No. They are both prime hands, but I think if they believe they are on the cusp, as it were, I might be able to shave a couple of points off their lay. Pay them less,' he added at John's blank look.

He took John's arm and they strolled up the street. 'I was referring to the new voyage,' John said. 'Are we really going to be departing as soon as possible?'

'But of course,' Owen said. 'Although it will take a several weeks; the *Wessex* isn't even fully unloaded yet, never mind patched up, provisioned, crewed and ready to sail.'

'Yet, what of life here? What of exploring this great land? What of . . . Isobel?'

'Yes, Isobel. We are very much attached, of course, but my wife will probably wish to see the back of me as I am, as usual, getting under her feet. Ultimately, she is a whalerman's wife. She is used to the life.'

A tight smile. 'Yet, already I chafe and yearn to be at sea. Do you not?'

John thought of the howling storms, almost being pitched overboard, the incessant toil, the lamentable food.

At the hesitation, Owen went on. 'This is partly due to my makeup. I was born to be on the waves, and feel uneasy and unwell if I do not have my feet on deck, feel the sea spray on my face, smell the tar. I know that can seem horribly romantic to some, but perhaps not to others. But the truth of the matter, John, is that I need you on this voyage.'

'Need me?'

'There is your expertise in whale-finding.'

'I—'

Owen held up his hand. 'I will hear none of your false modesty today. But that has nothing to do with it. No, to lay it bare.'

Owen paused, batted a stone back and forth with his cane. 'To lay it bare. I need your companionship, sir. You are my particular friend, and I find the thought of the next voyage without you unbearable. You will be treated as a supernumerary, by the by, as my friend on the voyage. We shall not expect you to engage in any sort of regular duties aboard. I think we shall enter you as the crew's translator and guide.'

John's last months with the People, the months of shunning, had been difficult. At first, he did not notice the shunning, so wrapped up was he in guilt and grief. He had been so numb he did not care, he felt his need for any kind of human interaction had been snuffed out completely. But as time wore on, the utter loneliness became as acute as his grief. Strangely, when he was actually alone — in his makeshift hut, scrambling about for roots and berries, out on a hunt — he could bear it better. Yet when he was amidst the People, with not one acknowledging his presence with even a word, a nod or a catch of the eye, nor a clasp on the shoulder or a hug, the loneliness began to destroy him. He longed to be touched, spoken to. Even in anger. A curse and a punch in the face would do. But even Torok would not accord him that. The first time, he realised, that he had human contact in months had been when he was hauled insensible from his kayak onto the *Wessex*. The first time he had been addressed was when Owen introduced himself.

Tears started to roll down his cheeks. 'I would be so very honoured to accompany you once again; nothing would please me more. You are my dearest, dear friend.'

John moved to embrace Owen, who stepped back, head swivelling up and down the street. 'Please, compose yourself, Mr Sackhouse,' he said in a harsh whisper. 'Compose yourself. I'm very glad, though, very glad indeed.'

Owen propelled John down a side street off of Main and they stopped in front of Saunders & Saunders, Incorporated. Its outside looked to John fussy and particular, at least compared to the other shops in town. Most had rugged weather-beaten frontages which looked designed to take on nor'easters, and were festooned with straightforward signage in simple script: Stephens the Chandler; Curtis & Sons, Ropemakers, est.d 1737; John Hampstead, Silversmith. Saunders & Saunders' sign was an inlaid brass plaque with very small lettering which you had to bend over to read. A single buff-shiny copper delicate and complicated whale lamp, unnecessarily burning bright in the middle of the day, illuminated the sign whilst behind the window was a painted screen with a turbaned man and sari-ed woman engaging in congress.

'And this is where one . . . gets clothes?' John asked.

Owen nodded and lowered his voice. 'Of course, given my druthers I would not use Saunders myself in the main, only for the odd alteration. I used to employ Paris tailors when I could, London ones when I could not. These damnable wars these past years, however, have certainly been inconvenient. Do you know I have paid custom to M. La Fitte of Rue Saint la Forgue and Mr Oswald of Regent's Street?'

'Indeed?' John hoped he had weighted the word with as much awe and respect as Owen seemed to be hoping for.

'Oh, yes. Still, we cannot fault Mr Saunders for his lack of panache. He is a creature of his environment. He is not without his flashes of style and none, none of the gentlemen tailors from the world capitals can match Mr Saunders when it comes to skill with the needle. That's a whalerman's education for you.'

Owen leapt up the small steps, pulled the bell and a teeny, tiny tinkling answered within. The door jerked open and an immense long-limbed, broad-shouldered man filled the doorway. 'Cap'n Chase,' a deep voice rumbled. 'I knew 'twas you. From the window I spied the tip of my damask hat, with my signature triple dip fold at the top, you see, so who else could it be?'

He ushered them inside. Saunders wore a red velvet suit with black boots that slightly eclipsed the knee. He was incongruous; a gorilla stuffed in gentleman's clothes, if that gorilla had his ensemble made to measure.

He pumped Owen's hand and then John's with shovel-sized mitts. He beamed at John, his eyes closing, crags and fissures forming as he smiled. 'And this here must be the Esquimaux everyone is talking about. Howdy do, sir?'

Owen made the introductions. 'John Sackhouse, Josiah Saunders. But how do you mean, Saunders, "everyone is talking about"?'

'Oh, come, sir. You know this ville. Someone breaks wind and the gossips start a-waggin'. But Mr Sackhouse here, well that will be a tale they'll be telling a long time. Mr Ellis and Mr Kane were certainly talking about it.'

Owen and Saunders talked on but John drifted away, walking toward the back of the shop, looking in awe at the shelves. Whenever he had gone to the sailing ships back home, his main task was to barter for the People. They wanted shiny things: silver and polished brass and glass. It did not matter that it was useful, although knives or tools were certainly appreciated, they just had to sparkle. John could never fathom the appeal. He once had given a slab of seal meat to a sailor for a shiny locket on a silver chain, encrusted with mirrored gilt which he in turn gave to Mary. She gasped when she took it in her hand, her smile wide, her eyes dancing. He shook his head and asked why she loved it so.

Why? she echoed. You idiot, look. It glitters!

Finally, he understood. On the walls of Saunders & Saunders were rows of buckled shoes and boots in variegated shades of blacks and browns. The subtleties of the colours of the jackets, the waistcoats, the breeches sang to him. The whites of the shirts and linen he had only seen before in untrammelled peak-top snow. The fabrics were a wonder, varying in thickness and heft, some sensuously soft. And pinned to the wall the accoutrements – pendants and brocades and canes, quizzing glasses and pocket watches – were all so detailed and delicate.

'I see something has caught Mr Sackhouse's eye,' said Saunders, now at John's left, a tape measure draped over his shoulders. 'That one is a bit European for our shores, but a wise choice, sir.'

John was standing in front of a suit and breeches made of dark blue serge, with a powder blue shirt finished with complicated ruffles on the cuffs and collars. 'May I,' John said, picking the shirt up with reverence, 'have something like this, but with more, far more, of the frilly bits on the end?'

The fittings for five outfits suitable for town, country, sea, evening and Sunday services took several hours with a bewildering number of decisions to make; style and colours were just two concerns. How many pockets, where to put the pocket watch, which way to dress, the thickness of the jacket, the lining material and on and on. Owen initially gave the orders, but John soon took over.

'And I have seen some fellows with tiny oblong pockets here,' John said to Saunders as they looked over a smoking jacket, 'in order to put a pipe or cigarillo.'

'Very good, Mr Sackhouse, very good. A reg'lar Beau Brummel, eh Captain? Tell you what, Mr Sackhouse, I've got a jacket, your exact size, here in the shop, which you're welcome to take away, on the house. It's a damn sight more respectable than the one you came in with, beggin' your pardon.'

'Why Mr Saunders, I would like that very much.'

Saunders jumped nimbly to the top of the sliding ladder on the side shelves, zoomed down to the end of the shop, plucked something from the uppermost shelf and bounded back flourishing the jacket.

'Where is the other Saunders?' John asked as he stepped into the jacket.

'Sir?' Saunders said.

'It's Saunders *and* Saunders.'

There was a slight pause. Owen stepped forward. 'John, I don't think—'

'No, no, Cap'n, you're all right,' Saunders interrupted. 'This is an intimate job. I've after all had Mr Sackhouse's goolies in my hand this half glass, so why shouldn't he know?'

Saunders stepped behind John, began brushing down the shoulders and back with the lint brush. 'There's no other Saunders. At least not in this shop. It was my boy, named it after him, you see. Twenty years I was a-whalin', from a spit of a boy until I made first mate on the *Osprey*, one of Mister Ellis and Kane's tubs. Actually, she was a good ship, or would've been if they fitted her out correctly, the penny-pinching whoresons. Anyway, I took my son Henry out on his first voyage, aged fourteen. A good lad; I wanted to keep him on my crew, but no, he said, he wanted to work his way up the natural way, so he started on the coofs' boat.

'A normal enough cruise – but it came a blow and we lost the coofs' boat, swept clean off the deck. So we had to use the spare. The leaky, hardly sea-worthy spare. I said to Captain Withers, "If we spy a whale, we need to keep them coofs in, that boat won't stay afloat." He shook his head and said we would have to risk it, it was Mr Ellis's and Kane's business, see, and there would be hell to pay if it ever got back that he left a boat in. 'Sides, his nephew was on the coofs' boat, too. As it would have it, next day we see a cow and a calf. Now, if you don't know, that's when the real danger is. Give me a bull what's twice the size of a momma whale protecting a youngster any day o' the week.

'We set out after it, and I saw over my shoulder almost immediately that the coofs' boat was takin' water. I hoped they could bail as quick as they could row. And that the killin' would be done darn quick. We're halfway to the cow and the calf decides to run towards Henry's boat. So the momma follows, and well, you can see where this is leadin'. The calf misses the boat, but the cow breeches right into it, and the boat doesn't just shatter, it explodes. Boom. Just splinters. When I picture it in my mind's eye — and I do every night — I see Henry at the crest of that explosion, being blasted twenty, thirty feet skywards, planks and broken oars all around him.

'I was about half a mile away. We rowed hard, but it was so far. I saw Henry bobbing a few moments, but there was nothing big enough to float on, and he couldn't swim, you see. I watched him go under, helpless.

'I didn't blame Withers. I blamed Ellis and Kane. We had seven more months on that cruise. Seven months of me plannin' every day to walk up into their offices and run them through. But when we finally came home, I stepped off the quay and there was Rebecca, my wife, with a daughter in arms. A babe I'd never seen. After doing the maths — she was mine — I couldn't run them through. What would that serve, leaving Rebecca husband-less?'

He paused. 'All right, I did make that decision after storming into Ellis and Kane's offices and throwing a harpoon in Mr Ellis's general direction that stuck into the wall just above his head. And left when my shipmates and the constable bodily pulled me out of there.

'But that was it. No more a-whalin'. So here I am.'

'I will take that, Saunders,' Owen said softly, holding his hand out for the lint brush as the tailor had stopped brushing moments ago.

'Oh, really, sir, I thank you,' Saunders said stiffly. 'I'll, I'll box up that hat and . . . ' He trailed off, running to the back of the shop.

'Seafaring's loss is sartor's gain,' Owen mumbled. He smoothed down the jacket — rather too vigorously for John's liking — unbuttoned the bottom waistcoat button, frowned into the mirror, then redid it. Adjusted and readjusted the point where the breeches and hose met. He placed the top hat on John's head, tip-tapping the brim until it was just so.

'There,' he said, a workman pleased with his labours. 'The port side of hat — of this particular type of hat — should be a point or two off North North-west, you follow?'

John nodded vaguely, too entranced by what he saw in the mirror to really hear. Owen went on: 'The mirror, not the eyes, is the window on the soul, for this is how the world sees you. How is that?'

'Jesus fuck Almighty,' John breathed. 'I do look astonishing.'

Nantucket

John stood just outside the sitting room door watching Owen scribbling on sheaves of paper. John marvelled at how he glowed with an inner radiance. He looked dashing, heroic even, as he carried out this mundane task.

And he was so clean — he was writing over-elaborately, wild flourishes of the arm when he reached the end of a sentence, plunging the pen savagely into the inkwell to refill. Yet not a drop of ink stained his fingers, nor touched his clothes.

Isobel was a few feet away from him on the daybed, her feet tucked up under her dress, reading. She held the small book with her left hand close to her face, two tiny furrows creasing her forehead. Her right hand ran through her hair, fluffing it up, making it seem as if she was wearing a giant wig.

A small fire was lit, somewhat unnecessarily on this warmish late summer evening, but its light was less harsh than the whale lamps, giving the room a snug glow. In front of the fireplace, Nero the cat lounged. Something swelled in John's breast, a tear came to his eye. Here, he thought, was home and hearth and family.

He stepped into the room and smiled broadly. 'Ah, what a lovely Chase-ian tableau this is.'

Owen and Isobel looked up simultaneously. Things were not, John realised immediately, fine. Something hung in the air between Owen and Isobel — a disagreement, a tension — that was almost physical. Their smiles at him were strained, they did not look at one another.

At length, Owen stood up. 'Forgive me, John. I am writing away my account, my great work, and I am in the midst of a particularly good passage. Perhaps my dear wife could extract herself from her novel to play at being a hostess, whilst I finish.'

Isobel smiled tightly. 'Why yes, my dear husband, your scribbles I am sure are far more important than whatever I am doing.'

John shuffled awkwardly over to the fire and stroked the cat, neutral territory in whatever war he had just stumbled into. He turned back to the Chases.

'Nonsense. Please, the both of you, turn back to what you were doing. I can find ways to amuse myself quite easily.'

John went to the bookshelves that he now knew were Isobel's — the literature, poetry and philosophy — and selected a handful at random.

'Ah, Sir Walter Scott, Boswell's *Johnson* and Smollett's *Expedition of Humphry Clinker*,' Isobel said. She was smiling at John, a bit more at ease. 'A full night's reading for you, then, Mr Sackhouse.'

'Which would you recommend?'

'I would recommend you read them all, as they all have merit. Which you should read first is the question. The Scott is full of derring-do, of the high-minded sort. Boswell is astute though you may tire of Doctor Johnson after a while for he is a bit of a trying soul. But Mr Smollett! Oh lord, it is rapturously funny, a terrific work of true genius.'

Owen looked up from his work. 'Of course, what truly recommends these books from my wife's point of view is that all three of their authors have had the good fortune to be born in Scotland.'

'Almost all of my books come from the British Isles and France, Mr Sackhouse,' Isobel said quickly, with a bantering lilt in her voice. 'And, yes, many of the volumes happen to come from Scottish writers. But that is not because of any bias on my part; what can I say but that the greatest writers at the moment just happen to be Scottish. Besides, what am I to do? There are not, I am afraid, many authors of note here in the former Colonies.'

Owen groaned theatrically. 'Oh, please, my dear, not again. We are but a young country. In time, we shall be as much a match for England — for Britain.'

'Hmmm,' Isobel murmured. 'A Shakespeare from the wilds of Kentucky? A Milton from the swamps of Florida? A Walter Scott being born in the backwoods of Vermont? In a millennia's time, perhaps.'

'Your Mr Smollett, I believe, was born in the Dumfries and Galloway, was he not, Isobel?' Owen countered. 'An area I heard you once say was populated by in-bred sheep and in-bred people, with the sheep a far more clever lot than the people.'

'I may not have been serious. Or at least entirely serious. But, I will grant you Owen, that one day America will produce great authors. For I am reading a book' — here Isobel brandished her volume in her hand — 'written by a lady from one of the most savage and inhospitable places on this earth: the west of Ireland. If that land can produce someone capable of writing a book, than anyplace can. Why—'

Isobel stopped, noticing that John's face had fallen. 'Mr Sackhouse, whatever is the matter? I was jesting. I hope I have not offended you in any way.'

John leant forward and took the book, *The Sligo Town Sinister*, from her. 'No, it's not that.' He held the book reverentially in his hands.

'It is not a solemn book, I assure you,' Isobel said. 'A bit of a ripping read, unbelievable in parts, but a nice bit of frippery. Do you know it?'

'Partly. I certainly know *of* the author. In fact, I knew her son, Father James Kelly, and I never met a better man.'

Greenland

It was three days after John and Mary's mother had died that Father Kelly first appeared. The brother and sister were walking away from the high crags where their mother rested under a cairn, crisscrossing down the slope of the finger inlet.

Shush, Mary said. Listen.

A moment, then John heard it too, a nasally, howling sing-song lament. Mary clutched John's arm. Mary, bravest of hunters, hated shaman tales, was frightened when anyone told her a ghost story. Her fears were exacerbated in the deep of winter, when permanent semi-night made everyone look like wraiths.

Mother is coming for us, she whispered.

John said, Oh, calm yourself. It cannot be.

John never believed any of the shaman stories, particularly when Oooonoooo told them. Not that the shaman did not tell them well. He told them too well. His mannerisms — the hoarse *sotto voce* at a dramatic moment, the eyes bugging in mock fear — all felt a bit too affected to John. Besides, John was about the here and now, what he could see, what he could feel and taste. He sometimes had trouble believing that things out of his sight even existed. He knew there were other countries and places and villages where people lived their lives though he was not there to see it, but still . . . it was difficult to imagine.

The ghostly singing got louder. Then the sound shifted, no longer echoing around the top of the inlet's hills but coming from over the water. John lifted Mary's hood back and pointed out a sail. As the boat bobbed closer, the singing grew louder and louder.

The boat was much smaller than the usual sailing ships that visited the island. As it neared they could see the singing was coming from the man in black who haphazardly clutched the tiller and the rope that worked the sail. He wasn't so much singing as shouting, a hoarse shrieking that only stopped as the boat ran aground with a crunch at John and Mary's feet.

With the collision, the man yelped and was pitched onto his backside into the middle of the boat. He blinked up at John and Mary.

'FECK! Look at the state of me,' he said, picking through the splintered boxes of whisky and poteen he had fallen into. 'Conformin', as it were, to the image of the typical Irishman. Might as well have a pig under me arm or shamble around like a hairy ape as we're envisaged in all those English cartoons.'

He staggered out of the boat up to Mary and John, putting a hand on both of their shoulders. 'Drink, FECK. They say, you know, that's all we are capable of doing.'

Father Kelly then laughed, a long 'guh-ha-ha', his whole body and face twitching violently. He fell, in slow motion, first bending over, then on to his knees, finally sprawling out prostrate before them, the laughs slowing to hiccups then changing to snores.

Mary bent down and gently shook the priest, but he did not wake.

What's wrong with him? Mary said to John. Where did he come from?

John looked at Mary as if to say, *How should I know?*

What shall we do now? Mary asked.

Let's get the dogs and a sled and bring him back.

Mary nodded her agreement and they left the man in the snow.

***

By the time Mary and John got back to the village, most of the people were lighting their dinner fires. It took a while to corral the dogs as the entire pack had been sleeping and were fractious. They were hitching the team to the sled amid much barking and howling when Torok's bellowing brought all the People out of their huts and into the village meeting space. Torok was dragging the singing man along by his coat collar, trailed by his two sons, Kelak and Sapok. Roaring, Torok flung the man down so that he was surrounded by a ring of the People.

I caught him trying to sneak up on me, trying to kill me, Torok bellowed.

Kelak giggled. Trying to kill all three of us.

Sapok nodded in agreement, kicking at the man and swinging a club menacingly by his side.

The man sprang to his feet. Mary could see he was no longer drunk. No, he was snow cold sober. It touched her; he was as vulnerable as John often was, as she could never be.

'Please, good CUNTING people, please,' he cried, the words coming out fast and jumpy. 'I am Father James Kelly, of Sligo Town. You may not know me, but surely you have heard of my good mother, the authoress, the Lady of the West? *The Sligo Town Sinister? Beasts in the Belfry? The Seas Are for Killing?* She uses me as the model for her main characters often — you know, the feckless patricidal son? No? Her books haven't travelled here? A pity, they seem to be so popular wherever I go.

'I digress. I mean no harm. I've merely lost my way. FECK. I don't know which way to go. A storm came, I lost me bearings, I'm no seaman after all. If you could just point me in the direction of the Isle of South Uist, and possibly give me a boat, or help with the repair of my vessel for it seems to have sprung a leak . . . '

As Father Kelly's babble of foreign talk and curses increased to a torrent, the People's eyes, except Torok and his sons', drifted to John.

John let the tension build, playing it out, and finally said, He is from somewhere else.

You are wise and all-seeing, Torok snorted. What would we do without your powers, Bright Eyes?

He is from somewhere else, John repeated testily. He is here by accident. His mother is a . . . storyteller? His boat is broken, he would like another. He is in the middle of a journey.

He is an out-of-islander at the end of his journey, Kelak giggled and kicked out, sweeping the priest's feet away putting him on his back in the snow. The other two waded in, kicking and punching.

NO! Mary screamed and rushed between them. She held her hands up and Kelak stopped his club mid-swing, looking at her curiously.

You will not kill him, Mary said, jutting her jaw out.

He attacked us, Torok said.

Mary squared her shoulders up to him. Is that right?

Torok made to push her aside when Oooonoooo sauntered out of his hut, singing a low song. As he moved, a scent drifted over to John. It was from the smoking of leaves of the smiling plant, the stuff the

169

shaman traded from the whalers to help his visions — which he laced with bits of the mushrooms found in the lower valleys. It made him move at half speed, speak with strange pauses.

These leaves . . . it is like I'm time-shifting in different colours, he once said to John. Too beautiful for words, really.

John eyes had widened eagerly. Can I try?

No, no, noooo, Bright Eyes, Oooonoooo had drawled. Only for shamans.

His full name was Ononoko, but the strain of four syllables had become unbearable; too much hard graft. Oooonoooo just rolled off his tongue.

Stay your hand, brother Torok, Oooonoooo said.

Torok faltered. I was just . . . he attacked us.

Oooonoooo sauntered up to Father Kelly and casually brushed Torok's club aside with a finger. Father Kelly shivered on the ground, a darting eye visible through the hands that covered his head. Oooonoooo prodded him gently with the toe of his boot, finding frail bones and emaciated limbs.

Oooonoooo sucked on his pipe, holding it in, then exhaling deeply in the direction of the mountains.

He attacked *you*?

Yes, Torok answered defiantly.

Oooonoooo finally swivelled his head towards Torok. He tried avoiding looking directly at the People when smoking. Now, Torok had two extra heads sprouting out of each shoulder, one topped by caribou antlers, the other was a polar bear's face. He stared at the normal Torok face in the middle. He said, *This man* attacked the three of you?

Torok, Kelak and Sapok shuffled their feet.

It doesn't matter, Torok blurted at last. He can't stay.

Why?

Are you going to hunt for him, Ononoko? You who rarely hunt.

Oooonoooo's eyes snapped out of their fog, boring into Torok's.

Not, not, not that you don't deserve it, Torok went on in a rush. A shaman *should* be provided for by the People. That is the way it has always been. No, I mean we cannot have another here living off nothing.

Torok turned around the circle, looking for agreement. He stopped at John and smiled.

I mean, we already have some among us that live off what others hunt.

He can live with us, Mary said, stepping out of the circle and kneeling near the priest.

You have one too many to look after, Torok laughed – and, following his lead, Sapok cackled like a crake, Kelak looking on silently. Mary ignored everyone, cooing to Father Kelly.

A good idea, Oooonoooo drawled, stifling the laughter. She hunts well. She can keep him in food, if he can't look after himself. We cannot do better than that, can we?

Nantucket

Mr Sackhouse had not come down for breakfast.

Kathryn had tried to wake him, but when she knocked at his room he merely groaned: 'Then when I looked in, Miss-sus, there he was, splayed out atop the covers in his altogether. His altogether, Miss-sus! So I thought it best not to go in.'

'Then we should leave him be, shouldn't we, Owen?' Isobel said across the table.

Owen grunted, barely looking up from his toasted cheese, immersed in a pile of paperwork. A moment later, he swigged the last of his small beer, stood and absently kissed Isobel on the head.

'You will look after my shipmate this morning, will you not?' he said. 'There is much to do. Obviously he needs to be kept from harm's way and particularly out of the sight and clutches of Ellis and Kane.'

'Well, yes, I suppose, however, I have much—'

'Excellent! Please, Isobel, if you could deliver him to me at the quay sometime this afternoon. I shall see you anon.'

He turned and rushed out of the house. Isobel sighed, took the unfinished toasted cheese from Owen's plate and chomped it, opened her book and slurped a deep draught of sugary tea.

Nancy bustled in. 'I believe I shall go to work in the garden shed,' she said, slowly emphasising the last bit of the sentence.

'Do not worry, he's away to the ship,' Isobel answered. 'I'm right behind you.' She took one last shot of tea before she sprang out of the room and mounted the stairs to collect the tools she kept hidden in her dressing room.

'Abominably hot,' John said.

Isobel looked up. John was on the first-floor landing, sitting on the banister, legs dangling over the side. He was shirtless, shoeless, sockless, wearing only white breeches, the laces on the legs undone.

One of Isobel's abiding memories of her mother — she had few — was of the times they made tablet together. She would help her mother stir the pot, a mixture of sugar and butter ('the primary cause of many a Scotchman's rotting teeth', her mother would say with a chuckle), that would later be cooled on a flat tray and cut up for sweets. Isobel loved the stage when the butter was melting with the sugar and it was turning into a mixture of caramel brown. Isobel would slyly stick her fingers into the pot, despite the burning, and lick the sweet goo. John's skin was the colour of that tablet.

Isobel averted her eyes. 'I suspect where you come from, Mr Sackhouse, that this is a roasting day. But it is quite cool for summer, I find.'

She looked at him again. He carried a patchwork quilt of pale and pink rivulets of scars across his upper body. But also tattoos: of hunting scenes on his sides and across his chest, ravens on either shoulder.

John shifted under her gaze. 'I am sorry. I forget that you people tend to be quite . . . the word is priggish? Yes, priggish about going about as God made you.'

She walked up the stairs to the landing. 'Forgive me, it is not that. Well, it is not just that; it is not the done thing to go traipsing about a house bare-chested, Mr Sackhouse, I can assure you. It is not the done thing a'tall. But it is just that — I shall show you something.'

She unbuttoned her sleeves and rolled them back. On one of her forearms was a school of sea turtles, on the other seashells, all weaved together by intricate wavy lines. John swayed and had to steady himself on the banister for the images were strange but the patterns somehow familiar; they reminded him of home. Before he knew what he was doing he reached out and traced the seashells with his fingertips.

Isobel snatched her arm away.

'Oh, forgive me—' John mumbled.

'Oh, think nothing of it,' Isobel said, hurriedly buttoning her sleeves.

John slid off the banister, suddenly acutely aware of his lack of clothes. 'But I didn't think people here . . . My ship-mates, the *Wessexes*, a few of them are "marked". But I didn't think well, women in particular here would—'

'Oh, it's not that unusual on this island. Though, I still must keep them hidden away. I had them done a long way from here, where it is common for women to do this.'

The raven on John's left shoulder looked particularly fierce, wise yet somehow comical. It had raised lines, bumps, and she resisted the urge to stroke it. 'Did these hurt?' she asked. 'Mine were exquisite pain, it took some hours.'

'I cried like a baby. And fainted. There was much blood.'

A bang on the back door and she took a step away. They heard Nancy, singing softly to herself, rustle around in the kitchen and go back outside again.

'I must get dressed,' John said. 'I fear I may have missed breakfast. Is there any more about? And then I would like to explore this fine town.'

Isobel pursed her lips. 'There is breakfast. But Owen is concerned about you going out alone. He said I should take you down to see him at the harbour.'

'As I understand, for the next week or two there will be the very arduous task of unloading the *Wessex*, followed by the loading of it. I want to be as far from that as I can be.'

'Well, Nancy and myself could chaperone you.'

'Mr Sackhouse!' Isobel half-yelled, half-whispered. 'Please do get down from there.'

John stood on a barrel at Widow Matthews' house, eyes cupped on a window, peering in at the startled widow who had been taking a leisurely dish of her tea in the parlour.

'I cannot believe the luxury,' he said, looking at her seriously. 'It is not just your house and Mr Mather's, Mrs Chase, but everywhere we go. A world of plenty.'

John had raced up and down the street from house to house, vaulting over fences to look inside the windows, poking in yards, examining farm objects, taking fistfuls of flowers and herbs to his nose. Nancy and Isobel kept having to forcefully pull him back to the street.

He bounded off the barrel, skipped over to the Kimballs' yard. He looked into a side window. Two women were inside, warped and wavy through the bubbly glass.

The younger of the two women stirred the big pot over the hearth, gave a spit a half turn and, as she put a pie on the sideboard, looked straight into John's eyes.

'Oh!' she exclaimed.

John waved and smiled at her. The older woman called over her shoulder as she hacked at the vegetables. 'For goodness sakes, what is it this time, Betsey?'

'There is a blackamoor at the window, Missus Garvey.'

Mrs Garvey looked up from her task. 'Aye, so there is. If that black-amoor is going to come in and help us get this roast ready for Mr and Mrs Kimball by suppertime, let him in. If not, you get back to work.'

Isobel and Nancy reached for John's shoulders, hauled him back. Isobel looked up and down the street. 'Mr Sackhouse, please, you must not peer in other people's windows.'

John looked at her curiously. 'Must I not? Why?'

Isobel and Nancy exchanged a glance. 'Well,' Isobel said at length. 'It is simply not the done thing. It is considered bad manners.'

'By whom?'

'General opinion. Custom.'

John smiled archly. 'So you are beholden to this general opinion and custom?'

Isobel bit her lip. 'There are surely traditions, ways of living, mores, where you come from? Some that seem absolutely absurd, but you just do them? That chafe you, that you rail against in private? Yet you do them, adhere to them because you cannot bear to fight against the world about every little thing?'

Isobel's cheeks had coloured, her voice rose and she advanced incrementally towards John, so that he stepped back.

'My apologies,' he said.

John plucked up a swirly candy cane and sniffed it dubiously.

'Try it, you will find it delicious,' Isobel said.

He stuck a tentative tongue out and, when it made contact, his eyes widened. He started chomping greedily.

Isobel laughed. 'Slowly. You're supposed to suck it.'

'Are they all like this?'

'No, there are many different concoctions, different flavours.'

John looked around Pandi's Sweet Shop. He had to squint for he was overwhelmed by the profusion of colours, some shades he had never seen before — pinks, lime greens, vibrant violets, a shocking yellow. And all these bits of sugary colour were then somehow squeezed into different shapes — thumbnail-sized squares, spheres the size of your cheek, a rocky dust that popped and fizzed on your tongue, an amber brick called the Never-ending Beast which was flavoured with something called sarsaparilla.

John darted to the shelves, scooping handfuls of lemon drops, anise balls, marble swirls, grape ingots, strawberry stars and began stuffing them in every single available pocket.

Isobel tried to stop him. 'We have to pay for those first.'

Mr Pandi shuffled over. A Lisbon-born sailor, he joined up with the *Endeavour*, one of the Mather fleet, when it was watering in Rio some twenty-five years ago. He opened the shop shortly after meeting his future wife Martha two minutes after stepping ashore from that first voyage. 'How can I leave someone as beautiful as this for months on end?' he once said to Isobel. 'I would have to be mad.'

Isobel shot Mr Pandi a wary glance. The children of the town called him Old Barometer because of his variable moods. He was most often kindly, but given to rages, particularly if someone helped themselves or upset the order of his shop. Last week he had banned the young Curtain boy for two months for breaking a jar of gumdrops. 'Forgive us, Mr Pandi. Mr Sackhouse here is perhaps ignorant of our ways. I can certainly pay—'

'Not at all, my dear, not at all,' Mr Pandi cut in. 'Mr Mather has let it be known generally that he shall pay all expenses Mr Sackhouse incurs.'

John crunched a lemon drop and looked around the shop. 'All my expenses?'

He and Isobel regained the street shortly after, John hauling a hefty sack over his shoulder, meeting Nancy who had crossed to the butchers.

'Lord, someone has a sweet tooth,' Nancy laughed.

'A sweet for a sweet,' John said, handing her a gumdrop. He then stopped short, looking at the general store across the road with mirrors, knives and pots and pans glittering in the window. 'Merciful fucking Christ,' he whispered. The women jogged after him as he sprinted into the store.

A few hours later they were trudging back to the Chase home. John had had to borrow a handcart to carry all his booty including a brass bed warmer, four fire screens which depicted the killing and trying out of a whale, seven ivory snuffboxes, a wheat scythe and an iron killick.

Isobel looked at the cart dubiously. 'I know Mr Mather said he would cover your expenses, Mr Sackhouse. But I think there are limits to his generosity. He has never been overly generous before with anyone, I can assure you.'

'As mean as a one-eyed tom cat,' Nancy said.

John stopped. 'Ladies, I am the Son of Ham, anointer of those in blood and oil. Surely Mr Mather will look beyond the material in my case.'

The two women exchanged a glance. 'What do you mean "anointer in blood and oil"?' Isobel said.

'Truly, I do not know. But Mr Mather and your husband must have confused me with someone else, I do believe. And it's perhaps best to make hay until he finds out otherwise.'

Nancy said she had to visit Mrs Kitteridge, with a significant look towards Isobel, and turned down towards Bay Road. Isobel and John walked on. After a few minutes Isobel broke the silence.

'Are you telling me, Mr Sackhouse, that this fancy that was knocked into my husband's head by a bolt of lightning is still there?'

'It very much is, I am afraid. Please call me John. Sackhouse is not my real name.'

'Is John?'

'After a fashion.'

Isobel looked at his face. He was striding forward, a dollop of sweat trickling down his face. 'But I am curious . . . John. You were adrift at sea. But how did you get there? And why? Where are your people? Where are your family?'

John stopped walking. He blotted his face with his sleeve. Avoided her eyes. 'Gone.'

'Do you mind me prying? What happened?'

They had stopped at the crest of a small hill. They could see the arc of the harbour, masts poking upwards like reeds, men bustling about, small boats buzzing ashore and back.

Nantucket

Isobel stared up at the ceiling in the grey half-light, Owen slumbering deeply beside her. The third night of little sleep, and when it did come it was fraught and troubled. Och, why, why? Why was she so foolish? She tried counting the egg-shaped decorations in the cornices on the ceiling, following the same pattern every time. She began with the chipped one directly above her, moved to the left, down the wall towards the bedroom door, across to the windows and then back to her spot. This little trick used to put her to sleep as a child but now she was feeling vexed. Not only was she not getting drowsy, she was coming up with a different number each time: 436, 499, 505, 475.

She switched to counting the ticks of the grandfather clock, the sounds muted here in the bedroom from its position in the hall.

Then she found herself not listening for those tick-tocks, but the soft sounds underneath. If she concentrated — really strained — there it was: John Sackhouse's grinding snore, from one floor above. Which must be a veritable cacophony if one happened to be lying aside him.

A fancy. That was all this was. His strangeness, his exoticism, making her turn her head like a foolish besotted maiden in a novel.

Still, at odd times she found herself thinking about John's corporality. She thought of him not as a whole but in bits: his thick calf muscles made the more attractive by brand new hose; the striations of his forearm muscles; his neck tendons when he turned to look at her; his lips, the top one slightly plumper and darker than the bottom one; the hair, the sable-black thicket she yearned to run her fingers through.

And the eyes, those brown orbs flecked and whorled with blue and green, like a child's marble.

She slapped her forehead. 'Brown orbs'? God in heaven, she was being silly. No, a momentary fancy. She dared not think it any more or something else: his quickness of wit, his playfulness, the laughter hiding the melancholy, his wonder and curiousness at the world.

Isobel nudged Owen. Nothing, not even a grunt. She reached under the bed to the secret spot hollowed out under the frame. She fumbled around for a moment until she grasped it: Sir Roger, the oldest in the

He's at Home range, and still the most popular. Ridged, thick and made of wax 'for that closest to real feel', as they had it in the company literature.

She reached under her shift, shuddered slightly at the cool first touch of Sir Roger. After a moment, though, she put it aside. This would not do. She cast the covers down to the edge of the bed, then pulled Owen's gown up. She bent down, put him in her mouth, feeling him stiffen immediately. After a moment, she climbed on top of him, facing away. Owen finally stirred of mind as well as body with a 'Huh? Oh.' He clutched her sides and she reached back and put her hands on his.

'Baahz, why do you keep pallin' ahound wi' tha' dahky bahstahd?'

Barz leant in closer to Joe Cole, stared at him for a few ticks, eyes narrowing. He had berthed with Joe Cole for much of the last five years over three separate voyages, and still found his thick Bostonian street urchin accent almost incomprehensible — it might as well have been Mandarin or Xhosa — a stream of nasally, discordant vowels occasionally interspersed with seemingly randomly-placed consonants. 'I do beg your pardon, shipmate.'

Joe Cole frowned impatiently. He was unpredictable in his cups, was old Joe Cole, liable to become suddenly violent or overly friendly.

'Oh, oh, you mean our estimable messmate,' Barz hurried in when he had figured out a beat late what Joe Cole had said (he was never called 'Joe' or 'Cole', but always the two names squashed together, sounding like 'jocull').

Joe Cole, like most Bostonians, had an overly self-satisfied view of himself, combined with a particular dislike of the lower races. And yes, 'lower races' pretty much meant anyone not born in the Athens of America, but there was a particular distaste of the Bostonian for 'black bastards'. Why anyone would subject himself to commingling with them, apart from when being forced to do on ship, was a mystery to Joe Cole.

'I am a student of mankind, my dear sir,' Barz explained. 'It is merely an anthropological curiosity.'

'Oahr, ah you manoovah-in' him?'

Another slightly panicky pause. 'Manoeuvring him, you say? Are you asking whether I am spending time with the Esquimaux to try to learn his secrets? To discover whether he really knew that horde of blubbery treasure was there, or whether we just stumbled upon it? And if he does have this knowledge, to find it out and sell it on to the highest bidder? To Messrs Ellis and Kane, perhaps? The thought never crossed my mind.'

'You bahstahd!' Joe Cole smiled and clunked his pewter mug against Barz's. Bastard served as Joe Cole's highest term of endearment and deepest insult.

'Or am I merely repaying my debt to Captain Chase, and to a certain extent good old Ezekiel Mather, who saved me from certain ruination? Looking after and protecting the Esquimaux. My motives are inscrutable even to myself.'

'You ah still a bahstahd!' Joe Cole said amiably, then whipped his head round. 'Hey, whatta you lookin' at?'

Joe Cole's attention had turned to the table nearest, his eyes riveting at two men from the *Young Eagle*, recently paid off after a 21-month cruise.

'Well,' drawled the smaller of the two — the one with two knives in his boots, Barz noticed — 'a moment ago I was looking at Jensen here.'

Jensen, big, blond, bearded — Barz had a brief image of him in a horned helmet leaping off a longboat to sack a village on the British coast — cracked his enormous knuckles. Two Knives took a pull of his beer. 'Now, because you talked to me, I'm looking at you. Is that much of a problem?'

Joe Cole appraised the man for a moment, then smiled. 'It could become a problem. You ah Haleswoth, from the *Young Eagle*, eh? I heah it should be called the *Spread Eagle*, 'cause that's what you do to each othah below decks.'

Halesworth was reaching down for one of his knives when Barz said: 'A joy to see you both, fellow mariners. Excuse my colleague's uncouth behaviour. He's just off a cruise, like you, and is perhaps still not adjusted to the more genteel ways of life on land. Please, let's drink and be merry.'

Barz motioned to the passing barmaid and a moment later mugs were plunked down in front of Halesworth and Jensen. 'Your health and *skål*,' Barz said. The two hesitated a moment, but then put their mugs to their lips.

There was a squeak of the chair as Barz lurched up, striking with his palm at the bottom of Halesworth's mug and driving it into the man's nose with a satisfying crunch. An instant later, Barz was sprawled on his back, Jensen looming above him, throwing the table aside. Barz had a second to appreciate that someone so big could move so fast, when Joe Cole, bless that bastard Joe Cole, leapt on Jensen's back.

V.

Hang Impropriety

Nantucket

Ezekiel opened his eyes a minute before the cockerel — that infernal beast that had been guarding the Pimhills' henhouse two yards away for what seemed like an eternity — emitted his first impertinent blast of the morning. Judging by the watery grey light creeping in through the shutters, he reckoned it must not yet be five.

Rising before the cock crowed had been a constant since he became more or less an invalid. This was new. Sleep, or at least eight or so continuous hours of it, had been a precious commodity when he was a-whaling, and whenever he was able to get ashore, and particularly since becoming a ship owner and landlubber, it was a commodity he would trade with no one. He rose very late, and it was not uncommon for him to arrive at the quayside offices after a scandalous eleven o'clock in the morning. But since he was stricken, sleep came in fits and starts and when it did come, he would be jarred out of it far too soon, even given his liberal doses of laudanum.

The pain was scarcely bearable, an attention-seeking, unwanted guest. And it moved: his gut, his chest, the head and shoulders, and, God help him, sometimes the nether regions. The disease's namesake, the crab, was apt; Ezekiel could imagine it scuttling about his body, feasting on his innards, and then moving on to some other bit when it had had its fill.

Yet his eyes snapped open today with excitement not pain. The moment the cock crowed Ezekiel sat up, spun his legs out of the bed and stamped his feet upon the floor. He stood, feeling strength flowing through him. He felt powerful. A colossus.

'Thar she blows,' he said with some satisfaction, looking down at himself. 'It appears that the old mainmast is still fully rigged.'

'Mmm . . . what's that, Zekey Beaky?' Mrs Hummock murmured from the bed.

'Now, now, Hummy Pummy,' Ezekiel said, patting the mound of bedding under which, somewhere, Mrs Hummock lay. 'Sorry to wake you. You just go back to sleep, now. You need your rest.'

'Oh, that I do, that I do,' she chuckled dreamily before rolling over and snoring softly.

The previous night had been unexpected. Captain Chase had taken his leave after an exacting look at the books and he and Mrs Hummock sat back, slightly flush, staring at the evidence of the voyage's success spread upon the logs and ledgers on the desk.

'A prodigiously good haul,' Ezekiel said at last.

Mrs Hummock nodded. 'And immensely profitable, given the duration. No repairs to speak of, no replenishing stores, didn't even have to take on water. Our most successful cruise yet, Zekey Beaky.'

Ezekiel whirled around, looking at the door. 'Good God, woman, I told you never to call me that when others may—'

Mrs Hummock patted his hand. 'Shush, now. Captain Chase is gone, my love. A glass to celebrate.'

'This saves us.'

'Yes, yes I believe it will.'

Truth was, Mather & Co was overleveraged. There had been two wrecks in the past six months — the *Blackstone* ground to bits on rocks off Concepción, with the loss of all hands and cargo; the *Wampanoag* had vanished, last seen sailing into a hurricane near the Sandwich Isles. This compounded by two ships taken as prizes by the fucking Royal Navy at the tail end of the last war. Lloyds still would not pay the insurance for the *Wampanoag* — and he was currently conducting two costly suits against the United States and British war departments for compensation for his seized vessels.

A commanding fleet of ten prime whaleships was down to a minuscule six — and two of those were in dry-dock and probably not seaworthy for about 18 months — when the *Wessex* set sail. There was so little ready money that he sent the *Wessex* out uninsured (a fact he hid from Mrs Hummock for she would not have countenanced it).

His God had abandoned him to illness and ruin. But He had come back with Owen's vision of the Son of Ham. God was with him again.

Mrs Hummock came back with a bottle of Old Reliable and two glasses. She plunked them down on the desk, and while bending over and turning slightly away from him to pour, she bumped into his leg with one of her haunches.

Ezekiel instinctively flinched. Even the slightest of jolts and jostles had been causing him pain lately. But it did not hurt; instead, looking at Mrs Hummock's delicious backside — oh how he loved her rolling superabundance! — he felt the old stirring. He reached out and took hold of her hip, which made her pause mid-pour.

'Ezekiel?' she breathed. It had been some time.

He stood. 'Bend over the desk, amongst the manifests. And spread them out so I can see them, so I can read those glorious numbers.'

'Are you sure you can – oh yes, I see you can indeed.'

Ezekiel was back in his office, carefully ordering the manifests that he and Mrs Hummock left scattered across the desk. The Pimhills' cock was still going strong. He opened his double folio ledger carefully, tenderly. It was Catalonian, from the Barcelona printers de Robles, of which he received a crate every five years. A rather expensive vice, but still, the volumes were luxurious – the paper thick and handsomely made, the crack of the spine when opened gave him a shudder of pleasure.

He hunched down inches from the pages — damn these eyes — double-checking Mrs Hummock's fine work. Of all things he held dear with that woman, perhaps most was her exquisite hand. Her transferring of the *Wessex*'s own ledger to the official Mather & Co version was like a child's drawing compared to a John Singleton Copley portrait. The lines were crisp and exact, with tiny idiosyncratic flourishes (oh how he loved the curlicue on the end of her capital S!).

And what she did was his true joy. When he was a ship's captain, nothing calmed him more than putting the chaos of life on deck and ordering it in logs and ledgers. Commanding it. A treacherous day when the very survival of the ship involved hundreds of minute adjustments, a multitude of orders, the exacting of discipline, the variables of the men's moods, acts of Providence and just sheer luck could be contained with the sentence: 'Wind from N NE and immoderately fierce, 30 foot swells, calming towards six bells. '

There was the reality of what had really happened. Now he had created another reality in paper and lines of ink. The official version, what history would record whether it be true or no. And that power pleased him so.

He glanced up from the ledger, a pleasant smile on his face and looked out the window. 'What in holy hell!' he exclaimed.

He fumbled into the top desk drawer, extracted a spyglass and rushed to the window. There was Ellis and Kane walking down Main Street and — clad in a garish emerald-green coat and an overly tall top hat — Mr Sackhouse. And Kane was now putting his hand, his pudgy, covetous hand, on Mr Sackhouse's shoulder and talking, what Ezekiel was sure, were sweet, honeyed words.

'This will not stand,' Ezekiel muttered. 'By my Maker, this will not stand.'

'Why that is a rather natty outfit, Mr Sackhouse,' Ezekiel said. 'One of your hand-me-downs, Captain Chase?'

'Oh, no sir,' John cut in. 'A new ensemble. I put it in your name at Saunders and Saunders as per instructions.'

'Splendid, splendid,' Ezekiel said merrily, doing his able best to hold his smile. 'You are acquiring a fair number of items, aren't you?'

'I must confess, Mrs Chase, Owen, Mr Mather,' John said, 'that I went out early this morning to see Mr Saunders and ordered a further three breeches, a greatcoat and a cape. A cape, sirs and madam, which one can drape behind oneself and turn and flourish. Have you ever heard of such a thing? It is made of ermine.'

'Ermine?' Ezekiel repeated, forcing out a laugh. 'Is Saunders really making capes with such costly materials?'

'Oh, yes, Mr Mather. It is most valuable, the good man tells me — you can only get this particular type of pelt from the wilds of a place called Canada — and Mr Saunders assures me my cape will be a cape worthy of a king.'

'Splendid, splendid,' Ezekiel said with a rictus grin.

Isobel looked across at John and he lifted his eyebrows impishly. She hid a smile behind her hand; why was it so difficult for Ezekiel to realise he was being made game of? Though Owen seemed not to realise either; it seemed a private joke between herself and John.

A tray of Negus appeared in front of Isobel as John was detailing the exact expense of the ermine cape. She was glad for the distraction as she was at the point of chuckling aloud at the look on old skinflint Ezekiel's face. She reached for a glass and the tray was pulled back slightly, obliging her to stretch from the settee for it.

She sighed inwardly. All of the servants at the Mather household were young whalermen indebted to Ezekiel. They were first-timers on massively long lays — promised something like a 1/500th share of any profits of a voyage. The desperate, the green, the dreamers agreed to these ludicrous terms, perhaps not realising that there were costs against their lay — equipment, clothes, provisions — and that anything less than an extremely profitable cruise would end in them actually owing their employers.

Isobel sank back into the settee and glanced up. Ah, of course it would be young Bramfield, formerly of the *Miles Standish* and a Mather footman for this past twelve-month. His moving of the tray had less to do with sullenness and making things just that bit difficult for guests, and more that, from his vantage point, it would provide a better glimpse of her décolletage. Bramfield had been dispatched to the Chase house many times over the past year, and whenever he had a message to deliver directly to Isobel, he did so pink-faced and stammering, his eyes boring directly in on her breasts.

'Thank you, Bramfield,' she said softly, her voice causing him to snap out of his bosom-reverie and scuttle off.

John was just about to launch into tales of further sartorial extravagance when Barz was announced.

'Mr Millar,' Ezekiel said, his eyes roving to the grandfather clock in the corner. 'There you are at long last.'

An eruption of red crossed Barz's face and a scowl which he mastered after a brief moment. 'Apologies, Mr Mather, some affairs last night kept me unavoidably detained.'

'Brawling in the Tri-Pots is no excuse to keep me waiting, sir. I mark your surprise. You will be able to do nothing on this island without me knowing it. Given your discreditable former life I would have hoped this sort of thing would have been of the past. My eye is upon you.'

Barz made a short bow in an approximation of servitude, his face now bland and inscrutable. Yet, John, standing off to the side, could see Barz's hands clasped behind his back clench and release over and over, the skin alternating white and pink.

'They are Ellis and Kane's men, you do realise?' Ezekiel went on. 'That big galoot Jensen and that little schemer Halesworth.'

Barz rubbed his jaw. 'Well, good. We certainly gave them what for.'

'That was their design, do you not see?'

'Design?' Owen cut in. 'Come, Mr Mather. Surely, you are reading far too much into my cousin's unfortunate predilection for fisticuffs. Typical coof behaviour. No offence, cousin. Or, ah, you my wife. Or indeed you, Mr Sackhouse.'

Ezekiel sighed and folded himself into a large armchair, motioning for the other men to sit. Owen and John sat on either side of Isobel on the settee, Barz perched stiffly on the hard-backed Chippendale.

'I have been around this world many a time, Captain Chase,' Ezekiel said. 'Far more than you. I can assure you that there are people on this earth from outside this tiny island that can outfox or outthink a Nantucketer.'

Owen flushed. 'I misspoke, sir. I did not mean—'

Ezekiel held a hand up. 'What perhaps you meant to say was, even if it was by design, what of it? Mr Sackhouse is with us, through and through.'

Ezekiel turned to smile at John, who nodded back. 'Indeed, I am, sir.'

'Yet when Mr Millar was otherwise engaged, where was Mr Sackhouse? Being sweet-talked by Mr Ellis. On the very square this house sits upon, right under our noses. You were to be spending time with Mr Sackhouse this ante meridian, were you not, Barzillai Millar? To ensure nothing of this sort would come to pass.'

Barz looked down into his drink for a long moment. Isobel cleared her throat. 'Well, I am sure Mr Millar did all he could,' she said.

Owen leaned forward. 'What did you discuss with him, John?'

The three others, knowingly or not, aped Owen's posture, leaning forward, staring intently. John suddenly felt guilty. 'Ah, well, Mr Ellis promised me riches beyond my wildest imaginings if I joined up with him and Mr Kane and led his ships to the whales. I said that I have a very fulsome imagination. I also said that I knew not where whales could be found, that it was sheer luck we stumbled upon them.'

Ezekiel touched his nose and winked approvingly. 'Well played, sir, well played indeed.'

John, unsure what those signals meant, slowly copied Ezekiel's nose touch and wink. 'Yet, I am telling the truth.'

At this Owen, Barz and Ezekiel shook their heads and at once indignantly disagreed. 'Tut-tut, sir,' Ezekiel said. 'I know that you know. The Lord knows that you know. Or you will know, once a-sea. You are like a bloodhound; you need the scent to find your quarry.'

Barz and Owen nodded eagerly. John caught Isobel's eye, who shrugged and drained her Negus.

'This episode should focus our minds for the task at hand,' Ezekiel went on. 'Captain, how long do you anticipate before the *Wessex* can sail?'

Owen frowned. Ironically, if she was not at her home port, the *Wessex* could sail in the hour. Yet, touching home with a hold full of oil instigated a long string of unloading, checking for repairs, repairing, fitting out, and recruiting a crew. Given his druthers, he would like three months. 'She does need some minor repairs at dry-dock, though the *Standish* is due in before her.'

'I'll prioritise the *Wessex*.'

'Captain Palliser will not like that over-much, and we are not on the best of terms.'

'Captain Palliser will be spoken to. Believe me, he will make no fuss.' Not least because Mrs Hummock had discovered in her surreptitious reading of correspondence that went through the Mather & Co mail sacks a number of letters from the Captain to the second Mrs Palliser in Cape Hatteras in the Carolinas. Which would be perfectly fine had the first Mrs Palliser and her four offspring not been very much alive and well and living just two streets along in Bedford Row.

Owen considered. 'Then I should say twelve weeks.'

'Let us make it ten, Captain,' Ezekiel said, going on quickly to avoid Owen's objection. 'Now, Mrs Chase and Mr Millar. Captain Chase will be extremely busy, so I must call upon you. We must ensure Mr Sackhouse never comes in contact with Messers Ellis or Kane or any of their agents over the next nigh-on three months.'

'Truly, Mr Mather,' John said. 'I can handle my own affairs.'

'With the utmost respect, Mr Sackhouse, I fear you cannot. Mischief is meant for you from these two, I can feel it. If they cannot accomplish what they want via persuasion it will be by force.'

Ezekiel turned back to Isobel and Barz. John stood up and stomped to the side table feeling irritated. He held out his glass for another tot of Old Peculiar. It was overfilled, spilling onto his sleeve. Ah, it was that red-faced boy who had spent the entire evening staring at Isobel's breasts. John listened to Mr Mather drone, then slid to the back of the room.

'We need to protect Mr Sackhouse,' Ezekiel said. 'I would propose that there be a rotating system whereby one of you is in contact, direct intimate contact, with Mr Sackhouse at all times.'

'As much as I enjoy Mr Sackhouse's company,' Isobel began slowly, 'I do think there may be some . . . impropriety . . . in my and Mr Sackhouse being together with Owen not present.'

'Oh hang impropriety!' Ezekiel thundered, with so much force that Barz spilled his drink. 'Excuse the outburst, madam. But I am none too interested in the tattle of fishwives as getting Mr Sackhouse on the *Wessex*. It is a solemn sacred duty and I must ask, and implore you, to help. And you must do the bulk of it, dear Isobel, dear child, as cousin Millar here, though trustworthy when sober, is a sot at heart and must be used as little as possible. Oh, do not look at me with that injured face, you know the truth of it sir.'

Barz drained his glass, held it out to be refilled. 'Why not, then, keep Mr Sackhouse in-doors for the duration, under lock and key?'

Ezekiel shook his head. 'Mr Sackhouse must be seen about in town. He is the very embodiment of Mather and Co.'

'Besides,' Owen said. 'I will get the pick of whalermen. Even now you can see people coming in.'

Isobel drummed her fingernails on her glass, thinking of the number of He's at Homes that needed making.

'Of course,' Ezekiel said, his voice suddenly feeble as he leant back into his chair as if exhausted. 'I would do the task myself, but my disease, my weakness, I have not the strength.'

John appeared at Ezekiel's side brandishing a couple of folios. 'May I have these? I am afraid I have used up all the pages of the log book Owen gave me while we were aboard the *Wessex*. It will be a journal of these interesting times here on this island. And, of course, my deep and comprehensive knowledge of whales.'

'My de Robles ledgers,' Ezekiel said stiffly, the rictus smile returning. 'Specially made for me in Catalonia. Very dear, they are, oh so dear.'

Isobel sat up straight. 'I can think of nothing better to keep Mr Sackhouse occupied, when under my supervision, than in pouring his thoughts out on paper. Do you not agree, Mr Mather?'

'Yes, yes, I do,' Ezekiel said, the smile unflinching.

Nantucket – The diary of John Sackhouse, Esquimaux

It is hard to fully write my thoughts. Mayhap it would be easier 'twere I not so whelmed over. Everywhere is colour. Yes, back home there was colour, too, and to some extent on the ship. But I recognise now that was almost entirely of subtleties: the variations of blue in the sky, the shades of green in the sea, the minute shifts of white in the snow.

Here I am attacked: reds, yellows, pinks . . . they assault my eyes like a huge flock of honking birds would your ears.

I ache in my head. I sleep late not for laziness but I try to shut my mind of everything. Yesterday, I crawled into a darkened cupboard and stayed there, just letting my mind stay at ease.

I am hemmed in by the crush of people and sometimes find myself trying to catch my breath. The buildings loom above like mountains but are impossibly close together. It is like being trapped in a crowd constantly.

And will these people ever stop talking? I was always the loquacious one, but all of these people seem to say ten words to my one. I try to block them out but all I hear is an incessant stream of blah-blah-blahs, blub-blub-blubs, bleat-bleat-bleats.

I am holding on though, keeping my sanity, thanks in part to dear Father Kelly. It was his books and patient explanations — amidst the irritated FECKS and CUNTS and SWEET TASTY BUBBIES — that I first encountered things I am seeing day to day. Look, there is a chaise and four as in *Roderick Ransom*, or there is 'nodding beech' as in *Elegy Written in a Country Church-yard*, or there is a quizzing glass as in *School for Scandal*. Some of the objects are not as I imagined them — the chaise and four, in my mind's eye as big as a long hut, a quizzing glass I constructed as being as large as a full-length mirror.

And there are such riches. There is something new each day, each hour, each minute. Something to taste, something to eat, something to smell, something to touch. Howsoever, these sensations are not always pleasant. These people, particularly those who live less exalted lives than the Captain or Mr Mather, are rather whiffy. I had thought the reek of the *Wessexes* was due to being a-sea; there is little chance of hygiene aboard ship, littler chance to get rid of that infernal whale blubber smell. But no, a-land these people stink, too. It is not just a lack of washing. Do they not realise they stink of those things they eat, the milk of the cow, the beef, the beer?

Do I smell like them now? I pray I do not.

I make more allowances for the scents of the women who, on the whole, tend to be far more scrubbed than the men and also more liberal with pomades, perfumes and scents. Oh, the women. Such riches. Not merely the sheer number of them. I am forever conducting myself about the town with mouth gaped. I am afraid this has affected my virility. I am in a constant state of readiness, or near readiness with the merest of stimuli enough to send me off. This is rather em-barrassing given the tightness of the trousers.

Amid all these people, this hubbub, the profusion of talking, I have somehow never felt so alone. I hide it, I think well, with jollity and exuberance, for I sense that this is the part I am meant to play now. I am the prize, the spectacle, the jewel to be paraded and shown off. And I am doing it for them, playing to the gallery and they laugh, and they applaud. And underneath, I am thinking of Mary. Of Father Kelly. Of their faces when last I saw them. They haunt me still.

I am sure I am not the only actor in this farce. Owen plays the part of Captain, but I sense his striking down has mangled him somehow. Not his wits, but something has been reordered and shaken up inside. He is often dreamy, distracted. I sense, and this is only a sense, that he is trying to marshal his forces to stay tethered to reality.

Barzillai is forever trying to keep his anger in check, a spark away from exploding. What did Mr Mather mean about his 'discreditable former life'? I did fear he would lash out at the old man. Mrs Chase I find beguiling.

I did not want to tell her of my parents' deaths. My mother carried away by fever, my father gone away hunting to never return. It is something I have held deep, deep inside of me. Even Mary and I never spoke of it. But somehow, I felt I could to Isobel. I finished my tale in the Chase front parlour, which had grown gloomy as the sun had dipped below the horizon some time ago. She lit a whale lamp on the table, then the two above the mantelpiece, like she needed to make the place full of light again.

She dabbed an eye, arranged her hair, that hair. 'You will excuse me, John,' she said, 'I did not wish to bring up so many painful memories.'

But, strangely, I did not feel sad. It was curious. My heart was lifted. Maybe stories about our family, even the bad ones, the ones with the endings, keep them alive. I told her that and she flashed me a painful sweet-smile.

Then she said, 'I am glad. Then, may I ask, what of your sister and this priest?'

Then Owen burst through the front door and I did not have to answer.

Mr Mather is, at least, straightforward. He requires riches and some sort of spiritual succour. Although I do believe his quest for succour may be fast losing out to the idea of more riches. Or perhaps riches are his spiritual succour. So is gaining the upper hand with his enemies. Why he and Owen and Mr Ellis and Mr Kane — and it seems the entire populace of this island — believe I am the way to this whaling pot of gold despite my frequent, unequivocal denials I shall never know.

Does greed and avarice blind to such an extent?

This writing eases my mind, and is becoming easier. My pen flows.

Nantucket

Isobel stepped through the back door, comforted by the heft of her tool bag in her right hand. She stepped towards the shed, stopping suddenly. Mr Sackhouse was doing a handstand on top of the back fence. He held it there for a moment, then launched himself forward, somersaulting in mid-air and landing on his feet with nary a sound. She was struck by a memory of seeing a Felicity Islands lynx dart through the jungle and bound up a tree, all sleekness, grace and musculature.

'Are you . . . ' She stopped for she found her throat suddenly dry. 'Are you practising acrobatics, John?'

John looked over to her and bowed gravely. 'I didn't see you there, Isobel. Your Ancient Greeks called it *kallosthenos*, I have been told. Making the body strong keeps the mind intact.'

'A hard day's toil down on the *Wessex* might also keep the mind intact.'

A quick glance at the house and John whispered, 'Is he gone?'

'Owen is down at the ship. Would you care to join him?'

'Oh, no.' John walked up to her, took her free hand. 'I would like to explore more of this fine town. I have come to yearn for our walks. Will you show me? Let us "hang impropriety!" as Mr Mather might say.'

She let her hand go limp then squeezed his slightly, surprised at its warmth. A despairing glance at the shed, then she looked into his eyes and put her tool bag down.

'Stop.'

They had ambled a short way down the street when Isobel halted. The sun was shining down warm and insistent, the heat alleviated by a gentle breeze.

'I always pause at this very spot when walking this way,' Isobel said. 'There is a confluence of aromas — Mrs Kitteridge's flower beds there, the Bealings' herb garden over here, those rose bushes on the common.'

Isobel closed her eyes and turned her face toward the sun, inhaled deeply through her nose. John, watching her closely, did the same. 'Most wondrous,' he said, after a moment, breaking the spell.

Isobel smiled, blinking away the sunlight. 'Yes, now attempt to hold fast to that bouquet, John, for when we turn that corner, we will be assailed by the stink of the Nantucket quayside at midday: blubber, fish innards, the sulphurous harbour at low tide.'

The smell did not come gradually, but at once, like running into a wall. And with it a cacophony of noise: a babel of voices, banging and yelling from the quayside, clip-clopping horse hooves, the grind of wagon wheels, the screech of pulleys. John shrank back, clutched Isobel tighter, moving his arm around her back.

'Courage, Mr Sackhouse,' Isobel whispered.

'Apologies. I admit I am a tad overwhelmed,' John said sheepishly.

'Fear not,' she said, gently but firmly putting his arm back on hers. 'You shall get used to it.'

As they walked, John felt discomfited by the number of eyes upon them. There were a few sidelong glances, but most people just stopped what they were doing and stared. John could hear them saying 'the Esquimaux, the Eesquimaux, the Esquimaux', the soft sibilance making it perfect for whispering.

Isobel was busy acknowledging the bows, hat doffs and curtsies. 'You are famous, Mr Sackhouse,' she said lowly. 'Or I have suddenly become the most popular woman in Nantucket. Och!'

Isobel's grip tightened and John followed her gaze to a black-clad woman stomping down the walk, her fists pumping vigorously at her sides, with two servants puffing away at her heels.

'Mrs Chase,' the woman halloed when she was within a few feet in a voice that would have served at a hundred paces. 'I am heartily glad to see you. I believe we have some business to discuss.'

'Mrs Kitteridge,' Isobel said. 'May I present Mr Sackhouse?'

'Ah, yes, the Esquimaux,' Mrs Kitteridge said flatly, as if Isobel had introduced her to some commonplace inanimate object: 'Ah, yes, the horseshoe. Ah, yes, the street cobbles.'

John made to doff his hat when she boomed: 'We must, Mrs Chase, speak of He's at Home. There are orders to fill, dear lady. I am ready to transport, but I have not enough product to deliver.'

Isobel shot a none-too-subtle significant look at John. 'Perhaps, Mrs Kitteridge, we could speak another time?'

'I need answers immediately.'

'Let's speak, then, away from Mr Sackhouse, who will assuredly find this less than exciting.' Isobel turned to John, looking at him imploringly. She whispered: 'I must discuss something with Mrs Kitteridge. It should not be a moment. Pray, do not stray.'

He agreed and, as soon as the two women turned a corner, a man shot out from the shadows of a nearby alleyway.

'Mr Sackhouse, Obed Swain of the *Nantucket Intelligencer.*' The man's voice was quick, rat-a-tat-tat aggressive. 'How would you describe your first days on the island?'

Mr Swain was short — John had half a foot on him — with a strange combination of an over-large head but small, slightly indeterminate features: a slit of a mouth, smallish, grey almost colourless eyes. He looked up at John over square-rimmed spectacles perched at the tip of a snub nose. He held a notebook and a stub of a pencil close to his face. There was something grubby about him, John thought, and not because of the ink-stained hands and cuffs. It was the look, an almost nakedly carnal leer, as he waited for a response.

'Mr . . .'

'Swain, Obed Swain of the *Nantucket Intelligencer.*'

'How can I hope to answer that question, Mr Swain? I am being subjected to a multitude of stimuli — internal, external — a riot of colour, a profusion of noise. It would take days to answer your question fully. Indeed—'

'Is it true you will accompany Mr Ellis and Kane's *Gay's Head* when she sails in three weeks?'

'Why, no. I am due to sail with my good friend Captain Chase on the *Wessex* in ten weeks.'

'That's ten weeks, is that?'

'Come, come,' a voice thundered. 'Do not abuse our illustrious visitor, Obed.'

'Alderman Stevens,' Swain said, switching over to the newcomer. 'Who have you assigned to conduct the inquest of the suspicious death of Alexander Coffin?'

Alderman Stevens majestically swayed into John's view like a fat merchantman tacking into a gentle breeze. A large man with a whale-barrel stomach and jolly, jowly face, he stopped in front of John and took a wide-legged stance, as if setting himself up to break into a belly laugh.

'You will not know me, Mr Sackhouse,' the alderman said. The voice was rich and luxurious. John felt he could almost wrap himself up in it. 'I am Eldred Stevens and you will forgive the intrusion, but I thought I would save you from the attentions of our Obed and his mongrel rag.'

'The only paper to print the truth,' Swain interjected.

'I had been meaning to pay my respects to you, sir,' Stevens said to John, rolling over Swain's words. 'On behalf of the Aldermen of Nantucket, let me officially welcome you to the island.'

He reached forward and enveloped John's hands, shaking them ceremoniously and turning so that the thirty or forty who began to gather round could get a better view. The alderman addressed the crowd. 'In fact, the island is so enthralled by your exploits, sir, that we want to recognise them officially. With a ball, a proper fete in your honour!'

The crowd cheered lustily at this and the alderman beamed. He extended a hand to the air for quiet and brought it down on John's shoulder. 'First we need your agreement, sir. What say you, Mr Sackhouse? Would you like a fete thrown in your honour, and you the guest of the entire Island of Nantucket?'

'I have one serious question to ask before I give my answer,' John said solemnly, and the crowd held its collective breath. 'Will there be dancing and drinking?'

'Mr Sackhouse, you will imbibe to your heart's content, you will frolic and gambol until your feet ache.' Here a rumble of approval from the crowd.

'Then I say, yes!' John raised his hands in triumph and the crowd roared.

'There is your story,' Stevens said to the newspaperman. 'In four weeks the fete to end all fetes in honour of Mr Sackhouse.'

A tug on John's coat and he looked back into Isobel's worried face.

'Mrs Chase!' John cried. 'This plumptious fellow here has promised a party in my honour.'

'That is very kind, Alderman Stevens,' Isobel said.

'My dear Mrs Chase,' Stevens said, bowing lowly.

'I hate to leave but Mr Sackhouse and I must away,' Isobel said, offering her arm to John.

As he took it, she propelled him out of the throng, dodging quickly down several side streets, her legs moving so briskly that John had to half-trot to keep pace. Soon they were well away from the quayside, skirting the coast, rounding a bend in the sea-walk to come along a beach. Isobel shook her arm free and strode from the pathway onto the golden sand. They were alone on the mile curve of beach, save for a couple of anglers on a rocky outcrop at the other end of the half-bay. The breeze was stiffer here, and Isobel undid her bonnet and shook her head. Her hair was cropped close to the scalp at the back, but voluminous on top and the sides. She rolled her neck, her tendrils catching in the wind. She lifted her face to the sun, closed her eyes. John watched her for a long moment, his heart beating triple-time.

'Have I done something wrong, Mrs Chase?' John asked. 'Should I not have agreed to the dancing and drinking?'

Isobel basked in the sun a moment longer before turning. 'Och, well. Alderman Stevens is Ellis and Kane's creature, by and large, so I am sure it's part of their master plan at your seduction, in luring the great Mr John Sackhouse to their bosoms. Mr Mather will undoubtedly be hot about that. And it will be interesting to see what that newspaper fellow conjures up. Mr Swain may be the greatest inventor of fiction in all the Americas.

'But, no, Mr Sackhouse. You did nothing wrong. I needed some fresh air, and a bracing sea breeze after my talk with that high-strung bint.'

'What is He's at Home?'

Isobel took a step towards John, fixed him squarely in the eyes. 'A venture of sorts between myself and Mrs Kitteridge, nothing more. No need to mention it to anyone.'

She bounded away, in four or five lithe steps, John following clumsily in his Hessians. She held her arms out as if embracing the breeze. 'Does it not make you feel free here?'

John looked up and down the beach doubtfully. 'Free?'

'Oh, I know you sea-folk, even you seal-folk, must feel this all the time. But here, and maybe only here, do I feel the endless possibilities of what may be over that horizon. Ahhhh!'

A gust kicked up, Isobel squealing with laughter at its sudden ferocity. John watched her as the dress was blown tight to her body, only snapping out of his reverie when the bonnet was whisked from her hand and he clomped unsteadily through the sand to retrieve it.

Nantucket – The diary of John Sackhouse, Esquimaux

22nd June 1816

A day with Barzillai Millar.

The previous times I have written that line I have done so with sadness and, if I am not being overly dramatic, despair.

Barzillai — I find I cannot call him in the diminutive — seems entirely certain I have either forgotten or forgiven him for trying to do nothing less than murder me. I have not forgotten. Perhaps I will never forgive. On board the *Wessex*, I put it out of my mind, for what could I do? I could not go anywhere.

Yet here he will come banging on the Chase door — he refuses to use the knocker, but hammers the door with fists — greeting me with a hearty, 'Well met, shipmate!' and a robust slap on the back. I play along and endure, as it means that the next day I will be with Isobel.

Still, I have had less time with Isobel than I thought I would. She is constantly occupied with those 'domestic duties', which from my observation is mainly to do with the shed in back. The one packed with all the, what were they called here, widow's comforters? Dil douls?

Owen has been distracted as well by *Wessex* duties and the Great Work. He often will leave home at sunrise, burdened by folios and a satchel stuffed with paper, arriving back at sunset, after which he will shut himself up in the office until the wee hours.

I have avoided Mr Mather as he has been in a fury about the fete, Owen said to me as he passed. 'So he is fetefully angry,' I retorted, but not a smile, not a flicker of a response. I thought it was a good sally.

So, then Barzillai, who comes to parade me about the town and 'keep me out of mischief'. He is normally bright, bubbly and, if I am being honest, an enjoyable companion, in the morning. But around about twelve of the clock he becomes sweaty and pale if he does not fortify himself with a tot of rum or mug of beer, so we frequent the alehouses — despite Mr Mather's particular injunction to stay away from them. The colour returns to his face after just a few sips, but his demeanour after a full glass or two switches to angry, sullen and quick to take offence. It then becomes awkward and I am forever trying to mollify and pacify until I am free of him.

Then, today, Barzillai entered the house with a sly grin. 'I have a special treat for you, shipmate.'

'Another visit to Mother Molly's? I think Mr Mather would not approve if word got out we were becoming habitués.'

I do not know why I cannot say it is I that does not approve, hang whatever Mr Mather would think. I knew of the cathouse in the theoretical — from Mr Defoe's *Moll Flanders* and Mr Cleland's *Fanny Hill* (despite Father Kelly trying to destroy the latter when I brought it back from a Hull whaler) — and I had assumed that either the moralising of Mr Defoe or the sensationalising of Mr Cleland would be close to the truth. Yet the experience was mostly dispiriting. The working women at Mother Molly's, an ordinary-looking house two doors down from Deacon Brodie ('handy, he is one of the best customers,' said Barzillai), are in all shapes and sizes, some beautiful, some not. They all, however, seem dulled behind the eyes; all are young-ish but seem *worn out* by life and, undoubtedly the ungentle attentions of the clientele.

I let Barz go upstairs with his chosen whilst I pretended to dither perusing 'the merchandise'. I then scuttled out the door and hied back to the Chase's.

Barz shook his head. 'I'll not subject those lassies to your immense James Madison again, sir. You must have spoiled them for all others, I am sure, if you were still going strong when I left. No, today you are meeting old shipmates.'

He brought me to a shack that lay on the edge of the North Quay and who should emerge out of it but the McKeever brothers. On the *Wessex*, I stayed clear of these two brutes after they conspired with Barzillai to murder me. Here I let myself into similar circumstance: a lonely spot, a sea to be pitched into.

I brandished my walking stick at them and advanced. I would go down fighting this time. They held up their hands and retreated, Barzillai stepping in between us.

'A lot happened out at sea,' Barzillai said. 'I was not without blame.'

'You were the schemer these idiots followed,' I said.

Barzillai smiled playfully as if acknowledging a minor *faux pas*; a boy caught raiding the biscuit tin. 'It's time to make amends. The boys have something to show you.'

I was relieved, as my walking stick has an exquisite gold handle which I would have been horrified to see damaged. I let them lead me into the shack. The McKeevers simultaneously bowed and directed me to a couple of objects in the middle of the room.

My kayak.

My sealsuit.

Emotion surged through me and I confess I had trouble not swooning. 'But my kayak was destroyed,' I said. 'My sealsuit thrown overboard.'

'Well,' the uglier of the McKeevers said, 'Cap'n kept the kayak hidden from you so you wouldn't wander. And I am sorry about your sealsuit. But we tried to make this one as close to yours as possible, near as we could.'

The suit was folded neatly across the kayak, which was propped up on two benches in the middle of the shack. They had made me two new paddles. Two toggle-harpoons were fastened snugly to the sides.

I picked up the sealsuit, put it to my cheek; it had that same soft toughness. A remarkable copy. I burst into tears and, before I knew what I was doing, I had embraced all three of these men who had tried to annihilate me just a few months ago.

'All right, all right,' Barz said, disengaging himself from my bear hug. He nodded at the harbour. 'Fancy a go?'

I did. Oh, yes, I did.

The McKeevers sewed me into the kayak and launched me off the quayside. I splashed down, going under momentarily then popping to the surface.

I breathed deeply, but froze. It all seemed so foreign — the paddle in my hands, the seal skin against my own. I looked up at Barzillai and the McKeevers, grinning down at me from the dock. I made a tentative paddle and then another and it came flooding back. I shot through the water, I dived, I spun, I whirled. I crested a high swell, using it propel myself upwards in order to twist mid-air. As I landed I heard applause.

Scores of people were now flooding forward on the quay. I whooped and held my paddle over my head and they roared. I then gave the crowd a 360-degree mid-air spin. Then I dipped the kayak's nose down in the water, holding myself upright for several heartbeats before slipping down and propelling myself underwater at the dock, and thence popped up so high, I was able to plant a buss on the cheek of a startled young lady.

The cheering was magnificent.

Barzillai yelled at me but I could not hear him over the ruckus. He made a throwing motion with his hands, and I understood. I manoeuvred about 100 yards out and he and the McKeevers catapulted a ship's barrel out into the air and with a prodigious flick of my arm, I drilled it dead-centre with my harpoon mid-flight. The crowd erupted.

I then proceeded to dazzle the audience, which continued to grow, by piercing a number of thrown objects in decreasing size: a goose (from the butcher, already deceased), a gentleman's top hat (plucked off his head by Barzillai; he was very sore at losing it), a lady's parasol (she threw it into the air with a spirited heave), a belaying pin, a ship's biscuit, and finally, a silver dollar.

At the last, I took a few turns paddling up and down the now choked quayside, revelling in the hooting and hollering. Glorious!

Nantucket

'Captain Christ!' Owen bellowed. 'Captain Christ!'

He ran down the hallway in his heavy boots, bursting into the library. He had a roll of the *Nantucket Intelligencer* jammed under his arm. 'Read this!' he cried, thrusting a copy at Isobel and John. They were on either side of the room, each engrossed in their own books.

John and Isobel shot each other a look as Owen stomped to one of the bookshelves, resting on it arms folded. 'It appears you are famous, John.'

'"Baldness: A beautiful head of hair is the grandest ornament belonging to the human frame",' John read. '"Oldridge's Balm of Colombia applied to—"'

'Towards the bottom of the page, Mr Sackhouse,' Isobel said.

The Nantucket Intelligencer

A sketch concerning John Sackhouse, the Esquimaux Indian
By 'Pilum Oceanus'

See him, readers, the personage with which the ISLAND is a-gog: John Sackhouse, the Esquimaux, late of the icy realms of Ultima Thule brought to these shores by Mr Cotton Mather's whaling-vessel THE WEE SIX (had by Captain Christ) with a hold full of whale oil of UNFATHOMABLE wealth.

He walks down the strand and is, like most of his SAVAGE and underdeveloped race, well-made in corporal form. Though on the shorter side at perhaps five foot six inches, he is a squat muscled beast, robust and active. His complexion is copper-coloured, his visage is made of a fixed, amiable expression of the IDIOT CHILD. He is docile most times, we are told by his shipmates, though known to fly into a rage when deprived of sweat meats and candied corn, of which, during his time on the Wee Six he became most attached.

Like most of his unfortunate race, he has his uses, though is of little understanding. His shipmates have been able to make him understand the rude basics of MOTHER ENGLISH. His hand, we are told, when he is given enough encouragements of the sweet meat line, can eventually be made to make a tolerable 'X'.

The men across the quaysides and in the taverns say he can point the way to new, untouched and lasciviously fertile whale-grounds. Though it would stretch credulity that anything behind that thick cranium and furrowed brow could actually contain KNOWLEDGE. No, he may be like a divining rod which points to blessed water; a tool.

Galumphing about the quayside, he makes an impressive figure. Yet not one for illumination. Asked whether he is enjoying his time on this FAIR ISLE, he scratched his cranium and said: 'Me like it here. Me don't know where me are, but me know where whales be.'

Though his mental dexterity is not prodigious his athletic prowess is a sight to behold.

Using his 'KAY-ACK' — a slim craft formed of skin of the sea calf about 15 FOOT LONG which he fastens himself bodily into with the intestines of the spermaceti — he performed a number of feats in the Harbour, marveled upon by a throng in the hundreds.

He propelled himself through the waves in his primitive craft performing trick upon trick. Moving in advance or retreat with the most surprising swiftness and far superior to that of any four oared cutter. What is the most astonishing of all his manoooverse, is he can give to his vessel all the properties of a diving machine and shelter himself like an ACQUATIC FOUL in the most stormy weather. He lays the 'kay-ack' entirety on one side and is totally plunged under the water while his canoe still following the same direction has its keel turned upward: he then goes on the other side and places himself as before: what renders this movement the more extraordinary is that during all this time he never lets go his paddle.

He then shoots out of these positions to throw his dart at a variety of objects big and small hoisted from the quay. He never misses his aim, throwing the lance a scarcely believable distance.

The fete in his honour approaches. See him yourself Nantucketers at the Quaker Meeting House in just a few weeks' time.

'Captain Christ!' Owen repeated as they both put the papers down. 'This is disgraceful!'

'Oh, tut-tut husband, you should not be vexed,' Isobel said. 'We call it the *Nantucket Ignorancer* for a reason. Your name was hardly the only error. *Cotton* Mather? The *Wee-Six*?'

'Why am I portrayed as a monosyllab?' John asked. 'And "squat and muscled beast"? I believe I am rather tall and my figure is most elegant; Mr Saunders said so.'

'Do you both not see,' Owen said with asperity, his voice notching up an octave, 'that this is a direct insult? Not only the "Wee Six", but Captain Christ most of all. It is clearly a ridiculing of all that has happened to me. And that is the only mention of me. The Captain of the *Wessex* for which the island should be a-gog. As a-gog as they are for you, John.'

'Owen,' Isobel said, her tone warm and placating. 'I think you are getting over-vexed. I do not see any reason for you to be over-vexed.'

'No, I see you do not.' Owen turned on his heel and strode out the door.

Nantucket

John walked into the sitting room holding the Woolly Mammoth — thick as his wrist, long as his forearm — in his hand.

'Ah, John, wonderful, you have found my rolling pin,' Isobel said as levelly as she could.

John handed it over to her. He leaned forward. 'A rolling pin? That device is for baking? This is unlike the others I have seen in the kitchen. The ridge running down the, what shall I call it — shaft, is it? Yes, the shaft. What purpose does that serve? And I notice it is rounded on one end and not the other.'

Isobel could feel the flush in her cheeks. She stood and turned away from him, searching through volumes on her bookshelf.

'No, no,' John continued in a lilting tone. 'Do not explain. As you know, I am no dab hand in the culinary arts, and I wouldn't understand the implications. Nor would I understand the uses of the various sized and shaped *rolling pins* in the woodshed.'

Isobel straightened her back and whirled around. 'Then you know, Mr Sackhouse, that they are not rolling pins. Very good.' Her cheeks were rose red now, certainly, with anger and her Scots accent became more pronounced. 'If you must know, these are products of my business, the He's at Home Company. I am proud of what we do, and am unashamed, though you may sneer and mock. I—'

'Mrs Chase,' John said softly. 'Isobel. Do forgive me. I was merely teasing; I realise I sometimes go too far. These, ah, items are not unknown where I come from. In fact, my mother and sister used to—'

Isobel held up her hand. 'Please, Mr Sackhouse, I am a free-thinking woman, but I do believe there are some limits to information that I would like to have shared.'

'I see,' John said, though he did not. Most of his time with these people seemed to entail discovering the little boundaries that he was not supposed to cross. 'I suppose I was teasing because you seem so furtive about it, with Owen, I mean. Yet, it does not take much to discover what you are doing. Nancy in particular is hardly discreet.'

Isobel sat down. 'Owen assuredly does know about He's at Home, but chooses to ignore it. He once told me that a wilful ignorance of some of the things the crew is doing on board ship is an even better way of dealing with them than active engagement. He even burst in on me in the shed once — he had left to go to the mainland but had to return home for some reason — and I hadn't covered up my work area and there were several unfinished Lady's Friends on the bench. "Ah, good stout ship's pegs," he said, grabbing two in either hand. "Workmanship is even better than my master carpenter, my dear."'

Isobel's spot-on impression of Owen's all hands voice made John chuckle. He picked up the Woolly Mammoth again. 'I do think, however, that if Owen saw this beast, he would have had a harder time dissimulating.'

'Hm . . . yes. Still, our clientele has varied needs and we need to accommodate them all.'

'The lady who requested this object certainly has particular needs.'

'That, in fact, is for a retired commodore.'

John puffed his cheeks out, whistled lowly. 'God's teeth. That is difficult to comprehend.' The two were silent as they contemplated the Woolly Mammoth with renewed interest for a moment.

Isobel stood up, flexing her hands and fingers. 'Since my secret is out, Mr Sackhouse, I will no longer be coy. My husband's return and you, my unexpected houseguest, have put me far behind schedule and there is work to be done.'

'But wait,' John said. 'I may not be a dab hand in the kitchen, but I am a singular craftsman. Let me help.'

'Oh, thank you no. I do not think that would be at all necessary.'

'Nonsense, madam, nonsense. To the shed!'

John rubbed his hands together. 'Now let us get to work, shall we?' He plunged into the shed and pulled out several of the hidden boxes from the back. He picked up the box of tools — plane, auger, rasp, chisel, knives – and meticulously laid them out on the bench.

He shook another box, rattling its contents, and looked inside. 'Now, I assume these are the near to finished ones. This here' — kicking another box — 'the just begun. What shall I do? How am I best employed?'

Hearing nothing, he turned round. Isobel stood just outside the shed's door, backlit by the midday sun so that he could see her only in silhouette. Isobel hovered there for a long moment, not answering but running her fingers through her hair, ruffling it, making it puff out.

'Could I ask you,' she said coolly, 'to replace those tools?'

When John hesitated, she strode into the shed, plucking the nearest tools up, cradling them tightly to her body. 'Would you please step aside?' she asked, her face flush with anger. 'In fact, it would be best if you would get out of the shed.'

'As you wish,' John said as he retreated to the garden. He stood somewhat uncertainly as she bashed things about inside, putting the boxes back in their places. He took a few steps toward the house, then a few back to the shed, performing this awkward shuffle dance a couple of times.

He stopped when Isobel emerged. She looked at him, frowned, and snapped the padlock shut. She smoothed her dress down, fixed her hair.

'Mrs Chase, I—' John began, but Isobel held up her hand.

'Do you think we can take a turn?' she said.

Ten minutes later they were outside, John offering his arm. He moved to go towards the quay, but Isobel turned him away from the seafront, guiding him up the slight slope on Liberty Street where the houses petered out, before steering him into the black gates of the Newtown Burial Yard. There they strolled through the middle of the somewhat haphazard and untidy rows of grave markers. The tombstones were of varying size and repair, some were crumbling, cock-eyed, on the verge of falling over; some were sturdy, robust monuments obviously designed to stand the test of time; a handful were new, looking somewhat shocking and out of place. The grass between the tombstones stood tall and unkempt, a dazzling verdant green interrupted by dots of yellows and purples and reds of dandelions and wildflowers.

'This is my favourite place on the island, probably a result of too much Radcliffe as a girl.'

These were the first words Isobel had spoken. John exhaled gratefully. 'I do not know this Radcliffe.'

'They are books of the most unsuitable sort, a corrupter of morals, particularly for young ladies,' Isobel smiled. 'Or so my father told me. So I would read Mrs Radcliffe and Clara Reeve, and their tales of the super-natural *sub rosa*, hidden in my bedroom closet, a candle held close to the page. Reading tales meant to terrify and horrify in a largely darkened, enclosed space added a piquancy, and made me want them all the more. And since, I have always been drawn to the Radcliffian. A ruined castle seen in moonlight, a deep spooky wood and a walk in a yard amongst the dead.'

John plucked a dandelion, a buttercup, a New England blazing star and handed them to Isobel. 'And yet it seems so overgrown, this place, so alive.'

'We may die but life goes on, I think is a better way of looking at it.'

John had stopped by one tomb, with a double-winged death's head etched on top. He read: 'In memory of Shubael Coffin, aged ten years, and Peggy Coffin, aged twelve years, taken from this earth, 7th May, 1801.'

'The son and daughter of Mr Coffin. That's Owen's and your ship-mate, Mr Coffin. They drowned when their rowboat overturned in Hummock's Pond. His wife is over there somewhere, with her parents. She died a month or two after, from grief, they say.'

'I did not know he had a family.'

'He was a-sea. He only found out of their deaths almost a year after the fact. I like this epitaph over here, you will see it on more than one: Remember me as you pass by/As you are now so once was I/As I am now so you must be/Prepare for death and follow me.'

'What a dispiriting, wretched piece of doggerel.'

'You haven't a heart, Mr Sackhouse, though it is no Rabbie Burns. I think the sentiment is worth heeding: you, reader, are going to die. Perhaps it is an exhortation to live your life to the fullest.'

They strolled on through the yard. Isobel said, 'Let's sit under the shade of that tree and get out of the sun.'

John scampered over, pleased to escape the unbearable heat. He plopped himself down, looking out onto the harbour. Isobel smiled. 'Please, after you sir,' she said.

John looked at her quizzically as she sat down next to him, near enough so when she smoothed her dress out, a portion near the hem flopped over on to his leg. She did not seem to notice and he let it linger there and John fought the urge to reach out and touch it.

'I appreciate the sentiment, John, of you trying to help me,' she said after a pause. 'And I am sorry for becoming cross at you. But the . . . enterprise . . . that I run from that shed is mine. Mine and Nancy's and ours alone. We do not really need help. But I thank you for the offer.'

'You know how adverse I am to manual labour, Isobel. To be honest, I only suggested it to be closer to you.'

Isobel blushed deeply and he went on quickly: 'And by that I mean, I enjoy your company. Particularly as Owen, Barz and Mr Mather talk incessantly about whaling, which grows tiresome.'

She glanced tentatively over to him and their eyes locked for a long moment before she broke away. 'Well, here we are. Let us rest in silence and drink in this pleasing aspect.'

'Yes, let's,' John said, clearing his throat. They both looked out to the sea. John then slowly reached out and touched the hem of her dress that still lay on his leg, stroking the soft fabric. Isobel reached her hand out and placed it by his. After a moment they touched, but just a caress with the tips of their pinkies. It was so light John felt more the heat of Isobel's hand rather than the solidity of it. John stole a glance at Isobel. She was steadfastly staring out at the harbour, but her lips were parted, her breathing shallow and cheeks turning pink. John looked back at the sea.

Nantucket

Isobel was awoken with a start. Was that something, or someone, banging around downstairs? She paused for a minute, hovering somewhere between sleep and heightened alertness. *Thump.*

It was something.

She bolted out of bed, did not bother trying to wake Owen, because she knew it would be useless. Ashore, she could yell, 'Rape! Thief! Fire!' in his face, perhaps even shoot off a musket above his ear and he would not rise. But, and she had seen this on the *Wessex* after they left the Felicity Islands, at sea he could somehow feel even a half point deviation of the course and he would jump out of his cot from a deep sleep.

She crept out of the bedroom, grabbed a cutlass and dirk from the cabinet on the landing before she stole downstairs. She held the cutlass before her, the dirk down at her side. She was always surprised by the heft of these weapons which she always attributed, ridiculously she knew, to some sort of latent magical power of objects made for solely for killing.

The sounds were coming from the larder. She relaxed. Just rats, then. But then she saw the glow of light underneath the larder door. She touched the cutlass to her forehead, breathed deeply and bashed the door in. 'Hah!'

John was on the floor next to an oil lamp, a layer of rosemary, basil, mint, sage and thyme spread beneath him. He seemed to be . . . luxuriating in the herbs. Rolling about on them, moving his arms and legs back and forth as if making snow angels, his face close to rapture.

John sat up quickly. 'Ah, Isobel. I, ah, well. This, I know must seem most, ah irregular. I cannot explain myself, really. It is just, I've never smelt anything so exquisite.'

He got up, dusted himself off. 'I may have ruined these herbs . . .'

Isobel smiled, brushed a few leaves off his shoulders, and then put the cutlass and dirk on the sideboard with a clank. 'I think we shan't put that rosemary on our roast beef tomorrow, at any rate.'

'Do you often go around in armour?' John said, eyeing the cutlass and dirk.

'Oh,' Isobel said, 'I had an altercation a few months ago with a couple of, well, they would perhaps call themselves whalermen but common burglars is what they were. They knew Owen was a-sea and stole in here in search of ambergris, ivory and whatever valuables we might have.'

'And they found?'

'That cutlass up the backside of the one who was slowest back out the window. Nothing else, I am glad to say.'

'Apologies, again, it is just that everything, everything . . . ' John looked abashed as he searched for the words. 'Everything is new. The tastes, the smells.'

'You won't know Edinburgh, John. It is a cold city. Not as cold as where you come from, but it is wet and chill. We even have a word for it: *dreich*."

Isobel drew the word out, the 'ch' lingering on the back of her throat. John immediately felt transported to somewhere stony, slate grey with rainy winds that made the bones ache.

Isobel went on: 'But we have a monotony of weather all year round. I had never, for example, seen true snow — deep blizzardy snow — until I came here. Which I suppose you cannot imagine.'

'It does not snow all the time where I am from. In fact, in summer we have grass, the flowers bloom.'

'Really? I've always assumed that Ultima Thule was a complete ice-locked barren wasteland. In Scotland, as I say, we have a monotony of weather, and of food. The taste is grey, bland. Even the colours of what we eat themselves can be so unattractive: pale yellow neaps, grunge-grey oats, dirty-white tatties. But when I went to the Felicity Islands, I could not believe it. The explosions of colours, of the fruits. The smells just assaulted my senses with pleasure, they were so powerful that I felt faint at times. Passion fruit, mangoes, kiwis, pomegranate. Oh I loved pomegranate. Have you ever? No? It is this combination of sour and sweet which at the first bite transported you to every emotion you could think of.'

Isobel trailed off, then collected herself. 'Excuse me. I seem to have drifted into a sort of reverie.'

John got up and moved over towards her. 'I know exactly what you mean.'

'Everything is new.'

'Everything is . . . wonderous.'

John moved closer to Isobel, so close he could see, even in the half-light the two tiny moles on her shoulder that peeped out of her night dress. So close he could smell her, something vanilla and sweet. His hands were shaking slightly. To do something with them, he reached across her to a shelf for a jar of raspberry jam. He opened it with a *thock*.

'In my rummages here — this is not my first incursion into this den of delights, I will confess,' he said. 'In fact this is one of my nocturnal rituals. I am quite addicted to this larder. But, I have discovered this.' He put a finger in and scooped out a bit which he placed on his tongue, letting it linger there for a moment before swallowing. 'It tastes of Eden.'

He put his finger in again and held it out to Isobel. 'Taste it.'

'Well, thank you, Mr Sackhouse, but I hardly need to as I made it.'

'Taste it.'

After a slight hesitation, Isobel nodded. She took his hand in hers and guided his finger into her mouth.

Nantucket – The diary of John Sackhouse, Esquimaux

27th June 1816

I avoided Isobel for the entirety of the next day. A significant achievement, I think, as neither of us left the house or the grounds. She breakfasted; I remained in my room. She went out to the shed; I went into the dining room. She returned for lunch; I slunk into the library.

And so on. Cat and mouse. Or rather, mouse and mouse. Although I am unsure if she was actually avoiding me or merely going about her daily business.

Later in the afternoon, whilst I lazed in my bedroom, I heard her say 'Will Mr Sackhouse not be dining with us?' to Kathryn.

'No, miss-us, his apologies but the gentleman says he has a dicky tummy.'

Isobel's reply was soft, indistinct, though I strained to hear it. Was that relief? Disappointment? Or worse, ambiguity?

I dozed and woke in the middle of the night, my stomach a-roil. I wanted badly to see Isobel. Oh, let me not shirk the truth in this journal or it has no use. I wanted to see her, yes, but touch her, taste her. And all the rest.

But I cannot see her. Strangely, I feel little guilt for my strength of feelings and that troubles me for I know how they would disconcert Owen so. Or would they? He seems detached and disinterested. In everything. No, I avoid her because I realise she must think it a mistake, why else did she flee from me? She perhaps has no feelings for me at all and I have mis-read her entirely.

I was famished. Earlier, I asked Kathryn to fetch me dinner to my room, but she refused. 'Oh no, Mr Sackhouse sir, a dicky tummy has no business intercoursing with a roasted beef.' And she left me a warm glass of milk and a desiccated biscuit that tasted of caked earth.

Damn my lies. I listened. Not a thing stirred, there was no sound but the tick-tock of the clock in the hallway.

I lit my taper and tip-toed down to the kitchen, heading for the pantry.

'I thought you might come down.'

'Ah!' I jumped and spun round, extinguishing the taper in the process. Isobel stood in the kitchen door. I tried to compose myself. 'How did you sneak up on me?'

'I could not sleep. I was sitting, in the dark, in Owen's study.'

My eyes adjusted to the gloom and I could make her out better. She remained hovering by the door, looking backward to the stairs. 'Are you here to make a digestive tonic?' she asked.

'A tonic?'

'For your stomach problems.'

I looked over on the sideboard and could make out the outlines of an enormous wheel of cheese. The scent of the roasted beef lingered in the air. My stomach gurgled. 'Yes, yes of course.'

She moved into the kitchen, brushing by me, her night dress grazing my hand as she passed. She rummaged around in a cupboard, finding a tinder box. Two strikes and she ignited a lucifer, placing it to a whale oil lamp. The wick seemed to hesitate and think about it before flooding the room with light.

'Dearie me, that is bright,' she said. Her head was bare and her hair was voluminous, as if she had been running her hands through it. She patted it down. 'You will forgive my state.'

I think I mumbled that I would. She was furtive and fidgety, looking randomly about the kitchen, picking a non-existent crumb or two off the countertops. She would not catch my eye. 'Oh, I have something for you.'

I managed to croak a few unintelligible words, and as she stepped toward me my heart went *bumpbabumpbabump*. She then handed me a mug filled with liquid. 'Oh,' I said. I took the mug in hand and sniffed. 'Jesus fuck Almighty.' It smelled of low tide and overripe fruit.

'I was in the larder,' she said, looking shyly down at the word, 'earlier thinking of you. I mean, that you might come down sometime today and be in need of a cure. When in doubt, I always revert to Culpeper's *Herbal*.' She reached over to the counter and tapped an old, weighty tome. 'This is his cure-all for any stomach ailment. A bit of purgative, I will warn you.'

She watched me expectantly. 'I'll take this concoction to my room upstairs, thank you so much,' I said, fully intending to chuck the brew out the window.

'I sense a reluctance. You will not. Drink it now.'

'Isobel, I think—'

'Down in one, John Sackhouse.'

I steeled myself and tilted the mug back. I coughed, spluttered and barely kept the rancid mixture down. I could feel it coursing down my insides like an invading army to my gut, and I had to stagger to the table and sit down.

She nodded approvingly. 'The best physicks are vile going down. That is how you know they will cure you.'

'I imagine the best poisons are vile as well.'

'You are a horrible patient, John. I would advise you staying down here for a half turn of the clock or so, in order to be closer to the privy. Good night.'

I could barely give her a bow or respond and she flitted out of the kitchen.

Nantucket

'Dearie me, dearie me, dearie me,' Isobel recited like an incantation, rocking back and forth on the low stone wall in the back garden, her forehead pressed on the butt end of a hoe. How could she let this happen? How could she? Whilst Owen slept, as well.

Yet it meant nothing, surely. She was just tasting some raspberry jam. Off a man's finger. In the middle of the night, in the pantry. Yes, she could hear herself telling Owen: 'Why, you'll never guess the most outrageous thing happened last night, husband. I heard a ruckus downstairs, got up to investigate, and would you countenance it, but Mr Sackhouse was in the pantry practically bathing in herbs. What are they like, these savages? The strange thing, he offered me some jam from his finger — I assume where he comes from they haven't much experience in using a spoon, ha, ha — so I took it into my mouth. For an overlong time, during which I became weak in the knees and had the most base thoughts. Oh, la! Do you not agree, husband, *très amusant!*'

She shook her head, trying to drive the images of the previous night out of her head. It meant nothing, of course. In Mr Sackhouse's world they perhaps fed each other by hand all the time.

'It meant nothing, nothing at all,' she said aloud.

'What meant nothing?'

Isobel rose and spun quickly, the hoe still in her hand, whipping around and knocking Barz's top hat off.

'God Almighty, you Scottish doxy,' Barz snarled as he picked the hat out of the muck. He stood in the pathway on the other side of the wall. 'What did you do that for?'

'Cousin Millar,' Isobel said flatly. 'Apologies. If I was a bit further south, this hoe could have done some serious damage.'

'Which you would have undoubtedly regretted.'

Isobel shrugged. 'It would have taught you a lesson about sneaking up on people.'

Barz looked theatrically up and down the pathway. 'Is this not a public thoroughfare? Am I not walking with these keys to deliver to Mr Mather that jangle as if I am in fetters on Shutter Island? Hardly sneak thief behaviour.'

'Mr Mather's is in the opposite direction.'

'First, there is business to be had here.'

'What business?'

'Och, aye, wimmon. Aren't you just the cheeky wee besom?'

This did raise a ghost of a smile. 'That is the worst Scottish accent I have ever heard.'

'It is about our Esquimaux, of course. After our meeting the other day, I had another one in private with Mr Mather and convinced him that I should take a greater role in keeping a weather eye on Mr Sackhouse. I pressed home to the great man that John and I have been shipmates with an unshakeable bond. If we can face the struggles of the sea together, surely I can pilot him through temptation on land.'

'An unshakeable bond formed in three months?'

'Forged in steel over three months! You could perhaps never understand the intimacies we mariners have when aboard ship.'

'I have a fertile imagination.' Isobel nodded toward the house, turned back to her work. 'Owen and Mr Sackhouse are in the study, I believe.'

A doff of the hat. 'Madam.'

Isobel glanced back to watch Barz round the fence and make for the front of the house. She leaned on the hoe for a moment or two after he disappeared from view, then lifted it and drove the blade into the ground.

After near an hour, Isobel realised she had done very little except bash the living bejesus out of the turf. She walked to the shed, and noticed with a start that she had not padlocked it. She stepped inside, unnerved. At first glance everything seemed in order, the He's at Home equipment safely stowed and hidden behind the garden implements at the back. But hang on, no. One of the boxes was missing. Heart beating quickly, she charged into the house, startling Kathryn as she rushed into the kitchen.

'Is Nancy not about, Kathryn?' Isobel asked.

'Ah, no, miss-us, but she told me to tell you something,' Kathryn said. She then arranged herself into an oddly stilted actress pose. 'The package is setting sail. Then she told me to do this.' Kathryn winked over-exaggeratedly.

'Hm. I am flummoxed by her subtlety. *What* could she have meant by that?'

'I am sure I don't know, miss-us.'

She thanked Kathryn and walked away, slightly relieved but still worried. Orders were piling up; she and Nancy must get working again in earnest, fear of discovery be damned.

She heard voices from Owen's study, the door of which was slightly ajar: Owen's a deep and soft murmur, Cousin Barzillai's urgent and penetrating, a note or two higher. She trod lightly down the hall and peered in the door through the crack. Owen and Barz were on either end of the table, talking lowly and passionately, both men hunched forward and gesticulating. John was between them, facing the door. He looked side to side as the two men volleyed back and forth, but he was clearly not attending. After a couple of moments, he ended the pretence of following along and became engrossed in examining the stitching of his new blue and green serge waistcoat. Far too heavy and totally inappropriate for this weather, Isobel thought, but the colour suited him very well.

John's eyes snapped up. He looked right at her and somehow she realised he knew she had been watching all along. Isobel caught her breath, retreated a half-step. They held each other's gaze for some time before John stretched, but then discreetly held his hands above Owen and Barz's heads, miming their flapping jaws with fingers. Isobel smiled, dropped her eyes and ducked down the hall.

Nantucket – The diary of John Sackhouse, Esquimaux

9th July 1816

I have offended Owen. Does he see into my soul? Does he know my thoughts?

He avoids my company. He goes to the dock-yard at all hours carrying folders stuffed with reams of paper. Yesterday, I offered to accompany him and he steadfastly refused, not meeting my eyes, almost angrily rejecting my companionship.

Does he know of the other evening? Did Isobel tell him? I know not what it means to her. But she is furtive with me. There is something of a heightened, strained politeness. She avoids seeing me alone. Yet, even when I am with her in company, I think of her lips around my finger and become woozy. I also think about the mad dash away she made an instant later, bang-banging up the stairs.

Although we are not often together with Owen, it is a blessing. He is in the study writing until all hours, a sliver of light burning beneath the door. I can hear it though — he is scratching so fiercely I wonder how the paper does not rip. He left the door to the study open the other day and I stole in. He turned the sheaves over quickly and greeted me with a tight nod.

'Yes?' he said curtly, adding 'John' a second later.

I hovered by the chair in front of his desk, not sure if I should sit. 'You seem rather busy at the moment, Owen,' I said, deciding to remain standing.

'The burden of being a ship's captain.'

I gestured at the papers. 'Am I disturbing your . . . '

He placed his hands upon the top of the pile of papers. 'Great Work.' That is how he says it, as if in capital letters. 'Quite frankly—'

'What happened when you were struck?'

'Happened?' He looked surprised at my interruption and change of tack.

I pressed on. 'Yes, happened. How did you feel? What did you experience?'

He put his pen down. He examined his hands at length before going on. 'I was struck and purified,' he said in a whisper.

I did not quite catch it, he said it so low. 'I beg your pardon?'

'Not really struck in the normal sense, but I was embraced. A white light, a warm white light lifted me up. I cannot explain it really; words do it no service, but it was all-encompassing, rapturous, and wondrous. He sang to me—'

'Who?'

'Why, God, of course. He sang to me. He still does, all the time. I can hear His song in the background even as I talk to you.'

He stared at me for an uncomfortable moment. I shifted on my feet, searching for something to say. 'I've heard a few good ones lately,' I said at last. 'A country farmer going across his grounds in the dusk of the evening found a young fellow and his lass very busy indeed near a five-bar gate. "What are you doing there?" cried the farmer. "Don't worry, sir," said the fellow, "we are only going to prop-a-gate."'

Nothing. 'How about: there was a famous teacher of arithmetic who had long been married without getting his wife with child. One friend of the wife said to her, "Madam, your husband is a tremendous arithmetician." The lady demurred: "Yet, he cannot multiply."'

Owen merely stared. I said: 'A hellfire sermon was being preached at a county church, which made the men and women all fall to weeping, except one man who remained unmoved. "Why are you not affected, sir?" said the vicar.'

'Good night, John,' Owen said to me and went back to his manuscript.

I bade a quick good-bye and mumbled: '"Oh, because I come from another parish," said the man.'

11ᵗʰ July 1816

Isobel and I were in the breakfast room this morning, Owen in his study.

A knock at the door and a man delivered a box for Owen which, judging by how Kathryn's legs buckled as she struggled with it down the hallway, was rather heavy. A moment later, Owen burst in on us. He planted a kiss on Isobel's cheek, shook my hand warmly.

'Isobel, John. Forgive my moods these past several days. I have been labouring on a Great Work, and have been distracted. Indeed, you may say I have been possessed. But that has made me fractious and irascible with you both.'

He went on: 'But here it is. The first of my masterpiece.' He solemnly laid a pamphlet down on the centre of the table, delicately smoothing down the page edges to stop them from curling upwards.

Isobel and I shot a glance at each other, and bent over the table to look. 'Purified by Fire,' she read. 'Part the First.'

Owen took over: 'In Which a Sea-Captain Is STRUCK by GOD's Righteous Hand of Fury; only to RISE AGAIN.'

'This is what you have been doing,' Isobel said. She was arranging the pamphlet in front of herself, squaring it over and over.

'I'll confess in all hours,' Owen said, drumming his fingers on the table. 'I have let Mr Coffin get on with the business of *Wessex*. My Great Work has consumed me. I hear the voices urging me to write at all times. Even when I sleep. Please, read it.'

'Here? In the breakfast room?' Isobel looked uncomfortable.

'Certainly,' Owen nodded. He handed me a copy. 'You as well, dear John.'

We bent to our task but, try as I might, I find it difficult to really remember much of it beyond the first sentence: 'Lo! The Lord burned me with brightness and in turned plunged me in the DARK.' I soon became confused, though, and recall little of the narrative or argument save for Owen's being abused by a very pugilistic God, variously describing his encounter with a lightning bolt as a slap, a punch, a throttling and a thumping fist. I could see Isobel struggling as well, worry lines spreading across her forehead.

Eventually we both finished, and turned to the eager and expectant Owen.

'It is a powerful statement,' Isobel said at length.

'Most forcefully argued,' I said.

Owen nodded at us. 'Good, good. I mean to tell this story far and wide.'

'Yes?' Isobel asked.

'I have instructed Mr Stoughton to start an initial print run of ten thousand.'

'Ten thousand, you say,' Isobel said, her voice hitting a higher register. She cleared her throat and went on, 'That must be a significant sum. And you have not yet been paid off by Mr Mather.'

'Oh, I know, and that's just the beginning!' Owen said eagerly and cheerily, then moving over to take Isobel's hands in his. 'Do you know how much it costs to ship products from here up and down the coasts?'

'It can vary greatly, but if you have a good partner and know which port-masters to avoid you can make significant savings,' Isobel said matter-of-factly.

'A small fortune!' Owen cried, seeming not to hear. 'Still, the Lord's will be done.'

14th July 1816

Another day, another huge sack of post. Just days after Owen shipped out 'Purified by Fire' the letters started trickling in. First from Fall River, New Bedford, then from up and down the coast and further inland. They were letters of admiration, requests from preachers and ministers to speak to their flocks, quite a few gushing and borderline improper notes from housewives.

'How about this, Isobel?' Owen cackled, holding one letter aloft. 'A proposal of marriage! Oh, what a sweetheart.'

The entire first run had sold out instantly — perhaps Mr Stoughton's inspired idea of putting a woodcut of Owen's chiselled features on the frontispiece had something do to with the success.

Owen has become unbearable, reading the letters aloud incessantly: 'Listen to this one,' he said across the dinner table last night. 'From a Maxine Levender (Miss), of Hanover, New Hampshire. "My Dear Sir: As I take this opportunity, I quiver, and I cannot suppress my hand from trembling for I am writing to a man who speaks the truth, whose righteousness burns through me. I wish I could have stood on your great long pole and have been welded together with you as one in God's glory . . . "

'And on and on she goes in a similar fashion for a number of pages. Isn't that marvellous? And look, she has enclosed a lock of hair. What a right little soldier of Christ.'

'A right little something,' Isobel mumbled.

'And look, another one,' Owen said, opening a new letter. 'A request to go speak to another church. But I am but a simple mariner not made for speechifying. Lovely to be asked, though, is it not?'

He beamed at us but he became more thoughtful when reading the next missive. 'This one is from Moses Brown. He is asking me to speak to his "little gathering of Friends".'

Isobel perked up. '*The* Moses Brown? Providence Moses Brown?'

'The one and only,' Owen said. 'And not only that. If it goes well, perhaps a few other gatherings might want to hear what I have to say.'

I looked at both of them. 'Who is this person?'

'An important man,' Owen said, rubbing his chin as he re-read the letter.

'But surely you are a humble mariner,' Isobel said.

'Not made for speechifying,' I chimed in.

Owen did not laugh. 'Mr Mather might be persuaded,' he said, dreamy and faraway. 'If I am away a short while. To be linked with Moses Brown would be a glorious thing. For me. And Mr Mather.'

Nantucket – The diary of John Sackhouse, Esquimaux

16th July 1816

I have acquiesced to Mr Mather's confinement and supervision, at least on the surface.

But I have had the need to strike out, to explore. So I do so at night. It is easy enough. The Chase household retires early. The door is bolted and creeping down the stairs would surely make too much noise. So I open the window in my room, and climb up to the roof to scuttle down the trees on the opposite side of the house.

And then I am off.

It is beautiful. There is a brightness to a Nantucket night, the darkness pricked by pools of whale oil street lamps. I like the relative quiet: Nantucket in repose. But it never really stops. There is always work being done out on the quay. And while the decent upright citizens sleep, the less than respectable carry on.

The taverns are almost always open. I avoid Tri-Pots, the Harlequin, the Mermaid, the more respectable places near the centre of the town. I go to the meaner, shabbier, shambling wrecks of places. Insalubrious places. Coof hidey-holes where my celebrity gets me drinks from the seamen. I imbibe. I convive. I revel. I am not alone.

This night in my ramblings I went north of Nantucket-town for the first time. About a mile up the coastal walk is a hamlet of houses, the most run-down I have seen on the island. There are a handful of sturdy-looking and respectable structures, but they are few and far between, here amidst slovenly shacks and hovels.

Though late, the streets were milling with shapes. I write shapes because I could not make out any faces, for the lighting was bad — in contrast to the rest of the streets on this isle — and when I moved towards people they would slink away.

I turned a corner and suddenly there was light spilling into the street. I followed the shaft, and saw it came from a low-slung building almost implausibly constructed of ship's planks and driftwood. Along with the light, a hubbub of voices leaked out of the window — or, to be more accurate, the hole in the wall.

I looked inside. It was a tavern room, smoky and crowded, groups of people gathered around various objects — boxes, barrels, a mountain of burlap sacks, a scuttlebutt — serving as tables and chairs.

It took a moment for me to realise that everyone inside, from the barkeep to the patrons, all looked like me. Or had some variation of my hue: brown, black, red or somewhere in between.

When I entered, all stopped talking and looked my way. It may have been my magnificence of dress. I was clothed in my skulking outfit of head to toe dark emerald green, set off with a black cloak with a hood for maximum stealth and disguise.

I nodded to all and sundry and sauntered to the bar, letting the denizens admire both my form and equipage. A large African with a voluminous crown of nappy hair stood behind the bar.

'May I, my good man, have a spot of your finest ale?' I asked. 'Or barring that, perhaps a nice claret would do.'

He fixed me with a stare. After a moment he bowed, low, over-elaborate. 'I do beg your pardon, your Grace,' he said. 'But I am aggrieved to say the cellar is lacking in fine ales or wine. Or, indeed, ales and wine. I regret I cannot oblige you.'

I knew I was being made game of but pressed on. 'What do you have, then?'

'Gin, rum, my own concoction called Wreck the House.' He looked me up and down, not unkindly, with a half-smile. 'You would best be safest with the rum.'

'Nonsense. The Wreck the House, please.'

He shook his head, pulled a tumbler full of a suspicious-looking amber liquid from a stone jug. 'You had a fair warning.'

I slid a coin across the bar and investigated the Wreck the House with a tentative sniff and was rewarded with a sudden rush up my nose, a stabbing pain. Eyes watering, I raised the tumbler to the barman and took a small sip that was like a slap across the cheeks and punch to the stomach.

I spun around. The patrons had gone back to their own conversations, though many kept stealing a covert glance in my direction. Then in the dark recess of the far corner I spied a man and a woman looking boldly at me. They were reclining together on what looked like a day bed fashioned out of ship's cable and hammocks, the woman stroking the man's inner thigh. My heart did a quick triple-beat. My own islanders, no, but surely these were of the People, my People.

In three strides I was a-fore them. 'Greetings friends, so far from home,' I said in the language of the People.

I could see now that he was a tad younger than she. He was thin, lithe; a tension within him suggested a coiled spring, though that spring was much lubricated at the moment. She was perhaps in her fortieth year, very striking, piercing eyes, high-cheekbones, her beauty largely untouched by time. She wore a dress as demure as any of the respectable ladies about town — though this was at odds with the corncob pipe clenched between her teeth and her hand that lolled lazily on the man's crotch.

'Can you believe this coconut?' the man drawled at length. 'What a fool.'

'Stephen Talhanio, manners,' the woman said, sitting up primly, setting her pipe aside. 'You are Mr Sackhouse the Esquimaux who is on everyone's lips. I am Lascivia Turner. Mr Talhanio here, you have just been insulted by.'

She motioned for me to join them. I looked around and spied a squat barrel not much over a foot high nearby and rolled it over. I flipped it up and struggled for a second or two to sit upon it.

'I am pleased to make your acquaintance, Miss Turner and you Mr . . . ' I hesitated as Mr Talhanio seemed to have dropped off into a deep slumber. 'Why coconut?'

'A poor jest,' she said.

'Brown on the outside, white on the inside,' Mr Talhanio mumbled, eyes still closed. He sat up, peered at me blearily. 'Maybe apple is more accurate here. Red on the outside . . . '

He trailed off and slumped back.

'Oh . . . I see,' I said. I understood and made to get up. 'Apologies. I merely thought you were of my people.'

'No, please stay,' Miss Turner said. 'Stephen should be apologising.'

'Stephen won't,' Mr Talhanio said.

Miss Turner shook her head. 'Impertinence is his currency. We don't speak the old languages, I am afraid. He's a Wampanoag, mostly — his people lived on this island before *they* came. My parents were Nipmuc, I think. From the mainland, anyway.'

Mr Talhanio sat up again. 'How are you finding New Guinea?' I looked perplexed so he went on, 'Darky-town as they calls it, mostly. The 'ville you are in now. Salubrious, ain't it?'

I said I did not understand. Mr Talhanio said: 'This is where they allow us the dregs to live. This is where we are cast to. You think you are special, Mr "I Know Where All the Whales Are"?'

'Actually, I have no idea where—'

'You are not! Once your usefulness is done, they'll discard you. Do you know how many whales I killed for Mr Mather?'

'A prodigious amount?'

'One hundred and thirty-two with this arm alone. Then I get trumped up for stealin' because my lay was becoming too high.'

'Stephen was on the *Standish* for five cruises,' Miss Turner explained.

'Never stole a thing in my life,' he went on. 'Leastways, no more than the next. Now where am I at? Even Ellis and Kane won't have me.'

'I know little of these matters,' I said, 'but surely an able seaman, a good harpooner, would find employment somewhere?'

'They'll toss you aside, Esquimaux,' Mr Talhanio whispered. 'They'll toss you aside.'

I smiled, stood, bowed quickly to Miss Turner and downed my Wreck the House in a gulp. I barely made it to the door, stars exploding behind my eyes. Once outside, I strode quickly away, turned the corner, then stopped to collect myself before I was able to go on.

I walked back to the Chases' unsteady on my legs, my stomach roiling — from the drink or what Mr Talhanio had said, I know not which.

30th July 1816

Since going to New Guinea I have stopped my nocturnal perambulations.

I am torn, torn, torn.

Does Owen not want me as a friend for who I am? Does Isobel not value my friendship? I am under no illusions that Mr Mather looks at me and sees nothing besides a sack of gold and not a living and breathing man (though an excellently attired one).

I have been taciturn to mine hosts. Cross and querulous. But Owen has been distant. Twice, I have attempted intercourse to try to broach the very subject and have been rebuffed, Owen pleading insistent business, and out the door he went.

I angered Isobel. Yesterday morning she suggested an expedition to the bluffs on the opposite end of the island for the following day. The weather, she said with an admirable flush to the cheeks, was to be most clement.

She had found me in the library, and stood by the door smiling expectantly for my acquiescence. I turned back to my book and said tersely: 'I thank you for the invitation, madam, yet tomorrow will see me in the library once again.'

I could sense her hovering there at the doorway. I sneaked a glance and saw her feet rock back and forth. She took a step back to the hall, then back to the library as if she was going to say something further, then she was away. I rose to chase after her to apologise, but stopped myself, not really knowing why.

VI.
The Great Awakening

Nantucket

'A formal dinner,' Isobel said. 'I am overjoyed.'

'Mr Sackhouse to be the guest of honour, of course,' Owen nodded happily, reading Mr Mather's invitation. 'Will that not be exciting, John?'

John looked up from the book he was reading and studied Owen for a long moment. 'I shall hoot and holler and perform like a trained gibbon.'

Owen's smile wavered but held. His brow furrowed. 'Yes, yes. That will be very well received, I am sure.'

'It is to be tomorrow?' Isobel asked as she took the invitation from Owen, her voice rising in incredulity. 'But I haven't a stitch.'

'I am sorry for the short notice,' Owen rushed in. 'Apparently Bramfield was to have delivered this three days ago but he, in the young man's own words, was "carried away to distraction whilst conversing with Kathryn and Nancy"'.

'I imagine there were four reasons for his distraction,' Isobel muttered.

'How do you mean?' Owen asked. When Isobel remained mute, Owen crossed to her, held her hand. 'You say you have nothing to wear but, whatever your costume, you will look glorious.'

Isobel shook her head at the facile understanding of men, whilst thinking of the mini-alterations and hours of preparation suddenly thrust upon her.

'John and I are also caught as unawares as you,' Owen said.

'Oh, I have a whole array of suitable attire to choose from,' John said absently, not looking up from his book.

'Thank you, John, you are most helpful,' Owen said stiffly, before beating a retreat to his study.

233

Isobel looked out of the window, alternately biting on her nails and chewing on her lower lip. John watched her, finding himself impossibly bewitched by the crease of a frown on her forehead, the dark, serious look in her eyes. He felt an urge to get up, put his arms around her, make it all better. He cleared his throat. 'Owen's heart is in the right place, Mrs Chase. Isobel. Or his sentiments are. He is so very correct: you will be the most beautiful woman there.'

He said the last bit looking down at his book. Isobel chuckled. 'You misheard him, John. He said I would look glorious, not the most beautiful.'

'That is what he meant to say.'

'Your insincere flattery is improving, John.'

'I have been practising assiduously.'

Isobel blushed ever so faintly, looking over at him. John felt a tremor in his chest, reached for the bumper of Madeira at the table next to him and drained it in one.

'We must arrive in style,' Owen said. Yet, the Chases had only a two-seater barouche — a pacy and impractical little thing, but both Isobel and Owen loved to zoom around in it — so a grander carriage was borrowed from Henry Esmond, the elderly bachelor lawyer who lived two doors down. This struck Isobel as wholly impractical as Mr Mather's home was but 400 or so paces away. Yet it did save her shoes. Good Mr Esmond must not use his carriage much, or at least his stable man was completely incompetent: the axle was rusted, groaning and shrieking for the entirety of the short journey.

'Well,' Owen said, 'at least all will know when we arrive.'

Isobel smiled faintly, then felt her stomach burble with nervousness, but not down to concern for her dress. She wore blue chiffon patterned with stars, a pearl necklace and matching earrings. She knew it sufficed. Although she could not hope to match Mr Sackhouse's grandeur. His mustard and orange ensemble certainly caught the eye — she first was minded of a spectacular sunset — yet it blended ever so well with his skin colour. Owen, in his demure powder blue coat and yellow breeches, looked fairly dull in comparison; Isobel caught one or two of Owen's sidelong glances at John and knew this vexed her husband.

As per Mr Mather's instructions they were the last to arrive, ushered out to the veranda where the other guests were enjoying iced rum punch in the fading heat of a summer evening. John and Owen were immediately swept into Mr Mather's long, bony arms, Ezekiel herding them into a press of black-clad men, all bobbing their heads hello. Isobel had an image of the men being led into a murder of hungry rooks.

Isobel realised she had drained one glass of punch and was on her second before she had descended the stairs to the women. Mrs Hummock caught Isobel's eye and moved to welcome her.

'Dear Mrs Chase,' she said, pink and happy of face, her voice an octave higher than usual. 'Welcome, welcome, welcome.' She embraced Isobel and kissed her heartily on both cheeks, presenting her to the knot of women. 'You know Mrs Chase, of course.'

The women closed and chit-chattered around her and Isobel smiled and interjected a pleasantry or two but mostly sat back and observed.

Some of these women were smart and powerful. Mrs Hummock's name may not have been on the sign above the Mather & Co offices, yet she all but ran the business. Mrs Kitteridge's name was above the door; she owned a fleet of a dozen whalers, which she built up from the mere two she inherited when her wastrel of a husband passed away ten years ago. Yet they were letting the conversation be dominated by the group Isobel called the Sisters Mothers: Missuses Kenabeck, Oatmen and Yarlin, three wide-hipped siblings whose main accomplishments were birthing a brood of children for their sea captain husbands.

All three had sired this past twelvemonth and the ladies nattered on in the smug manner of recent motherhood. They told of little Nathan's amazing progress in walking, cute Lucinda's prodigious appetite, young Josiah's surprisingly copious shitting. Marvellous, it was all just marvellous!

Was anything more tiresome than hearing of someone else's children?

Yet one had to *pretend*. Isobel asked about Lucinda's suckling, which gave Mrs Oatmen a platform to expound at length about her child's astonishing capacity to extract milk from a ready teat which,

Isobel thought, hardly set her apart from all the mammals on this earth.

Isobel's attention wandered to the men. At these gatherings, she sometimes wished she could be among them. Though perhaps it was just as dull; all their talk would be of whaling. Which it seemed to be now, as John was in the centre of the half-moon of the rooks, miming a harpoon throw. Ezekiel beamed at him like a proud papa. Owen stood a bit further away, his smile strangely rigid.

'And you, Mrs Chase,' Mrs Yarlin said, bringing Isobel back to the ladies. Mrs Yarlin was the plumpest and smuggest of the Sisters Mothers — she had produced seven remarkable healthy tots in as many years. Isobel steeled herself, for the Question loomed. 'Do you and Captain Chase have any happy news, perchance?'

Isobel absolutely loved children. When spying a cute, fat baby she longed to squeeze and hold it. She loved to play with older children, was confident she could be an excellent mother. Yet, she was not sure she wanted to bear any. She did not want to become like these women, for one: she wondered if one's brains turned to mush so one is solely capable of talking of one's off-spring. Dearie me, how dreary. Then there was the curtailing of the freedom she so cherished; which, with Owen away often, she had much of. Plus, and this she told no one, the thought of something the shape of a mid-sized cannonball bursting out of her actually made her queasy. She had confided in friends a few times of her reticence. But she felt she was not taken seriously. 'Oh you'll come round,' was the dismissive reply, always in a stern tone that made her feel that she was letting the rest of womanhood down by not yet breeding.

But this is what womankind was *meant* to do. And she did not want to do it. The Great Mary, of course, had written on the difficulties of motherhood and how it weighed down their sex. And she had died in childbirth, irony of ironies. Or perhaps Mrs Wollstonecraft was merely going to extremes to prove a point?

Luckily, and she realised this was unusual for a woman of the middling to upper classes, her father's natural philosophy lessons had given her a clear-eyed understanding of the reproductive process from an early age. Owen wanted children but in the vague sort of way

236

of most men, assuming that it will happen when they least expect it. But she took precautions and potions and douches and she had not yet fallen.

She had practice in handling The Question and stopping follow-up inquiries. It involved looking away with a hurt, troubled expression on the face (it helped now with Mrs Yarlin in that she could squint into the setting sun which brought something close to a tear to her eyes) and saying querulously: 'We have not yet been so blessed and we will wait for God to shine His light upon us. And I hope he will soon.'

The uncomfortable silence was broken by the bell for dinner.

Isobel pushed the Mather library door and it sealed with a *thwick*, the sound making her unduly happy. She looked around the vast room. Empty. She breathed in and out, unclasped her pearls, took off her gloves and placed them on one of the reading tables. The key was in the door and she turned it with a snap.

She massaged her neck and rolled her shoulders. She kicked off her shoes and dug her feet into the red carpet. 'Thank merciful Christ,' she said.

'Ahem,' someone coughed.

'Oh,' Isobel cried.

John had been sitting with his legs crossed on a high-backed chair which faced away from the door. He put his feet on the floor, stood up and saluted Isobel self-consciously.

'John,' she said. 'I thought I was alone.'

She moved to gather her things and began putting them back on.

'Please, Isobel,' John said. 'Don't don your armour again for me. You are among friends.'

She hesitated a moment, then put her pearls and gloves next to her shoes and sauntered down the room. She plopped on the chair next to him, smoothing out her dress. 'And what are you doing here, honoured guest?'

'I have read about parties like this,' John said. 'Or what I imagined this party would be like. It has been far more raucous than I thought.'

Isobel nodded. 'These are whalermen. Gentlemen whalermen, but

237

that is like being a gentleman pirate. We are always a hairsbreadth away from a tavern brawl.'

'Are you much recovered?' Isobel's eyebrows went up questioningly and John added: 'You seemed not yourself.'

Isobel looked at John levelly for a moment. 'I had a cosseted up-bringing, John. My mother died when I was small and my father spoiled my sister Ali and me. We were coddled, lived in a closeted atmosphere and, before I knew it, it seemed we were going to the opposite side of the world. So I am unsure of how I should behave here. There are codes I do not read, cues I miss. Most of the women, the other women, do not like me.'

'Oh, that is surely untrue!' John cried, leaning forward and clasping her hand. 'Surely no one could have that perception of you?'

Isobel shook her head. 'I guess I mean that they regard me as strange and wish I was not there. And I am no good in crowds. I am not good at making myself heard above the hubbub. You may have perceived this already, John, but in our society it matters not so much what you say, but the volume at which you say it. Blab whatever tosh you like and you will be feted if it rises above the din.

'In these gatherings, my wits desert me. As I search for something telling to say I am always a beat behind everyone else. So I tipple too much, and my wits desert me more! And I become more taciturn, thus underscoring my reputation as either haughty or a simpleton.'

Since he had taken her hand, Isobel had been half-concentrating on what she was saying, and the fact, the physical fact, of his hand. He was not just holding but softly kneading between the fingers so that she was becoming limp with relaxation.

Their eyes locked. Isobel put her other hand around John's wrist. She could feel his warmth, his pulse. 'I was most impressed by you tonight, John. You were the life and soul of the party. You entertained, you told stories, you were magnificent.'

'With my tosh that rises above the din?'

Isobel laughed. 'It doesn't necessarily have to be nonsense that you say loudly. It does impress me, your being able to command a room like that, to make people hang on your every word.'

'Entertaining like a dancing gibbon.'

Isobel looked at him curiously. 'That is the second time you have used that phrase.'

'Last week I found myself in what I think you might call Darky Town.'

'Did Mr Millar take you there?'

John shook his head. 'It was in the dead of night. I have been having a few nocturnal emissions away from you all. Why do you laugh so? But I have been escaping your confinement and exploring the town on my own.'

He told her about the mean tavern, of meeting Miss Brown and Mr Talhanio, of Mr Talhanio's opinion of him.

'Am I being used horribly, Isobel?'

'Owen loves you like a brother. I am much attached to you. You should not trust anyone else. You should make your escape from this place.'

'You could come with me.'

She dropped his hands and smiled brightly. 'Aye and Owen, too! What a trio we would be!'

The handle turned on the door. Isobel rushed to pick up her belongings and quickly put them on before unlocking the door.

Bramfield stood at the entrance-way. 'Mrs Ch-ch-chase,' he stammered. 'Captain Chase said I might find you here.'

Isobel extended her finger to under Bramfield's chin, guided his head up towards her eyes. 'That's better, is it not, Bramfield?'

'M-m-ma'am. Carriages, ma'am. Captain Chase said carriages.'

Nantucket

Mr Kane ambled down the steps into the gloom of the warehouse basement, each stair creaking objections at his weight. Reaching the foot of the stairs, he patted his stomach contentedly, inhaling deeply with satisfaction. Mr Ellis followed a moment later carrying a whale oil lantern, muttering to himself as he picked his way down.

'Why must we always meet here?' Ellis sighed, swinging the lamp to illuminate his partner's face. 'It smells like the bowels of hell.'

Kane inhaled again, more theatrically. 'Tosh, Lambert. Breathe, breathe in deeply, and take a great snuffle with that great snout of yours. That is untreated spermaceti, pure whalebone, and rendered blubber. Literally the spine, the guts from which our empire is built.'

Ellis grunted and the two walked to the opposite end of the warehouse, the light throwing shapes of dancing marionettes on the walls and making the rats squeak and scurry between barrels.

'We can smell the guts and viscera of our "empire" from the offices upstairs,' Ellis said at length. 'Indeed, we can still smell it in our homes in town. In fact, there are few places on this blessed island where you don't get that particular aroma. Only not as noisome as it is down here.'

'The offices upstairs, even the one in town,' Kane said equably, 'are susceptible to the prying eyes and ears of our enemy.'

Ellis grunted to concede the point. They reached a rough table in the corner and swung the lamp onto the desk, a dull thud echoing throughout the chamber. The flame guttered then burned bright again.

The two men both rolled a barrel to serve as chairs, and plunked themselves heavily upon them. 'Now then, the Esquimaux,' Kane said.

Ellis shook his head. 'Not being let out of sight by the Chases or Millar.'

'Can Millar be gotten?'

'I had thought him weakest. And habitually in need of funds. But, no, not yet. Although brother Ezekiel must have had some notions about not trusting him fully. Mrs Chase seems to be doing the bulk of the supervising.'

Kane lifted an eyebrow. 'Oh, really?'

'Nothing like that, Hereford, I am almost certain of it.'

'Hm. Still, every avenue must be explored. It will be, what, twelve weeks before the *Wessex* will sail again?'

'They are saying closer to nine, though that will be a difficult task.'

'We must redouble our efforts. I will have that blackamoor in our possession, you understand, Lambert? If he is not leading our expedition, I will ensure he does not lead any others. Upon my word, he will certainly not board any ship in Ezekiel Mather's fleet.'

Mr Ellis sat back, his face moving into half-shadow. 'This . . . feud between yourself and Ezekiel. Has it been worth it? I go along with some of your carry-ons as at some level it is in the interests of our business to have a weakened Mather & Co. But is the bitterness over one woman worth it?'

'That brute does not deserve her, my dear Mrs Hummock. I know where your predilections lie, so I will ignore your implications about my motives. For how can you know the true love of a man and a woman? How can you understand that depth of feeling? And how can you know what it was like to lose that woman, with the grace of Napoleon's Josephine, the beauteous visage of Lady Hamilton, the body as could only be imagined by Peter Paul Reubens? And, yes, twenty-five years and it hurts as much as it did the very day he spirited Mrs Hummock away to make her his, what? Concubine? I made an offer to wed and she turned me down to be his mere Jezebel.'

Mr Ellis shifted in his chair, regretting asking the question. It always worked old Hereford up to such a lather. Mr Ellis also considered reminding his colleague that while Hereford started cosying up to Mrs Hummock a few days after old man Hummock was planted, she never seemed at all interested. And that Mr Kane's offer of marriage came after Mrs Hummock was ensconced in the Mather home for some six months; it must have seemed to that formidable lady as an extremely poor late-in-the-day proposal. Still, we all have our narratives that we ascribe to our lives. The jilted, wronged suitor was probably a better character for Hereford to play than the reality of the podgy no-hoper whose suitability to the marriage bed was so repulsive to at least one lady that she would become no less than a whore than take his hand.

Mr Ellis allowed Mr Kane to fulminate a bit more about Ezekiel's ghastly treatment of Mrs Hummock. He finally said: 'To reiterate, giving Ezekiel Mather a bloody nose is in our interests as a whaling company. He is our fiercest competitor. I am not entirely sure, however, that murder is in our interests.'

'Murder?' Mr Kane said, mock-offended. 'I was thinking of nothing of the sort, Lambert. There is a range of persuasive methods at our disposal. Bribery, extortion, threats to the body of a person. Murder? You insult me, Lambert. That would be so unimaginative. Although accidents have been known to happen to people, as well.'

Mr Ellis looked at his partner for a long moment and nodded. 'Let us have Jensen and Shattuck see what they can find out.'

Mr Kane clapped his hands and drew the lantern in towards himself. 'Excellent! That's the spirit. Now — when shall we two meet again/In thunder, lightning or in rain?/When the hurly-burly's done/When the battle is lost or won.'

And with a witchy cackle, he extinguished the flame, leaving the two in utter darkness. A few heartbeats later, all was still. Then came a weary sigh. Mr Ellis struck his tinder, once, twice, thrice before it lit. He opened the lamp's window, set the wick alight.

'Must you,' Mr Ellis said, as they tramped back across the warehouse, 'do that every time we are down here?'

Nantucket

'Have you a paramour, John?'

John glanced at Owen, but the Captain was looking out on the harbour, shifting uneasily from side to side. Isobel was making arrangements with the man who ran the packet just by the gangplank and was out of earshot. Further along the quay, Barz was helping Nancy with Owen's dunnage, to the maid's clear irritation.

'Or did you? Perhaps even, forgive me, had a wife?' Owen went on. 'I do not know how you people do these things. Is there marriage of a sort?'

John tried to steady himself. Perhaps this was merely the white man's curiosity about savage customs. 'My people have a ceremony you would probably not recognise as marriage as such. There is an attachment, a bonding between a man and a woman.'

'Ah.'

'But there can be commingling, of course.'

Owen coughed and looked further out to the harbour, as if trying to see beyond the horizon, over the curve of the earth. 'Commingling, you say?'

'When I was a child, whenever the East Islanders and the People came together for the caribou hunts, one of the East Islander hunters, who was called Massak, would stay in our hut with my parents. And there was much, very much, commingling.'

Owen finally turned around to look at John, staring him full in the face for several beats. 'By commingling . . . I am sorry, are you telling me that your father allowed this other man to have relations with your mother? There? In his own home?'

'This is only my assumption. I was young. But there was much groaning and grunting going on behind the partition.'

'Hang on. Do you mean to tell me that your father was in there and . . . taking part as well?' Owen had gripped his hands behind his back and was running a bit pale.

John had once witnessed Utuk tumble down the sheer ice face of one of the small mountains near the encampment, a long four-minute slide from top to bottom. Utuk later said that within two seconds he knew he had done something stupid, but there was no handhold, there was no way to stop himself, so he just had to hang on and ride it out until he got to the end. John now knew how he felt.

'Well,' John continued a bit unsteadily, 'my mother was very fond of Massak.' He was going to add that he thought his father was rather fond of Massak as well, but Owen's demeanour suggested this might not be prudent. 'Something of that sort would not be countenanced here, I suppose?'

John asked the question softly and now he turned to look at the horizon.

'Good God, no,' Owen barked, pink burning bright in his cheeks. 'We would not, this is not that kind of place. What sort of man would countenance anything like that? Share his wife, his rightful property?'

Owen's eyes burned into John's. 'No disrespect intended to your good father, of course.'

Owen moved a few steps up the quay and John followed. The wealth of Nantucket was spread before them. John stopped counting at seventy-five ships of sail of various sizes spread across the harbour. Rowboats skimmed in and out between the vessels ferrying people and cargo. Across the way was the *Wessex*, hove to on its side on the dock, its copper-bottom exposed. Mr Coffin was leading a team of twenty men chipping away at the barnacles underneath.

'Take care of her whilst I am gone, would you please, John?' Owen said.

'The *Wessex*?'

Owen laughed. 'Well, if you feel moved to try to. I imagine Mr Coffin will not let you anywhere near her. No, Isobel.'

'Your wife?'

'Is there another? You are being peculiar, Mr Sackhouse. My wife, yes. I fear she will pine for me and will need you. She is very fond of you, John, I can tell. Please try not to leave her side much these next few days.'

'I will do as you wish.'

A yell. Mr Coffin had stopped to barrack poor young Isiah Folger, who in his zeal at removing the barnacles had chipped away two of the *Wessex*'s copper plates. Mr Coffin's booming voice echoed across the water, both John and Owen privately marvelling at his inventive use of oaths.

John, Barz, Isobel and Nancy stood on the quay waving at the *Monadnock* as the pilot towed it out to the roads. Owen responded with a quick nod from the taffrail, then turned his back on them to look out to sea.

'He is not one for the long good-bye,' Barz said. 'He thinks it unlucky.'

Isobel turned to John and Barz. 'Cousin Millar,' she said, her voice thin and trembling. 'It was Owen's desire that Mr Sackhouse would stay at your lodgings while he is away.'

Barz looked at her curiously. 'He said nothing to me.'

'It must have slipped his mind in the preparations. I believe he must have said something to you, Mr Sackhouse.'

Isobel spoke to John but did not look directly at him, fixing her gaze somewhere at the end of the pier. 'Yes,' John said. 'Just before he left he expressly asked me to move to yours. For propriety's sake.'

Isobel nodded. 'Nancy, would you mind arranging for Mr Sackhouse's belongings to be sent to Mr Millar's lodgings?'

'Do you think that is a good idea?'

Isobel turned to Nancy. 'Yes, actually, I do.'

Nancy shook her head. 'It is just that I am sure Cap'n Chase would want Mr Sackhouse to feel most comfortable and surely he's at home where he is now.'

'I have decided. Now would you do as I asked?' Isobel regarded Nancy coolly for a long moment until the maid bobbed her head and sullenly walked away.

'Well, gentlemen,' Isobel began.

'Shall I, shall I then come by tomorrow?' John asked.

'Certainly. But I think it is best if Mr Millar accompanies you. Don't you? Well, good-bye.'

The two men bowed. Barz watched Isobel as she walked away with his hands on his hips. He looked at John, then back at Isobel. He put his hat back, scratched his head, chin and under his arms. 'Tell me true: are you putting it to her?' he said.

John glared. 'Of course not, you cankerous scoundrel. She is a model of virtue.'

'Hm. Well, I'll be.'

John gave an exasperated snort and shouldered by Barz. 'Wait, John,' Barz called, then trotted after him. 'Apologies. I am completely in the wrong.'

John stopped, considering Barz. 'Let's go and get banjaxed.'

'And this, Mr Esquimaux, is The Great White. What I would call a *real* pub.'

Barz bowed lowly, swept his hand majestically towards the dumpy assemblage of discarded planks and driftwood that seemed to list dangerously over the quayside.

John looked at the entrance uncertainly. Two massive jawbones with deathly-looking serrated teeth gaped open above and below the door. Two laughing sailors burst out the door — or rather through the jaws — arm in arm, tripping down the stone steps and sprawling at John and Barz's feet. The sailors got up, one began pissing on the Great White's side, and the other retched over the railing and into the harbour.

'And do you go to this . . . establishment . . . for fun or some sort of penance?' John asked.

Barz patted John on the shoulder, ushering him inside. 'To be brutally honest, my friend, a little of both.' John steeled himself for a malodorous foul-smelling den, which would undoubtedly bring to mind the sickly-sweet vomit-inducing cloyness of blubber.

'Forget your Tri-Pots with its airs and graces,' Barz enthused. 'This is a perfect drinking den. Mostly because this is a *talking* pub. No music. Why do pubs always have to have music? Who wants some fuckwit sawing away on a fiddle, or a lugubrious Irishman burbling a ballad about the last rose of summer or a love who was just hanged — so you can barely hear yourself think, let alone what your neighbour is saying? If I wanted to hear music I would go to Faneuil Hall.

'And yet, people will only bother you if you want. If you want to chat, there are people who will do so. If you want to be left alone to the oblivion of drink, then you'll be left on your own.

'And last, but perhaps foremost, this is their brew: Sea Lion, Nantucket's finest ale.'

Barz plunked two pewter pints on the table, a bit of foam leaping out and splashing on the sleeve of John's emerald jacket. John snatched his arm away, wiping the cuff, irritated at Barz's clumsiness.

John leaned down, put his nose near his pint and sniffed expansively. 'Smells like a ship's biscuit edging towards mouldy.'

Barz shrugged, taking a long happy slurp. 'It may be an acquired taste.'

John brought the pint to his lips and took an exploratory sip. It was cool but not cold, bitter with a sweet honeyed aftertaste, a little hint of something like raspberries. He felt a warming spread through his stomach. He took another, longer pull. 'You have acquired it already, I believe, my friend. Yes? Yes?'

John nodded, a foamy moustache ringing his smile. 'Yes. Oh, yes, indeed.'

They careened out of The Great White into the dimly lit street, and John collided with a solid wall of flesh, which knocked him backwards, sent him stumbling and rolling into the mud.

'Jesus fuck Almighty,' John managed to squeak.

'I beg your pardon, sir,' came a gruff voice somewhere from the heavens.

John rolled in the muck, aghast. 'Ruined. My jacket, my new breeches. All of it.'

John regained his feet. Barz had found his top hat half sunk in a puddle. 'And my hat, sir,' John said, exasperated.

The bulky figure continued to stride away. 'I do believe I begged your pardon, sir.'

'You did not do so sufficiently, you English galoot,' Barz shouted after the man.

The figure stopped suddenly as if struck, whirled round and rushed back up the street, bellowing: 'I am Scottish, sir.'

He came under the lamp where John and Barz were standing, towering above them, his large, round eyes aflame. His head was uncovered and the light reflected off a completely bald pate. As if to compensate for his lack up top, the man's ginger beard was voluminous, reaching down almost to his mid-riff. And it was extravagantly groomed: the mustachio was wax-stiffened, protruding the length of a hand on the man's face, each side curved slightly so together they resembled a bird's wings in flight. The beard itself was oiled — with seal blubber John could now clearly smell — combed, manicured and trimmed to a point at the very tip.

John gasped. He knew the beard. How could he forget it? 'As I live and breathe. Captain Veitch.'

The man peered closer, his fire doused. 'John? John Sackhouse?' he whispered. 'Is it truly you? How in God's name is this possible?'

The two men stared at each other.

'It has been some time,' said John.

'Seems like but a day ago for me,' said Captain Veitch. He shifted on his feet. 'How did you find yourself here?'

'By the most extraordinary of circumstances.'

'You are the Esquimaux, the one they are all talking about! The *Wessex* Esquimaux.'

John acknowledged the fact with a bow. The Captain shook his head in wonder and said, softly, 'I am truly sorry for what happened last we met.'

John looked back at his hat, tried to wipe some mud off the brim. 'We all are,' he said evenly.

After a pause, Captain Veitch cleared his throat. 'We find ourselves in Nantucket after being horribly shot up in a dreadful blow. Luckily, I have some friends here, but the repairs will take some time. The *Thomas and Ann* is being fitted out on Edwards Quay, if you would like to pay a visit.'

'I shall do that.'

The Captain bowed and made to move on but thought better of it and shook John's hand vigorously. 'I am so pleased to see you again, Mr Sackhouse. And pleased to see you thriving and well.'

After he had gone, Barz patted John on the shoulder. 'How do you know that goliath?'

'I've met him on a number of occasions.'

248

Nantucket — The diary of John Sackhouse, Esquimaux

10th August 1816

They all talk about the heart here. Affairs of the heart. My heart was broken. Preposterous. That organ — so deep inside — seems not to come into it when sadness strikes. I feel it in my legs, the blood draining away where I could hardly stand. And in wooziness of the head. And most of all my stomach, as if I have been punched and kicked in my midsection, so I cannot fully stand upright.

She is right to do it, to send me away. To dismiss me until Owen returns was for the best. And yet I cannot stay away.

Each night after Barzillai retires, I am outside the Chase home, in the darkness, peering in for a glimpse of her. I climb the sturdy elm outside the Gardners' to get a good look over the back yard, or am in the bushes across the way.

I am aware this is most ungentlemanly. But I thought from the moment Isobel and I met that we were meant for each other, that it was in the stars. A foolish, childish notion. Suitability and love and consanguinity matter not a whit in this world I have come to.

So I deal with it with my nocturnal excursions. They are a comfort. And I am rewarded, from time to time. There she will be, flashing across the window, a book in hand, or stepping out across the yard to the shed (in which she spends a lot of time) or opening a window fully from time to time to look skyward at the stars for long periods, contemplating I know not what.

Which she was doing tonight, perhaps because it was a crystal-clear night, the Great Bear shining so brightly it seemed just above the Chase roof. She then sighed and looked across to the bushes where I skulked. 'Will you come in?' she said.

I shrank back and remained quiet. 'Mr Sackhouse, will you come in?' she said again. A moment later the door opened a crack and I crossed the street.

She stood halfway down the reception hall. 'I was hoping you would stop this,' she said.

'What do you mean?' I asked.

'John, do you know how disconcerting it is to have a man creeping about in the bushes every night?'

I mumbled an apology. She blinked rapidly, eyes misting. 'I hope you are prepared,' she said.

'For what?'

'For what comes next.'

She turned and I followed as if in a fog. She undid her outer gown and left it on the bottom of the stairs. She shucked off her pannier and dropped it outside the door to her bedroom. She turned around inside the room in just her chemise, thin and gauzy so that I felt I daren't touch it lest it disintegrate in my hand like that flossed candy from Mr Pandi's. Whale lamps burned behind her, and I could see the faint dark of her nipples.

She looked at me, her chin pointing downward, her eyes tilted up. I stood in the doorway for a long time.

'Why do you not come?' she said at length.

'You are,' I said, stepping towards her, taking her hands in mine, 'you are most beautiful, most desirable. But I am afraid.'

'I am, too.'

She pulled against me. Our lips met, our tongues met. I took a handful of the chemise, ripped at it as she tugged and clawed at my clothes.

As I write this I remember every moment, every sensation from the ginger-jasmine scent behind her ears to the salty-sweet taste of her breasts, to the way her eyes widened when I first entered her. I cannot mark it all down for it overwhelms me.

Then I shuddered and I held her for a long, long while. And then we rolled apart. We did not speak or look at each other for some moments. I stared up at the covering on the four-poster bed. I realised it was made of sailcloth. From the *Wessex*?

'Can you . . . ' Isobel began.

'Yes, yes, of course,' I said, stiffly as if I was taking her leave after dinner. I gathered my things, held them in my hands, wondering if I should dress there or leave. I finally skulked out, leaving Isobel staring up at the awning.

Providence

Captains of short-run packets to the mainland tended to be either competent but elderly whalermen grown tired of years-long voyages or green fuckwits who should never be put in charge of anything afloat. Captain Saxton, Owen determined after less than five minutes aboard the *Monadnock*, was the latter.

The crossing to Providence was interminable as young Saxton — Owen assumed by the man's spotty face and yardarm-thin frame that he could not have reached his twentieth year — contrived somehow to add hours to the voyage, despite favourable backing winds and smooth seas. At one point, Owen had to grip the taffrail with both hands in order to stop himself from shouldering the young Captain out of the way and barking orders to the crew.

'I know I have a command here, Captain Chase,' Saxton said, offering a hand as Owen disembarked on the rickety gangplank to the Providence quayside. 'But I am keen to go a-whaling, and I would, as you have perhaps noticed, be a tremendous asset to the *Wessex*.'

'A most gracious offer, Captain,' Owen said, struggling to break free of the young man's over-eager grip. 'Your abilities have certainly been noted these last twelve hours. But, as you may be aware, I am swamped with offers of men eager to crew with us.'

'Ah, yes, owing to the Esquimaux.'

Owen stared hard at Saxton's grinning mug and the word *glaikit* popped into his head, one of Isobel's Scotch words for the vacant and foolish. 'Mr Sackhouse has certainly been part of our success. But there is not a little bit of credit that should go the *Wessex*'s Captain. I found Mr Sackhouse, I was led to him, and it was I who was baptised by lightning.'

Now it was Captain Saxton who tried to free himself from the handshake and step backwards, but Owen held fast and firm. Owen collected himself, noticing that the *Monadnock*'s crew and the stevedores unloading the merchant ship at the next mooring had stopped to gawp.

'But I will see what I can do to find you a berth,' Owen said, hurriedly. 'Come and see me when I return.'

Owen bowed, walking hard and fast from the quayside. He had gone a couple of hundred yards when he slowed, realising he had headed the wrong way. He hesitated. Retracing his steps would mean passing the *Monadnock* and he did not want to do that, foolish as that was. Perhaps there was another way through this warren of back-streets?

As he vacillated, he contemplated the town. He had not been to Providence for nearly a decade and it was different. At first he could not quite figure out what it was but then he realised that it was louder. Yes, the port was bigger, busier — he counted 15 merchantmen variously loading or unloading cargo on the Long Wharf alone with another dozen vessels out in the roads of the harbour. Business was booming. But the change was in the city itself. It banged, clacked and clanged with industry. Whistles blew. Steeples were far outnumbered by smokestacks which belched black into the sky, leaving a haze which pinched nostrils and eyes.

'Captain Chase, Captain Chase,' a voice cried.

Oh Jesu, was that Saxton? Owen, affecting not to hear, plunged into one of the roads leading up Federal Hill. His name was called again, so he quickened his stride, but became aware of the sharp tapping of boots closing behind him. He was contemplating whether breaking into a trot or even an outright sprint would be overly unseemly when a hand tugged at his coat. He spun round.

Staring up at him was a young woman. He took her face in in flashes, piecemeal: wisps of auburn hair flying out of her bonnet; rounded pale cheeks flushing pink; a tiny mole just above full lips. The pieces slid together like a jigsaw when he looked at her eyes, deep green, penetrating and knowing.

'I beg your pardon, sir,' she said, puffing. She hooked her arm through his, steadying herself. 'A moment, if you please. I have not had a mad dash up this hill like that for ages.'

She puffed a bit then went on, smiling up at him. She squeezed Owen's arm more tightly and suddenly everything else in the world went away, it was just she and he. 'There, better now,' she said. 'You are, I hope, Captain Owen Chase. You did not respond to our hails, but I knew, felt it must be you.'

Owen managed a bow. 'I am. I can not have heard your call.'

'Goodness, they must have heard our calls from Newport to Woonsocket. I am Violet Brown. My grandfather is waiting for you.'

'*Violet* Brown?'

A furrow of vexation appeared on her brow. 'Yes. Thank you, mater and pater. Mix them together and you get black.'

'A dirtier brown, I should imagine. A very muddy brown.'

'A more gallant gentleman would perhaps have made an allusion to the flower, comparing my beauty to it. You are terribly ungenteel, sir.' Her smile bloomed.

'Forgive me, Miss Brown. I am but a crude sea captain.'

She gave him another smile that seemed to say, oh, I know all about sea captains, then pointed down the street. 'My grandfather awaits.'

She pulled him back towards the quay where they came upon a man who looked about fifty, but robust and active. He was a shade over six feet, wide shouldered, with strength in those thick arms. His features were pronounced — hawkish nose, jutting ears which propped up an overlarge Quaker-style broad-brimmed hat. His well-cut suit was sober, in varying shades of brown. He held a silver-topped stick with both hands behind his back; it looked more weapon than walking aid.

'Captain Chase?' the man boomed. 'With the *Monadnock* so overdue we were anxious some calamity had befallen her, so we came to the harbour to get any news. And when we found her, we saw what could only be you dashing away hell for leather. And my granddaughter here took it upon herself to sprint after you in a most foolish and uncouth manner.'

'Oh, fie, Grandfather,' Violet said, playfully hitting his shoulder. 'We are amidst the hustle and bustle of the port. No one saw that I was dashing about.'

'I am sorry,' Owen said, bowing to the man. 'But you *are* Mr Moses Brown?'

The older man looked at him curiously. 'I assumed my granddaughter would have said as much. I am indeed your humble correspondent and host.'

'Forgive me, but I was sure you were at least in your seventy-fifth year, sir.'

'My seventy-eighth, actually.'

'It is just, looking at you, I would not have put your age beyond fifty.'

Moses smiled, his eyes twinkled as he preened and stood on his tiptoes. 'Well, I admit you are not the first one to remark on my youthful features and figure. But I do not revel in it—'

Violet snorted. 'Pshaw, Grandfather. I love you dearly but you are as vain as the veritable peacock. Do you know, Captain Chase, that until Grandpapa lost most of his hair a few years ago — and *entre nous*, the lack of hair is why he wears that ridiculous hat even indoors — he put India ink in it to mask the grey?'

'Captain Chase,' Moses said, cheeks reddening, 'surely does not want to hear of my toilette, mistaken as you are.'

'My sister Almy and I caught him red-handed. Or should I say black-handed?'

'It was a careless accident, dear girl! I had merely spilled some ink on my hands doing my letters and had absent-mindedly run my fingers through my hair. I can assure you, Captain, my mane of black hair, a glorious mane it was too, was most natural.'

Owen smiled uncomfortably. This back and forth seemed to have occurred many a time and the old man was obviously enjoying the banter. But Owen was also sure that Moses might only appreciate chiding from this charming, precocious young woman who was clearly a favourite.

'You cannot fault God's blessing, sir,' Owen intoned piously, blandly. 'He has favoured you with hale and hearty good health.'

'Indeed, sir!' Moses said. 'Violet, the man has the very nub of it. I am not vain, I am merely chosen so that I can continue to do the Lord's fine works and do what I can to spread His word. And for that, I need vitality! Founding my little College, for one. But also, bringing the likes of you to Providence. Are you ready to tell your story to the world, my good Captain?'

Owen could not ever remember being truly nervous for any big moment in his life. Not on his first day aboard ship on the *Mercy Otis*; his first whale kill; the day he stepped on to the *Wessex* to take his first command; the day he bent a knee in front of Isobel half a world away. There was an emotion and a physical response, of course — excitement, a quickening of the pulse — but nothing that could be called anxiety or fear.

When he remembered those moments — the raised eyebrow of a young Mr Coffin as if to say 'Who the fuck is this little shit, now come aboard?'; the encouraging nod of old Jacob Campion as he handed over the harpoon for the final thrust; stepping to the quarterdeck for the first time and met by an older Mr Coffin's bow, then that of the junior officers and crew in succession so that it was like a rolling wave; Isobel's shimmering eyes and tears coursing down her cheeks — he knew, to his very marrow, that he would succeed. So why fret?

But this — this was terror.

He clutched at the sides of the State House podium to stop his hands from shaking. He was slightly blinded by the whale oil lamps burning impertinently bright in reflective white clamshells ringing the foot of the stage and shining upon him like an accusation. And above the lights, there was the crowd. It was one entity, moving and sighing together as if an angry beast. And it was large, this beast. Every seat on the ground floor and balcony was filled, people squeezed into the aisles and packed against the walls. Heads peeked in through the windows that ran down the hall's sides.

Owen moved his hands from the podium and interlocked them together behind him, pinching at his back. Maybe this bit of pain would stop his voice from faltering.

How did he get into this?

When Violet and Mr Brown were leading him into the heart of the city a few hours ago, Owen felt buoyant. Here was a Great Man of the Republic not only listening to what he had to say, but even deferring to him. Plus, the Great Man's rather comely granddaughter was hanging on his every word. Later, he would tell his story to Mr Brown's 'little gaggle of fellow co-religionists' and assuredly be feted and toasted until the wee hours. A pleasant evening.

'I told Grandpapa that we should take the carriage to meet you, Mr Chase, but he declined,' Violet said, once again interlocking arms with Owen.

'A carriage!' Moses cried. He stopped and walked five or six strides back towards Owen and Violet. Owen had been struggling to keep up with the two, who shuttled along at a great pace. Violet kept dropping back to Owen, but he suspected only to let him save face. Owen was glad they stopped; he was sweating profusely and out of puff, and had been dreading asking a man almost fifty years his senior to slow down.

'The carriage, sir, is a symbol of what will be this nation's downfall,' Moses went on. 'We have hewn the country out of rock. And how did we do that? Through hard work and graft.'

'Brace yourself, Captain Chase,' Violet said, smiling at her grandfather. 'The squall we are about to go through may last some time.'

'The carriage, the barouche, the gig, and any of those modern contrivances and gee-gaws are the symbol of our decline. We have built this nation, as I said, on hard work and graft – and what do we do in just a few short years after we have our freedom? Contrive to be ferried around like indolent wastrels. We are becoming soft, dear Captain, lovers of ease and comfort. To build this nation we need a new generation forged in iron. Not this generation which lazes around like gout-ridden English lords and ladies. The carriage, dear sir, is ferrying us to our doom.'

As Moses' pique crested, Owen tried to gauge if the old fellow was quite serious. The way he expostulated on it, mock-serious, suggested he might not be entirely convinced of his own argument. Violet's indulgent smile suggested she was not the least bit convinced.

'At any rate,' Owen said as Moses paused, 'I think the matter may be moot. Have we not arrived?' He motioned to a delicate arrangement of rickety clapboard and shingles that was impersonating a building. Outside a sign — more sturdily built than the rest of the structure — proclaimed it to be the Friend's Meeting House.

Moses blinked at him before Violet said: 'Captain Chase must have set sail before your last letter.'

'Dag, he must have, Violet, child.' Moses flipped his hat off his head — revealing a shiny domed pate — twirled it over a couple of times, then plunked it back on his head. 'You are in for a glorious surprise.'

He shot off, Violet trailing immediately behind. After a slight pause,

256

Owen somewhat reluctantly trotted after them. Moses and Violet rounded the corner and fully five seconds later Owen did the same, pulling up sharply when he realised that they had somehow come out to the city's centre. The two were walking up to the impressive four-storey building with a clock tower opposite. There they stopped and both threw their arms up like assistants presenting a conjurer at a county fete.

'The State House,' Violet said, face glowing.

'Our humble little meeting house was what we originally envisioned,' Moses explained. 'But after word began to spread upon your arrival, well, we needed the biggest hall we could find.'

'And how did word get out . . .' Owen trailed off as he got closer to the State House. On either side of the main entrance were bill posters, with an engraving of his face under the legend: *Embraced by the Light!!!*

And then, in various sizes of hysterical, screaming fonts: 'Hear! The world-famous Whalerman Captain Chase speak of his Communion with the ALMIGHTY! To save YOURSELF, to save YOUR SOUL. Turn out, Turn out and save your country from RUIN. One night only!!!!! For people of ALL faiths, colours and creeds.'

'We had these printed out almost immediately after you agreed to come,' Moses said. 'Violet did the design.'

Violet curtsied playfully. Owen said: 'My likeness, how did you . . .'

'Your cousin, of course,' Violet said. 'Mr Millar. He most kindly sent a sketch of you for which we made the engraving. At the time, I thought it was most impossibly idealised: rather too handsome. I see now, it is actually inferior.'

'Do not play the coquette, Granddaughter,' Moses said. 'Can you not see you are embarrassing the Captain?'

'Not at all,' Owen murmured, though in actual fact he could feel his cheeks warming. Violet had stepped closer to him, and he found he could barely meet her frank gaze. She was near enough for him to catch her scent, salty-sweet like flowers borne on a sea breeze when nearing land. With a slight panicky flip of his stomach he could feel himself . . . stirring.

He shifted away, closer to Moses, bit his tongue — an old trick to keep the monster down. He cleared his throat. 'How, how many people would you think will be attending this evening?'

'Oh, not above five hundred I should say,' Moses said.

It was, Owen estimated, closer to 1,000.

He cinched his hands tighter behind his back, took a deep breath and locked his eyes on the clock on the balcony at the far end of the hall and began intoning: 'On ninth of June last, I was in the process of fitting out the *Wessex*, a whaleship owned by Mather and Mather Shipping Incorporated and of 130 tons. My instructions were to prepare for a voyage of two years or sufficient time to fill the capacity of those 130 tons with spermaceti oil.

'It was the second day but one before we were to sail. We were nearing the last of our stowing and victualising the ship for our voyage. That day we were taking aboard most of the food supplies: fifteen times barrels of salt pork; fifteen times barrels of salt pea; twenty-five times barrels of ship's biscuit...'

After five minutes, midway through the recitation of the ship's roster and their duties, Owen realised that he was close to putting the beast to sleep. There was mass fidgeting and coughing. Some of those standing near the back began to drift out the exits. A man on the front row right was ostentatiously reading the *Providence Intelligencer*. He dared a glance over at Moses and Violet stage left. The old man was stony-faced, flipping his hat over and over in his hands. Violet stared directly at Owen, blinked slowly once or twice, as if trying to communicate something.

Owen unclasped his hands, brought them to the podium and touched his handwritten speech delicately with his fingertips. He folded the pages in half, then half again and slowly put them into his jacket pocket. He walked from behind the podium to the front of the stage.

'I am but a humble sea captain,' he said in a much softer voice, people having to lean forward to hear. 'I am not particularly good at speechifying, as I have demonstrated thus far.'

A soft ripple of laughter from the beast.

'I gather many of you may know my story – but here it is for those unacquainted: on a clear, cloudless day I was blasted off a yardarm of my ship into the drink by a bolt of lightning that came, literally, out of the blue. Unconscious, near death, I was revived three days later, pulled suddenly out of my catatonic state, with a vision, a mission burning in my mind: find the son of Ham, and I would be delivered.

'In truth, I did not, I will confess to you good people now, know what exactly that entailed. But I knew where I could find it, I knew I would know it, or him, when I saw it.

'And I discovered him. The Son of Ham, some little blackamoor abandoned and floating in the Great Drink some thousands of sea miles away from where anyone had any business to be.'

Owen had been prowling across the front of the stage, his voice rising, but now he went back to a stage whisper: 'As if by a miracle.'

Prowling again now, his eyes latched on to individual members of the rapt audience. 'Many of you know what happened next. The Son of Ham led my ship to the greatest find in any whaleship, one that countered the practices of marine fishery, the laws of nature herself. One that could only be there, by the will of the Almighty Himself.

'Now, let us not be coy. Many of you, I imagine, are here because of the . . . commercial nature of my experience. Perhaps you think, by listening to my words and my tale, you can enrich yourselves. People, like YOU, SIR!'

Owen boomed the last two words in his all-hands scream, pointing at the fellow in the front row who had been reading the *Providence Intelligencer*. The man started.

'Me, me, sir?' he finally managed to squeak under Owen's persistent, accusatory finger.

'There you are, reading a news-paper, undoubtedly for the latest happenings upon the 'change, when I am testifying to the glory of God.'

'But, sir, I—'

'Begone from this house, sir!'

Owen stalked to stage left, eyeing the man as he fumbled with his newspaper. In the back of his mind, in the very dark recesses, Owen conceded to himself that that was grossly unfair. The man had become slack-jaw rapt as Owen moved stage front, only holding onto the newspaper because he seemed unaware he still clutched it. Still, an affront is an affront.

He waited stock still, side on to the crowd until he heard the door close behind the newspaper reader. '"Embraced by the Almighty." That was what we have entitled tonight. But it was no embrace. It was loving, yes, but no hug, no cuddle. The Almighty did not embrace me. He baptised me by fire. He took me by the scruff of the neck and slapped me about the face. He picked me up on my wooden perch two hundred feet above the water and shook me to my core. Embraced? No, my friends. I was smote by the Almighty.'

Providence

Owen poured the port to nearly the top of the glass, and sidled over to the window, bottle in tow. His room was on the third floor, over-looking Unthank Street, a graceful curve down the hill to the quayside. In the town below, tubby merchantmen and a handful of slavers milled around, their outlines punctuated by lanterns fore and aft.

His hand shook, port spilling onto his fingers. He switched the glass to his left hand, sucked the tangy-sweet port off his knuckles. He took a big sip, then another and in a moment he was refilling the glass.

Where had that come from?

He had not allowed himself a moment to reflect until now. He had spoken for near to two hours, railing, ranting and reasoning. He talked of God's grace and wrath, of redemption and salvation. Or at least he assumed he did. He could remember little of the words themselves, and when he thought about the night, he saw himself not from his own perspective but that of the audience as he went through the actor's tricks. It was like when he first awoke from the lightning blast and felt he was being directed, puppet-style, by a greater force.

Yet he had them. The entire crowd, the beast, tamed. They laughed, they wept, they cheered. They adored.

A knock at the door. Finally. That fuckwit Saxton of the *Monadnock* had sent his dunnage to a Mr Moses' house in East Providence, not Moses Brown's city centre townhouse. 'Come.'

'I hope I am not disturbing you.'

Owen spun round, spilling more port on his hand. 'Ah, Miss Brown.'

Violet squeezed into his room, closed the door behind her. She had changed into what Owen preferred to think was a gauzy summer dress, but knew was an overlong night shift. He took another healthy swig of port.

'Am I disturbing you?' she repeated, not waiting for an answer, but walking into the middle of the room.

'Not at all, not at all. Port?'

She nodded. 'I hope you are not scandalised by my coming to you, but I felt I needed to see you immediately. I assure you it is most proper.'

Owen coughed as he drank. 'How could it be anything but?'

'I was much invigorated by tonight, Captain Chase. Thank you,' she said, as he handed her a glass. 'More than I have ever been in my life.' Her eyes shone in the candlelight.

'In a way, I was too,' Owen said. 'Invigorated.'

'And I felt I could not wait until the morrow to plan our itinerary for your excursion!'

'Ah, yes, about that . . . ' Owen hoped his voice did not betray the disappointment he had no reason to feel.

Violet whipped out a notebook from her shift — where it could have been, Owen could not imagine — and pointed to the desk. 'Shall we begin?'

After his talk — amidst the back-thumping, the congratulations, the adoration — Moses had embraced Owen warmly, bringing him aside. 'I knew you could do it, son,' Moses said. Then he explained his plan. He had taken the liberty of writing to various Friends' chapters throughout New England, wondering if they would be interested in hearing Owen's tale first-hand. 'And most of them responded with a resounding yes! Would you be so good as to spread the word to them, too?'

'Well, yes,' Owen began, meaning to go on that he would love to, of course, but there were whales to kill, his friend John to meet, his wife Isobel to return to. But then he was swept aside by a tide of well-wishers and did not finish his thought.

'Miss Brown, your grandfather's plan is sound, but I cannot spend too much time on the mainland,' Owen said.

Violet closed on him, placed a hand on his chest. 'That would be disappointing.'

'Perhaps a few dates could be accommodated, but . . . '

'Let's have a gander at this schedule and see what you think.'

Ten minutes later Owen had agreed to a three-week tour of Rhode Island and Massachusetts, travelling to every hamlet and village up the Blackstone River as far as Worcester – although his agreements were in the form of grunts which could be taken as yesses, for he was lost in contemplating the sway of Violet's breasts beneath the shift, the earlobe he yearned to reach over and suckle, and her sea-breeze floral scent.

Again he stirred, and no amount of tongue biting stopped him from reaching full mast. He was certain it was obvious — damn these tight trousers, normally they certainly stood him in good stead. He tried to mask it by contorting his sitting position, hands over his lap, bending over to a figure C. He wished she would leave, but wondered how he would negotiate walking her to the door. Claim stomach cramps and say he had to remain seated?

Violet underlined the last item on the itinerary (Gosnold House in Troy, twenty-four days), then put the pad on the desk. 'I am so glad we have done that, Captain Chase. You do not know how these matters were pressing upon me.'

'I understand pressing matters all too well, Miss Brown.'

She appraised Owen for a long moment. She brought her face closer to his, looked into his eyes levelly. Oh, those knowing eyes, piercing into his soul! He felt as if she could read his every depraved thought.

'Captain Chase,' she said, placing her hands on his knees. Owen straightened his back, leant his upper body back into his chair. But he kept his knees exactly where they were. 'Captain Chase,' Violet said again. 'You have nothing to fear from me.'

'Fear? Of course not, I could never fear you, Violet, oh—'

Her hands were slowly, inch by inch, travelling up his thighs.

Fall River

10th August 1816

Bonhomme Richard Inn
Fall River
Overcast; a moderate breeze from SSE

My dearest Isobel,

I cannot truly convey how much I miss you and I thank you for your indomitable forbearance for my being away these extra three weeks. I trust Mr Sackhouse — how fares dear, dear John? — has not given you much bother and you have been able to chaperone him about town, and keep him out of reach of those brigands Kane and Ellis.

I think back to when I agreed to this expedition and I must have been addled, or so caught up in the moment that I lost leave of my senses, for it has been the most trying of times. I have repeated my story, and John's story, to a handful of yokels as we travelled from moderate-sized hamlets to poky wee villages. I realise I had never been so far inland than I have been on this journey and find I am wholly unnerved by not being able to hear or see or smell the sea. And do you not find that the further away from the coast one goes the more simple the folk are?

I grow tired of my companions, it pains me to write, for they have been exceedingly generous. Oh, Mr Brown is a tireless champion for his causes, for his University, for the state of Rhode Island and the Republic in general, but like a lot of Great Men, particularly those whose greatness is at some level driven by the Almighty, is a frightful bore in company. And his granddaughter, whom I think I have not mentioned yet, but is a plain, rather mousy spinster who acts as Mr Brown's hostess and companion, is worse. Supper is hardly convivial, it is like dining with the Puritans of yore.

I finish in haste for the messenger boy has arrived to say the Nantucket packet is soon to hove-to. I will be on the wing tomorrow, for which I can hardly wait. I do so ever like our homecomings.

Your loving husband,
Captain Owen Chase

Owen sealed the letter quickly and handed it and a quarter-dollar to the boy, whose eyes lit up at the coin. Owen watched him belt down the street towards the harbour through the tavern's bay window. He sighed. That the boy was there and the packet was sailing soon was perhaps the only bit of pure truth in that letter. Actually, there was indeed a moderate breeze coming from the South South-east, though the clouds just parted and bright sunshine shone merrily on the town.

And Fall River, of course, was officially known as Troy — changed a couple of years ago by a handful of town fathers with ideas far above their stations (naming your town after a place most famous for being hoodwinked into being sacked and pillaged struck Owen as tempting fate) — though none of the locals seemed to call it by the new name.

A mug of ale was plunked in front of him. 'Oh, that is very kind,' Owen said, starting from his reverie, reaching into his pocket.

'No sir,' the barmaid said. She was young, sixteen perhaps, had a broad, pretty, freckled face with baby soft skin which contrasted with the chapped red and rough hands that lingered on the mug. 'My husband says you are not to pay a penny.'

She nodded at the owner behind the bar, the obsequious flit who showed them to their rooms last night, bowing and scraping as if they were aristocrats. The owner was, Owen conceded, not an ugly man. A full head of hair, most of his teeth, no obvious pox marks. But he had to be knocking on fifty, and here he was married to this young pretty creature, whom judging by the state of her hands, did most of the labour in the Bonhomme Richard. In matters of the heart, Owen thought, women are either wholly practical or wholly stupid.

'I, I saw you last night, Captain Chase,' the barmaid said shyly. 'Well, we did, my husband and I, at Tiverton.'

'Did you now?' Owen said, flushing with pleasure. 'Well, I am afraid I cannot recall seeing you, forgive me.'

'La, sir! Don't you think anything of it at all! There must've been near two thousand people there.'

'Three thousand, more like,' Owen said quickly, almost inaudibly. There had been 2,982 tickets sold and undoubtedly there were probably a few stragglers who managed to get in without paying. It was his largest crowd yet; it had to be held in a huge tent, hastily staked on the outskirts of town.

'I was transported, Captain,' the barmaid went on. 'Simply transported. I hung on every single, solitary word.' She stepped closer to Owen's chair, and said lowly: 'My name is Clare, sir. I hope you enjoy your stay here. Do let me know if you need anything, anything at all.'

She whisked away in a flutter of skirt. Without exception, this had happened everywhere he had spoken. He was speaking, preaching really, about the purity of God's love, God's stern hard love. But after each meeting, he was surrounded and accosted by dewy-eyed women (and some dewy-eyed fellows) saying they wished to further question him about the Lord, but really wanted to bed him from now to Kingdom Come. He watched Clare move away and found himself wondering what sensation those chapped and raw hands would have pumping up and down on his cockstand.

'Wanton thoughts about the comely young barmaid?' came a whisper in his ear. Violet had sidled silently up. Owen rose as she sat. Her eyes glittered. 'As erotic fancies goes that is rather dreary and common. I expect far more imagination from you, Captain.'

'Oh, it was nothing of the kind,' Owen said quickly. 'She was at Tiverton yesterday and was expostulating on the Glory of the Lord.'

'Ha, ha, ha!' Violet trilled in her wonderful, fluting laugh which never ceased to make him laugh too. This woman! He could not dissemble with her, she saw through him, saw into his very soul.

These past three weeks had been the best of Owen's life. First, he acknowledged to himself that he adored adoration. Being the centre of the crowd with all eyes upon you was not terrifying, it was bliss. To move people, to be the most important person in their lives for even a couple of hours was heaven. And all the rest of it: talking to the newspapermen afterwards, his speeches being reproduced and hurried to the next town before his arrival, the crowds growing. And being besieged wherever he went by, yes, comely young barmaids, highborn ladies and ladies of the night; being deferred to by wise old men, idolised by children. Was there anything more felicitous and beautiful than pure Fame?

And good Moses Brown! He was like some fantastical hero: indomitable, blessed with so much energy. Which would have been irritating if he was indeed a bore as he told Isobel. But he was not. Owen had never laughed as much at table as these past weeks, listening as Moses recounted anecdote after anecdote, necking glorious quantities of wine and flip and gin which eventually led to singing and, on one occasion in The Fir Tree in Uxbridge, the old man doing a jig on the table until he cracked his forehead on one of the beams.

He was more impressive when out amongst the people. Owen had never seen anyone so comfortable talking to people from any walk of life, partially because he was so insatiably curious about everything. They were delayed half an hour leaving Millbury as he stopped to ask a farmer ploughing a tobacco field about crop rotation and what was his yield per acre. Owen rounded a corner into the stable yard at The Drover's Rest in Taunton to hear Moses quizzing a local wet nurse: 'So, madam, if I can recapitulate: the suckling itself is what prolongs the process. You are essentially deceiving Nature into believing you have recently brought forth a child, hence your life-giving milk needs to flow unheeded?'

'That is about the size of it, yer honour,' came a throaty, laughing reply.

'Fascinating! Fascinating!'

And Violet. Owen had lain awake after she slipped back to her room on that first night in Providence. He had not felt particularly guilty, not for Isobel or his host Mr Brown in that he had just rogered his granddaughter. No, he was mostly dreading the awkwardness of seeing her the next morning, and over the next three weeks. There was nothing for it; he would have to cancel the tour, invent some excuse: the *Wessex* shipping early, perhaps.

He rose early in order to avoid her and Moses at breakfast, but he found the old man in the sitting room. 'Ah, Captain,' Moses said warmly. 'Up with the cockerel as myself. I trust you are ready to spread the word on our little tour of the provinces. I take it you and Violet have already worked out the logistics.'

Owen stood at the door uncertainly. 'Well, we discussed them, before we retired.'

'Did you sleep well, Captain Chase?' Violet chimed, sauntering past him into the room, pecking Moses atop his bald pate on the way to her chair.

'Tolerably well, yes, thank you Miss Brown,' Owen mumbled.

'I for one slept gloriously,' Violet said, stretching her arms out like a cat. 'Do you know, Grandpapa, I believe it was the good Captain who was entirely responsible for it.'

'Oh yes?' said Moses.

'Oh yes?' repeated Owen.

'Sure, Captain, I was left positively sated by your, what can we call last night, your performance, perhaps?'

'Perhaps ministrations?'

'Ministrations, yes! Grandpapa! In every sense of the word, I was left sated by your ministrations, Captain. I have not slept as well this fortnight.'

This *fortnight*, Owen thought wildly.

And Owen thought: ah, this is . . . tolerable. We shall get along just fine.

As they traversed up and down the Blackstone River, they did get along just fine: in a Woonsocket hayloft, a broom cupboard in a Pawtucket inn, a canoe in Millbury, up against a dog-cart in Uxbridge. And when they met in company afterwards they exchanged sly, meaningful looks – but most of all, there was an understanding. Owen felt terribly sophisticated. For this was what English kings and Dukes had (or Parisian men of all classes). That little uncomplicated courtesan on the side.

Although, Owen guessed, it remained uncomplicated if you did not become besotted with your mistress. Everything about Violet thrilled him, and he found himself physically restraining himself — self-administering a pinch to the thigh was best — when in company to refrain from touching her. When they did not get a chance to lie together — eight out of the twenty-one days of touring, he was counting — it was utter agony.

Owen looked at Violet. The light was streaming in from the Bonhomme Richard's windows, seeming to light up just her. Good God, I am in love, he thought.

He realised it was not just love for Violet. In the last week or so he had wild fantasies about being unattached, no Isobel — in fact, in the last week when he thought of his wife she had an incompleteness in his memory, missing all the details, as if she was an artist's pre-portrait charcoal sketch, not the finished oil — and being welcomed into the Brown family fold on their wedding day. Owen: 'Thank you, sir.' Moses: 'Sir? Call me Grandpapa.'

Owen moved violently in his chair, lurching towards Violet. 'Miss Brown, Violet, I need to speak to you urgently.'

'Whatever for?' Violet asked, turning from the Bonhomme Richard window. She looked into Owen's eyes and stopped, leaned back slowly. 'Alas, whatever it is, dear Captain, will have to wait, as I believe Grandpapa has arrived and we must away.'

New Bedford

'Thank you for coming out tonight, my brothers and sisters in the Lord,' Moses yelled above the clapping, hooting and hollering. 'Captain Chase has left the premises.'

Just left, thought Owen, as he burst through the side door of the Athenaeum. As he stood on stage a few moments ago, soaking up the applause, he had seen Violet leave her grandfather's side and melt towards the back of the hall. Now, he looked up the alleyway towards the main street and saw Violet flash by in the direction of the Bonhomme Richard. He took off after her.

He rounded the corner quickly, checked his trot into a more or less decorous shuffle, affecting not to hear calls after him from the crowd. She was halfway up Ananwan Street when he caught sight of her — that woman can walk!

'Miss Brown! Miss Brown!' he called. 'Violet!'

She put her head down, quickened her pace. Hang propriety, he thought as he bolted up the street. She turned as he neared, obviously hearing the drumming of his boots on the cobblestones.

'Violet,' he puffed, coming to a stop. 'I have been calling you.'

'Yes, I heard you, Captain,' she said, her face inscrutable.

'Oh, yes? I assumed you did not hear. At any rate, I shall escort you to the inn.'

He gave an arm and she took it. They walked in silence for a few paces, Owen's thoughts roiling.

Eventually, Violet said: 'I was most anxious to get back to make sure of the arrangements for tomorrow. That is why I was bowling along heedless of your calls. Our departures, that is. You to Nantucket, my grandfather and me to Providence.'

Owen stopped short, turning to her. 'Violet, I need to say a few things to you most urgently.'

Violet looked up into his pleading, dewy eyes and touched one of his cheeks. 'I know you do, dear Owen.'

'You do?'

'I suspect it is something along the lines of: "I love you as no man has ever loved a woman. I shall move heaven and earth to be at your side. I shall divorce my wife, she never meant a thing to me, do away with my position and station, because love, love will conquer all.'"

There was a plunging sensation in Owen's stomach, as if leaping from a great height. 'You mock me?'

Violet shook her head and took both his hands in hers. She squeezed them tightly, looking down. 'No, of course not, Owen. Forgive me, I have been so very selfish. I knew your feelings were shifting to something . . . greater than I had planned, than what I imagine either of us had planned, if we planned anything at all. I should have ended our assignations. I thought you understood.'

'Yet we do not have to end them, that is the very thing! I will swear to them in court as proof of my adultery and thus the divorce is granted. Even my very career as a ship's captain with the months and years I am away might be cause for abandonment.'

'You fellows seem to become quickly acquainted with divorce law. Bigamy and impotence are the other two grounds, though in my experience none of my gentlemen would considering lying to the court about the latter.

'What we had was beautiful and exciting and of necessity finite. I am so, so sorry, my dear, dear Owen. I will cherish every moment we have been together. You are an amazing creature, Owen Chase. But tomorrow we must part.'

She offered her arm again, but Owen merely stared at it. After it became clear he was not going to take it, she smiled sadly and began to make her way to the inn.

'"Fellows?"' Owen said. '"Gentlemen?" How many has it been?'

Violet pivoted slowly, glaring at him with a look of true anger that surprised him. 'Ah, there it is,' she said. 'The nub as it almost always is, the need to conquer virgin territory. How many? Oh dear, I suspect not above two or three hundred.'

'Now I understand how you know all those skills you have. Slattern.' Owen spat the word and then, for effect, spat in the street. 'This was not pure. This was not pure.'

Violet stepped back and visibly marshalled her features until her face was blank, a mask. Owen wanted her to yell, scream. He wanted anger, rage, passion. There was nothing there.

271

'I will take my leave of you, Captain,' she said and, with a quick curtsy, strode towards the door.

Nantucket

John turned the corner out of the Tri-Pots feeling very merry indeed. Seven ales. A new record. And, in the process, he managed to leave old Barzillai a-tangle with Nancy in a darkened corner.

This was new. Nancy had previously seemed to regard Barzillai with distaste, as something to be endured. Since he moved from the Chases', Nancy had taken a shine to Barzillai, flirting with him outrageously when she popped by their lodgings — which she did so frequently on the pretext of delivering one of John's belongings or a message from Mrs Chase. John had woken the previous night to bumps and groans, following the noise to Barzillai's room then peeking through the gap in the door to find the two in a clinch.

'I wear them down, you see,' Barzillai said to John the morning after. 'I am not blessed with comeliness, fortune or witty repartee. But I am always *there*.'

Tonight, Nancy had boldly joined them at the Tri-Pots — not the done thing, at all — plying Barz with two drinks to their one. 'Go on then, Mr Sackhouse,' she whispered as Barz approached insensibility but remained *compos mentis* enough to enjoy a vigorous nuzzle into her ample bosom. 'Have a stroll on your own. Mr Millar needs a little bit more of Nancy tonight.'

Well, who was John to deny him? As John walked away from the Tri-Pots he put his top hat on his cane, thrust it skyward and caught the hat on the way down with a dexterity that pleased him greatly.

Seven ales, a new record. By number four, he found that he had been able to stop thinking about Isobel. He would have to try for eight tomorrow and maybe she would be permanently banished from his memory.

He sauntered over to the quayside, took a hearty pinch of snuff and then lit a cigar. Both these vices did little for him — his eyes teared, his nose ached, he coughed — but he now found he could hardly stop doing them, particularly after a few ales.

Scurrying below him were several mudlarks, picking through the muck for scraps. These children roamed the harbour floor at low tide, scavenging for crabs, clams and whatever man-made treasures had fallen off a ship. None of these boys seemed to have parents, as if they were begotten from the seabed, from the very muck they trod about on.

'Mr Sackhouse, Mr Sackhouse!' one of them yelled up, hoisting a rather thin and sorry-looking crustacean. 'Would you be wantin' any crabs? They're good eating.'

'Alas no, lad, I am full up,' John said, patting his stomach.

One of the mudlarks scrambled up a pier post nimbly as a monkey and vaulted over the side, to stand directly in front of John.

'Sir,' he squeaked, 'I have something you want.'

John smiled and pulled a penny out of his coat. 'I think I told your friend that I am not requiring any seafood, but here's something for your trouble, young 'un. Go on to Mr Pandi and get yourself something nice.'

The boy snatched the coin but did not leave. 'It's from Mrs Chase.'

John looked about the quay. There were carpenters scrambling about the deck and the sides of the *Young Eagle* a couple hundred yards away. A few fishermen were at the end of the pier unloading a catch, but none was within earshot.

John bent down to talk lowly to the boy. He was painfully skinny, his hands and feet puckered from being in the water, a nasty red sunburn scorching his neck.

'What do you mean, from Mrs Chase?' John said. 'I have just left her lady's maid. Whatever could it be?'

'I was told it was a very special letter and to make sure I gave it to you before you started for home. That in particular was emphasised. Before you started for home.'

John's stomach flipped. Was Isobel calling him back? 'Well, give it here, please.'

'I don't have it here, sir. I have it in a special place. You'll have to follow me.'

The boy took off, padding off the pier, skipping across Harbour Street and ducking down an alleyway next to the chandler's.

'Jesus fucking Christ,' John muttered and ran after him. He made the alleyway, saw the boy's heels disappear down a corner. John made for it and rounded the corner when the lights went out.

The burlap bag was ripped off his head and John was thrust back into a hard-backed chair. He was in a windowless room, but judging from the smell of whale oil, the barrels, the manifests on the table in front of him and the harbour water showing through spaces in the floorboards, it was one of the warehouses on the quays. Mr Ellis and Mr Kane's warehouse, judging by the two men who sat across the desk.

John ran a hand through his hair, adjusted his vest, his shirt. 'You gentlemen do realise that you need only have asked and I would have been happy to meet with you.'

'Aye, and take our food and drink again without any recompense,' Mr Ellis burst out.

'I was only responding to what I thought was your good-natured hospitality,' John said primly and started to rise. 'Now, if you could direct me to my hat and walking stick I shall be on my way.'

Mr Kane lifted a pudgy finger and someone moved out of the shadows, shoving John back down by the shoulders.

'Thank you, Captain Jensen,' Mr Kane said, then smiled at John for a long moment before going on. 'This bit of skulduggery is a nasty piece of work and it does no credit to any concerned. Still, needs must. We needed to speak to you, Mr Sackhouse, unbeknownst to others to negotiate once more.'

'I told you gentlemen, I do not know the whereabouts of—'

'It is not your knowledge we need,' Mr Ellis broke in. 'We do not know of the exact point on the charts but we know, simply by overhearing chatter in the pub, the general area.'

'No, what we need is you,' Mr Kane followed up. 'What I will risk my life, my career on is that you are the talisman, you are the good luck charm, you are the thing that brought that shoal of spermaceti to the *Wessex*. And you will now deliver a similar one to the *Young Eagle*, captained by dear Jensen here, when it leaves in three days' time.'

Jensen smiled wolfishly at John through his thick blond beard, tightening his hold on John's shoulders with his thick arms.

'Gentlemen,' John said with some asperity, trying to break free of

Jensen's grip. 'As I have said previously, I simply cannot oblige you. Nothing has changed.'

'Oh but it has,' Mr Ellis put in.

'I know of your loyalty to Mr Mather and your great, dear friend Captain Chase,' Mr Kane nodded. 'But if you do not join the *Young Eagle* in three days' time — the morning after the fete thrown in your honour, what a great send-off that will be! — we will be forced to tell your friend, show your friend, that you are, how shall I delicately put it?'

'Fucking his wife,' said Mr Ellis.

John shrank bank into his chair. Mr Ellis glowered with triumph, Kane rolled a pen back and forth on the table, eyes downcast, giving away nothing. 'Owen would never believe the two of you,' John said. 'Would not believe such a tissue of lies.'

'I believe you are right,' Mr Kane said. 'He would not. However, there have been whispers around town; the usual tittle-tattle that gossips spread whether it is true or nay. And Captain Chase, I imagine, has heard it, but has put it down, like you say, as a tissue of lies. But when he reads these fascinating pages, then he will believe.'

Mr Kane nodded and Mr Ellis reached under the table and brought out a folio. John's heart sank to his knees.

'The diary of John Sackhouse, Esquimaux,' Mr Ellis read.

'Do you have a favourite passage, Lambert?' Mr Kane asked.

'I do, Hereford. From just a day or two ago. 'Tis the one that begins with Mr Sackhouse mooning outside the Chase household, spying on Mrs Chase. Yes, there is a sauciness, but a *tendresse*. "I remember every moment, every sensation from the ginger-jasmine scent behind her ears to the salty-sweet taste of her breasts to the way her eyes widened when I first entered her."'

'Stop, Lambert, I think I need a cool drink of water,' Mr Kane said, fanning himself with his hands.

'It is not real,' John said, staring at his boots.

'Come again?' Mr Ellis asked.

'A passing fancy. A narrative.'

Mr Ellis and Mr Kane stared at each other, then burst into guffaws. Captain Jensen, still holding John fast, chuckled, a sort of rasping heh-heh-heh. 'That is a most pathetic defence, Mr Sackhouse,' Mr

Kane said, wiping his eyes as his laugh wound down. 'But here it is in black and white.'

'Enough bantering, Hereford.' Mr Ellis leaned menacingly across the table. 'You have your choice, Mr Sackhouse. Your world here in Nantucket is destroyed no matter what you do. Leave with the *Young Eagle* and you may destroy your friendship with Captain Chase, but you will preserve his marriage.'

'How did you . . . ' John began.

'Domestics are such a burden to the mistress of the house,' Mr Ellis crowed.

'Nancy?' John said, disbelieving.

Mr Kane shot his partner an angry look. 'I see no reason for you not knowing. Now that Lambert has shot off. Miss March in the past few months has become overly familiar with one Jemmy Martin and has fallen. Mr Martin is not the marrying kind. And whilst Mrs Chase would do everything to protect Miss March, I do not think Captain Chase, the purified Captain Chase, would countenance an unwed pregnant maid in his household. We have given Miss March a sum of money—'

'A vast sum of money,' Mr Ellis chimed in angrily.

'A vast sum of money. She has now, as it were, crossed the aisle and is working as a spy for Kane and Ellis.'

'It's Ellis and Kane, Lambert,' Mr Ellis said irritably.

Mr Kane smiled. 'You are quite right. My point here, Mr Sackhouse, is that in our world, everyone has their price.'

'You have found mine,' John said, shrugging himself out of Captain Jensen's grip and standing up. 'Now, may I have my hat?'

It was only a fancy. The truth was he did stand outside Isobel's house of an evening, longingly looking inside, his mind a-whirl. But all the rest of that entry, all those other . . . things — complete fantasy. He had taken to writing fiction. Why had he written it? Because he wanted them to happen? Oh yes, undoubtedly so. It was not real, but he had now, ridiculously, seemed to make it so. It was only his fantasy. And now he had created this reality out of this fiction, which a maid found — who was probably only being nosy — to use to her profit. And now he could deny all he liked, but no one would ever believe that it was not true. The prospect of leaving Isobel, and Owen, made him feel like he was about to jump down into a gaping black void. Yet he found himself also thinking about Mr Ellis and Mr Kane pawing over the pages of his diary and felt violated and used.

John silently closed the Chases' front door behind him, leant back to the wall and slid down, feeling as if the floor was slowly being pulled away. Sitting down, he bent his legs, folding his arms over his knees to bring them close to his chest.

He breathed uneasily, his stomach guttering. Yesterday, no not even yesterday, today, just one hour of the clock before this very moment, all was different. He rolled over and laid down onto his side. He wished he could just disappear, become part of the floorboards.

A door opened and closed from the back of the house, and he heard a heavy, impatient tread boom through the kitchen into the hall. John got to his feet. Nancy paused as she reached the foot of the stairs on the opposite end of the hallway.

'Ah,' she cried, when she spied John. 'You startled me there, Mr Sackhouse.' Her voice faltered as she went on: 'I had no idea you would be back here this evening. But if you require nothing, I should be getting on . . . '

John rushed down the hallway in four great strides, stopping just inches from Nancy. 'Why?'

Nancy backed away a step, stumbling slightly as she caught her heels on the first stair. But when she righted herself, she squared her shoulders and puffed out her chest. John instantly thought of the *Wessex* when she turned into the wind, sails filling fully to life. 'What I am doing,' Nancy said levelly, 'is protecting the missus and Captain Chase.'

'Are you? That is extremely high-minded of you.'

She jutted her chin out. 'Sure, I am also helping myself. Do you think I would have been able to remain here when my situation became obvious?'

'I do, actually. I see no reason why you would not be able to.'

'A savage would not comprehend.'

'Under Mrs Chase's protection you would have been able to stay.

The Captain will be many miles away before you ever began to show signs of being with child.'

'Would he now? Would he go a-whaling after you scarpered off with the missus?'

'How? What? We would not—'

'I have eyes, though Captain Chase is blind. I haven't betrayed her. I'm protecting her. You do not understand. This would ruin her, him. Maybe even Mr Mather. You would destroy them. It would then hurt Kathryn, me. But you do not have a conscience for this, do you, Mr Esquimaux? You have lobbed a bomb in, but you will be the only one to walk away.'

A squeak upstairs of a door opening. 'Oh, Mr Sackhouse,' Isobel said, peering over the banister. 'Are you returning already? Has your dunnage been collected?'

John moved away from Nancy, watching Isobel as she descended the stairs. 'I was just collecting one of my things. Returning?'

Isobel reached the bottom, turned towards Nancy.

'Ah, sorry, ma'am, I shall leave you two,' Nancy said, making a quick curtsy then boom-booming up to the first floor.

They stood in silence. Isobel concentrated on her hands held in front of her, clasped tight together. 'Isobel, I—' 'John, I—' they both began simultaneously and laughed nervously.

'I am sorry I sent you away,' Isobel said at length. 'I was frightened.'

'As was I,' John said. 'But I am to return?'

Isobel cleared her throat. 'Owen is back on the morrow, or even tonight, with fair winds.'

'Ah.'

'In time for the fete. Your glorious night.'

'It will be an affair to look forward to.'

Nantucket

The man's hat came at them first, end over end, whizzing by John's head. Then the man himself, arms flailing, as he was propelled down the stairs by three meaty Kane and Ellis men. He hit the floor, tumbled and rolled, coming to a stop so close to Isobel she had to hike up her gown and skip out of the way.

Owen came to her side. 'Captain Gosnold,' he said, looking down.

'Captain Chashe,' the man slurred, attempting to rise, then slumping back. His hand searched the ground until he found his hat, and he raised it in shaky salute. 'And you, Mishush Chashe. Your humble shervant.'

John was hovering a few paces behind and Isobel reached over and took his arm. 'Welcome, John, to a Nantucket fete. This is as decorous as it will get.'

John assembled his features into an approximation of a smile. No warmth, though, and no happiness. Isobel sighed inwardly. Since she had told him of Owen's imminent return, John had been sullen and morose, shutting himself up in his room as much as possible. Oh, why could he not *pretend*, at least for her sake? She felt as he did, surely he knew that. Did he not understand that she was pretending and that was the only way to survive?

A hand around her waist and she was pulled away from John. 'Tut, tut, John, do not monopolise my beautiful, beautiful wife,' Owen beamed. 'My dear, I hear the players tuning up and your card is full — you dance with me all night!'

He turned her around and marched her up the stairs. 'Owen, this is most unseemly,' Isobel whispered, with a glance over her shoulder at John.

'Oh, hang impropriety!' Owen laughed, leading his wife into the Meeting House.

A wave of heat and the smell of sweat not entirely masked by perfumes and eau de colognes assaulted them as they entered. The musicians were drowned by the babel of voices. Isobel actually loved these Nantucket gatherings for their incongruity. A mixture of classes and sometimes races. But the real discordancy was between the rough and ready whalermen, full of the usual carousing habits of the seamen, and the soberly-clad slightly more abstemious Quaker folk. Although, truth be told, the only real difference was that, while the seamen might end an evening like Captain Gosnold, the full-blown Quakers tended to end a revel on two feet.

'What larks, eh?' Owen said, pointing to the decorations.

Dearie me. The Meeting House was a shrine to Mr Sackhouse. Hung from the ceiling rafters were about twenty effigies of him, straw stuffed into mini-Esquimaux costumes. On the walls were paintings of John in various heroic poses: leaping onto the back of a spermaceti, loosing a harpoon, bursting through waves in his kayak. None of the paintings bore much of a resemblance; they were obviously done by Tristram Greenleaf, the island's jobbing portraitist who rendered all of his subjects with square jaw, slightly too-wide eyes and a flattened nose — in short, made them look much like Tristram Greenleaf.

'A punch for the lady!' Owen trilled and ducked through the crowd towards the refreshments table. Well, thought Isobel, as she saw Owen approach a gaggle of fellow whalermen, that's him gone for half an hour in conversation. But no, a few quick nods to the various gentlemen and he was back at her side.

He handed her an iced rum, toasting her with his. 'To you, my sweet love.'

Since he had returned from the mainland, Owen had been like this. By her side and attentive. *Interested* in her — beyond the usual 'return rogering'.

'Tell me about the mainland,' she had said. 'By the newspaper accounts you were exceedingly popular. You must have many a tale.'

He waved his hands dismissively. 'Oh, it was a rather tiresome slog, hard travel on muddy roads, spewing out the same old speech to cowhands and rustics. You know how these papers exaggerate. Let us talk about you. About John. Oh, how I missed you and this island.'

For the last three days he had always been underfoot, excitable and looking love-sick. But it was the wrong note, so obviously false she wondered what had happened on his tour. She wondered if he believed the things he was saying to her now, all the sweet nothings and pourings out of affection. But perhaps false notes were a recurring theme. She tried to think of a time in their marriage when he opened his heart or even told her of his true feelings. But then, maybe she had never done so to him.

A crash of strings and the crowd stirred. 'The quadrille begins,' Owen said, putting his glass down and offering his hand. 'My lady.'

Barz came up behind John and clapped both hands on his shoulders, following John's gaze as he watched Owen and Isobel disappear into the crowd.

'Pecker up, good Mr Sackhouse,' Barz said. 'Two words to you. Fish, sea. Fish, sea.'

John spun on Barz and something in John's face made him retreat a step, put his hands up. 'You are right. I am sorry to tease you so about my unfounded suspicions. I apologise.'

John shook his head. 'I was just thinking about when I take my leave of this place.'

'Were you? Come, we sail in a few weeks, there is still plenty of time for us two young bucks to sow our oats. I would especially like to sow my oats into that minx Nancy, who has been avoiding me for a few days now. Has she arrived?'

Barz stood on his tip-toes, scanning the faces. John said: 'I am not sure she will attend.'

'What? The fete of the year? Perhaps of the century? Come now, our gal Nance would never miss this. I will confess, John, normally I do not go for the more full-figured lassies. But, oh, Nance is so . . . bouncy. Do you know what I mean?'

Barz mimed several obscene gestures to explain, then straightened up. 'Look lively, shipmate, the USS *Stevens* has just tacked towards us.'

John turned to the plump form of Alderman Stevens gliding through several knots of people. 'The man of the hour,' he bellowed, drawing up to John. 'The man of the night. The man of the year!'

A ripple of applause came from those milling about the front of the Meeting House as the alderman stepped over Captain Gosnold to pump John's hand. John did feel a bit better for the clapping and raised a hand to acknowledge it, a smile dying on his lips as he saw Kane and Ellis hove into view.

'He is indeed the man of the year,' a voice barked out.

John turned and Mr Mather and Mrs Hummock were striding from their carriage towards them. Ezekiel reached him, and clapped his big claw on John's shoulder, trying to draw him away from Alderman Stevens. The alderman, however, still held fast to John's hand.

'Mr Mather!' Alderman Stevens said. 'I had not expected you here.'

Ezekiel affected surprise. 'Would I miss a chance to gallivant around for a reel or two? Especially in honour of my find, Mr Sackhouse.'

'Splendid, splendid. Let's not tarry, then. I shall lead Mr Sackhouse in so that I, Alderman Stevens, organiser of this occasion, can honour him.' He said this at the top of his voice so he was heard not just by the people close by, but many in the Meeting House.

'Wonderful!' Ezekiel matched the alderman's volume. 'And I, Ezekiel Mather of Mather & Co will be right at the side of my charge, John Sackhouse.'

The alderman led John in, Ezekiel on their heels. The crowd at the front of the hall did not notice them as the quadrille was reaching its denouement and all eyes were on the dance floor. Owen and Isobel had just done an exchange so were with different partners, but Owen still smiled wolfishly at his wife. Isobel appeared to be concentrating deeply on her steps (this may have been self-preservation; her new partner Mr Cullen, who owned the rope-makers, had in this quadrille alone trod on three ladies' toes) but John could sense she noted his entrance.

They reached the front and Alderman Stevens gave a slight wave at which the players stopped. The alderman spoke above the groan of disappointment of the dancers. 'Friends, people of Nantucket, I formally welcome you to this fine fete in honour of John Sackhouse, the Esquimaux.'

The alderman bowed and majestically presented John, who was assailed with a chorus of 'huzzahs' and 'hoorays'. The alderman raised a hand for quiet: 'I should inform you that magnificent refreshments and glorious decorations have not emptied the town coffers by one red cent. Yes, you should well applaud! We are indebted to Messrs Kane and Ellis whose largesse has given us tonight's entertainment in order to pay tribute to Mr Sackhouse and in respect for their brother whalerman Mr Ezekiel Mather.'

283

Now there was genuine applause from the crowd, for Mr Kane and Ellis were hardly known for their generosity of wallet or spirit, led by Ezekiel himself who tried not to look too triumphant over his competitors. The benefactors gave a number of bows to the audience, Mr Kane blushing shyly, Mr Ellis preening. As the clapping died down Mr Ellis shot John a quick lascivious wink.

The alderman raised another hand. 'Friends, that is what this island is about. Generosity. We can celebrate the individual — like we do tonight with this fine young Esquimaux, who it seems has been sent by God Himself — but it is our collective strength that makes this great isle the wonder of the whaling world.'

Alderman Stevens grinned, expecting a crescendo of praise at his finale, but only received muted cheers. The alderman had never whaled — he passed the Bar at eighteen and had practised the law since — and was mostly unaware of the animosities and feuds that coursed underneath the surface throughout the room.

'Well,' he continued, a bit deflated, 'I give you John Sackhouse. I am not sure he is much for speechifying, but I wonder if our honoured guest would like to say a few words.'

'Speech, speech, speech!' the crowd bellowed, but John shook his head. The last thing he wanted to do was to speak, tonight of all nights. Then, in the back corner of the hall, he spied Obed 'Pilem Oceanus' Swain of the *Intelligencer* smirking and scribbling in a notebook. John stepped forward and prepared to speak.

'Me like it here,' he said. 'Me don't know where me are, but me know where whales be.'

A confused silence fell over the crowd. Barz, a few paces away, mouthed, 'What are you doing?'

'I jest, my friends,' John went on. 'I was merely repeating what I am purported to have said by one of your newspapers, one that is used in privies thoughout the island. *The Ignorancer*, I believe it is called.'

'Ha!' someone snorted and slapped Swain on the shoulder. The hack shrugged and kept writing in his pad.

'But I am not the grunting, monosyllabic savage as I have been portrayed. If I were, I suppose I would be thinking of becoming a newspaperman, although that would make me overqualified. I apologise if that is what you came here to see: some darky; some dancing gibbon to entertain you; something for your amusement.'

The crowd was looking discomfited, though Barz was grinning with pure delight.

John paused. 'I am sorry. This is a fete, a celebration. And I am here to celebrate! I was plucked from near-death by dear Captain Chase, taken in the bosom of the Chase home with open arms. I have once again found a family which I thought I would never have. I rediscovered what love and loyalty mean and, for that, I am eternally grateful.'

John dared a look at Owen and Isobel, both of whom were tearing up. He bowed to Alderman Stevens, who motioned to the musicians. 'C'mon you idiots, play something, now, now!'

A reel started and Mr Ellis snatched at John's arm. 'Lovely words about love and loyalty, Esquimaux,' he said lowly. 'You had better not be double-crossing us.'

'Ease up, Lambert,' Mr Kane said, sliding up. 'And keep your voice down.'

'It is because of love and loyalty that I will go with you,' John said. 'It is the kindest thing.'

A shadow loomed above. 'What do you two vultures think you're doing?' Mr Mather said. 'Get your hands off Mr Sackhouse. You cannot bear that I have bettered you, can you?'

Mr Kane and Ellis looked at Ezekiel for a beat, then simultaneously burst out laughing.

'Yes, you've beaten us, Ezekiel,' Mr Kane wheezed, 'you've beaten us good.'

'Do not bother with them, Mr Mather,' Mrs Hummock said, coming up to Ezekiel's side. 'Let us go.'

'Henrietta,' Mr Kane said, his face draining. 'You are still the most exquisite creature on God's green earth.'

Ezekiel rolled his eyes. 'Give it up, Mr Kane. It has been twenty-five years.'

'Twenty-five years you have made her a whore.'

'What?' Mr Mather stepped closer to Mr Kane, seeming to grow several inches.

'You heard me,' Mr Kane said, undaunted. 'You have made her your whore for—'

Thwack. Ezekiel delivered a blow to Mr Kane's face and everything stopped. Mr Kane dabbed at the blood trickling from his nose. Then, Mr Ellis cold-cocked Ezekiel and all hell broke loose. Matherites and Kane and Ellis men waded in as if this was the dust-up they'd been waiting for all night. Women screamed, some running away, some joining the melee. John was shouldered aside by Barz who leapt on someone's back with a look of wild, gleeful abandon on his face.

John skirted to the door and headed outside, passing Swain who was madly writing in his notebook, his face aglow.

Where was he? Isobel had seen John scoot outside but he had disappeared. She looked left and right and caught a flash of his tangerine jacket heading up the hill towards their house.

She ran after him, against the flow of people emptying out of the taverns who were eagerly running towards what might turn out to be the biggest donnybrook in island history. She burst in the door just as John was pelting down the stairs, dressed now in a blue whalerman's coat, a duffel slung over his shoulder.

'I told you it would not get more decorous,' she said, trying to catch her breath from her sprint.

'Good night, ma'am,' John said and tipped his cap.

'You are not going out tonight?'

'I am.'

'To where?'

John hesitated, would not meet her eyes. He tried to move past, but she grabbed a handful of his jacket. 'Where are you going? Are you going away?'

'It is best this way.'

'Why?'

'To save you. Everything I touch, everyone I love, is destroyed.'

'That is not true.'

'Yes. Yes, it is. I shall tell you why.'

Greenland

John woke with a rush, jack-knifing out of bed. Oooonoooo, the shaman, stood above him, stern-faced.

Where, where? John said, blinking his eyes. Everything before him swam in and out of focus, before he recognised Oooonoooo's tent. Why am I here?

Oooonoooo turned his back to John, took a long flensing knife down from the ceiling and rubbed it briskly on a whetstone. He sharpened for five minutes, John watching the tattoos on his back become animated by the striations of his muscles. On and on he sharpened, not speaking. John searched his mind for what happened the previous night, could remember nothing beyond drinking rum on the deck of the *Thomas and Ann*, the reels of music, the dancing, the stars wheeling overhead.

John rose, stumbling as his head thrummed.

Well, he said uncertainly to Oooonoooo's back, I should be going.

Oooonoooo whirled and had the knife against John's throat.

You don't remember why you're in my hut?

John edged back a step, two, until he could retreat no further. No, he said slowly. I do not.

The shaman lowered the knife and went back to sharpening it. You're here because they would have killed you.

The sailors?

Sailors? You really do not remember? You do not remember a thing? Not the sailors. The People.

You're mad. Why?

John moved to shoulder past Oooonoooo, but the shaman stopped him with a powerful hand. His look was some combination of anger and disappointment.

I may be mad, he said. I saved you.

I'm going back to my hut.

It's not there anymore. Torok's sons destroyed it.

What? I'll kill them! Mary will kill him.

John tried to rush outside but Oooonoooo blocked the way.

No, he said, with a catch in the throat, his voice thin as a blade of grass. Mary is dead. Come now. You need to see this.

Mary was stretchered out on her favourite hunting sled, but John could sense she somehow was not there, or her spirit or soul or whatever you called it was not. She looked from this angle peaceful, sleeping.

Mary! John screamed and ran towards her. He pulled up in shock as he came to the sled. The other side of her face, the one facing away from him, was a pulpy mash, her right eye smashed, her skull stove in. Blood had dried black around her face and had painted the snow below the sled a ruddy brown.

No, no! he implored. He tried to shake her, scooped snow up to wash away the blood. Wake up, Mary, wake up! Jesus fuck Almighty, wake up.

After a moment he sat back on the snow, the world shrinking around him. The light seemed to go out, he could not catch his breath. He sank to his knees, crying out in great wracking wails.

He touched Mary's hand. How could she be so cold, so stiff? He shook her again, and a silver locket with crushed glittery mirror around the edges fell to the snow. He picked it up and squeezed it hard.

He turned to Oooonoooo. Who? How?

Oooonoooo was a few steps behind John. He packed some of his herb into his pipe, taking his time. He lit it from a box of long matches of the type whalermen use. He sucked deeply, looked off at the mountains, exhaled a great cloud. His eyes snapped on John.

How? A rock, a large one expertly thrown. Who? Why, who else could have done it? It was you, Bright Eyes, it was you.

Oooonoooo told John what had happened, at least as far as the shaman could piece together. The previous night on the deck of the *Thomas and Ann*, a sailor and Keetiak were both trying to dance with Mary, which had roused John out of his drunken stupor. He pitched up on to the deck, slamming into Keetiak, swinging wildly at this sailor in a frenzy.

Get away from her! he shrieked, taking out his knife and slashing out.

Mary was having none of it, trying to stop John. You idiot, John, you *eee-dee-ott*. I can take care of myself!

But he wouldn't stop, until Captain Veitch, immense and swelled with anger, came storming from his cabin. 'Belay there, belay you scum! There will be no fighting on this ship.' When he pushed into the melee he stopped short. 'John Sackhouse? This is unlike you. What are you doing? I appreciate you fighting for your sister's honour—'

'Sir, he came right at me, this darkie, with the knife out for no reason.'

'Stow it, Denham, the lady is lucky your pox-ridden cock has not come anywhere near her.' A big thumb jerked over his shoulder. 'Now get aft.'

He turned and looked down at John. 'Now Mr Sackhouse, I am going to have to ask you to leave, I am afraid. This is best for all concerned. All of your friends, too, off they go.'

John was the first to leave, sullenly going over the side, paddling his kayak furiously towards shore.

The people were none too pleased with you, Bright Eyes, Oooonooooo continued. They followed and soon Keetiak and Sapoch set upon you in your drunkenness. Yes, a cowardly thing, but they are cowards.

They caught you as you stumbled about on shore, kicked you, punched you, threw you into a snowdrift. Then they went off laughing. But you roused yourself and got hold of a pile of rocks. Big rocks, fist-sized, hefty rocks. You followed them to the encampment.

Just as you got to the encampment, you, marksman of marksmen, let fly at your two tormentors.

Oooonooooo stuck the pipe between his teeth and mimed the throwing motion. *Whhhppp, whhhppp.*

But your sister had beaten almost everyone to the encampment. And she came out of the hut and took the rock meant for Keetiak.

Thunk.

Oooonooooo mimed the motion of a rock hitting a head.

If it makes you feel any better, Oooonooooo said, death was instantaneous.

John collapsed sideways into the snow wailing, curled into a foetal position. He cried and cried until it felt like his insides would burst.

Oooonoooo looked down at him, drawing deeply on his pipe. John's crying tapered off. He sat up gingerly.

What about the other rock?

Ah, Oooonoooo nodded. Even in your state your aim was true. Torok came out of the hut after your sister and took the rock square in his face.

Did I kill him, too? John asked softly.

His jaw is broken. He will have to live on seal milk for a while, but he will live, I do believe.

Where, where, is Father Kelly?

Well, the shaman said. Well.

Father Kelly was nervous when the white whalers and fisherman came, but when a British ship hove into view, he became extremely disconcerted. It was a slight possibility, a very slight possibility, that if he went to meet with the ships someone might recognise him from home. But even if not, his appearance would assuredly lead to questions: why are you here? How long have you been living here? Where are you from?

And then who knows what would happen when these sailors met another ship when they put out to sea or when they got back in their home port?

Yet, this was strange; he thought he had shucked off long ago, or at least many months ago, his ability to care whether he lived or died. In fact he constantly thought of ending it all, though perhaps he was too much a coward to commit the act himself – the noble Roman way out – rather than live on in this fraught existence. Or maybe it was not cowardice but that his former faith and profession still had some kind of hold on him. He did still – and he knew not why and preferred not to think of the why – wear his ratty dog collar and rosary beads around his neck, hidden under the folds of the sealskin and caribou furs.

But he had some sort of survival instinct. He had not given himself up. Maybe it was solely down to a perversion. He would not give the

Crown the satisfaction of hanging him. After the rising he just got up and ran. And had continued running. First over to Skye, then to Orkney — the further north you got from Edinburgh, the more the Scotch were inclined to help an enemy of King George — then the Faeroes, off to Iceland, hitching aboard fishing boats and whalers. He had to leave Reykjavik in a hurry, on a stolen none-too-seaworthy boat and little clue as to how to navigate. It was lucky that he made landfall, even if it was to this frozen wasteland.

He walked out of the hut, looked towards the harbour, could hear the faint sing-sawing of a fiddle. 'That's Strip the CUNTING Willow,' he said to himself, and he had an image of when he was very young, four or five, and following his uncle into The Bull and Cock in Sligo Town, a roaring fire, clinking glasses, a whirl of skirts on a space cleared in the middle and Pat Fahey perched on a barrel, scratching this tune on his fiddle.

He shook his head to get rid of the memory. He seemed to live every day in the past, amongst dead people: his father, his old comrade-in-arms FitzGerald.

He hoped the children were all right. Heh. Children. They took care of him more than he them. He would have died without Mary and John. Or Mary at least.

But the two were . . . family. So he fretted like a sopping mother whenever they left. Death was a constant part of these people's lives, so much more so than back home. Or rather it happened far more suddenly here: innocently going about your day one moment, a polar bear's dinner the next.

The whole 'nobility of the savage' popular in literature the last decade or so always struck Father Kelly as rather fatuous or patronising. Though he did enjoy the narrative of Prince Lee Boo, probably because of the descriptions early in the piece of the nearly naked bronze-skinned native women. John and Mary's folk were neither noble nor savage, just people.

However, they were different. The proximity of sudden, violent death made them more like the ancients. Today is for living, tomorrow for dying. *Manducemus, et bibamus, cras enim moriemur, et cetera, et cetera.*

His fear for Mary and John's welfare had, he acknowledged with a pang of shame, more than a bit of self-interest. If they were gone, surely he would not last long. That big one — Torok — and his sons would carve him up like a seal pup, but slowly and with quite a bit more cruelty than they did to the poor seals. The shaman, would he step in to save him without John and Mary being around? Father Kelly thought not; he played the drug-hazed mystic like the seemingly permanently sozzled whiskey priests at home. Like those men the shaman had hard, hard little eyes that Father Kelly always had the impression were *working* — swivelling back and forth, particularly when the shaman did not think anyone was watching, so quickly that Father Kelly could almost hear them click and clack as they went side to side.

Father Kelly was going back into the hut when a movement caught his eye. He had thought he was the only one still in the village, but apparently not. The shaman had emerged from his tent, with that puffed-up regal mien of a minor noble that irked Father Kelly so. He looked around, for a long time directly at Father Kelly's hut. James involuntarily stepped backward. 'Did he see me? FECK!' Father Kelly wondered aloud. But then he shrugged. What if he had? He was not doing anything wrong. Maybe he should go out, say hello — or at least reprise one of their frequent exchanges, Father Kelly jabbering on in English and a few words of the People's language, the shaman looking at him with dead eyes.

He ducked outside but the shaman had turned, heading away from the village towards the harbour.

There was a hullabaloo in the clearing. Father Kelly sat up from his mat and looked at the dying fire dozily. Was he dreaming? Another clash of voices, a scream and yelling. No, he was not. He dressed quickly and stumbled out of the hut.

John was at the edge of the clearing, the shaman standing over his inert form. Mary was a hundred yards away, flat-backed, a halo of something dark staining the snow around her head. The two sons of Torok stood by her looking shocked, their father just beyond them, writhing about on the ground, roaring in pain.

'Mary, John!' Father Kelly yelled and ran towards the clearing.

His shout seemed to snap the two younger men out of their trance.

The taller one pointed at the priest, yelling something. This was the one Mary was spending more and more time with, Father Kelly knew not why. Yes, he supposed he was handsome — but in the way the Devil is. When he once asked Mary about it, she stared at him with that inscrutable look for an uncomfortable minute until he had to look away.

Handsome as the Devil was now wheeling towards Father Kelly, grabbing something long and sharp from the ground at his feet. An instant later, the stouter, shorter one also picked up something.

They both yelled at Father Kelly, pointing at the two prostrate on the snow, then back at him. For a mad instant, Father Kelly thought they must be calling for his help, but then Handsome as the Devil crouched, his face scrunched in fury and let fly.

The lance — Father Kelly actually thought, Ah, yes, a lance, I can see it now — zipped towards his head. He ducked just in time, the lance burying itself into the hut behind him. Looking back in wonder, he felt the lance vibrating in the wood, as if alive.

He turned and Short and Stout was upon him. How does someone so fat run so fast? he wondered, just as he was able to see now what was in his hand. That, he thought to himself, is a cudgel.

The cudgel struck Father Kelly on the side of the head, knocking him against the hut and down to the snow. A kick to the midsection expelled all the air he had in him as efficiently as a bellows. Everything slowed down as the two waded in on him. After another bash of the cudgel to the face, he heard the crunching of his nose far off, as if happening to someone else, watched the spurt of blood geyser across the snow. The last thing he saw was the big boot of Handsome as the Devil rising up above his face and rushing down, down, down.

Why didn't you stop them? John asked numbly.

Oooonoooo squinted at John. I was protecting you. They came for you next, but I stood over you and even in their fury they did not attack me. I let them destroy your hut, though. Let them drag the priest's body away to do I know not what to it.

293

But why Father Kelly?

Bad magic. Many evil things that have happened since he arrived.

You do not believe that.

Oooonoooo shrugged. No. But the People do.

You should have let them kill me.

A long puff on the herb, then Oooonoooo spat ruminatively and nodded. This I do not entirely disagree with.

John had told the last bit of the story in an increasingly soft voice, looking out of the window at the streetlights. He finally stopped and stared out for a long couple of moments, his hands clasped behind his back.

Isobel rose, pinched the bridge of her nose. She walked over to John, made to put her arm on his shoulder, but stopped at the last moment. She cleared her throat. 'What, what happened next?'

John turned around to her, but did not meet her eye. 'I buried Mary. I looked for Father Kelly's body, but could not find it. Then . . . well, my people do something you call, I suppose, shunning. No one would speak to me. No one would acknowledge me. It was like I did not exist. A ghost.'

'Even the shaman.'

'He spoke to me once more. To tell me to leave. So you see, Isobel, I am hardly a good luck charm. I am cursed, cursed.'

Here Isobel did put her hand on his shoulder, grasped his hand. She could not think of anything to say, just held his hand. Her heart burst for him. She touched his face, cradled his head, then pulled him closer, first lightly, but then urgently.

Nantucket

John watched her hands, clutching and re-clutching a little balled-up bit of sheet each time he thrust into her. He stretched over her, kissed her ear, put his hand upon hers, their fingers intertwining; brown, white, brown, white, brown, white. He gripped her hand tighter, thrust deeper, their breathing coming quicker. Then she stopped.

'What?' he asked. She was looking away. He followed her gaze and looked into Owen's eyes.

Owen stood stock-still in the bedroom doorway. He must have come up the stairs and moved the heavy door without either of them hearing. His body was not moving, but his eyes were flip-flopping from John to Isobel, Isobel to John. Owen took a step into the room then, as if reconsidered, backed up. He did this strange dance three or four times before turning his back to them. He took a huge breath and went down the stairs slowly, each step creak-creaking heavily.

'Oh my God,' Isobel whispered, eyes closed, pinching the bridge of her nose.

'What, what shall I do?'

'Go. Please, go.'

He was still inside her. He slid out of her, put on boots, shirt and breeches and had just placed his top hat on when Owen bounded up the stairs three at a time, his duelling pistols in either hand, aiming both at John's head.

John ducked as Owen raised to fire, the balls blowing two perfect eye-holes into his top hat and shattering the window behind him. The shots were amplified in the small room, and John could hear nothing but ringing. Not Isobel's screams, though her mouth was agape, nor the click of the hammer, nor the tamping of the powder as Owen reloaded.

Isobel was saying something to him, pointing towards the window. She got up and stood in front of Owen, who thrust her aside, sending her sprawling on the bed. Owen raised a pistol and fired as John dove out of the window, bounced off the roof of the shed below and tumbled to the ground. Owen leaned out of the window, but couldn't get a clean shot with the shed in his way. John ducked around the corner, burst through the yard and was on the street.

John ran towards the harbour and found himself reflecting that it is extremely difficult to run with an erection. Why wouldn't it go down?

And where to go?

He could see the *Thomas and Ann* moored out in the roads. Captain Veitch, dear Captain Veitch, would help him. He was about to untie a dinghy on the quay when he saw Owen turn the corner, walking slowly but purposefully towards his position. John did not think he had been spotted. He crouched, skulked along the quayside, tiptoed past a sleeping security guard and slipped into Mather's warehouse.

The overwhelming smell of the whale oil, piled in columns of five barrels, nearly made him retch. He stopped, noticing his wound for the first time. It was gushing, his shirt soaked, and he tried to staunch it as best he could with his hand. He worked his way down the warehouse slowly, to the exit at the opposite end of the quay.

He was halfway there when Owen stepped through a side door.

'You're easy to track, bleeding as you are,' he said.

John scurried down the aisle towards the rear exit. Owen fired, blowing holes in two barrels on either side of John, which spewed oil onto the floor. John slipped in the goo, regained his balance and reached the door. The rusted knob would not turn. John tried the door once, then again with his shoulder. It barely budged. He turned around.

Owen stood ten strides away, reloading carefully. What scared John most was the lack of expression. No outward signs of anger, no sense of betrayal, just some sort of calm.

'Here's one, John: A gentleman had married a fine young lady, and being terribly afraid of cuckoldom, asked her if she had considered what a crying Sin it was in a Woman to cuckold her Husband? "My Dear," says she. "What d'ye mean? I never had such a thought in my head, nor never will." "No, no," replied he. "I shall have it in my Head, you'll have it somewhere else."'

John said nothing.

'No? That does not tickle you, dear friend? How about this: An amorous fellow was making very warm Addresses to a married woman. "Pray, Sir, be quiet," she said. "I have a Husband that won't thank you for making him a Cuckold." "No, Madam," he replied, "but you will, I hope." No? I agree: that too misses the mark.'

'I'm so very sorry, Owen,' John said.

Owen had finished loading, stood looking down at the pistols. 'I didn't expect this from you.'

'What have you done to her?'

The question seemed to baffle him. 'Nothing. I expected something like this from *her*. A whore who makes and sells those . . . things. Not my friend. Women are weak.'

'She was right about that.'

'What?'

'You do not understand her at all.'

'My life has been the life of men; perhaps not. I guess you won't be with me on my next voyage, Son of Ham.'

'I am not—'

'Of course you're not. I realised that the moment I first spoke to you. But men's lives, particularly mine, are mostly a series of useful hypocrisies. You were one of them. I lead men. I have to pretend. I have to lie. It is something you would not understand.'

John moved to his left, shouldering over a column of barrels. Owen leapt backwards, barely avoiding the topmost one, which split open at his feet, covering his legs in oil. He scowled and fired the pistol in his right hand. The ball missed, blowing off the top hinge of the door. Owen shook his head, transferred the other loaded pistol to his right hand, slipped on the oil, and regained his balance. He steadied and fired, but the pistol buckled, exploding in the pan in a shower of sparks.

Owen and John watched the embers of wadding drift lazily downwards to the floor like fireflies. The largest spark settled into the oil pooled around Owen's feet. It sputtered then lit. Owen stamped wildly but the flames spread the more he thrashed about. John kicked the door, once, twice, thrice. At last, it burst open and he was out on the quay.

He looked back to see Owen fall over into the oil and then scramble to his feet, the flames leaping up, covering his body.

John took a step then another towards Owen, but the heat was pushing him back. Owen got up on to his knees and threw the damaged pistol at John's head. John hesitated. The flames were now spreading, moving up barrels of oil on either side of Owen. John turned and ran. He reached the end of the quay, was beginning to jump out when the vacuum sucked him back, like a giant intake of breath, and then expelled him as the warehouse exploded.

The blast propelled him out and upwards. It was a clear night, the stars incredibly bright; as he flailed about it was almost as if he could reach out and touch them, use them as handholds to swing across the sky, all the way back home. And he kept saying to himself: This is a good way to die. This is a good way to die. This is a good way to die.

Author's Note and Acknowledgements

This book is set 1816 and some of its characters are based on people who lived at the time, so in that sense it is a historical novel. Yet that term has always troubled me. I would argue that every historical novel no matter how well-researched or how high its degree of verisimilitude is a product of its time. There are some purely practical reasons for this — 'true' dialogue from a book set in Tudor London, for example, would be incomprehensible to the modern ear. But it is also difficult, and nigh-on impossible, to fully remove oneself from the sensibility of the age one lives in. If the past is a foreign country you can be proficient in its language but never have a native's fluency of it.

I relate this both as a warning to the reader and, quite frankly, a bit of 'insurance' – if I have anything 'wrong' in these pages I can say, 'hey, it's poetic licence'. But John Sackhouse (or Saccheuse as it has also been spelled) did exist, as did a Nantucket ship's captain by the name of Owen Chase. However, their stories bear no relation to what I have concocted in this book and in real life their paths certainly never intersected. And my Nantucket of 1816 — though based on the real topography and history — has been rearranged to fit my story.

I first encountered John Sackhouse in the Scottish National Portrait Gallery in Edinburgh. I was struck by his painting, somewhat out of place among all the Georgian *high heid yins* in the room. First off, the frame was round and modestly small — one could cover it with one's two hands. But he was the only person of colour in the collection and, apart from the occasional foreign-born aristo, certainly the only non-Scot.

Who was this guy? I wondered.

Turns out, someone extraordinary, though only the bare bones of John's story are known. A native of Disko Island off the coast of Greenland who was born around the turn of the 19th century, in his late teens John stowed aboard an Edinburgh-bound whaler. Arriving there he became a sensation — a performer of wildly popular kayaking and harpoon demonstrations in Leith Harbour who was taken up by the city's beau monde and intelligentsia, including his great friend the painter Alexander Nasmyth, whose portraits of Rabbie Burns and John now hang a few feet from each other in that Edinburgh gallery.

I originally planned to follow John's story as closely as possible but it is, as the semioticians might have it, such an open text with only a handful of contemporary sources that I decided to add more. What if John went to the New World? So, a detour was taken and in my version John meets Owen Chase. Owen is based very loosely on the man of that same name who was first mate on the *Essex*, the Nantucket vessel which was sunk after a collision with a white whale, the real-life basis for *Moby Dick*. The tale was wonderfully brought to life in Nathaniel Philbrick's *In the Heart of the Sea* (in non-fiction, Melville did OK, too) and I am indebted to Philbrick's book, not least for suggesting that there may have been a dildo trade among the women of 19th century Nantucket. John's journey towards Edinburgh in this volume is more my story than his real-life one.

In addition to Philbrick's book there are several recent titles I used as secondary sources or inspiration during the writing of *The Esquimaux*, including Wendell H. Oswalt's *Eskimos and Explorers*, Gretel Ehrlich's *This Cold Heaven* and Barry Lopez's *Arctic Dreams*. I accessed primary sources and made much use of the reading rooms at both the National Library of Scotland and the British Library, and I am indebted to the helpful staff at both institutions.

A brief note, too, on the word 'Esquimaux' (Eskimo), which came to English via the French – hence the Francophone spelling I've used for the title. As many will know, the indigenous peoples in the Arctic and Subarctic regions, particularly those in Canada and Greenland, have used the overarching term Inuit (meaning 'people') for some time with Eskimo being seen as perjorative. I've retained the archaic term and done so deliberately to underscore the culturally insensitive times in which John lived. Perhaps I shouldn't feel the need to explain this to my whip-smart readership, but I do hope no one has taken any offence. For the record, as a West Greenlander, John would have undoubtedly been a Kalaallit, which today make up the biggest group of the Greenlandic Inuit.

For getting *The Esquimaux* to market, my everlasting thanks must first and foremost go to Humfrey Hunter at Silvertail along with Rob

Dinsdale for his advice and keen editor's eye and Shona Andrew for her excellent jacket design.

Thanks to my agent Charlie Campbell (and his partner in crime Julia Kingsford) at Kingsford Campbell.

A tip of the hat to my friend Dr Jim Kelly (he's a doctor of literature, not a *real* doctor), who had the good humour to let me use his name for one of the characters — for the record, the real-life Jim is not an alcoholic priest with Tourette's. I am grateful to Mike Bennett for his friendship and cluing me in on Barry Lopez's work. But mostly and above all, this book simply wouldn't have been completed without the constant love, support and editorial nous of my Anna-Marie.

Lightning Source UK Ltd.
Milton Keynes UK
UKOW01f0803160218

317994UK00001B/284/P